Calling All Customers

by

Tara Ford

Is sanity a small price to pay for happiness?

© Tara Ford 2015
All rights reserved

ISBN-13: **978-1502808974**

No part of this publication may be reproduced, stored in a retrieval system, or transmitted in any form or by any means, without the prior permission in writing of the author, nor be otherwise circulated in any form of binding or cover other than that in which it is published and without a similar condition including this condition being imposed on the subsequent purchaser.

Other titles by Tara Ford

Calling All Services

Calling All Dentists

Acknowledgements

Thanks to Tracey Rawlings for challenging me to include the most ridiculous name you could imagine, in this book – but hey – I did it. Thank you to the following people for their show of support and encouragement throughout: Ann Faulkner, Andrea at EIS (you owe me a review or two and also, you look amazing with no hair), Veronica Hall, Cathy Parr and Nicola Elson.

Thanks to Sarah Bennett and Debbie Lewis for being patient ladies (although I'm sure that you both love to badger me at any opportunity, just for the sake of it) but here's the third one at long last.

Thank you to Caroline Fielder for the generous offer of living with her, in her picturesque new home, somewhere in the sticks. I will be taking her up on the offer, purely for writing inspiration of course… and maybe the odd meal thrown in for good measure. And the obligatory glass of wine.

A huge thanks to Jane Hessey who, once again, has had to endure the task of proofreading and going through my emails – you're a star!

Thank you to Nigel, Liam, Zak, Abbie, Megan, Benita and Ashley for putting up with my little, laminated, hand-made signs. However, I do think they worked well and I will continue to use them. 'I am working – pretend I am not here', 'Please don't talk to me, even though you can see me – I AM NOT HERE!'

Thank you to everyone who has read my other books.

My biggest thank you goes to those of you who have taken the time to leave a review on Amazon – I appreciate all of them (good or bad) as always.

Tara Ford

http://taraford.weebly.com/

Twitter: @rata2e

Facebook: Tara Ford - Author

For Jane and Luke

Chapter 1

Jenny Fartor (as in Fa-toar not Far-ter) sighed, stood up and stretched her limbs. Kneeling on the floor for half an hour had numbed her slim legs. The mound of letters, addressed to countless different people, did not look any smaller now that she had sorted through and placed them into categories. There were three piles of mail on the floor: 'No longer at this address', 'Junk' and 'Not sure what to do with it'.

Staring out of the four-paneled window front, Jenny pondered over the huge task ahead. She'd realised her dream when she collected the keys to her very own retail unit in the suburbs of Farehelm and now the hard work was really going to start.

It had been two months since she'd started the process of raising enough money for the deposit on the 15 year leasehold. A substantial amount of money had been required, not only to stock the shop but enough to cover the costs of shop-fitting, shelving, display cabinets, fridges and freezers as well. Her business plan had been welcomed by her bank manager but now she was in debt up to her ears. It was a challenging and scary place to be.

Jenny was made of tough stuff though and to lessen the burden of a huge loan, she'd been saving, here and there, for the past five years. Her previous job in the wholesale business had helped her financially, as well as equip her with a vast knowledge of the independent retail trade. These firm foundations had secured her business plan. And ditching her boyfriend, Calvin, had been the best move of all. She was free. Free to do what she'd always dreamed of – to own her very own convenience store.

However, it was still a terrifying place to be.

At the tender age of 28, Jenny was somewhat angst that she had wasted more than five years of her life with a hopeless, no-brainer like Calvin. They were still friends (amazingly) but their new friendship status was one-sided. If Calvin's controlling and insecure personality had anything to do with it, they would still be together. She supposed that he couldn't help being a complete and utter dork and she genuinely wished that one day he would find someone else to get his little claws in to.

Drawn from her reverie by the sound of her mobile ringing on the mahogany windowsill, Jenny reached for the phone. "Hi Dayna."

"Jen, are you in there yet?"

"Yes, been here about an hour, picked the keys up last night."

"Yay, when can I come over? I am so excited."

"Now if you like. I'll be here for most of the day, I expect, judging by the state of this place."

"Rubber gloves on as we speak," replied Dayna in her usual excitable, high pitched tone. "I'll be there in a couple of hours, going to drop Xaylan off at my mum's first. Is that ok?"

"Yes, great. Thanks Dayna, I could do with some company here."

"Ok, see you laters," she said and then hung up the phone.

Dayna Seeshy was Jenny's closest friend, confidante, and the first member of staff at *J's Convenience Store*. Having moved on from her ten year stretch of raising a child, claiming social security benefits, working voluntarily and several dead-end jobs in local fast-food stores, Dayna was now ready for the challenges that lay ahead. She was going to be Jenny's number one sales assistant, customer liaison manager, agony aunt, bouncer, security guard, comedienne, all-round entertainer, counsellor, psychiatrist, general dogsbody and anything else that Jenny saw fit.

The two women went back a long way, to their school days in fact, and had stayed in contact through the years, through the boyfriends and the ups and downs of bringing Dayna's son, Xaylan, up – sometimes between them.

Jenny had now joined Dayna's world of singledom, except, unlike Dayna, she had nothing to show for her years with Calvin apart from the proceeds from the sale of their small apartment. But she supposed that if it hadn't been for the small amount of profit she'd accrued from the sale, she may not be here, sifting through piles of letters and rubbish in her very own shop.

Jenny picked up the biggest pile of letters and proceeded to scribble out the current address and write across the front of each one in jumbo lettering, *No longer at this address*. The shop had been empty for over six months, having closed down as a failing tanning salon previously. So Jenny had a mammoth sized job now in the conversion process to turn the unit into a grocery store. Her plan was to convert the shop over the next six weeks and open up just after she received her alcohol license. *There must be over 30 letters here*, she thought to herself as she leant over the rickety old counter and continued to scribble.

Brilliant sunshine poured through the shop's front windows heating the interior, so much so that Jenny had to stop what she was doing and open the front door to allow the heat to escape. Peering up and down the road, she noted that there were not many people around for a Saturday morning, apart from the occasional dog-walker meandering past.

She'd studied the demographics of the affluent area before she had decided to purchase the unit and her services were definitely required in the area. Yet it seemed oddly quiet. She had expected the place to be a little livelier than this. Just the odd vehicle travelled up or down the road and there were very few pedestrians about, anywhere.

The nearest grocery store, *KO Stores*, was about a mile away and although it was part of a retail chain, it was much smaller than Jenny's shop would be. It stood alone, amongst a cluster of maisonettes and tatty looking garages. When she had visited, during the purchasing period, she had secretly checked out their footfall and been quite surprised by how many people were using it. In the hour that she sat in the car park, across the road, she'd counted 74 people using the shop. A rough estimation of the shop's traffic and likely spend per hour was favourable. Jenny's own shop looked promising if the *KO Store* was anything to go by.

Along the row of retail units, where Jenny's shop would be, there was an expensive looking ladies hairdresser come beauty salon, a recruitment office and the last three units were owned by a nursery. Each unit had three parking bays directly outside and there were further parking bays around the back of the building for the residents of the flats above. Across the side road was a small pub and just behind that, a car showroom and mechanics garage. The local school was a couple of streets away and the bus stop, in to town, was just across the road, a little further down. Jenny had speculated that her shop, along with the area it was situated in, would have far more to offer than the *KO Store* could and would see more traffic. A personal and friendly service was the top of Jenny's list of provisions. Upon her surreptitious visit to the *KO Store* previously, it had appeared that the staff were a right miserable bunch. They'd slouched around with hunched shoulders and a look of disdain on their faces.

Jenny would also be in a position to offer low prices on everyday products too. So a smile and a bargain were the name of her game – what could go wrong?

Upon further inspection, up and down the road, Jenny could only assume that the quiet streets were just a sign of it being too early on this sunny Saturday morning and the neighbourhood would be out and about soon enough. She breathed in the warm sweet air, tied back her mid-length, wispy brown hair, into a ponytail, then returned inside to continue the mammoth cleaning up and clearing out task.

"Yoo-hoo, only me," called Dayna from the front door. "I've got my mighty-mission-holdall with me and look at these, I just bought. Cool or what?" She waved a pair of long black, rubber gloves, with a red feathery frill around the tops, in the air.

Jenny peered around the staffroom door at the back of the shop. "Seriously? That's a worry," she said and tutted. "Where on earth did you get those from? And more importantly – why?"

"That new fancy dress/party shop in town, they've got loads of weird and wonderful things in there. And they're so cool – that's why."

"Dare I ask why you would go to a fancy dress shop on your way here?" asked Jenny, knowing full well that she was going to hear a ridiculous reason for why her best friend had been shopping in a party shop, so early in the morning.

"I just bought a didgeridoo. Mum told me they had some in there. I just had to get one, Jen, and Xaylan will love it too. I've just tried it out in the car park down town." Dayna grinned her usual quirky smile as she closed the front door and looked around.

Dressed in a pair of blue jeans, red plimsolls and a matching red t-shirt, Dayna's striking features and long, dark hair always managed to make her stand out in a crowd. She'd always liked to be noticed, right from an early age. In their younger days, it was always Dayna who would get sent home from school because she was wearing heavy make-up or false, painted nails or 'inappropriate' clothing, when she should have been wearing school uniform. The worst occasion was in their last year of school, when Dayna had to get changed for PE one day, and got caught showing-off her new nipple piercing. According to her, she'd offered sexual rewards to the tattoo man, in town, in exchange for an under-age piercing. They both got into a lot of trouble for that.

"Really?"

"Yeah. Mind you, I got a few funny looks sitting in my car playing a great big didge out of the driver's window."

"I don't doubt that," said Jenny and shook her head. "What am I to do with you?"

"I know, first things first, where's the kettle?" Dayna asked as she admired her new rubber gloves.

Jenny raised her eyebrows and tutted, "In here, but I forgot the sugar so we'll have to pop down to the *KO Store*. It's not far. We could go for a walk and check out the area. What do you think?"

"Sure, sounds like a plan," said Dayna as she walked down the length of the shop surveying the rubbish and discarded pieces of equipment and furniture. "Gosh, we've got some cleaning and clearing to do."

"Hmm, but I'm sure your mission holdall will have what it takes to do the job. Maybe we could even blow it all away with your didgeridoo," said Jenny with a wry smile. "Come on then, let's go."

As the girls left the retail unit together, Jenny peered back and grinned. "It's really happening, isn't it, Day."

"Not before we've had a cup of tea – with sugar – to christen the place." Grabbing hold of Jenny's arm, Dayna ushered her friend away.

"After the tea, I need to start thinking about looking for that third member of staff... we have got so much to do in the next six weeks."

"Tea first," replied Dayna, pulling Jenny's arm. "Then we'll find our dream team, third person."

Chapter 2

There had been six applicants, sent from the local job centre, two of whom had been so over- qualified that Jenny worried that they would take over her shop in no time. Another three were either, not quite right, for one reason or another, or, as Dayna put it, 'There's no way I'm working with a jumped-up tart like that'. The sixth person had been far more suitable and at just 19 years old she was perfect (well as perfect as could be, bearing in mind the other five, who were either 'Up their own arses' as Dayna had suggested, 'too geeky' or 'total sleaze-balls'). So it was final, Tasha Evans had been declared the third member of staff and would start her employment in one week's time, although Dayna still had some doubts.

Jenny sighed, only one week to go before the deadline. Just seven days before *J's Convenience Store* supposedly opened – there was still so much to do. The signage for the front of the shop had been delayed, due to an error, but Jenny was adamant that the apostrophe after 'J' really did matter. So the new, correctly punctuated sign was expected to arrive and be duly fitted in another two days time.

Keeping the whole business 'in the family', Jenny's dad and her older brother had been fitting the shelving, new counter, installing the electrics and countless other jobs that had needed to be done. They'd worked tirelessly over the last five weeks and had done so at a very reasonable rate of pay.

Dayna had spent a lot of her time helping Jenny with the menial tasks of clearing out and cleaning up, making tea for everyone and generally getting in the way of the men. Her saucy rubber gloves had been made good use of over the weeks and had certainly given everyone a good giggle. Dayna fancied Jenny's brother, Jacob, openly and even if he was happily married, which was questionable, she could still flirt outrageously with him.

"All I need, Jacob, is a rubber maid's outfit to go with these gloves and then I'll be well away. What do you think?"

As always, Jacob ignored Dayna's innuendos, he had no time for her and her antics.

However, Dayna's motto was, 'A little flirt here and there never hurt anyone'. But nobody was really sure just how much her 'little flirts' would amount to. She was a law unto herself.

"One week to go Jen," said Dayna excitedly. "Are you getting nervous?"

"I've been nervous for months. In fact, since the first meeting with the bank manager." Jenny tried to peep through a tiny gap in the window. "You keep putting that cream cleaner on so thick each week Dayna, guess who's going to be scrubbing it all off next week."

"Well you shouldn't let anyone see what's going on inside the shop – it's a secret. It'll be a great unveiling next week, you know, build the excitement and all that kind of stuff."

"Yes, I know. I've seen a few people pass by and try to peer through the window."

"See – they're curious aren't they. *Cif* is great stuff when it dries... until one of you lot go and lean all over it and rub it all off."

"Do *you* feel nervous?" asked Jenny, moving away from the window, as she could just make out a couple of figures walking along the path towards the shop.

"Not really, I can't wait. I'm looking forward to meeting all of our potential customers. I'll soon have them rolling in, Jen."

"Hmm, I thought as much, that's why you're here."

"Shush... they're talking." Dayna frantically pointed to two dark shadows on the other side of the window. "Listen." She suppressed a giggle and moved closer to the glass.

"What are they saying?" whispered Jenny.

"Something about alcohol."

"They might be the people who complained to the council." Jenny edged nearer. "Can you hear what they're saying?"

"Talking about the nursery up the road. Shall I go out there?"

"No." Jenny drew a sharp breath. "Come away from there, Day, I don't want to cause any more trouble around here."

The silhouettes moved away from the window and slowly disappeared.

"Bloody cheek, who do they think they are?" Dayna was in fighting mode already. "I bet they *are* the ones who complained, well at least two of them anyway."

Jenny had applied for an alcohol license during the leasehold purchasing stage. Upon good advice and her own knowledge of independent retailers, she knew that it was a sure-fire way to succeed if she could supply alcohol at reasonable prices. However some of the residents of Farehelm and in particular Millen Road, where Jenny's shop was situated, had disputed the application for an alcohol license. Eight of the local residents had written to the Council, as was the protocol for such matters, to air their views about why there should not be a license awarded to Miss Jenny Fartor, proprietor of 166 Millen Road.

Some of the reasons of disapproval were slightly ridiculous and had left both Jenny and Dayna gasping incredulously. The Council had made a terrible mistake and unbeknown to them, they had sent the copies of each dispute application, along with the names and addresses, to Jenny's shop. She was more than amused by the statements and also forearmed and ready for her review hearing, in which she would have to justify why she needed a license and why the local residents' concerns would not be a valid reason to deny such a privilege to the area.

Jenny and Dayna had read through the applications together and devised a covert plan of action to tackle the issues raised. Only one of the statements had a reasonable and valid point but the others would be kept for the sole purpose of hilarity, as Dayna had suggested.

The applications were as follows:

- I don't drink and neither do my neighbours, so we don't need alcohol shops round here.

- This will bring thugs to the area from the town, causing chaos, vandalism and crime. There could even be violence or murders – drink does that to some people you know.

- There will be drink cans littered around the area, which will make the place look untidy. And even if they do throw their rubbish away, alcohol smells horrible if poured into street bins.

- There should not be an alcohol license due to the fact that there is a nursery, just five shop units along. This would have a detrimental effect on the young children, should they witness folk purchasing alcohol or indeed drinking it outside of the shop.

- We are mainly elderly residents in Millen Road, apart from the huge, council housing estate that you decided to build, at the back of the shops, AGAINST our wishes and whilst ignoring our petitions, and therefore, we do not require a shop that sells alcohol, or the types of people that would be drawn to such a place. Let's hope that you will take notice of this one.

- Alcohol is an evil of this world and we don't want it

around here, thank you very much. I hope they won't be selling cigarettes either. That's another revolting, over-used substance.

- I won't be using the new shop, especially if it sells alcohol. I do not wish to be associated with a sleazy, small-time retailer who will attract the vermin of this town. I don't use the supermarkets either. I much prefer to get my requirements from the small butchers in town, have my dairy products delivered by our local milkman (milkmen need our support – they are a dying breed) and I grow my own vegetables.

- We don't need a convenience store of any description around here. We have other shops close by that will suffice. And we certainly have no need for alcohol as those that do require this can go in to town and buy it from the supermarkets. Why can't we have funeral directors here as there are many elderly people in the area and the nearest funeral parlour is bloody miles away?

Jenny had mulled over the statements for a considerable length of time, she wanted to be sure that she had the ammunition to fight against the complaints. Her dad and brother had given her some good advice, once they'd stopped laughing and she had been ready for the rather humiliating experience of sitting in a boardroom, being scrutinized by three very official looking men. It had been scary stuff.

She had won. The license was granted. So now Jenny had to prove that the local residents were wrong. And as Dayna had already pointed out, 'If the worst comes to the worst and things don't work out for your convenience store – just change it and open up a bloody funeral directors'.

"So, what's on the agenda today?" Dayna asked, smiling widely.

"The phone lines and internet are being fitted and then the final electrical checks will be done tomorrow. We should be stacking shelves and turning fridges on by Friday."

Dayna's eyes lit up, "Ooh, does that mean there will be lots of men in here today?"

"Yes, but it doesn't mean that you can prance around in your high heels and frilly skirts, ogling them all day long."

"Ok, guess I better get home and get the *Cinderella* gear on then. I'll be back by ten."

"See you then," said Jenny as her quirky friend walked out of the door.

Jenny could never understand why Dayna needed to dress up so fancily just to take Xaylan to school. She'd always been the same, whether she was going to the corner shop to buy a pint of milk or going to a pub for an evening out. She would put on her glad rags for any occasion. In contrast, Jenny was very plain, pretty boring and lived in jeans and trainers. She realised she would have to 'up' her game when the shop opened. Being the proprietor required some sort of formal wear surely, she'd wondered, even if it was just jeans and shoes or boots, rather than her trusted, tatty trainers.

Jenny sighed, there was still a lot of work to do before opening and her dad and brother would be turning up any minute with metal shelving racks to 'kit out' the store room at the back of the shop.

Another quick glance through the peep hole in the window and Jenny could see that there was no one around outside. She grabbed her keys, went out to the car, parked up in the first bay, directly in front of the shop, and proceeded to unload the boot of kitchenware for the staffroom.

The long hours she was expecting to work meant that she needed a microwave, plates, cutlery, a new kettle, mugs, a mini fridge, tea towels and two swivel stools with backrests. This was primarily going to be her home, at least until she had acquired a big enough customer base to afford another employee. Long hours lay ahead. The alcohol license had been granted for use during the hours of 7am to 11pm, however, she did not plan on staying open until 11pm every night – maybe just at the weekends. She was mentally prepared for the long, hard slog ahead of her. 'Determination' may as well have been Jenny's middle name, Dayna had always said. At the moment, however, Jenny privately thought that her middle name should be 'bricking-it'.

Chapter 3

Everyone had offered to help. The shop was buzzing with the hustle and bustle of footsteps, hurrying in and out through the doorway. Jenny, Dayna and Tasha (who'd been asked to start two days early, cash in hand) carried in the smaller packages and boxes of stock and placed them roughly, in their respective places, alongside the shelves. Ten year old Xaylan dragged his feet and followed behind the women, carrying the least amount possible. The ingrained scowl upon his young face suggested he was not amused by his mum's offer of him helping out. Wearing three-quarter length ripped jeans, *Converse* trainers and a *Lacoste* blue hoodie, Xaylan's facial expression, framed by a shaved head, blended in with his overall thuggish appearance.

Jenny's dad, John, and her brother, Jacob, hauled the crates of alcohol and the larger, heavier items into the shop. They had worked so hard to make Jenny's dream come true. Even Calvin had come along, uninvited, to help out with the stocking of shelves. Since Jenny's break-up with Calvin, he and her brother, Jacob, hadn't seen eye to eye, yet Jenny's dad still thought that the sun shone from Calvin's every orifice for some strange reason.

The dairy products would be arriving tomorrow, ready for the grand opening the following day and Jenny's head felt like it might explode. She had so many things to remember, to check, to finalise, to switch on, to start, to end and to do.

"We'll have to go out for a celebratory drink tomorrow night," said Dayna. "You won't get any time once the shop is open."

"That sounds like a plan," shouted Calvin, "I'm in."

Jenny tutted and rolled her eyes as Calvin walked back out of the shop to the Transit van.

"Don't worry, I'll think of something to get rid of him if you want me to," said Dayna, confidently.

Jenny noticed Tasha look round awkwardly. She wondered if Tasha had worked out the relationship between her and Calvin. She was also inquisitive as to whether Tasha had worked out yet, that Calvin was nothing more than a lecherous, obnoxious prick.

"Do you want to come with us Tasha?" asked Dayna, rather presumptuously. "You know, team bonding and all that sort of stuff."

"Thanks, that sounds great. I'd love to... if that's ok with you, Jenny?"

"Sure, no problem, it would be nice to get to know you a little more before we start." Jenny wasn't sure if it was a good idea, but she decided that one drink wouldn't hurt any of them and if Calvin did have to come along then she would make sure that her dad and brother did too. Safety in numbers.

"That's the lot then, Jen," said Dad. "We'll get back to the wholesalers. I reckon another two loads and we'll be done."

"Ok, thanks Dad." Jenny smiled and walked to the door to watch the three men drive away in the van.

"You could probably do worse you know..." Dayna's voice whispered over Jenny's shoulder. "I mean worse than Calvin."

"Dayna, there is no way on this earth. How can you say such a thing?" Jenny moved round her friend and walked over to the counter. "Don't even go there, Day."

"Ok, ok – I was just saying..."

"Well, don't say."

The problem with Dayna was that she had always settled for less. In her mind, Jenny was lucky to have a man around, even if he was a prize-prat. He could be made use of, he had money and he could do a bit of DIY, so surely he was worth hanging on to. Jenny however, did not agree with her friend's loose morals and would much prefer to be alone than pretend to like or love someone, just so that she had a well fitted-out home and someone to talk to at the end of the day.

Tasha was down the far end of the shop, carefully placing jars of price-marked pickle onto the top of a shelf. Already she had shown herself to be a hard and conscientious worker over the last two hours. She'd neatly filled two rows of shelving with condiments, sauces and tins which she had first labeled with price tickets, if they weren't already pre-labelled by the manufacturers.

The carefully thought out stock plan had been adhered to so far and the shop was really beginning to take shape and form. Jenny knew that the three women had a good hour or more before the men came back with another van load of stock. It was going to be a long, tiring day.

Xaylan hadn't been seen for over an hour, not that Dayna would have noticed. "Where's Xaylan gone?" Jenny asked as she tinkered with a till roll, trying to weave it around the machine whilst looking at the diagram on the instruction sheet.

"Dunno... I told him to go down to the other shop and check out their prices of bread and milk. He's probably hanging around somewhere, getting up to no good." Dayna laughed and continued to label tins of dog food.

"Did you really?"

"What?"

"Did you really send him to check out my competitor's prices?"

"Yeah, why wouldn't I?" Dayna looked up with a puzzled frown.

Jenny shrugged. "I'm just surprised by your forward thinking," she said. "Your entrepreneurial skills have shocked me."

Dayna laughed, "Well you know me Jen – it's all or nothing, right?"

"Right," agreed Jenny. "I suppose it is."

By half past three the final van load of boxes, crates and cartons had been carried into the shop and placed around the floor, directly below the shelves where they would go. Everyone looked tired and hot. The heat from the late September sun had penetrated through the smeared windows all afternoon.

"I can see you're going to have a bit of a problem here, Jen," said Dad, pointing to the shop front. "It's going to get hot in here, love. You'll be swimming in melted chocolate."

Dad had a valid point and one which Jenny hadn't thought of. It was very warm around the counter area, which was where most of the chocolate bars were going to go. "Well I can't afford air-conditioning, Dad – not yet anyway. I'll have to get an awning or something like that."

"Leave it to me, love – I'll get it sorted out. Call it my contribution to your future success."

"Thanks Dad, you're my hero." Jenny smiled and then flung her arms around her dad's neck.

"Get off woman," he said in jest.

Jenny's dad had been a rock since her mum died. At the tender age of 48, Jenny's mum had dropped dead from a massive and undetected brain hemorrhage, four years ago. It was so sudden and so very shocking for the family – for everyone who knew her in fact. She had been a vibrant and apparently fit and healthy woman until her demise. The family had bonded so deeply after the tragedy and Jenny's dad now devoted his whole life to his two children and his building business. He kept busy all of the time and was always attentive to the needs of others. Jenny had figured that this was his coping strategy but she did worry that he gave too much time to others and not enough to himself.

"Right, I'm going to the chippie in town. What do you all want?" Jenny called out across the shelving units. Holding a notepad and pen poised, she waited for the replies.

The last three hours of hard toil had really transformed the unit's appearance from a warehouse, filled with discarded cardboard boxes to a well set-out and reasonably stocked convenience store and newsagents.

Jenny reached down behind the counter and turned off the radio. "Chippie anyone?" she called again.

Xaylan bounded up the shop from the office at the back and skidded to a stop just short of the counter, which was already laden with warm chocolate bars and snacks. "Yeah, can I have some," he said, eyeing the sweets in front of him. "Mum, can I have chips?"

"I'm buying them – you don't need to ask your mum. And don't run through the shop like that, you could fall and hurt yourself or damage the stock, Xaylan."

Xaylan, like his mum, was a strong-willed character. At just ten years old he was already more than his mum or his grandma could cope with. Without a father-figure in his life, he was growing into an unruly and wayward child.

Xaylan shrugged. "Sorry... I want a cheese burger as well." He scuffed his feet across the newly tiled floor and tapped the side of the counter with his trainer.

"Yes, ok – go on then – off you go, back to your games," said Jenny, feeling slightly annoyed by Xaylan's nonchalant attitude. "And a 'please' and 'thank-you' might have been nice."

"Please – thank you," Xaylan added, before scuttling away.

"I'll get this," said Dad as he walked over to the counter, brushing the dust from his jeans.

"No Dad, this is my treat – you've all worked so hard today."

"Even so, I'm still getting the chips in – no debate."

Jenny knew that once her dad had decided that he would do something, there would be no argument. Whatever he said always went.

"Ok, thank you, Dad. You really don't have to do this though."

"Give me that pad and pen."

Jenny passed them to him and smiled lovingly. He was the most important person in her life and no one came anywhere near close.

"I think we should all nip down to the pub in town, tonight, rather than tomorrow. What do you think?" Jenny wiped her salty lips and looked around. "Don't know about anyone else but I could do with an early night tomorrow so that I'm ready for Tuesday."

Everyone nodded, smiled or mumbled in agreement as they scoffed the chips, burgers and fishcakes hungrily. Only Xaylan scowled but that was to be expected anyway.

"Yep, let's do that," Dad said as he winked at her. "Drinks are on me ok?"

"No Dad, I will get a round of drinks for everyone – please. You've all helped me out immensely and it's the least I can do to repay you all for your kindness."

"I'm agreed on that Jen, thanks hun," said Dayna.

"You're paying me though, so I should buy everyone a drink shouldn't I? I'm the one with the money…" Tasha piped up.

Everyone stopped eating (except Xaylan) and stared at Tasha.

Jenny thought it an odd statement to make, especially when Tasha had hardly said a word to anyone during the course of the day. Jenny had put it down to shyness.

"No, don't be silly… and you're not the only one who has been paid for their hard work. I will get them and that's that – right Dad?"

Dad nodded and raised his eyebrows. "If it makes you happy, love," he said and continued to eat his fishcake.

Jacob said nothing as was usual for him. The shy and quiet type, Jenny's brother took everything in but didn't give much out. Dark and mysterious was how Dayna described him, however, Jenny was sure that Jacob's wife, Becky, didn't have the same opinion, as she would often be heard or seen to be nagging the life out of him. Dayna and Becky hated each other with a passion, hence the reason that she had not been invited to help out with the shop. Jacob always seemed to be happy though and both Jenny and her dad couldn't ask for anything more. Although Dayna would, if she ever got her way.

As for Calvin, he was a little quieter than usual and especially in the presence of Jacob. It was clear to everyone that they did not like each other and even young Tasha was beginning to notice their strained relationship. Calvin kept a low profile and apart from his fixed gaze upon Jenny, he could only be described as a caged animal, watching and waiting for his time to pounce. Calvin's obsession with his ex was somewhat unnerving, but sadly, Jenny's dad didn't understand, or see, the harm that his undying acceptance of Calvin, was doing to her new and long awaited status of freedom.

Jenny's dad had the same train of thought as Dayna, 'she could do worse'. His own lonely existence, since losing his wife, had made him see things from a different point of view. Dad's view of 'be grateful for what you have got' included his daughter's ex-relationship and was spurred on further by the desire to have those, long awaited, grandchildren in the future.

In Jenny's eyes, however, Calvin just would *not* do and she would *never* settle for just being grateful for what she had. She would strive for the best. And one way or another, she would get it.

Chapter 4

The public house in the middle of the town was quiet. Just the regular Sunday evening locals, who were mainly men, dotted up and down the length of the bar. They all looked thoroughly miserable. Jenny could never understand why so many men spent their evenings (or sometimes the afternoons too) drinking beer by the side of a bar and usually on their own. Some picked at peanuts and other bar snacks, while others stared into space, clinging on to their pint glasses as if someone would come along and snatch it from them at any moment and the odd one just sat on the barstools, motionless, observing everyone else.

Jenny ordered a round of mainly soft drinks. There were just two alcoholic drinks purchased and those were for Dayna and Calvin – no surprise there. Jenny passed the drinks along the bar as the others said thanks and went over to a semi-circular seating area and sat down. They were all a little dusty and grubby from stocking the shop but had decided to have just one or two drinks before they all made their way home.

"Excited then, are you, Jen?" Calvin asked, still at the bar, even though he had his drink.

"Kind of – it's quite scary though as well."

"Well, I did say that you shouldn't go it alone…"

"No, I mean it's scary to think about that first moment when I open the door – when the shop opens for the very first time. That's what I mean. Nervous, I suppose – not scared."

"Still think you've taken a big risk, Jen."

Jenny had wondered for a long time whether Calvin might be jealous and she still thought the same now. "I'm a risk-taker Calvin, you know that. I have drive and ambition. If you don't take small risks – or even big risks – in your life, then you won't get anywhere."

Calvin didn't take any risks at all in his life. He was a plodder, same things every day, same routines, same job, same TV programs, same meals, same topics of conversation, same everything and same boring sex-life. "Well I still think you're taking on something too big here – just hope it's going to work out for you, Jen." Calvin huffed and walked away.

"Oh it will work. I'll make it work, even if it's over *your* dead body," she replied, under her breath.

Joining the rest of the group, around the long oval table, Jenny plonked herself down next to Tasha. "So, what did you think of your first day?" asked Jenny politely. "You've done a brilliant job getting those shelves stocked, down the far end. Thanks for coming in today, Tasha."

"That's ok, I liked doing it. I'll be in tomorrow to help clean up. I'd better get my frilly maid outfit on and bring my pink feather duster," she laughed, briefly, and then took a large gulp of her orange juice.

Jenny smiled, unsure of what to make of Tasha's comment. "Great – we need to get you and Dayna trained up on the till as well. There's nothing to it, it's pretty basic. And I'm sure that your feather duster would go remarkably well with Dayna's rubber gloves."

"Oh, better bring my cashier outfit too if I'm going to have till training." Tasha grinned wryly.

"Yes – great." Jenny felt uncomfortable. She thought Tasha's comments, to her new boss, were rather odd.

Dayna looked at Jenny, having overheard the conversation, and gave a puzzled look before she smirked. "You're gonna tell me next that you've got an air hostess costume as well," said Dayna.

"Yes, funnily enough, I have. Will we be flying then?" Again, Tasha smiled wryly. "And a policewoman's one as well – so no being naughty." Tasha giggled coyly and sipped her drink.

Jenny and Dayna looked at each other and then burst in to laughter. "Right, I think we'll leave it at that, shall we?" spluttered

Jenny. Slightly embarrassed by the strange and sudden change in Tasha, Jenny wanted to curb the conversation before it went a bit too far. However, she couldn't help thinking that the young girl hadn't even had an alcoholic drink and was saying rather unusual things, so heaven help her if she ever did get drunk.

"I'm gonna get going Sis – work tomorrow. Let me know if you need help with anything."

"Thanks, Jacob, you've been so amazing today. Couldn't have done any of it without you and Dad."

"You would have found a way," Jacob smiled warmly. "Good luck with the opening, I'll try and drop in during the week."

Jacob ruffled the top of Jenny's hair, said goodbye to everyone else, and left.

Pushing her bottom lip out, Dayna sulked as she watched him walk away. Jacob was a handsome man. He was tall and wide-shouldered with a shock of black hair, neatly styled and tantalizingly spiked on top. Jacob's placid disposition and inviting smile were appealing to many women, yet he had settled for Becky, his wife, who was the complete opposite. She had a fractious, child-like nature, was very plain, rather plump and not particularly attractive.

Turning back to Jenny, Dayna raised her eyebrows and rolled her eyes in the direction of Tasha, who was sat next to her.

Tasha was engrossed in something in the bottom of her glass and did not notice the puzzled expression on Jenny's face or indeed the renewed look of wonderment in Dayna's expression.

"I'd better go as well, Jenny," said Tasha. "What time shall I come in tomorrow?"

"Err... nine would be great if you can do that?"

"Ok, I'll be there... or be square," she giggled. "No, I'll be there... I wouldn't be square anyway. I'd probably turn out to be oblong... or even round."

"Great, I'll see you then and thanks for today Tasha," said Jenny, slightly concerned by this new, eccentric Tasha she was hearing.

Tasha stood up, tugged her t-shirt down over her slim hips, puffed up her short, brown hair and grabbed her jacket from behind her, "Bye then," she called out loudly.

Tasha had really grown in confidence since this morning, pondered Jenny, and she had suddenly become very familiar with her new work colleagues. "Do you want a lift home?" Jenny asked, standing up to let her pass.

"No, I only live around the corner don't I? I'll get my Batman suit on and fly home."

Jenny smiled, not daring to look in the direction of Dayna, for fear of letting out another burst of raucous laughter. "Ok, see you tomorrow then," she said calmly.

As soon as Tasha had walked out of the door, Jenny looked round at Dayna and the pair of them laughed hysterically. The hysteria rose from a predetermined dread of what on earth they were letting themselves in for with this new girl, Tasha Evans. She was not what she first appeared to be.

"Anyone for another drink?" said Calvin, draining the last drops from his pint glass.

"Oh, if you're offering, Cal – yes please." Dayna just about managed to splutter before she began to laugh again.

"That was quick, Calvin, are you in a race?" Jenny remarked, sarcastically.

Calvin smirked. "Thirsty work in that dusty shop of yours," he said. "Well, do you want one?"

"No thanks," said Jenny, "Don't think I'll be staying much longer."

Dad and Xaylan shook their heads. "No thanks Calvin, I'll be getting off soon too," said Dad.

Jenny nudged Dayna with her elbow, "Is it me or has that Tasha turned a bit odd?"

Dayna looked up, shook her head from side to side and then continued to laugh. "Jen..." she burst out. "I'm sorry, I can't help it. What's with all that dressing up stuff?"

"I have no idea. Was she trying to be funny, you know, to make us laugh or something?" Jenny shifted uncomfortably as she noticed her dad and Xaylan watching and listening.

"I really don't know – it'll be interesting to see what she's wearing tomorrow though, won't it?"

Jenny smirked and shrugged her shoulders at her dad and Xaylan.

Young Xaylan looked embarrassed by his mum's outburst and had stopped playing his game on his tablet. He tutted and rolled his eyes in disgust.

Jenny's dad had been engrossed in watching Xaylan play on his *iPad* but then his attention had been drawn by the two girls, laughing their heads off.

"Everything all right Jen?" he said, "She's a bit of an odd one, isn't she?"

"Think she was just trying to impress us really," replied Jenny, unconvincingly. "She's a sweet kind of girl."

"Hmm, sweet but odd I'd say," said Dad.

"Freaky weirdo," muttered Xaylan and then resumed his game playing.

"Well, she's on a three month trial period, so we'll see how she gets on."

Calvin returned with two drinks and passed the smaller glass to Dayna. "Are you back at the shop tomorrow?" he asked.

"Of course," replied Dayna. "It's all go from now on. We're gonna be a dream team, aren't we, Jen?"

"Absolutely," Jenny sighed. "Will you be ready to go after that one?" she said, pointing to the glass in Dayna's hand.

"No, you go now if you want to hun. I'll be fine here with your Calvin." Dayna grinned at Calvin before reaching over to peck Jenny on the cheek. "I'll see you in the morning," she whispered.

Before leaving, Jenny leant across to Dayna and breathed in her ear, "He's not *my* Calvin, Dayna – remember?"

Although Jenny appreciated all of the help she'd received today and valued every single one of her helpers – including Tasha and Xaylan, she couldn't help feeling relieved to be on her way home to the peace and quiet of her small flat.

Unlocking the communal front door of the building, Jenny then travelled the four floors, in the creaky old lift, to her one bedroom home. There were two flats on each floor and five floors altogether. Most of the residents were young couples but there were one or two lone, elderly people. Jenny hadn't lived there long and didn't really know anyone, apart from by sight or just to share a smile and a 'Good morning' each day.

Entering her flat, she threw her bag on the kitchen table, kicked off her shoes and slumped herself down on the sofa. Her flat was small but cosy. The open-plan kitchen/diner/lounge was the largest room, sectioned off by laminate flooring in the kitchen/diner and carpet in the lounge area. From the lounge, two doors at each side of the room, led to the bathroom and bedroom. Well designed and decorated by her dad, Jenny's home was modern and bright. But most importantly, it was hers – alone. Without Calvin.

Jenny flicked the television on and stared at it absent-mindedly. Her head was filled with thoughts of Tuesday, the grand opening of her shop. Yet there was nothing grand about it at all. Apart from a poster that had been displayed in the shop window for several weeks, informing people of the opening day and the types of products to be sold i.e. groceries, newspapers, confectionary, tobacco, alcohol, stationary and gift cards, there was nothing else 'grand' about it. Jenny wondered whether she had done enough to let the local residents know when she would be opening but worse still, did they even know she was there.

Posters or leaflet drops had both been mentioned over the course of the last few weeks but Jenny hadn't actually got around to doing either. Somehow she was hoping that it would all just happen naturally and everything would fall in to place.

Currently she had more pressing issues to deal with as her drooping eyelids gave in and closed. There was going to be a lot of hard work ahead so she made the most of the moment and fell asleep.

Chapter 5

J's Convenience Store sparkled. The girls had been hard at it for most of the day but the greatest transformation was when Tasha, very kindly, offered to clean the front windows to a smear-free shine. Daylight poured in, creating a bright glow along the aisles. It looked like a real shop.

Jenny stood in front of the central shelving unit, which stretched down the length of the shop, with her hands on her hips, and sighed. It had all come together finally.

The bakery and dairy wholesalers had made their first delivery, as expected, this morning, and after spending a couple of hours stacking items into the fridges or onto the bread shelves, Jenny hadn't been able to resist the temptation of a packet of six crumpets. The girls devoured them at lunchtime, along with a broken packet of chocolate biscuits.

"Hmm," said Dayna, wiping her lips, "I'm liking this working practice, Jen. Bring on the crumpets."

"Yes, thank you very much for the crumpets – they were really nice," said Tasha. "Would you like me to pay for them?"

"No, not at all. It's the least I can do to say thank you to you both."

Now everything was ready. The fridges and freezers were whirring away quietly, the electric metre, Jenny had noted, was spinning rather speedily and the old, second-hand cashier till was lit up and ready to go.

Both Dayna and Tasha had received some training on the till and between the three of them they'd worked out the best and quickest way to change the till rolls.

Already, Jenny had a pile of invoices and receipts, out in the back office, which would need to be dealt with and paid straight away, before they began to mount up. And a price list had been typed up for the items that could not be priced with the labeling gun.

It was really going to happen. *J's Convenience Store* was opening tomorrow.

"There's not much left to do now," said Jenny, still gazing out of the clean windows. "Dad's coming to hang the blinds in an hour, so it's just a case of preparing this front display shelf, ready to welcome the customers in the morning." Jenny felt a rush of both excitement and fear surge through her. "Shall we get the signs up and set out the tubs of lollipops and chocolates?"

"Yep, let's do it," said Dayna, clapping her hands together and walking off to the staff room to collect the plastic champagne flutes. "*Buck's Fizz* for the customers, hmm, we could have some drunks on our hands," she shouted back.

"Have you got any *blu tack*? I could put the signs up," said Tasha.

Jenny reached behind the counter and grabbed some sticky dots, "Here, these should do the trick." She passed them over and then stood and watched as Tasha carefully placed a sign at the top of the shelf. "Looks great, thanks Tasha."

Tasha smiled and then went off to display more 'Welcome' signs around the shop.

It was odd. It was almost like Tasha had two personalities. Today she had behaved in exactly the same way as she had during the day yesterday. She was shy, hard-working and very conscientious. She wasn't at all like the rather strange young lady from last night. Jenny didn't understand why Tasha could be so very strange in different situations. She was a lovely, polite girl and seemed to keep herself to herself and get on with her work. Yet last night, she was quite out of the ordinary and both Jenny and Dayna had thought the same, even though they had not known her for long at all. Jenny hadn't liked to ask Tasha about her comments the previous evening and Tasha certainly didn't mention them. Both Jenny and Dayna, however, were both relieved when she'd turned up this morning wearing nothing more than a pair of old jeans, a plain black t-shirt and white trainers.

Jenny stood watching the odd passer-by, outside on Millen Road. They didn't seem to notice that the windows were now clean and they could see in. They looked as if they were minding their own business, passing by with their heads down or turned the other way. Dayna had already said that she would stand outside tomorrow, in her bra, with a megaphone if she had to, to inform the locals that the shop was 'Now open!'

On the odd occasion that Jenny had bumped in to, whom she assumed, were the proprietors of the other units along the way from her shop, they had smiled and acknowledged her but no one had actually stopped to talk. Customers had pulled up in the parking bays at the front of the units to go to the hairdressers next door or was it the beauty parlour? And every week day in the morning, at lunchtime and late in the afternoon, hoards of parents, mainly mums, either took their babies and toddlers to the nursery or collected them. At those particular times of the day, Jenny had noted that practically every single parking bay had been used for the parents – even her three spots.

Dayna had, in her usual bolshie way, said that she would soon put a stop to that. It could jeapordise a potential sale if there was nowhere to park. Jenny just hoped that her dear friend wouldn't upset anyone in the process and jeapordise a potential sale through her, sometimes over bearing, actions or words.

"You want me to put all 50 of these out?" said Dayna.

Jenny jumped and quickly left her pondering hanging in the air – some worries resolved some not. "I was a million miles away then," she replied.

Dayna stood holding two boxes of plastic champagne flutes. "Thought so, with anyone nice?"

Tutting, Jenny shook her head and pointed to the shelves behind her, "Yes, we'll put them all out. At least that way it will look like we're expecting a lot of people for the opening."

"I've got one left. Where do you want this one to go Jenny?" called Tasha from the back of the shop. "I could stick it above this fridge?" she said, eyeing the chilled milk unit.

"Yes, that's fine – thanks Tasha."

Jenny was proficient in all things computer-ish and had made the 'Welcome' posters along with dozens of sheets of shelf price labels a few weeks ago. It had taken her several nights of copying and pasting, printing and trimming to create the colour coordinated shelf labels in every denomination conceivable. Jenny's forethought had come from her own frustration when she walked around the shops in town, only to find that there were no prices on the shelves for the items that she wanted. She was going to make sure that *her* customers knew the price of everything in her shop, even if the little price stickers had fallen off the products.

"That looks nice doesn't it?" said Jenny, stepping back and admiring the display of flutes, bottles of *Buck's Fizz*, chocolates and lollipops. "It looks very welcoming doesn't it?"

Dayna and Tasha stood either side of her, staring at the show of balloons, welcome banners and glitzy, curly ribbons hanging from the shelves.

"Looks good, Jen," said Dayna.

Tasha nodded her head and smiled just as the front door opened.

"Hi Dad, what do you think...?" asked Jenny as she turned round at the same time as the other two. All three of them dropped their mouths and peered questioningly at the stooped, old lady standing by the counter grinning.

"Oh, I'm not your dad lovey," she chuckled, "at least, I don't think I am."

The elderly woman was so tiny, she could barely see over the top of the chocolate laden counter displays on either side of the till. Carrying a large, woven shopping bag, she looked like she was waiting for some assistance.

"Can I help you at all?" asked Jenny softly. "We're not actually open until tomorrow morning but I'm sure that we could serve you now if you wanted something."

Dayna rushed behind the counter and stood up tall and all important looking. "May I?" she said to Jenny, beaming from ear to ear.

Jenny nodded and laughed and then watched and listened to her no.1 employee's first ever transaction with, potentially, her first ever customer in *J's Convenience Store*.

"I would like some sardines if you have any," said the old lady, tugging her bright yellow knitted cardigan, tightly around her. "And bread?"

Tasha headed straight round to the tinned food section and grabbed two tins of sardines. "We have got them in brine or tomato sauce," she called out.

"How much?" asked the woman.

"Two pounds and twenty pence," replied Tasha.

"Goodness gracious me," said the little lady. "That's far too expensive. What about your bread?"

"We're doing a fantastic offer on the bread," said Jenny, stepping in defensively. "It's just one pound and fifty pence."

"Hmm..." the woman muttered, "I'll have a half loaf of brown please."

"Ah, we're not selling half-loaves yet. I will almost certainly be getting some in though, if you could come back on Thursday." Jenny hadn't given it a thought to order in any half-loaves for the (more than likely single) elderly residents of Millen Road.

The petite old woman huffed and turned to leave. "I walked all this way and you haven't got what I want or it's too expensive. I will have to go down to the town now."

"I do apologise madam but as you can probably see..." Jenny pointed to the open/close sign on the door, "... we're not actually due to open until tomorrow. But by Thursday, we will have the half-loaves, if you would like to come back." Jenny hoped she didn't sound like she was begging for her first potential customer to come back.

"Hmm, thank you kindly. I will go to town before the chilly evening sets in. Good bye."

Dayna and Tasha were speechless as they watched the frail woman go out of the door and hobble away.

"What a bloody cheek," said Dayna, leaning across the counter top. "If she's anything to go by, we're gonna have a lot of fun around here, eh Jen?"

"I should have thought about half-loaves – especially around here," replied Jenny, slightly deflated by her first experience of a customer.

"We're not even open yet, Jen. She shouldn't have come in." Dayna was in defensive mode, "She obviously didn't look at the sign on the door which clearly says 'Closed'."

"I know but I could hardly turn her away, could I?"

Tasha stood silently by the side of the welcome display, propping herself up on a shelf. She said nothing.

"I can see there will be a lot to learn as we go through this. One step at a time I think," said Jenny and looked across to Tasha and smiled. "If you want to get home Tasha, that's fine. I think we're all done now."

Tasha nodded and then turned and walked away to collect her bag from the staff room.

"How about you, Day, I can manage here if you want to get off and pick up Xaylan."

"Yeah, was gonna get going now anyway. Mum texted me asking what time I'm picking him up. Don't think she can put up with him for more than a few hours these days."

Can't blame her, thought Jenny. "Ok, I'll see you at eight o'clock then – on the dot," she said, teasingly. "We could have crumpets for breakfast, yes?"

"Absolutely," replied Dayna and headed off to collect her things.

Thankfully Jenny's dad was the only other person to walk in through the door during the late afternoon. Three sets of silver coloured window blinds were hung quite quickly, between them. They added a finishing touch to the look of the shop front and could be closed to conceal the contents of the shop at night. Although Jenny had paid to have security alarms fitted, the blinds now had a dual purpose and would also protect the shop from the afternoon sun, which poured through the windows, causing the counter area to be a very hot place to work in.

"The awning will be here in about two weeks," said Dad. "Let's just hope it doesn't get too hot in here before it arrives."

"Wow – thanks Dad. I really appreciate everything you've done for me. I couldn't have achieved all of this without you."

"Yes you could – it would have just cost you a bit more," he laughed.

Chapter 6

It had been some time since Jenny had got up so early in the morning. Her alarm had gone off at 5am and she'd sprung out of bed, with a tummy full of fluttery butterflies.

Millen Road was peacefully sleeping as Jenny pulled up to the back of the shop and parked her old Jeep in one of the two spare bays. It was still early in the morning but her first ever newspaper batch had already been delivered and left, as previously arranged, in the lock-up cupboard (although it was not locked) at the rear of the store. Excitedly, she trotted round to the front of the shop and unlocked the door. She knew she had ten seconds to get to the alarm button, to disable it, before it would begin its incredibly loud ring. Although Jenny had disabled the alarm on several occasions since it had been fitted, it somehow felt different today. Everything seemed different today. It was all for real.

Jenny hadn't been at the shop at such an early hour before. It was quite an eerie place. When they had fitted the shop out, they all usually turned up at around nine o'clock to begin the day's work. However, J's would be opening at 7am today, ready to trade and ready to hopefully catch the early morning commuters as they headed down Millen Road towards the train station in town.

Once the newspapers had been displayed along the bottom shelf, Jenny tried to spread out the few magazines that she had, on the rack above. It would take a couple of weeks before she had the full range of weekly and monthly magazine that she had requested. But for now, she had enough to be getting along with and more would turn up as each day went by.

Taking a long, slow breath, Jenny sighed. The time was 6.45am, she had 15 minutes to grab a cup of tea, walk round the shop for the umpteenth time to check everything was in place and then prepare herself for her first customer.

Turning the open/closed sign round, Jenny checked through the hours of business. Mon – Thurs 7am – 8pm, Fri & Sat 7am – 10pm, Sun 7am – 6pm'. She had a long slog ahead of her but until she could afford more staff she would have to practically live at the shop.

The work rota had been set and agreed upon by both Dayna and Tasha, who would work six days a week each. They were going to alternate mornings and afternoons/evenings, with the option to switch over from time to time, if (and only if) everyone, but more so Jenny, agreed on it at the time. So Dayna and Tasha had a healthy 46 and 43 hours respectively, full time job each. There would be a cross-over period from Monday to Friday, where Dayna and Tasha would both work from 12pm until 2pm together. This would give Jenny a chance, each day, to either take a well-earned break, nip into town to do her banking or pop over to the wholesalers, if she ever needed to.

Wedging the rubber door-stop under the door to keep it open, Jenny dragged the large A-frame notice and poster board outside and left it next to the corner wall. The bold lettering on the poster, displayed in a deep blue print, read, *'J's Convenience Store – Now open!'*

Everything was set, the first shot-glass measures of *Buck's Fizz* had been poured in to just ten glasses – Jenny didn't want to be too presumptuous and she could always fill more, if and when she needed them, and the till had a £100 float in it.

Peering up and down the road, Jenny noted that, apart from the odd motorist or builder's van passing by, there was no one around. Stepping back inside, she went round the counter and plopped herself down on the high stool, which the girls had all decided would be a good idea to have behind the counter for those moments when they needed a breather. Dayna had said they would need to sit down after the long periods of serving countless customers, whilst rooted to one spot. Jenny had sighed at Dayna's remark and momentarily thought to herself, 'wishful thinking', but then quickly brushed the negative thought away.

At 7.15am Jenny slid off the stool and casually walked back to the front door and scanned the length of the road. The traffic had picked up slightly and now there was at least one car or van every minute or so, traversing either up to the top of the road, which ended in a large, circular housing estate, or down into the town.

In the distance, some two streets away, Jenny could see an elderly lady walking along the path with a small brown dog. Jenny darted back inside the shop and returned to her stool. Waiting in anticipation, she watched through the window to see if the lady was heading up to her shop.

A few minutes later the white-haired woman arrived outside the shop. Jenny's heart raced as she slid off the stool again and stood to attention at the till.

"Hello?" called the old lady as she strained her neck to peer round the opened door. "Do you have any dog hooks out here?"

"Err... sorry, dog hooks?" Jenny left the counter quickly and went to the door.

"Yes – hooks my love, to tie the dog lead to."

"Err, no sorry, I don't." Jenny tutted, once again she didn't have what the customer wanted. "I could pick some up this afternoon – I'll have them fitted by this evening." Jenny followed the woman outside and looked at the wall underneath the windows. She was sure her dad would be able to pop over this evening to fit some hooks on the wall if she went to buy them in her lunch break. "Could I bring something out to you? What was it that you wanted?"

"Oh nothing – I was only coming to have a look round my love."

"Ah, ok," said Jenny scanning the length of the road one way and then the other for any more potential customers. She looked down at the lady's little terrier type dog. "Would you like me to hold on to your dog for a moment while you have a quick look round?"

"Ooh would you mind, my dear? Wilbur's a very good boy – aren't you Wilbur?" the woman said as she bent over to ruffle the top of his head. "Here," she said, passing the lead to Jenny, "I'll just be a moment... and please take good care of my Wilbur."

Taking hold of the lead, Jenny stepped back to allow the woman to pass. Wilbur attempted to follow his owner but Jenny pulled him back and then stood outside the door and watched the lady slowly saunter around the shop. Smiling to herself, Jenny wondered what Dayna would think if she saw her standing outside her own shop with a dog, while someone was having a look around inside.

The woman stopped now and again to pick up items from the shelves. She held the goods in her hand and seemed to study the labels on them. Then she would plonk it back in its place and move along the aisle further, to do the same thing again.

Jenny was just wondering how long the lady was going to be when a tall man appeared from round the corner of the shop. "Good morning to you. Are you the owner?" he asked in a very eloquent voice.

"Good morning," Jenny replied politely. "Err yes, I am." She smiled awkwardly. "I'm just holding this dog for a lady in there. She's having a look around."

The very upright and strong looking man had to be in his late 60's or even early 70's, Jenny guessed. "Would you like to go in?" she said, feeling unsure of what she was going to do if the man wanted to buy something.

"Thank you," he said and smiled as he passed her. "Ah – young Dolly," he bellowed. "I thought that was Wilbur at the door." Gazing around the interior, the man took great strides down the first aisle and met up with the lady, whom Jenny now assumed was called Dolly.

Jenny continued to stand and wait at the front door with Wilbur, who was indeed a very good dog, just as Dolly had said. She looked along the road and could see another elderly man heading her way.

"Morning," the stout, red-faced man said as he walked up the slope to Jenny's shop. "This your shop?"

Jenny nodded and smiled weakly, this was not how she had planned to meet and greet her first customers.

"I've come to see what you've got," he said with a wide smile across his face. "Is that yours?" he asked, pointing to Wilbur.

"No, I'm just looking after it for the lady in there. She's having a look around and I don't have any dog hooks yet."

"Ah, is that Dolly in there…?"

"Yes, I think that's her name."

The elderly man raised his eyebrows and tutted, "Thought she might be the first to get in here. Do you have papers?"

"Yes – absolutely." Jenny ushered the man through the door and then wondered what she was going to do with Wilbur while she served him. Wilbur looked like he could be quite a mean dog if he felt like it – one of those nasty little ankle-snappers, so Jenny decided against picking him up and carrying him into the shop.

The rotund man had gone straight to the newspapers and grabbed one from the bottom shelf. "I'll leave the money on here," he called, as he placed some change on to the counter.

"Thank you," Jenny replied, rather gratefully, as she watched him walk down to the end of the shop to join the other two. Peering down at Wilbur, Jenny smiled as the thought of her first transaction, albeit in an unusual way, had been made.

"Good morning," said another elderly man, who was walking a weary, old, half-dead looking, overweight Labrador. Jenny jumped, as she hadn't seen him approach the shop and could only assume that he'd also come from round the corner. Wilbur pulled on the lead with his tail wagging frantically. The Labrador panted and drooled and then plonked itself down on its wide bottom, when the man stopped. "Are you the dog-sitter," he laughed.

"Yes, you could say that," Jenny laughed too. "I'm holding it for a lady while she takes a look around in there," Jenny pointed inside. "I haven't got any hooks to tie dog leads to at the moment but I do hope to get some fitted this evening." Jenny wondered if the man also wanted to go in. "Do you want to have a look?" she asked presumptuously. "I can hold yours too." *Why have you just offered to hold on to another dog, Jenny Fartor – stupid woman?* Jenny tutted, discreetly, to herself.

"That's very kind of you. I've seen you come and go from this place and I suspected that you may have been the new owner. The name's Stuart – here and thank you." The man gave Jenny the dog's lead and went straight into the shop, leaving Jenny wondering whether *his* name was Stuart or the dog was called Stuart. She decided not to use the name at all, just in case she offended the man by calling him by his dog's name or indeed, offended the dog (Jenny had doubts as to whether the fat animal would last through the whole day, judging by its size and lethargy, let alone be offended by anything). Wilbur and possibly Stuart, stared at each other but made no attempts to play, fight or sniff each other out, or indeed do anything that she thought normal dogs would do.

Shrugging her shoulders, Jenny huffed and shook her head slightly. What a completely bizarre situation to have got herself in to. She was standing outside of her own shop (although it *was* a gloriously beautiful morning), minding both Wilbur and the fat Labrador (possibly called Stuart), while three elderly people stood down the far end of the unit chatting and laughing. They all seemed to be oblivious to the fact that the proprietor of the new shop was standing outside, doggie-sitting. Or were they aware but just didn't care?

Jenny watched as a petite woman appeared from a side pathway running between two houses further up and across the road. She headed down towards the shop, scurrying along like a tiny mouse on a mission. She must have been at least 70, Jenny noted, as she drew closer. The elderly woman screwed her face up and grinned as she approached. Without a blink or a word, she hurried straight past Jenny, did a sharp 90 degree turn and entered the shop. Jenny watched in amazement as the petite lady hurried down the first aisle, scooted around the group of three people, still chatting away at the end, and then turned down the back end of the shop and out of sight.

Standing on tiptoes, Jenny craned her neck to see where the old woman was going or what she was doing, as she held on to Wilbur and possibly Stuart's leads.

Bloody ridiculous, thought Jenny, *I've got four customers in my shop and I'm stood outside with a half-dead dog and Wilbur the mollycoddled, potentially hazardous, ankle-snapper!*

Suddenly, through the window, Jenny spotted the tiny-framed woman skittering up the far aisle with a pack of toilet rolls in her hand. She stopped and peered into one of the freezers. Reaching down into the icy unit, on tiptoes, she grabbed a tub of ice-cream.

Jenny became uneasy, knowing full well that this was probably going to be her first 'real' sale. She scanned Millen Road, searching for anyone else that might be passing by. Then she desperately peered around the frontage, looking for somewhere that she might just possibly be able to tie the dogs to.

There was nowhere.

The little woman plonked her goods on the counter and walked away. She then proceeded to scurry around the shop for a second time.

"Are you ok in there? Do you need any help?" called Jenny from the front door.

The woman didn't hear her and continued to look at different items, along the shelves.

The other three people continued to talk and laugh amongst themselves, still supposedly unaware that they had left Jenny, inconveniently, outside the shop. Wilbur and possibly Stuart panted, drooled and dripped in the warm, morning sunshine. They didn't seem to have a care in the world and would have probably been quite happy to stay outside *J's Convenience Store* for the rest of the day. However, Jenny was not happy and suddenly decided that almost 15 minutes of waiting was getting to be a bit of a joke.

Moments later, Jenny spotted another man walking towards the shop... with yet another old and well-worn looking dog. The big black dog walked along beside the man, without a lead. Now and again it would stop, sniff a lamppost and then waddle along, behind him again.

"Morning," said the elderly man as he approached Jenny. The man eyed Wilbur curiously. "Is that Wilbur – Dolly's dog – you've got there?"

"Yes," said Jenny. "She's in my shop having a look around."

Apart from a few weary wags of tails, the dogs didn't stir as they all came together. *Old people – old dogs*, thought Jenny. It was like the dogs all knew each other.

"Ah, so you're the new owner. Well, I hope you do better than old Jim," puffed the man. His glowing, wrinkled face suggested that he'd walked a fair distance with his dog. Or maybe he was just very old and out of breath.

"Err... yes I am." Jenny peered, sharply, back into the shop to see where the petite old lady with the toilet rolls was. She was down the end aisle again but this time she was hugging a pack of kitchen paper towels in her arms whilst perusing the information on the backs of crisp packets and other savoury snacks. "Who's Jim?" Jenny enquired.

"He used to own this place, some years ago. He had a newsagents like this."

"Oh, I see. So he didn't do very well with his business then?"

"No, he scared the kids around here and they wouldn't come in. He only had one arm." The man beckoned to his dog to sit. "He had a hook, instead of his left hand and the kids had teased him for years."

"Oh dear."

"He started wearing an eye-patch as well, after an operation on his cataracts and told all of the kids that he was from a ghost pirate ship."

"Oh, I can see why that might have frightened the kids," said Jenny, feeling slightly bemused, not only by the story she was hearing but the whole situation that she had come to find herself in.

"When the parent's heard the stories, they stopped using the shop too. Then poor old Jim did a flit one night. He'd been struggling to make ends meet for a while. He was never to be seen or heard from again."

"Oh gosh. Well hopefully, it will work out ok for me... I do hope so anyway... and especially as I have an alcohol license – that helps."

"I'm sure it will my lover. The name's John." The man stretched out a hand.

"I'm Jenny," said Jenny, holding out her free hand to shake his. "Call me, Jen."

"May I have a look around?"

"Sure." Jenny eyed the big dog which was obediently sat by John's side.

"Don't worry about him, he should stay there and wait for me. You don't need to hold on to him." John laughed, turned to his dog and said, 'stay' and then went into the shop.

Now this is getting totally bizarre, Jenny mused and mumbled to herself, *there are five people in my shop and I am stood outside with three antique pooches. What on earth would Dayna think if she turned up now? She'd laugh her bloody head off and probably go inside and join them.* Jenny was growing more and more frustrated. Not so much by the fact that she was stuck outside, but more so, by the complete lack of consideration of the group of people, yakking, down the end of *her* shop.

Chapter 7

The ringtone stopped, "Hello?"

"Dad – it's Jen."

"Hello love."

"Dad, I need some dog hooks fitted..."

"Dog hooks?"

"Yes – to hook dogs on."

"On to what love?"

"I mean, dog leads. I've just had a nightmare Dad – you wouldn't believe it if I told you."

"You're selling dog leads?"

"No Dad." Jenny rubbed her brow and then peered through the window to see if anyone was coming up or down the road. All clear. "I need some hooks for the outside, under the windows somewhere. So that the customers can hook their dog leads on them."

"Oh, I see. I'll pop in this morning and have a look. I may even have something in the van."

"Thanks Dad, you're a superstar. I'll explain when I see you about my doggish nightmare of a morning so far."

Jenny's dad laughed down the other end of the phone, "It's only just ten to eight, Jen, and you've had a nightmare morning already?"

"Yeah Dad – there are some weird characters around here, I tell you."

"Ok, I'll see you in an hour or so, love."

"Thanks again Dad."

Placing the phone back in its base, under the counter, Jenny sighed. She hadn't even been open for an hour yet but she was already stressed out. Peering up at the 'Welcome' display, Jenny noted that two of the champagne flutes had been knocked over and a dribble of *Buck's Fizz* rested on the shelf. She grabbed a cloth from under the counter and proceeded to clean up the display.

"Yoo-hoo, only me."

Jenny smiled as she heard the familiar, shrill cry of a very welcome friend.

"No customers yet then?"

Turning round, Jenny watched Dayna totter into the shop and over to the counter – primarily to hang on to it for dear life – wearing her usual, four inch high stiletto shoes.

"Are you seriously going to wear those in here all day?" asked Jenny, shaking her head and grinning.

"Nah, brought my flip-flops. Had any customers then? It's a bit dead in here. I was expecting to make a glorified entrance into a shop full of people."

"Huh... you won't believe it, Day."

"What?" Dayna began to rummage through her oversized bag and pulled out her yellow flip-flops.

"Go and make a cup of tea and then I'll explain all," replied Jenny. "You're going to love this, Day – it's been like a bloody community centre, forward slash, *Battersea Dog's Home*, forward slash, *Alcoholics Anonymous* group meeting in here this morning."

"Blimey," said Dayna, chucking her flip-flops on the floor, sliding her disfigured feet (disfigured from years of wearing terribly high shoes) into them and then grabbing her bag and heels. "I'll be right back," she said as she flipped and flopped her way down to the end of the shop.

"I'm not kidding you, I think that she was drunk by the time she left here," said Jenny, sipping her tea, behind the counter.

"I'm coming in early if it's going to be that much fun in here at seven o'clock in the morning."

"No, seriously, Day... she's a bit odd you know. The little old Irish woman bought toilet rolls, kitchen towel for her birds to play 'nest-building' with, bleach cleaner to clean their cage out, six packets of crisps – in case she runs out of bird seed (they like ready-salted crisps) and a tub of vanilla ice-cream which she may share with her birds, if they're good. It was already starting to melt by the time she left."

"Well at least you've sold some stuff then," said Dayna, cheerily.

"Yes, I suppose I should be grateful. Think I heard her life story in ten minutes flat as well."

"So you've had an eventful morning so far, made some sales and some new friends –exactly what you wanted." Dayna laughed, just as a new customer walked through the door. "Good morning," Dayna bellowed.

Jenny smiled at the woman and greeted her with the same.

"Thank heavens your dad's coming to sort out some dog hooks though. Seriously, if I'd seen you stood outside, caring for the local pack of canines, I would have laughed my head off, Jen."

"Oh, I know you would have... that's what I was more worried about."

The girls giggled and then stopped suddenly as the short woman, dressed in a navy blue fleece and black trousers, came up to the counter with six, 2-litre cartons of milk. "It's cheaper in here. Think I'll get it from you each morning."

"Each morning!" replied Dayna, "How much milk do you go through?"

"I run the nursery up there," said the woman, pointing with a finger.

"Oh right, nice to meet you then. I'm Dayna... and that's Jenny."

"Cool, I've seen you both around here just lately. Suppose you've been helping to get the shop done up. It looks good."

Jenny smiled politely and nodded her head.

"It's her shop..." Dayna pointed to Jenny. "She owns it."

"Oh, I see," said the woman. "Well my name's Andrea Doo-Glass. I'm the manager of 'Small Steps'."

"Nice to meet you," said Jenny, offering a handshake.

Shyly, Andrea returned the gesture with a delicate hand and then her face flushed. "Have you met any of the other owners along here yet?"

"No I haven't. I've seen people coming and going but I wouldn't know who is who."

"Oh," replied, Andrea, before bowing her head and looking down into her purse. "There are all sorts along the way. I'm sure they'll all come in here at some point."

"Ah good. I look forward to meeting them."

"Hmm..." muttered Andrea. "I'll have a receipt as well please." Passing a debit card over, she appeared to wait nervously. Shuffling from one foot to the other, scratching her head and rubbing her nose, Andrea looked impatient as well. "Well I must be off – the children will be waiting for their breakfasts. Goodbye. Oh, and good luck – you'll need it round here."

"That sounded a bit ominous," said Dayna. "Don't you think?"

"I'm really not sure what to think about this place at the moment, Day. Seems to me, there are a few odd characters around here, so far."

"Ah, it'll be fine Jen. Have faith. In what? I don't know yet."

"Psst... Dayna..." Jenny stood on tiptoes, peering over the shelving unit. "Psst," she said, holding her pointed finger in the direction of the tiny lady who had just walked into the shop.

From behind the counter, Dayna looked up and frowned at Jenny's frantically pointing finger.

"That's her... the woman from this morning. Toilet roll woman," she tried to whisper, as she edged towards the front of the counter.

"Oh – is it?" Dayna watched the old woman scurry down the length of the shop.

"Yes, she must have forgotten something. She was only here an hour ago."

"Could turn out to be your best customer, Jen – don't knock it."

The two girls watched the woman through the large, circular mirror above the door, which gave a bird's eye view of most of the shop floor, when standing at the counter. The little old lady picked up a pack of four toilet rolls and tucked them under her arm.

"What does she need them for?" whispered Jenny. "She bought a pack of those an hour ago."

Dayna cupped her hand across her mouth and giggled. "Looks like she's getting some more kitchen towel too – she must have some bloody big birds, that's all I can say."

Jenny couldn't help herself and let out a snort of laughter. "I'm going," she breathed, "you can serve her this time... you might get to hear her life story too." Jenny sneaked off down the other aisle and out to the back office.

Seated at her new office desk, Jenny could hear Dayna asking the woman if she would like any help. She strained to listen to the conversation that Dayna was striking up with her and again, it was about the woman's life story. A few minutes later, Jenny heard the till make beeping noises and she assumed that Dayna was serving the woman.

Glancing at the small pile of invoices on her desk, Jenny screwed her nose up and then pushed them to the back of the desk. She did not want to be doing paperwork on opening day. She wanted to be out on the shop floor, meeting and greeting customers and having a laugh with Dayna. She decided that the real hard work could start tomorrow. Standing up, she moved over to the door and listened. No sound. Jenny walked back out to the shop floor and along the aisle to where Dayna stood, behind the counter. "Did you get her life story in three minutes flat then?"

"Oh yes, and I asked her why she needed more toilet rolls and kitchen towel. And we'll have to take that bottle of champers off the shelf – she took a swig straight from it."

Jenny looked over to the display and could see that one of the bottles, behind the champagne flutes, had been moved to the front of the shelf.

"Oh gosh, wonder if she's an alcoholic. What did she say when you asked her about the loo rolls?" asked Jenny, curiously.

"She said that she didn't know what I was talking about because she'd never been in this new shop before."

"Really?"

"Really," Dayna replied, "Guess that either you have been telling me little fib-lets, she has got a twin sister or she's completely insane."

Jenny laughed out loud, just as a couple of elderly men walked through the door, beaming and peering around the interior of the shop.

"Morning," said one man, "Looks nice in here – done a good job."

"My bet is, dementia," whispered Dayna, with a smile, before she proceeded to chat to the two men in what Jenny thought was a most flirtatious way.

Chapter 8

Lunchtime couldn't come soon enough for Jenny. Although the morning had gone very quickly, she felt like she had expelled a vast amount of nervous energy – unlike Dayna, who was taking everything in her stride. And that was why Jenny had wanted Dayna to work in the shop with her in the first place.

Dayna did have some failings when it came to a courteous manner or tact but her finer qualities were exactly what Jenny thought the customers would want. A humorous, flirtatious and sometimes quite rowdy person, Dayna could get on well with practically anyone and certainly with men of all ages. She loved to dish out cheeky remarks to anyone that cared to listen. She could also stand up for herself, should a situation arise. She was clever and strong-minded and the leaning post that Jenny may just need to lean upon should any hair-pulling moments arise.

Tasha turned up promptly at five minutes to twelve with a wide grin on her face. "I'm excited but nervous," she said quietly, leaning over the counter.

"We haven't had that many people in this morning but let's hope the word is spreading that we're open now," said Jenny.

Tasha nodded, "I'll just go and put my stuff in the staff room. Be right back."

"Yes sure and feel free to make yourself a drink and bring it up, if you'd like."

"Is that ok?" remarked Tasha.

"Yes, of course. We've been on the tea all morning – haven't we, Day?"

Dayna poked her head around the shelving unit where she had been rearranging the ready salted crisps. "Yeah – if you're making one, Tasha, then I'll have one please."

Tasha smiled again and walked off.

"You might need to get some extra ready salted in, Jen. If that woman runs out of bird seed, she could clear us out."

Jenny laughed and then wrote 'Ready salted crisps to replace bird seed?' on her homemade order sheet which she kept under the counter for everyone to add items to. "I'm going for my lunch break, Day. Hold the fort."

"No problem," replied Dayna and stepped up to the counter, looking like a woman on a mission to cajole and entice the next unprepared person that walked through the door.

Opening her sandwich bag, Jenny picked up the limp bread containing grated cheese and salad cream and proceeded to eat it. After the second mouthful, she placed it back into the bag. She really wasn't feeling that hungry. Having shared yet another pack of six crumpets with Dayna at 9.30, she was still full. Leaning back in the office chair, Jenny placed her hands on top of her head. This was day one of her new business and it hadn't quite gone as she had imagined. She could hear the till making its kerching noise from time to time but there hadn't been as many people through the door as she had expected. Now and again, Jenny listened to the strange, unknown voices talking as they went around the shop and the sound of Dayna's laughter resonating along the shelving units. As long as Dayna was making a raucous noise everything had to be going well out on the shop floor.

Closing her eyes, Jenny stretched back in the reclined chair. Fifteen minutes of her two hour lunch break had passed and if she thought about it hard enough, she knew that she had lots of things to do. The only problem was that she had no inclination to do any of it. It had been a long struggle over many months to get to this day and now she felt slightly deflated and worn out. These extended lunch breaks were designed to be her time to catch up with things, nip into town if she had to, but also they were meant for catching up with some much needed sleep. So that was what she would do – have a quick nap.

Her dad wasn't due back until around 5pm, with the dog hooks. It turned out that he did have some hooks in his van but they weren't big enough, by far. Jenny had offered to nip into town to get them herself, in her lunch break but her dear old dad was going to the builder's wholesalers anyway and had said he would get the right ones.

Grabbing her sweatshirt from the back of the chair, Jenny wrapped it around her shoulders, lifted her legs up onto the desk and reclined the swivel chair as far back as it would go. Then she slept.

Some 35 minutes later, Jenny awoke to the sound of Dayna's voice, just outside of the door.

"Oh, her name is Jenny, she's on her lunch break at the moment."

"Ah yes… Jenny… young Jenny, I know her."

"Yes, you met her this morning. She served you with toilet rolls I do believe," said Dayna, in what Jenny thought was an amplified way, just like when she talked to people who were hard of hearing. Jenny imagined that Dayna would also be pulling faces and speaking with distorted, over-exaggerated mouth movements too.

"Oh no – I know young Jenny from a long, long time ago," replied the old woman.

"Really?" remarked Dayna, "she didn't tell me she knew you before."

"Yes, yes I know Jenny – dear girl."

"Shall we put that ice-cream back in the freezer until you decide what else you would like, Marj?"

"Yes please… I need some toilet rolls. Have you got any?"

"Oh, I think you bought toilet rolls this morning." The volume of Dayna's voice had increased and Jenny suspected that it had been done so, purely for her benefit.

"Oh, silly me. I don't know where I might have put them dear. I'll take another pack – you can never have enough toilet rolls. I do have two toilets you know."

"Are you sure? I think you may have bought two packs already this morning, Marj."

Jenny now assumed that the old lady was called Marj. Smiling, Jenny pulled herself up in the chair and stretched. Peering at the clock, she was surprised to see that she'd been asleep for at least 30 minutes. She felt far more alert and ready to take on whatever the afternoon might bring. If the morning was anything to go by, the opportunities for the afternoon were endless, Jenny thought, as she shook her head in disbelief.

"Oh no, I have only ever been here once before," said Marj. "I've just got back from Ireland, you know. I've recently lost my dear husband, Neville... and my mother too."

"Oh dear, I'm so sorry to hear that."

"Oh yes, I'm sorry too. My poor mother was only 59 when she died of cancer. It was just last week and I'm heartbroken you know."

"Really? Oh, I can imagine how terrible that must be for you," replied Dayna. "And how old are you, Marj? You look like a fine, strapping woman, I must say."

Jenny could detect a hint of sarcasm in Dayna's voice. She could also hear the distant sound of the till ringing which gave Jenny a sense of euphoria each time it made a noise, because it meant that she had made another sale. Happy that Tasha was at the till, serving lots of customers, Jenny revelled in being the proverbial 'fly on the wall' or the 'fly behind the door', listening to what was turning out to be a very amusing conversation.

"Ah, I'll be 83 now... I think... yes, coming up for 84 in November."

"Ok..." Dayna replied, "Hmm... you say your mum died recently... she would have had to of been a lot older than... did you say 59?"

Marj mumbled something incoherent and coughed loudly.

"Right, anyway Marj, what else was it that you wanted today?"

As the voices drifted away from the door, Jenny rolled her eyes and tutted. *That woman has lost the plot,* she thought, before picking up the cheese sandwich, discarded on the desk, and taking another nibble. She then decided to try and finish it even though it tasted like cardboard in her mouth.

A moment later, there was a gentle tapping noise coming from the other side of the door.

"Come in," called Jenny.

The door opened slightly and Tasha poked her head into the office. "I'm making a cup of tea for Dayna, would you like one?"

"I would love one, thank you."

Tasha smiled and started to go.

"Oh Tasha..."

"Yes?"

"Firstly, you don't have to knock the door but thank you anyway and secondly, is Day still with that woman, Marj?"

"Yes." Tasha giggled and rolled her eyes up. "She's been in the shop for about half an hour, walking round and round. She must have a family that looks out for her – surely – she's not all there."

"Hmm, I do hope so, she needs someone to look out for her, doesn't she?"

The corners of Tasha's mouth drooped, "Yes... poor old woman."

There was still just less than an hour of Jenny's lunch break remaining. She had managed to finish the last bit of her cheese sandwich before it turned in to a soft-centered brick. Picking the pile of invoices up from the back of the desk, she shuffled them in to a neat pile and placed them back down again. It was no good, she wasn't going to even bother to look at them today. They could wait until tomorrow. Glancing up at the clock, she made a mental note that there were almost seven hours of 'open' time left of the shop's first day. A rush of excitement and then fear rumbled around in her tummy as she anticipated the end-of-day takings and what small fortune it may or may not bring her.

Strolling out onto the shop floor, earlier than expected, Jenny took a view of the stock loaded upon the shelves. Some things had been moved or touched and there were gaps here and there, while other items didn't look like they had been disturbed at all, since they were first placed there. A very rough calculation of the gaps suggested that Jenny's new shop really hadn't sold many items as of yet. She began to pull jars and tins forward just as Dayna appeared from the staff room.

"It's not that time already is it?" said Dayna, glancing down at her watch.

"No, I was bored. Thought I'd come out early and have a look around at what we've sold so far."

"I reckon you're gonna do all right, Jen. Tasha just served one man who wanted a hundred fags."

"Oh really, mind you, there's not a lot of profit in tobacco products."

"Nah, I suppose not."

Jenny looked up and realised that there were two people in the shop. "Let's hope it picks up a bit more this afternoon," she said and gave, Dayna a wink.

A blue taxi pulled up to the corner of the shop, turned around and then reversed up the side of the building to the small car park at the back of the shops.

Jenny was outside trying to figure out which one of the large wheelie bins was hers. She had ordered her own one but there were three identical bins from the same company. Peering inside each one, she noted that they all had rubbish in them. Feeling slightly peeved that someone else may have used her bin, Jenny pulled the least full one round to the back of her shop just as the taxi came to a halt, directly in front of her.

A tall, gangling, middle-aged man levered himself out of the back of the taxi in a most awkward way. Dressed in a tatty, green sweatshirt and grubby, grey trousers the man looked disheveled, dirty and disgruntled, by the way his forehead creased into deep folds, between his eyes. He dragged a large holdall out from the back of the car and then joined the driver, at the boot, to collect a small suitcase on wheels. The angry looking man gave Jenny a cold stare and then proceeded to ascend the metal staircase on the side of the building. Huffing and puffing, he struggled to get the holdall and the suitcase up the stairway, at the same time.

"Would you like a hand with those?" called Jenny, wondering if the man was one of the residents of the flats above the shops.

"Yeah, whatever," he replied without meeting Jenny's eye.

Joining the man on the fifth step, Jenny took the suitcase handle from him, "Here, I'll take that up for you…"

"Ta, live just there." The man told Jenny, as he pointed to the first flat at the top, which was directly above Jenny's shop.

Jenny noticed that the man limped as he climbed the stairs, "Would you like me to carry the holdall for you as well?"

"Nope."

"My name's Jenny, I own the shop below."

"Good for you," replied the man as they reached the top. "And, ta, for helping."

"That's not a problem at all. Those stairs are hard work when you have lots of baggage."

"Huh."

Jenny felt a little awkward and unwelcome, "Well I'll be off, got lots of things to do. Let me know if there's anything I can do for you. I'm only down stairs."

"Nothing you can do for me."

The man had completely avoided eye contact and left Jenny feeling slightly confused by his harsh persona as he unlocked his door. Throwing the holdall in the hallway, he then limped inside, dragging the suitcase behind him. Closing the door, with what Jenny considered to be a slam, the man could be heard muttering to himself from inside the apartment. Jenny turned and travelled back down the stairs two at a time – yet another weird, eccentric character had presented themselves to her and this one lived right above her head.

"Hello love, sorry I'm a bit late," whispered Jenny's dad. Scanning the length of the shop he could see that several people were walking around, looking at, or picking up the products from the shelves. "How's it gone today?"

Jenny leant over the counter, "Ok, I think," she whispered back. "Thanks for getting those Dad." Jenny glanced down at the small bag of hooks in her dad's hand. "I don't think I could cope with another morning like this morning. There have been another two people this afternoon, both with dogs. They also wanted to know where they could tie their dogs up and weren't very happy when I said they couldn't."

"Guess dogs must be popular around here then."

"Yes, certainly with the older people. I expect they have all taken their dogs up to the park today and then wanted to pop in here and have a look."

Dad nodded. "Any chance of a cuppa, Jen? Then I'll get these hooks put in."

"Yeah, of course, I'll call Tasha. She's having a quick break in the staff room. She should have had her 15 minutes at four o'clock. But we had a bit of a rush on with the school kids getting off the bus and also parents from the nursery."

"Ah... sounds good though. I mean, plenty of customers then," said Dad, smiling warmly.

"I suppose so but you can't class lollipops and penny sweets as a roaring trade, can you?"

Dad laughed, "It's a start, love. It's a start."

Three sturdy hooks had been placed along the length of the shop's front, underneath the window sill. Jenny and her dad stood outside, admiring the gleaming, metal protrusions as the late afternoon sun shone down furiously, penetrating the shop's windows in a rage of heat.

"Are those blinds doing the job?" asked Dad. "It's a hot one again today, how's it been by the counter?"

"It's way too hot, Dad. We put the fan on at about one o'clock. I'd only just turned it off before you arrived."

"Well hopefully you won't have to wait too long for the awning, love."

Jenny laughed, "Well it's supposed to be autumn now but I think we're having an Indian summer. I bet when the awning arrives, it'll start snowing."

Dad put his big arm around Jenny's shoulder and squeezed her tightly. "I'll give you a call later. You can let me know how you got on today, once you've cashed up."

"Ok, and thanks again for the hooks. There had better be some bloody dogs tied up to these, come the morning." Jenny laughed and then kissed her dad on the cheek, before he left.

J's Convenience Store bathed in an eerie glow as the sun dipped below the rooftops of the houses on the other side of the road. Jenny hadn't seen her shop look like this before. Although the lights inside the shop had been on all day, they hadn't been noticeable until now. As twilight cast an orange glow in the sky, the crisp, white lighting in the shop began to brighten.

Jenny peered out through the opened blinds. Dusk was starting to creep along the road which had become void of traffic and pedestrians and although it was only 7.30pm, the residents of Millen road had already disappeared. An autumn chill had set in as Jenny closed the front door and shivered.

"Ooh, it's got chilly," said Jenny, before joining Tasha along the first aisle. "We'll just get this lot tidied up then you can get off, Tasha."

"Oh no, I'll stay here until eight. I can get all of those papers tied up and put out the back for you."

"Thanks Tasha, you've been wonderful today. I'd say that it hasn't been a roaring start to trading but you have been amazing anyway. Thank you."

Tasha looked down at the shelf, coyly, and then pulled the bottles of washing gel forward, two spaces. "Sold two of these today."

Jenny laughed, "Well I hope that's not all that we have sold."

Tasha smirked, shook her head and then began to pull more items forward, stepping sideways along the shelving as she went.

Thump... thump... thump! Jenny followed the sound of heavy thumping noises which vibrated through the ceiling above her. *Thump, thump, thump.* Quicker this time. She traced the thudding along the whole length of the shop, above her head. Slightly unnerved by the obviously, deliberate thumping noises, coming from the flat above, Jenny checked the front door was locked again and then headed down the shop to the office at the back, with the till's cash tray in her arms.

Alone and uneasy, she began to count out the float money for tomorrow, from the tray. *Thump, thump, thump.* The noises resonated through the ceiling. This time the noise travelled in the opposite direction, away from the back of the shop and towards the front. Then it stopped.

Puzzled by the strange thuds, Jenny pondered for a moment as to what they could be. It sounded as though someone was jumping along the length of the flat above. Inconsiderate, she thought, and then continued to count out the coins from the tray.

Apart from the whirring of the fridges and freezers, there were no other sounds to be heard. Jenny wasn't sure that she liked this bit of her working day. Although she was excited about the unexpected takings, which were just under what she had forecast for the first few days, Jenny didn't feel comfortable being in her semi-lit shop alone. She supposed that she might get used to it in time. It may have not been so bad if there were people and cars rushing past, along the road outside, but there didn't seem to be anyone around. Even the pub, just across the access road by the side of her shop, appeared to be very quiet when Jenny had gone outside to fetch the A-frame newspaper display board in.

At five minutes past nine, Jenny turned the computer off, stood up and stretched her legs. It was way too late and she knew that she would need to be much quicker at cashing up and logging the day's takings into her computer. By the time she arrived home it would be getting on for half past nine. But this was her first day of trading, it was a bit special, she'd been pleased with the takings and the till roll's report had married up with the cash and card transactions, to the penny. Result!

Pushing the alarm button in, Jenny rushed towards the front door, flicked the lights off and got out of the shop, quickly. She knew that she only had ten seconds to do this part of her day and racing against the alarm's timer was quite scary. In time, she supposed, it would become easier and far less daunting. Double-locking the door, she stood back and peered up at the large lettering on the sign. She'd done it. Day one – complete.

Chapter 9

Today was Tasha's early shift and Dayna wouldn't be in until twelve o'clock. Jenny wished that Dayna was in this morning, just so that she could have a good old natter about everything but it would have to wait until this afternoon. Tired from a sleepless night, Jenny turned the 'open' sign round, dragged the A-frame out to the pavement and checked that the dog hooks were still firmly in place.

Glancing down Millen Road, she could just see the lady with the small terrier, who she had dog-sat for yesterday. Darting back inside quickly, Jenny tried to look busy by removing the last bottles of *Bucks Fizz* and plastic champagne flutes from the 'Welcome' display and then grabbing a duster from under the counter to clean the shelves.

With her back to the door, Jenny stopped and listened as the door opened slowly.

"Excuse me... when will you be getting some rings?"

"Rings?" Jenny turned and smiled.

"Yes – rings – for leads."

"Ah, do you mean something to tie the dog to?"

"Yes – like a metal hoop. When will you be getting some? You could lose customers if you haven't got anywhere for their– "

"I do have hooks out there now." Jenny placed the dusting cloth on the shelf and moved towards the door. "My dad put three in, last night." Stepping outside, Jenny brushed past the elderly lady. "Look – there... and one there and there," she said, pointing to the three hooks, proudly.

"Oh, they're no good for me, dear," said the woman, shaking her head. "The lead will come straight off of that and my sweet Wilbur could run into the road and get hit by a car. You wouldn't want to have that on your conscience now, would you?"

Jenny disguised her irritation and looked down at the hook nearest to her leg. Perhaps the woman did have a point. "Yes, I see what you mean. I suppose the hooks would be ok if you didn't have a thick lead but I can see that yours is very thick and probably wouldn't fit into the hook."

"You need rings, my love. Like a door knocker – that sort of thing."

Jenny nodded. "You did ask for hooks yesterday..." she sighed, loudly. "I'll see if my dad can pick up something like that today. Hopefully we can get them fitted, ready for tomorrow."

"Ah, good girl, good girl," said the woman. "My name is Dolly by the way. What is your name my dear?"

"Er, Jenny. Jenny Fartor. I own the shop."

"Oh do you – oh my goodness. You're very young to run a business like this, dear. I hope it succeeds for you... shops like yours haven't ever done very well here before."

"I know. I did hear about a man who owned a newsagent here, some years ago – before the tanning salon. Didn't he have a hook or something?"

"Oh yes, he did. Before him, err, Jim was his name I think, anyway before Jim there were two other men who ran a shop a bit like yours. Asians, I think." Dolly paused for a moment. "Anyway, they had the shop for about six months and then one night they just vanished – gone. All the stock was cleared out overnight – gone. I believe they hadn't paid any of their bills either. I hope the police caught the little rascals." Dolly peered up and down the road. "Well, I'd better be going. I must nip in to town today. I need to buy some new jumpers for church. I'm in the choir you know – gets a bit chilly in the church."

"Would you like me to pick up anything from the shop?" said Jenny, pointing over her shoulder with a thumb, "Or I could hold Wilbur again, just for a moment, if you'd like me to?"

"Oh no, that's fine my dear. I got my paper and a loaf of bread from *KO Store* earlier. I just came up here to see if you had fitted any dog rings yet."

"Oh I see," said Jenny, feeling put out by the fact that the woman hadn't had any intention of buying anything from her shop, much the same as yesterday and Jenny had gone to all the trouble of fitting dog hooks too. "Well I do hope to have some rings fitted by tomorrow, if you'd like to get your paper here."

"Oh, we'll see. You might close down by tomorrow." Dolly sniggered and then turned to walk away. "Good bye dear and all the very best to you. You'll need it."

Thump, thump, thump, thump. Jenny stood in the centre of the aisle and traced the noise along the ceiling again. *Thump... thump, thump, thump... thump, thump... thump.* Convinced that someone was jumping around in the flat above, Jenny made a mental note to investigate the strange happenings and even confront the rather odd man upstairs. The shop was empty, luckily, but how would she explain the strange noises to any curious customers. It could be embarrassing to have that racket going on when there were customers in the shop.

The hooks were good for most of the early morning dog walkers who travelled up the road to *J's Convenience Store* to collect their papers. Some people even thanked Jenny for supplying them. So it seemed that Dolly was the only one who had any complaint about the hooks. Jenny wondered why she had to have such a thick dog lead for such a tiny dog. Weren't those types of leads for Rottweiler and the like? Wilbur was just a scrawny, little Jack Russell type.

"Morning," chirped Tasha as she glided in through the door. "Shall I make a cup of tea?"

Jenny nodded her head profusely and continued to make small talk with a group of several elderly men, gathered around the counter. A middle-aged woman, who had popped in to pick up a paper, joined in the light-hearted, friendly chat, at the front of the shop, as she knew two of the men already.

As Jenny began to serve another woman, the chatty group moved away from the counter and continued to natter.

"It's like a community centre in here," the woman said in a hushed voice.

Jenny giggled, "Yes, I know. I think they all know each other from years back."

As Tasha came waddling up the shop towards the counter, with two cups of tea in her hands, the front door opened again and in tottered the tiny, ancient woman, Marj. Ignored by the friendly OAP's huddled in their garrulous group, Marj hobbled down the first aisle and out of sight as Jenny completed the transaction with the woman she was serving.

Tasha looked at Jenny and raised her eyebrows. "That woman is here again. The toilet roll one," she said, carefully placing the two steaming mugs of tea underneath the counter.

"Oh, you mean Marj?" Jenny whispered.

"Yes," Tasha laughed discreetly, behind a hand shielding her mouth. "Hope she's not buying more toilet rolls."

"She is." Jenny looked back from the shop's mirror. "Just seen her pick a pack up."

"Oh no," said Tasha, "should I go and talk to her?"

"Well you could try," replied Jenny, before rolling her eyes.

After 15 minutes, the small community centre of chattering pensioners began to drift away. Jenny watched from the office door, at end of the shop, as Tasha served each one of the group with a newspaper, before they said there cheery goodbyes and left. Marj was hovering around the frozen desserts freezer, obviously pondering over the idea of buying some more ice-cream. Jenny frowned and shook her head before turning to enter the office.

Leaving the office door slightly ajar, she plonked herself down in the chair and began to finger through the paperwork, already piling up on her desk.

"Ooh, hello." A voice came from the door. "How are you?"

Jenny looked up, startled by the unexpected visitor. "Oh, hello Marj, have you got everything you want now?"

"I need some bird seed... do you sell bird seed?"

"Ah no we don't I'm afraid. I could certainly have a look to see if I can get some in for you though."

"Today?"

"Oh no, it wouldn't be today, Marj."

"I need it today you see."

"Where do you normally buy it from?"

"Well, here of course," said Marj, screwing her face up in a huff.

"But I only opened yesterday, Marj." Jenny shifted in her seat and wondered why she hadn't put the 'Private Staff Only' signs up on the doors yet.

"I'll have some salted crisps then please."

"Yes, we have those. If you go up the aisle, straight in front of you, you'll find them on your left."

"Could you show me please? My eyesight is not as good as it used to be."

Jenny heaved herself back out of the chair. "Yes, follow me, Marj," she said begrudgingly, "and then I need to get back to my office and get some work done."

"Your office? Where do you work?"

"I work here Marj – that's my office," said Jenny, turning round and pointing to the room she had just left.

Marj said nothing and walked off to the crisps section as Jenny stood in the middle of the aisle, half way along the shop, with her hands on her hips, shaking her head despondently.

"I think you might be losing some customers," said Tasha.
Jenny stared at her perplexed. "Why do you say that?"
"Well, all the parking bays outside are full and I just saw a couple drive past, slow down, look in the shop and then drive off again."
Jenny peered outside and could see that every parking bay was indeed full but not because of any customers in her shop. The cars all appeared to belong to parents from the nursery, a few doors away. "Well, I'm not having that," said Jenny sharply. "Those are my bays, for my customers. I'll have to have a word with that woman who manages it."
Tasha pulled the corners of her mouth down, "I'm sure the couple in the car did want to park up and come in here, possibly to buy something" she reiterated. "Maybe you should buy a 'No Parking' sign to put outside or something like that."
"Hmm," replied Jenny, pleasantly surprised by Tasha's entrepreneurialism. "Perhaps I should... problem with that though, is... well, no one would park here at all if there was a 'No Parking' sign."
"Oh yes," replied Tasha and giggled embarrassedly.

Somewhat later than yesterday's time, Andrea Doo-Glass walked into the shop with a piece of paper in her hand. "We're going to buy everything we need from you." She pulled her shoulders up and grinned widely. "You're a bit cheaper than *KO Store* and a lot nearer," she puffed.
"Great," replied Jenny. "What do you need?"
As Andrea reeled off the list of items needed for the nursery's daily menu, Tasha hurried round the shop and collected them.

Jenny put each item through the till and then bagged everything up, whilst trying not to show the excitement on her face.

"That will be £27. 30 please," said Jenny, as she took the debit card from, Andrea and examined it. "Oh, it's Douglas, Andrea Douglas... I thought you said your name was Doo-something."

"Yes, Doo-Glass. That's how it's pronounced." Andrea's face flushed and her eyebrows crinkled into a frown.

"Right – apologies – yes, of course, Doo-Glass."

Andrea grinned falsely. "It's a bit cheeky of me to ask but would you be able to get this all ready for me each day?"

Jenny gulped and composed herself before saying, "Yes, sure, no problem."

"Don't suppose you do a tab, do you?"

"Err..." Jenny laughed nervously, "I haven't been open long enough to even think about anything like that."

"Oh it doesn't really matter... I just wondered you know... well maybe some other time." Andrea took the debit card and stuffed it into her purse. "I can bring a box down if that would help?"

"A box?"

"Yes, to put our stuff in."

"Oh, I see," said Jenny. "Yes that would be a good idea, thanks."

"Here's a list of the things we need every day. Are you sure that you wouldn't mind?" Andrea passed the list to Jenny and smiled.

"No, no that's fine. No problem whatsoever." Jenny was already calculating the amount of extra stock she would need, to cover such a hearty list every day.

"I'll let you know if it changes any time. Thank you so much. Sorry, what was your name again?"

"Jenny... and this is Tasha."

"Ah yes, Jenny. Well, thanks again Jenny."

"You're welcome, please, don't mention it."

"Don't suppose there's any chance of delivery is there?" Andrea laughed out loud. "Only joking... well, unless you do deliveries..." Again, Andrea laughed, but with more vigor.

Jenny thought it rather odd that Andrea should laugh so raucously and couldn't quite see what was so funny. She smiled politely. "Again, it's not something that I have thought about yet. I'm just getting used to running the shop at the moment. I may well branch out to other ventures in time though, so don't dismiss it altogether."

"Branching out eh?" said Andrea, leaning over the counter and staring hard at Jenny and Tasha. "You getting more shops then?"

"No – not at all. I mean branching out in respect to other services that I might offer in the future."

Andrea burst in to laughter again, almost hysterically, before stopping short. "Oh you're funny. I know where to come now, should I need a good giggle."

Jenny grinned uncertainly, although behind her smile hid a puzzled frown and thoughts of *'oh dear, not another strange person'*.

"I dread to think what other services you two young ladies might be offering," Andrea guffawed. "Will you be offering services out the back of the shop?"

"No, I think you've got the wrong impression. I meant things like deliveries, groceries and newspapers – that kind of thing." Jenny's tone of voice had changed, conveying annoyance.

"Ooh, I was only having a little joke with you. Hope I haven't offended you in any way. I just thought..." Andrea paused and frowned, "well, I thought, you know, girls together, having a little laugh to make the day go by quicker."

Jenny smiled, "Oh absolutely, I'm always up for a laugh. Apologies, I didn't mean to sound rude."

"No offence taken. Right, I'd better get back, they'll all think I've gone and left them," said Andrea, picking up the four carrier bags, laden with milk, bread, margarine and sandwich fillings. "See you tomorrow morning, my friend."

"Did you forget to mention about the parking?" asked Tasha, quietly.

"Yes I did. I was a bit surprised by her daily order request, to be honest."

"That's good though isn't it?" Tasha fumbled with the chocolate bars, tidying and straightening them.

"Oh yes, very good. I just had it going around in my head about how much more I would have to add to the bakery and dairy quantities, that's all." Jenny picked up a note pad and pen. "I'd better go and put an order in quick actually, otherwise we will run out of things by tomorrow."

"Good morning," said a cheery middle-aged lady as she strolled past Jenny, who'd just exited from the office.

"Morning," replied Jenny, absent-mindedly, as she hurried up to the counter, having just been summoned by the buzzer which connected the counter area to the rooms at the back of the shop. It had been lovingly fitted by Jenny's dad, for the purpose of emergencies or to call another member of staff, should one of them be out the back of the shop.

Tasha was talking to an elderly man who was leant over the counter, huffing and puffing. "Sorry to call you, Jenny, but this man wants to know if we do newspaper deliveries."

Jenny looked at the heavily breathing man, who appeared so frail, and she wondered for a moment whether he should sit down. "Are you ok?" she asked, trying not to stare too much at his grey, gaunt face.

"A chair if... you have one please, dear."

"Yes of course," said Jenny and grabbed the stool from behind the counter.

The elderly man slumped down on the stool. "Thank you my dear," he breathed, hard. "Asbestos... fifty years ago." The man leant over to one side, resting against the side of the counter. "Not too long left."

"I'm so sorry to hear that," said Jenny sympathetically. "Could I get you a glass of water or anything else?"

"No dear," sighing heavily, the man continued. "Paper delivery. Could you drop one... round to me... every morning?"

"I'm sure we could manage that somehow." Jenny's empathic nature had dropped her right in it, as usual, and she knew it. "Do you live nearby?"

"Cornerstone... Close."

"I'll check where it is on the map. Afraid I'm not that familiar with the area," Jenny replied.

"I know where it is," said Tasha. "It's only two streets away from here."

The tired old man nodded his head and grinned a brown toothed smile.

"Ah good, well I err... Yes, of course. That shouldn't be a problem at all," said Jenny before she had time to think about it. Grabbing the notepad from behind the counter, she asked, "Could you give me your address and the paper you would like?"

Writing down the details, Jenny suddenly worried how she was going to get a single paper delivered each morning. *It's plainly obvious*, was her second thought. She would have to do it herself, once one of the girls turned up to work.

The old man panted, "How much... will... delivery be?"

Jenny hadn't even thought about that. "Erm, will that be delivery every day, including weekends?"

The man nodded.

"I haven't thought about this to be honest with you," she admitted, "How does 70p a week sound?"

"Seventy pence? That's... daft."

Jenny frowned in puzzlement, "Oh, I thought that might be ok. Ten pence a day?"

The old man shook his head and smiled. "Far too cheap."

"Oh really? Too cheap?"

Nodding his head, the old man continued, "*Shaw's...Newsagent...* two pounds... and fifty... pence."

"Oh I see what you mean," Jenny laughed. "Well, I'm happy to start at 70p – if you're all right with that?"

The man nodded again. "Paperboys... not reliable... at *Shaw's...* monthly bills are... wrong too." The man pulled himself up and drew in a deep breath. "Rubbish service."

"Ok, so you came here to see if *we* did deliveries then?"

"Yes. Drove past... last night... thought you opened... yesterday."

"Yes we did," said Jenny, "I closed at eight."

"No lights on... outside... thought you opened... today."

Jenny frowned and shook her head whilst wondering why the man had thought she was closed yesterday. "What time did you come past yesterday?"

"Seven... picked up my... wife from church."

"We were definitely open at that time, weren't we Tasha?"

Tasha smiled widely. "Oh yes, it was my first shift here."

"Looked dark, thought... you were shut" said the man, struggling to breathe, to the point of looking quite scary and on the brink of death.

Jenny suddenly realised, "I haven't got any outside lighting. So you say the shop looked closed from outside?"

The man nodded again.

"Wonder if a lot of people thought that?" said Tasha. "We didn't have many people in last night."

"Well, we don't know that, Tasha. After all, we may not have many customers any night." Jenny laughed. "I'll have a look outside tonight. Thanks for letting us know."

"You are welcome," said the man. "Could we start... delivery... tomorrow? I'll pay a month... up front... in case... I should die."

Jenny was stunned momentarily, by the poor man's last comment. "Err... yes, that will be fine. Would eight o'clock be ok? I'll have to wait for one of the girls to start work."

"Would have preferred... earlier but if you can't... I'll wait. Here..." said the man, passing a payment card to Tasha. "One month."

Tasha looked, wide-eyed, at Jenny and shrugged.

"Right, well, we'll have to set up a separate payment system for this one, I think, Tasha. Leave it to me."

Tasha backed away from the till and stood watching as Jenny recorded the transaction in her notepad, grabbed the calculator and a calendar from under the counter and began to work out monies to be paid.

"Dad, hi – it's Jen."

"Hello love. Everything ok?"

"Well not really, there are two things, Dad. You're not going to believe this but the hooks were just not good enough for one woman this morning, she'd already bought her paper from the other shop. So I really don't know why she'd bothered coming up to mine anyway. She said she'd only came to check whether I'd had the dog hooks fitted. Can you believe it? Bloody cheek if you ask me."

"Oh dear, you will get funny people like that, Jen. So what are you thinking of now then?"

"A ring of some sort, well that's what she said anyway – not that I'm bowing down to her demands or anything like that but I suppose she could have a point about those thicker types of dog lead which may not fit into the hooks. Something like a door knocker, do you know what I mean?"

"Yes, I know what you mean, love. So a heavy-duty ring pull, is that what you need?"

"Ha ha, yes Dad. Couldn't think what they were called. Do you have any in your stash?"

"Not sure that I do, love. I've got a lot on this afternoon but I will have a quick look during lunch. If not, I'll get Jacob to run over to the wholesalers and pick up a couple for you. I can drop in on my way home but it won't be until about seven. Is that any good to you?"

"That would be wonderful, Dad. Don't know what I'd do without you sometimes."

"Not a problem, love. What else?"

"I think I might need some kind of lighting for outside the shop. Something above the sign, to illuminate it somehow."

"I had thought about that at one point but forgot to mention it to you, Jen."

"Do you think it would be expensive?"

"Not sure, I'll have a look in to it. I suppose you'd need it quite soon, what with the dark evenings drawing in."

"Yes," replied Jenny, nodding her head and twiddling with a pen. "Someone came in earlier and said that they thought we were shut last night because there were no lights on."

"Oh, that's not good. I'll ask Jacob to source them for you. I'd imagine you'll need some downward-facing, strip lighting."

"Thank you Dad. I really appreciate everything you do for me."

"I know you do, love. Isn't that what dads are for?" He chuckled.

Chapter 10

Giggling among themselves, in the afternoon sun which poured through the slits in the blinds, Jenny and Dayna had to stop abruptly, each time a customer walked in. Once again, and if yesterday was anything to go by, Marj's appearance at the door was not a surprise at all. She hobbled in, waved her dainty little fingers toward the girls and then scuttled off down the first aisle. Dayna looked at Jenny, raised her eyebrows and grinned knowingly.

"This is *only* the second time she's been in today, I'm sure," Jenny whispered, "unless Tasha forgot to mention any other visits this morning. Hope she's not buying more toilet rolls... we'll have to stop her somehow, if she is."

"You can't really decide on what she does and doesn't buy, Jen."

"Yes, but if she has got dementia, or something like that, we can't just let her keep buying the same thing all the time. It's not fair."

As the two friends watched Marj through the mirror, their eyes were suddenly diverted to a tall, sleek and handsome man, dressed smartly in a dark grey suit, who walked through the open doorway. He smiled and acknowledged the girls before heading down the same aisle where Marj had just disappeared.

"I'm serving him," whispered Dayna, nudging Jenny with her elbow.

"No you're not – I am," breathed Jenny. "Go and do some menial task – he's mine."

Dayna stared, with a downturned mouth and wide eyes, "Pleasey-weasey."

Letting out a short burst of laughter, Jenny cupped her hand to her mouth and tried to discreetly contain the giggles. Up in the mirror, she could just see the reflection of the young man slowly moving along the shelves, looking from side to side.

Nudging her friend in the ribs, Dayna tried to push her out of the way of the till. "Come on, move. He's mine I tell you."

Both girls giggled too loudly and simultaneously covered their mouths with their hands, to suppress any guffaws.

"You win," said Jenny, "I've got stuff to sort out. You can have him." She winked a long-lashed eye at Dayna, turned to leave the counter area and then stopped sharply, when she saw Marj and the young man talking at the end of the shop. Turning back to Dayna, Jenny whispered, "Think I'll wait until Marj has gone."

At the end of the aisle Marj could be seen holding on to the man's jacket sleeve and giggling. She was whispering to him while he leant over to catch what she was saying. Then he would laugh or smile and try to edge away from Marj's grasp. The young man looked up the aisle towards Jenny and Dayna, and smiled awkwardly, before raising his eyebrows and rolling his eyes. Marj pulled him over to one of the freezers and began to point to various products.

"Oh no, what is she doing?" asked Dayna, rhetorically. "She's hooked herself up to him. You can see by his face that he wants to escape." Dayna shook her head and tutted.

"I'll go down and ask if Marj needs any help," replied Jenny. "He might be able to escape her then."

Dayna shook her head again, in disapproval. "Bloody ridiculous, she shouldn't be allowed out."

"That's a bit harsh, Day. The poor woman can't help it." Jenny sighed, "I'll sort it out."

As Jenny approached the couple, the man turned and smiled at her warmly. Smiling back, she felt herself blush slightly – his deep brown eyes seemed to penetrate straight through her. "Err... Marj, is there anything I can help you with? I'm sure this young man has got things to do." Jenny smiled again and raised her eyebrows.

"Oh, we're just having a friendly chat. Must you rush off?" asked Marj, staring up at the man's face.

The man nodded and grinned, "I'm afraid I must," he said in a gentle voice.

"Come on then Marj, let me help you get some things," said Jenny, tucking her arm through Marj's arm and trying to steer her away. "Now what is it that you want today?"

"Excuse me, could I just ask whether you sell *Milk Tray*?" the man asked politely.

Letting go of Marj's arm, Jenny looked round and was instantly aware of the man's eyes burning deep into hers. "Err... well... err, we only sell milk in poly-cartons... I mean, I don't know if you can get it in a tray... how much is in a tray?" Jenny pointed to the milk fridge, further up the aisle. "That's the only kind of milk we do I'm afraid," she said, coyly.

Dayna had sauntered down the aisle to join the group, just as the young man burst into laughter and began to shake his head.

"That's a good one." He managed to say before laughing again.

Stopping dead, Dayna had overheard the conversation and stared disbelievingly at Jenny, before bursting into uncontrollable giggles too.

Marj continued to look into the freezer, mumbling to herself about whether she should have the ice-cream or one of the cheesecakes which were further back in the icy chest unit. She was oblivious to the comedic situation going on behind her.

With a flushed, puzzled gaze, Jenny looked at Dayna and frowned. She had missed something.

The young man stopped laughing and grinned at Jenny. "I'm sorry, that made me laugh," he said. "I meant do you sell boxes of *Milk Tray*? You know, the chocolates, *Milk Tray*, made by *Cadburys*."

"Oh my goodness. Oh no, I'm so sorry – how stupid of me." Jenny cringed as her face burned to a deep scarlet. "Yes, they're over there, on the top shelf."

The man looked at Jenny sympathetically. "Don't worry about it." He smiled warmly, "it was funny though," he said as he walked off, still chuckling to himself.

Jenny looked towards Dayna, who was biting her bottom lip, and shook her head despairingly, before rolling her eyes to the ceiling. What an absolute idiot she'd been.

"Why do you always do that when you see someone you fancy?" whispered Dayna.

"I don't fancy him. I don't know what I was thinking – I feel so bloody stupid."

"Well you did sound stupid. I'm sorry but it was so funny, Jen. Never mind, don't worry about it. But I think you do fancy him though." Dayna laughed and walked back up to the counter.

Jenny followed behind, having already decided that she had to see this through to the end, in order to save face. She would serve the man with his box of *Milk Tray* and apologise to him again.

"Shall I make a cup of tea?" asked Dayna. "You look like you could do with one."

"Yes please. I will serve him now – I feel so bloody stupid."

"I'm sure he found it quite hilarious and doesn't think you're mad." Dayna picked up the two empty cups from under the counter and left.

Marj was leaning over the side of the freezer, still muttering something under her breath. Her tiny frame, with outstretched arms, could barely reach the ice-cream, let alone anything else.

The tall, and most definitely handsome, man had found the chocolates and had already picked up one of the larger boxes of *Milk Tray*. With the box tucked under his arm, he moved up the aisle to the magazine rack and stood with his back turned to Jenny, as he perused the titles.

A few minutes later, the man turned and strolled over to the counter. "Is this a new shop?" he asked.

"Yes, we've just opened," replied Jenny, feeling her face begin to heat up again. "Sorry about that, a minute ago, I must have been on another planet."

"Don't worry about it." The man grinned again. "Sorry I laughed so much – it was funny though. Is it your shop?"

"Yes," Jenny gulped as her face continued to heat up.

"How long have you been open?"

"Err... one day... precisely."

"Cool – nice shop. I see you've got an old till there," said the man, pointing to the old, electronic till.

"Yes, I got it secondhand. I need to get up and running before I can spend any more money on it. It's a bit of a sad looking till, I know." Jenny laughed nervously.

The man smiled. "Ah ok, cool. Well let me know if you want to upgrade later, I sell EPOS systems to independent stores like yours." The man fiddled around, searching his pockets. "Don't think I've got a card on me at the moment." He tutted.

"Oh, is that why you came in?" asked Jenny suspiciously.

"No – not at all. I didn't know this shop was here actually. I don't do cold-calling. I have a company online. I gain business by recommendations or by word of mouth but mainly jobs come directly through my website. I run a retail systems support network too."

"Oh, that sounds interesting. I might just contact you once I'm doing a roaring trade," Jenny spoke jokingly. "Marj, down there, my number one customer on day two, should help." Jenny laughed, nervously.

"I'll drop a card off to you, I don't think I've got any in the car either. Stupid really." The man smiled again, "See, we're as bad as each other."

"I'm sure you couldn't be as silly as me. I live on planet Zog sometimes."

"The name's Aaron – Aaron Frey," said Aaron, stretching out a hand towards, Jenny, "nice to meet you."

Discreetly, Jenny wiped her perspiring palm on her thigh, took his hand and shook it gently. "Jenny Fartor," she replied shyly. "Nice to meet you too." She gazed up into Aaron's deep brown eyes and momentarily, she was transfixed by them. "Err... right, shall I take that for you?" she said, reaching for the box of chocolates.

"Sure, thanks." Aaron passed them over the counter...

"Ooh... oh... argh! He...e...e...e...lp..."

Both Aaron and Jenny turned their heads at the same time.

Their mouths fell open as they both peered down the aisle.

Aaron threw a horrified glance at Jenny, dropped his box of chocolates onto the counter top and shot down the aisle at a surprising speed.

Jenny's heart thumped in her chest, as she too, followed Aaron towards the tiny pair of 40 denier, beige coloured legs, sticking out from the freezer, frantically waving around in the air.

Marj's whole torso was inside the freezer.

She scrambled around, right at the back of the unit, trying to push herself back out as the boxes of frozen desserts crumpled and moved aside. Her little, stocking-clad legs swayed back and forth as she desperately tried to grasp on to anything to help pull her out.

Having heard the commotion, Dayna walked out of the staff room with two mugs of tea in her hands and halted, mid stride. Gawping at the sight of Marj's legs poking out of the freezer, Dayna was frozen to the spot as she watched the young man lean over the freezer unit, grab Marj around the waist and carefully drag her out whilst talking to and reassuring her all of the time.

A disheveled heap of frailty, Marj's face had turned deep pink. She grimaced as she rubbed her right hip but remained silent.

"I'll grab a chair," said Jenny, flying past Dayna, who was still holding two cups in her hands and staring, wide-eyed at the scene before her. "Bring her in here," Jenny called out.

Supporting Marj's slight frame, Aaron guided her past Dayna and into the staff room.

Pulling a high stool towards her, Jenny lowered the seat and helped Aaron ease her up onto the seat.

"Have you hurt yourself anywhere?" asked Jenny, nervously. "Marj, could I get you a sweet cup of tea or something else?"

Marj remained silent, but shook her head slightly, while staring absent-mindedly across the room.

"Are you sure that you're ok Marj?" Jenny leant into Marj's face, trying to get a coherent reply or even just some recognition in the poor old woman's dull, grey eyes.

Dayna had turned and followed the trio's exit into the staff room, whilst still holding the steaming teas. A moment later she was pulled to her senses sharply, as a couple of mothers and toddlers walked into the shop. Swiftly, Dayna placed Jenny's tea on the sink and then hurried up to the counter with her own.

Leaning on the doorframe of the staff room, Aaron watched as Jenny tentatively responded to Marj's needs.

"Here, Marj, have a sip of this," said Jenny, passing a small glass of water to her. "You've had quite a nasty shock. Is there anyone I can contact? I think that your family should know that you've had a bit of an accident."

"Haven't got any family. I'm all right. I'll sit here for a moment, thank you. Do you have any biscuits?"

Jenny turned and looked at Aaron despairingly. "Would you mind picking up some biscuits from the shelf up there." Jenny pointed to the first aisle, on the opposite side from the freezer units. Turning back to the poor old woman, Jenny asked, "Which biscuits do you like, Marj?"

"Oh, I do like a chocolate digestive, thank you."

Aaron headed off up the aisle to find the digestive biscuits, like an obedient dog. Jenny watched after him, admiringly, before he disappeared around the corner.

"Marj, is there anyone at all who I could contact? What about a friend or neighbour?"

"No there's no one my dear. I am fine, really I am. You don't need to call anyone. I'll finish this water and then be on my way."

Jenny nodded her head, "Ok, well if you're sure... Can I get your shopping for you then?"

"Shopping?"

"Yes, what did you come into the shop for Marj?"

Marj chuckled, "Oh yes, well my dear. I need some toilet rolls. That is all."

"Ok, I'll get them for you. Do you want the same as usual?"

"Yes please. The nice turquoise ones."

"Ok and they are on the house Marj – you can have them."

"Are they free?" asked Marj, looking surprised.

"Yes, you can have them for free." Jenny was somewhat relieved that Marj did appear to be all right.

Returning with the chocolate biscuits, Aaron passed the packet to Jenny and their eyes met again. *There's something in those eyes*, thought Jenny, briefly. They excited her and created little bubbles in her stomach. She did fancy him.

"Is there anything else I can get for you?" asked Aaron. A warm smile spread across his faultless face as he gazed at Jenny.

Jenny then knew that he liked her too. She could feel it. She could see it. She could hear it and she thought she could smell it. "Are you sure you don't mind? Marj would like some blue toilet rolls." Jenny whipped her gaze away from Aaron and looked at Marj. "Do you want a two pack Marj?"

"A two pack?"

"Yes, toilet rolls. You wanted some toilet rolls. Would a two-pack be enough?"

"Oh no, I'd like four please, the nice turquoise ones."

"Nice turquoise ones it is then," said Jenny. "Are you sure you wouldn't mind?"

"Not at all, I'll go and grab them," replied Aaron, before turning to leave. "Urgh... I'm sorry," he grunted, as he walked straight into a woman carrying a small child.

Jenny pushed the staff room door to, as the two women and their young children in tow, tried to peer into the staff room to see what was going on. Tutting and rolling her eyes upwards, Jenny leant back on the sink unit with her arms folded, as Marj nibbled on a chocolate biscuit. "How did you manage to fall in the freezer, Marj?"

"Fall in the freezer?"

"Yes, we've just pulled you out of the freezer, Marj. Do you remember?"

Marj giggled, "Oh my goodness, yes. Those cheesecakes are in too deep, dear." Marj extended her biscuit out in front of her. "May I?" she asked, before submerging the digestive into Jenny's cup of tea and letting it go.

"Err... yes..." Jenny replied, surprised. "Yes... go ahead." Picking the mug up from the sink, she passed it to Marj. "Here, help yourself..." she said, peering down in disgust, as the soggy, chocolatey biscuit floated on the top.

"Thank you." Marj gave a wide, biscuit grin. "Do you have a spoon? I need to get the rest of the biscuit out."

Slightly irritated that Marj appeared to be making a meal out of her accident now and had messed up her cup of tea, which she had been longing for, Jenny continued. "I realise that the freezer is too deep now... but how did you actually get in there, Marj?"

"I climbed up. I called you but you were too busy talking to your husband."

"He's not my husband Marj, he's just a customer," replied Jenny, defensively.

A moment later there was a tapping noise at the door. "Come in," called Jenny.

"Toilet rolls." Aaron's tall and slim figure stood in the doorway. "Is she ok?" he asked, eyeing the little woman, perched on the stool, pecking away on pre-dunked digestive biscuits, like a caged bird.

"Yes, she's fine. Thank you so much for all your help."

"It's not a problem at all. I've never seen so much drama in a shop before." Aaron grinned and then winked his eye at Jenny. "I'll leave you to it then... are you sure you'll be ok?"

Jenny nodded and smiled. She didn't want him to leave but she couldn't think of any reason for him to stay.

"I'll drop that business card in to you sometime," said Aaron.

"Great, thank you. I'm sure I could use your services in the future."

"Is this your husband dear? I'm dreadfully sorry. Here..." said Marj, beckoning Aaron to come inside the room, "would you like to sit in here?"

Jenny and Aaron looked at each other and burst into laughter. "Marj, I've already said that he is not my husband. This kind man helped to pull you out of the freezer. He's a customer, like you."

"Oh yes, of course. Well maybe you two should stop beating about the bush and just get married."

Aaron's embarrassment was quite apparent but endearing too, Jenny noted, admiringly.

"Maybe we should," Aaron mocked and then winked at Jenny. "Anyway, it's been nice to meet you Marj," he said, leaning in through the door. He stretched out a hand towards hers.

Peering up sharply at Aaron, Marj did not take his hand but shrugged her small shoulders and climbed down from the stool. "I'd better be off. My birds will be waiting for their tea," she said, pushing past him and into the shop.

"Did you want these," Aaron called after her, "toilet rolls?"

Marj turned and snatched the packet from Aaron's hand.

Jenny peered round the door and could hear the till ringing as Dayna scanned one item after another. The two young Mums were by the counter, chatting and laughing. "The toilet rolls are on the house Marj, like I said before, a token gesture to express my apologies."

"Pardon?" said Marj.

"Never mind – have the toilet rolls Marj, they're free."

"Oh, yes, thank you very much."

Hugging the turquoise toilet rolls close to her chest, Marj tottered off down the aisle and straight out of the shop.

Aaron and Jenny both stared at each other in amazement and then quickly averted their gaze. "Right, I'd better go and pay for those chocolates," said Aaron. "Good luck with your shop."

"Huh, think I'm going to need some good luck. I've only been open two days and already a customer has had an accident."

"I don't think you need to worry too much, she didn't hurt herself."

"No thankfully, but if we hadn't seen her, I could have been removing a frozen, dead customer from my freezer unit."

Aaron burst into laughter again. "Sorry, it's not funny really," he managed to say, "I've never seen anything like it before though. Maybe you should put a sign up."

"Good idea."

"It could say something like, 'Please do not get inside the freezer, due to the risk of freezing to death and turning into a stiffy'."

Feeling guilty momentarily about her pending reaction, Jenny just couldn't stop herself and burst into a loud roar.

The two Mums left the shop and Dayna walked down to the end, to see what all the noise was about. Outside the staff room, Jenny and the tall man were bent over in fits of hysterical laughter. "Don't know if Marj paid you for her toilet rolls," said Dayna, slightly disgruntled that she may have missed out on something highly entertaining.

"I told her she could have them," said Jenny, before bursting into laughter again.

"She seemed ok when she left," replied Dayna, huffily.

Jenny nodded and looked at Aaron who then began to laugh again whilst shaking his head and looking up to the ceiling.

"Those chocolates are on the counter if you still want them." Dayna stared despairingly at the two guffawing clowns. Irritated by the fact that she didn't really know what was so funny, Dayna puffed out her cheeks and walked back to the counter.

"Right, I'd better go and pay for them," said Aaron. "It's been great to meet you, Jenny."

"You too." Jenny couldn't help feeling forlorn as she began to walk up the aisle towards the counter with him. "You can have the choccies. No need to pay for them. I don't know what I would have done without you here."

"Well, I suppose you may not have realised, for a while, that you had a customer hanging out of your freezer." Aaron laughed. "Your customer service wouldn't have looked very good when those other two women came in with their kids."

With that, both Jenny and Aaron burst into laughter again, just as they reached the counter.

Dayna stared at the two of them in puzzlement.

As Jenny walked behind the counter, she placed a hand on Dayna's back, "I'll explain all... in a minute," she said.

Aaron took his wallet from the inside of his jacket, "I want to pay for these," he said. "Maybe I'll come in another time for some of your free turquoise toilet rolls."

Again, both Jenny and Aaron guffawed but Dayna just stared unknowingly.

"Sorry Day, this is Aaron. He sells EPOS systems."

"Oh, hi Aaron. Nice to meet you, although I have no idea what a he-pos system is."

Aaron and Jenny's eyes met once more and there wasn't a hope in hell that they wouldn't start the cachinnation again. So they did.

"I'm sorry, Day," said Jenny again. "I've got a fit of the giggles today."

Dayna shrugged, "Nice to see you happy again."

Jenny stopped giggling abruptly as Dayna's words made it sound like she hadn't been happy for a long time.

"What do you mean – happy again?"

"Well, you could do with someone in your life, who makes you laugh a lot like this."

Jenny frowned at her dear friend and poked her in the side.

"Right, I really must go," said Aaron, sensing the awkwardness. Passing his payment card to Dayna, he smiled warmly at Jenny. "I'll drop that card in to you, as soon as I can."

"Ooh, chocolates. I bet there is one lucky lady going to receive these," Dayna said as she began to process the card.

Aaron grinned before looking down, embarrassedly. "Yes, my mum... I forgot her birthday."

"Oh dear, that's not good. You'll need to buy her more than a box of chocolates," said Dayna.

"Oh don't worry, I have." Aaron smiled, "I've got a boot full of garden gnomes – she loves gnomes."

"Ooh, one happy Mama!" said Dayna, laughing exaggeratedly. "Give me the creeps – I'm sure they walk around the gardens at night."

"Maybe they do… but she still likes them." Aaron met Jenny's eye. "Thanks… and… err… nice to meet you. I'll pop the card in as soon as I can. Bye."

Jenny gave an acknowledging smile and watched him walk out of the shop as tingly, flutters flipped around inside her. There was no mistaking it. She most definitely fancied him.

Chapter 11

"Day, I don't get it. Why did you say that I wasn't happy? That well embarrassed me in front of Aaron."

"Ah, you're not getting my motive are you, Jen?"

"No, I'm not."

"I was trying to give him subliminal messages."

"What do you mean, subliminal messages – about what?" Jenny huffed as she watched three lone and potential customers walk straight into the shop and down the first aisle, one after another.

"That you're single and up for grabs."

"What?" Jenny gawped at her friend and colleague. "I thought *you* fancied him."

"He's all right. You do though – most definitely."

"He's really nice, Day. I'm not ready for that kind of stuff again though. I've got a shop to run now. And besides, he's probably already spoken for."

"Nah, I reckon he's single too. No ring – I looked." Dayna slurped her cooling tea. "You need to have a life too though, Jen."

"I've got a life. I'm devoted to making this shop in to a successful business. I don't need men... well, not at the moment anyway."

Dayna cleared her throat. "Huh, well it's nice to have the option."

The three customers were spread around the shop now, perusing the well-stocked shelves. Jenny watched as they picked up items, placed them back and then moved along the aisle to something else. She hadn't seen these people before, which was great news for the shop's footfall. Jenny suspected that no amount of advertising would bring her customers quicker than 'word of mouth'.

"You liked him too. Why don't you go for him? Well, that's if we ever see him again." Jenny sighed and really hoped her words would not be true.

"No point," said Dayna, just as one of the people approached the counter...

"Blimey, news travels quickly around here, doesn't it?" Dayna checked the details she'd written in the note book and then placed it back under the counter.

"Yes, at this rate I'll need to hire a paperboy."

The second person, of the three people who had walked into the shop, one after the other, had been told by 'a friend' that *J's Convenience Store* provided a newspaper delivery service.

"Or girl," corrected Dayna.

"Yes, or girl. I've got no problem with delivering two newspapers in the mornings but if we get any more, I'll have to consider it."

"So you're going to leave Tasha here on her own, on the mornings that she works?"

"Ah, well I hadn't actually thought about that," said Jenny, placing a thoughtful finger to her lips.

"I've got no problem with you going off to deliver a couple of papers, Jen, but Tasha is very young. I'm not sure that you should be leaving her alone to manage the shop at all."

"Hmm..." Jenny pondered over Dayna's statement for a moment. "I could ask her if she would drop them off, I suppose."

"Well yes, you could but she'd have to walk wouldn't she? I don't think she'd be too happy to do it if it was chucking it down though." Dayna left the counter and went round to the front of it, to tidy the chocolate bars. "You'll have to ask her Jen – see what she thinks."

"Yes... I wonder whether she's got a bike."

"Still get soaked if it's peeing down," said Dayna, fiddling with the chocolates needlessly.

"Well I'll just have to leave her in the shop then. How long can it take to deliver two newspapers?"

Dayna shrugged. "Dunno," she said, before walking off to the magazine rack to do some more unnecessary tidying.

"Anyway," said Jenny, joining Dayna by the magazines, "why did you say 'no point' earlier, when I said about you going for that man, Aaron?"

"Oh Jen, it's so obvious that he fancied you."

"Really?" Jenny felt a bubbly sensation in the pit of her stomach. "How do you know that?"

"The way he looked at you. Didn't you notice?" Dayna turned to face her best friend. "No, you probably didn't – you were laughing your head off too much."

"Well, we may never see him again," said Jenny, pulling her bottom lip down and staring wide-eyed.

"We will – I know it... even if you can't see it."

Dead on seven o'clock, Dad arrived, beaming as usual. "You're right love," he said to Jenny, "it doesn't look like you're open from outside."

"Thought so. The light from the street lamp on the corner seems to wash out the lights inside here. I'd better get something sorted out, pretty soon."

"Never fear – Father is here," said Dad. "Jaycob picked some outdoor strip lights up for you."

"Oh, bless his little cotton socks," said Jenny. "Dare I ask how much?"

"No, you dare not. Call them a complimentary gift from both of us, for pulling off your dream."

"Ah, thank you Dad." Jenny leant over and kissed him on the cheek.

"Well before you start shouting my praises..." Dad wiped a hardened, builder's hand across his face, "...we can't fit them until Friday. We've got too much on at the moment."

"That's fine. I'll stand outside the shop in the evenings, with a torch, if I have to." Jenny laughed and kissed her dad's cheek again.

"I could have asked Calvin to give Jacob a hand, they could have got it done tomorrow afternoon... but you know your brother... he screwed his nose up when I suggested it and said, 'No thanks, Jen can wait'."

"Well you are the only one that seems to like Calvin, Dad. I'm well and truly over him and Jacob never really liked him from the start," said Jenny, defensively.

"I always say you could do worse, love."

"Yes, I know. Dayna tells me that all the time as well." Jenny shuffled uncomfortably. "It doesn't matter what anyone says, Dad – I'm prepared to give 'worse' a chance."

"You've got to do what is right for you, love. Now make me a nice cup of tea, while I get the stuff from the van."

"Ok... oh, and Dad, did you get the ring thing?"

"All in hand, love," said Dad as he headed back towards the door. "You can tie an elephant to the front of your shop, when I've finished."

Both Jenny and Dayna, who had been busy filling up the savoury snacks and crisps, laughed.

"I'll make the tea, Jen," said Dayna, getting up from her knelt position and dusting off her trousers. "I'm all done with this lot," she said, picking up two boxes of crisps and waddling off towards the store room.

Dad returned with two lengthy boxes and a carrier bag of bits and pieces. "I'll get the elephant-rings fitted now, shouldn't take too long," he said, as he rummaged around in the carrier bag. "How's it gone today?"

"Blimey, where do I start?" said Jenny, raising her eyebrows. "I can't believe I've only been open two days – feels like a lifetime."

"Oh dear, why's that?" Dad found what he was looking for and pulled the rings and their attachments from the carrier bag.

"You won't believe what has gone on today." As Jenny proceeded to tell her dad about the day's events, he listened intently to her remarkable tale.

After 20 minutes of drilling, screwing and banging, Dad poked his head round the front door. "All done, love."

"Coming," shouted Jenny, from behind the counter, where she was jotting down the two addresses for the newspaper deliveries. She had to double-check the whereabouts of her customers' homes on the computer, in order to ensure a quick delivery in the morning.

"Ooh, they look good. Bigger than I thought. I see what you mean – you could definitely tie a horse to that," said Jenny, pointing to one of the rings.

"Elephant," said Dad.

"And an elephant!"

Another day was drawing to an end. Dayna had been very helpful in removing coins from the till and bagging them into their correct bags, before the shop closed – they were ready for tomorrow's float. It would save Jenny the job of doing it later and hopefully allow her to go home a bit sooner, once she'd cashed up.

"I'm getting off now, Jen," said Dayna, glancing up at the clock on the wall. "Got to go and pick up the little rat-bag."

Dayna's mum was babysitting once again, although the task was proving to be tetchy and tedious, as far as everyone was concerned. Dayna's mum didn't approve of Xaylan's late-night game playing and the distinct lack of homework, and rightly so. Xaylan didn't agree that he should ever have to do any homework as he did enough at school and as he was going to be a game-maker when he grew up. So there was no need to do anything else, apart from play games. Dayna was on the fence and not in any position to preach about the benefits of doing homework. Having played truant for most of her school years and certainly never considered doing any school work at home, she wanted to keep her mum sweet, hence the reason for the constant arguing between Dayna and her pre-hormonal son.

"Is there anything else, before I go?"

"No, that's fine, thanks, Day. It's ten past eight already – you get yourself home. I've nearly finished here, thanks to you. I think we should get the next day's float ready every night."

"As long as we're not too busy," replied Dayna, grabbing her coat from the hook in the staff room.

"Well, I hope we will get busier, once Dad and Jacob have put the lights up outside. We might look open in the evenings then."

Jenny was praying that this was indeed the case. She needed to have more than four customers in the evenings if staying open, keeping lights on and paying staff was going to be financially viable. The last two days had not paid for themselves in the slightest, but Jenny had allowed for a slow start in her financial forecasts. Things would have to pick up quite sharply though, if her targets were going to be met by the end of month one.

"See you in the morning, Jen," said Dayna, waving the back of her hand as she went out of the door.

Jenny left the paper bundles for a moment and went to lock the door behind her friend. She felt safer knowing the front door was locked as she sat out the back in her little office, counting out the day's takings, checking the cash and card slips against the till report and then inputting the information into her spreadsheets.

She finished five minutes earlier than the previous evening. Shrugging her shoulders, Jenny made a mental note to get much quicker at the cashing-up. By the weekend (when she would be open much later), she needed to get home as soon as possible. She wanted to feel like she at least had a tiny, even microscopic, bit of life at home, especially at the weekends. Only two days had passed and already Jenny felt like she lived in the shop... and she practically would be by the weekend.

Wrenched from her muse, Jenny's heart thumped as she listened with bated breath. She had heard a knock at the far end of the shop and assumed it came from the door.

Who could be there?

For some unknown reason, she felt uneasy. If there was a stranger at the door, what would she do?

Open it?

Would it be a customer?

Surely not. The front sets of lights were turned off. Realising, potentially, just how vulnerable she was, Jenny made the decision to go to the door and call out to anyone there, that the shop was closed and of course, she would also say sorry.

Nervously, she pulled herself up from the chair and headed down the semi-dark shop, as the knocking came again.

"Bloody hell, you scared the life out of me – you idiot," said Jenny as she pulled the door open wide. "What are you doing here?"

"I was passing. Thought I'd drop in to see how you're doing."

"I close at eight o'clock. Did you know that?" Jenny began to feel somewhat agitated at the lack of consideration shown.

"Like I said, I was just passing. I saw your car round the corner and thought I'd come and see how you were. What are you being a stress-head for?"

"Stress-head? I was just getting ready to go. You scared me, Calvin. You could have just text me or phoned," said Jenny, angrily.

"All right, keep your hair on. I wouldn't have bothered if I'd known I was going to get this reception. I guess it's not going too well, by the sound of it."

"It's going fine, Calvin – thank you."

"Good, pleased to hear it. Do you want to go for a quick drink before you go home?"

Calvin had softened which made Jenny rethink her momentary, irrational fear. "Thanks for the offer Cal but I need to get home. I'm worn out. And since when do you go for a drink on a Wednesday night?"

"Well, I can start can't I?"

Jenny laughed, "Look, I'm really not up for it. I'm gearing myself up for day three and my papergirl duties. Maybe another time. You know, I'm not sure that this can work…"

"What?"

"Well, this being 'just good friends' bit. I know it's what you want but… well, it's just a bit odd, don't you think?"

"Why should it be odd?" Calvin was frowning now.

"Well how are we… you, ever going to move on, if we're 'good friends'?"

"I'm happy where I am, Jen. I don't need anything else. Are you trying to say that you do?"

"Calvin…" Jenny lowered her voice, "…my only interest in life now is my new shop, my business. End of – Finito!"

"Yes, I know. I'm only trying to be supportive, Jen. You're a bit of a stress-head at the moment aren't you?"

"No, I'm not… I just need to get home, Calvin. I'm sorry – I don't mean to be snappy." Jenny cringed at her nasty thoughts and sharp words. "Pop in again at the weekend, if you must. I'll be less tired during the day."

Calvin huffed and turned towards the door. "We go back a long way, Jen. I can't just stop caring about you straight away."

"I know… I'm sorry Cal. Let's go for a coffee on Saturday. I get a two hour lunch break."

Calvin grinned.

"But that's it. A coffee and a catch up, Calvin."

Nodding his head and smiling like a pathetic child, Calvin went to leave.

"Hang on, wait for me. I was just about to lock up." Jenny ran back down the shop, turned off the computer, grabbed her coat and bag and switched off the bottom rows of lights. It was much nicer to have someone waiting at the door as she switched all the lights off and ran to the door before the alarm went off.

Thump, thump.

Jumping into her car, Jenny wondered whether she had imagined the two 'thumps' coming from the ceiling, as she left the shop. Perhaps she had invented them in her moment of being a 'stress-head', as Calvin had called her... or perhaps the strange noises had happened again.

Chapter 12

The rain poured down heavily, in diagonal bands as the wind whipped across the car park at the back of the shop. Wrestling with the swinging doors of the newspaper shed, Jenny attempted to get the bundles of papers inside, as quickly as possible. Last one in. Only the top paper in each bundle was wet and as Jenny hadn't managed to sell any more than half of them to date, she could spare several damp ones.

Thump... thump, thump. Thump... thump... thump.

Jenny stood dripping in the back of the store room and peered through to the shop's ceiling. She could trace the pathway of the thumps, each one growing quieter as they led away to the front end of the shop. *Thump.* And then they stopped.

Peeling her coat off, she puzzled over the noises, once again. It seemed that the thumping only happened at night, when she was closing up and early in the mornings. Or had she just not noticed it during the day? She decided that she should ask the other two girls if they had heard any strange thumping noises, at any time.

At 7am, Jenny went to unlock the front door. She didn't expect to see many shoppers this morning, due to the weather conditions – and certainly not any dog walkers.

Just moments later, a car pulled up in one of the parking bays outside and out stepped Dolly, clad in a lime green, waterproof jacket. Flicking the elasticated hood up and over her head, she went to the windows and walked along the outside, with her head down.

Jenny watched from inside, somewhat amused by the old woman's obvious display of checking whether or not the rings had been fitted, purposefully, for her dog.

Bloody cheek, thought Jenny as Dolly then came hurtling through the door with a gust of wind behind her.

"Ooh, are you ok?" asked Jenny, desperately suppressing a giggle.

"That wind is incredibly strong, dear." Dolly turned and tried to close the door but the wind refused to let her shut it, now that it had got its foot in the door. "Ooh," cried Dolly as another gust pushed against the door and almost won. "It's ridiculous! Do you have another door open somewhere dear?"

"No," said Jenny, as she rushed around the counter, to help Dolly close the door. "I've got the staff room window open slightly though. Maybe I should go and close it."

"Yes, you should dear, you've got a wind tunnel travelling through the shop."

The moment Dolly had finished speaking, the door burst open again and the wind swept in, tearing down the aisle, taking several magazines and papers with it.

Lunging towards the door, Jenny just managed to close it properly, ensuring the catch clicked into place. "Phew," she said, turning to see Dolly dripping all over the floor. "I'll be back in a moment." She then shot off down the aisle to the staff room and closed the security-grill window. She'd opened it every day, since the fridges and freezers had been running, due to the excessive amount of heat created by them, which always seemed to accumulate down the far end of the shop.

On her way back, Jenny grabbed the mop and a hazard sign. "The window is shut now. Sorry about that Dolly, are you ok?"

"Yes thank you." Dolly looked down at the tiled floor. "You'd better get this cleaned up before someone slips."

"Yes, that's just what I'm going to do. Dreadful weather out there isn't it?" Jenny began to mop the area around Dolly's feet.

"You need a much bigger doormat dear," said Dolly, eyeing the small, household sized mat behind her. "*KO Store* has a huge one, six times bigger than yours."

Propping the mop up against the counter, Jenny sighed. "I'm learning every day, Dolly. I realise that there are still things I need to get and sort out." She walked over to the newspapers and began to collect the papers and magazines which had been blown-to-bits. Lightening the conversation, Jenny said "Did you see the rings outside?"

"Rings?"

"Yes, for your dog."

"Oh, those things – yes I did. They're not any use in this weather, my dear. I won't be bringing my little Wilbur out in this," said Dolly, pointing to the front door.

"No, I guess there won't be a need for any of the rings today. I'm guessing that no dog would want to step outside their front door, this morning." Jenny feigned a laugh, of sorts, in a vain attempt to bring about a friendly interaction with Dolly, or even just a smile on the old girl's sour face. It didn't work. "So..." said Jenny, picking up the last sheet of newspaper, "...what can I get for you, Dolly?"

"Oh, thank you dear but I don't need anything. I must get home to my little Wilbur. All I need is a nice cup of tea while I read the paper."

"Do you need a paper?" asked Jenny.

"No, no. I picked one up at the *KO Store* today, as I had my car. It's often a dreadful chore, trying to get a place to park up here when I go to the beauty salon."

Beauty salon? Is there any hope? "I agree. During the day it can be busy, but surely not at this time of the morning?"

"I wasn't prepared to take the risk my dear." Dolly edged towards the door.

"Oh, that's odd. May I ask why you're here now then?" Jenny could feel the exasperation growing inside her.

"I was passing dear. I saw the parking bays were free so I popped in to see how you are doing."

"Oh, ok. Well thank you for your show of kindness. However, I do need people to buy their paper from me, rather than the *KO Store*. And as you must realise, the independent stores need as much support as they can get," Jenny blurted out before she could stop herself. Dolly was a crotchety old woman and could possibly take offense at anything Jenny said. But it was too late – Jenny had said exactly what she was thinking.

"I'm sure you'll get everything right soon enough, my dear. Support comes with respect" Dolly placed a hand on the door handle. "I'm going to brave that terrible weather again, I must get back to my Wilbur. He doesn't like the wind and rain you know. Goodbye dear."

With one tug of the door handle, Dolly was sucked from the shop as the wind continued to play havoc with anything that stood in its path.

Jenny watched through the window, as Dolly battled against the force of the wind to open her car door. She climbed in, slammed the door shut and drove off.

"Stupid old bag," muttered Jenny, under her breath. She grabbed the mop and hazard sign and took them behind the counter, in case they were needed again later. Hopefully, Dolly's swift visit, just to gloat and whine, and not buy anything because she'd been to another shop, was not a sign of things to come.

Gazing out of the window, Jenny watched the raindrops plopping onto the pavement, each one creating its own perfect circle. The road was deserted and she had hardly seen any of the usual customers (usual – as in, over the last two days). Most of the early morning customers were dog-walkers, who came in to get a paper and have a natter. Jenny guessed that they were probably avoiding the weather and hopefully, not avoiding her shop.

Jenny looked up at the clock, it was ten minutes to eight – Dayna would be here soon. At least she could have a giggle with Dayna, to lift her spirits, which felt a little damp right now.

Suddenly, Jenny jumped up – *papers!*

Rushing round to the newspaper piles, Jenny picked up the papers required, took them back to the counter and checked them off in the book. She had forgotten all about the two deliveries. *Great weather for delivering papers*, she thought to herself.

A moment later, Dayna pulled into a parking bay at the front of the shop, which was unusual as she normally parked round the back. She slammed the car door shut and ran into the shop, holding on to the hood of her coat.

"Phew," she said, as she stood by the door. "Have you got those papers ready? I may as well do them, as I'm already suited, booted and wet."

"Are you sure, Day? I'd actually forgotten all about them until a minute ago. You're doing better than me."

"Give 'em here," said Dayna, reaching out a wet-sleeved arm. She took the papers from Jenny. "Have you got a carrier bag, they're going to get soaked?"

Jenny pulled out a bag from underneath the counter, took the papers back and placed them inside the bag.

"Right, I'm off. If I'm not back in half an hour, call for the cavalry." Dayna winked and then hurriedly left the shop like she was on her greatest mission of all time.

Jenny watched her go and wondered just how she would manage her new shop without Dayna around to make everything seem so simple.

At 8.30am the rain had stopped, although the wind continued to batter at the front door and try to get in every time a customer walked in. On several occasions, Jenny or Dayna had run down the aisle, collecting papers and magazines. So the fact that the window, in the staffroom, was now closed had nothing to do with the wind whipping through the shop.

"In hindsight, I should have had the papers and magazines further down the shop," said Jenny, as another customer walked in and several magazine covers opened up.

"Why don't we move them today?" asked Dayna, always the spontaneous one.

"That's a big job, Day, and where would we move them to?"

"Here," said Dayna, propping herself up by the central display unit.

"And where would all the promotional stuff go?"

"There," Dayna said, pointing to the magazine rack.

"Not enough room."

"Papers here then... and magazines opposite, on the second bay down."

Dayna was a determined character, Jenny would give her that. "There's an awful lot of work involved in it, Day. We'd have to move all the stationery up to the front."

"Yes, I know. We'd do it all in a day though, between us."

"What about the customers though?" Jenny thought for a moment. "The place would be an upside-down mess."

"One section at a time, Jen. Shall I make a start?"

"Yes go on then. I could regret this later."

"Needs must Jenny... needs must," said Dayna as she began to remove items from the promotional shelves and carefully place them in neat piles, behind the wide counter area.

"Come to pick up the nursery stuff," said a miserable looking young woman, as she leant across the counter.

"Sorry?" replied Jenny.

"Stuff – for the nursery." The woman stared straight through Jenny. "Bread and milk stuff."

"Oh – yes. Oh my goodness. Hang on a moment – Day!" Jenny tried to locate Dayna through the mirror's bird's-eye view. "Dayna!"

Popping her head round the end of the aisle, she smiled. "Is that the nursery?" she called.

"Yes, we need to get their stuff ready."

"Just coming, I have it all here." Dayna walked up the aisle carrying three carrier bags filled with bread, milk and other items. "Sorry, we haven't got any spare boxes," she said to the young woman, as she plonked the bags by her feet. "Your manager did say that she would bring a spare one in."

Jenny was speechless. Dayna must have got the bags ready earlier.

"I've tallied it up on this sheet, Jen. How is it going to be paid?" said Dayna, looking from Jenny, to the other woman, as she passed the piece of paper over.

"Boss said it comes to about £115 a week. Here..." The woman handed over a wad of notes, "fink that's right."

"Oh, thank you – that's great. We'll make sure that you have everything you need throughout the week. Could you tell your boss that I will make up an account... so that she can see what she's had and what she's paid for?" Jenny smiled at the straight-faced woman and wondered for a moment how she had got a job working with children – unless she was just having a bad morning.

The young woman picked up the bags and walked straight out of the door without a goodbye or anything.

"Miserable cow," said Dayna. "Could at least smile – might make her day a bit easier."

"Hmm." Jenny agreed. "I thought we'd forgotten to get the stuff ready for the nursery. Everything seems to be happening so quickly round here."

"No, *you'd* forgotten – whereas, I hadn't."

"I honestly don't know what I'd do without you," said Jenny, "I'd be pulling my hair out by now."

"That's why I'm here," said Dayna, nonchalantly, before walking away. "Now stop pestering me, I've got newspapers to move."

"Love ya," called Jenny. Picking the piece of paper up from the counter top, she began to put the items through the till and then took the money owed from the wad of notes. She then found a money bag and put the rest of the money, including change, inside it. Then she stuffed the bag at the back of the cash drawer, in an empty section. Although it was only day three of *J's Convenience Store*, Jenny now realised that she had to get serious and put some form of accounts into place – not only for the nursery, but also for the paper deliveries.

By the time Jenny had finished her two hour lunch break, she'd eaten a hearty meal of chicken and sweetcorn pasta, a chocolate bar, two mugs of tea and also, she'd made two new spreadsheets on the computer. She was extremely pleased with her lunch break and her efficiency streak and felt ready to take on whatever the afternoon might bring.

Dayna had moved over half of the magazines and all of the newspapers, during the morning. When Tasha turned up for her shift, she'd received strict instructions, from Dayna, on the completion steps for the project. Dayna had then proudly announced that she was *J's*, fully appointed, logistics queen.

Jenny left the quiet, calm of her office and sauntered up to the hive of action around the counter. "Day, have you seen the time?"

"Yep... I know," she puffed, "...we're just going to clear this section and then Tasha has only got those shelves to fill up." Dayna pointed to the new stationery section, by the front door.

"You've done an amazing job girls – thank you." Jenny looked out of the windows at the glistening, watery houses across the road, lit up by the afternoon sun. "The weather looks better now. Still, at least we won't have flying newspapers or magazines the next time it's windy."

At twenty past two, Dayna said her goodbyes and left. She wouldn't be back until tomorrow afternoon and Jenny knew that she was going to miss her. It wasn't that she didn't like Tasha; on the contrary, she was a hard-working, thoughtful girl. It was just that Dayna was her best friend, her confidant, her level-headed storm-trooper with a loud mouth. But all in all, Dayna was a kindred spirit, they'd come a long way together and still had a long way to go.

"Dayna told me what happened to Marj yesterday." Tasha giggled. "How is she?"

"I haven't seen her today. I thought that perhaps the bad weather kept her away this morning. I do hope she's ok though."

"Yes, me too. She's sweet isn't she?" Tasha continued to place packs of envelopes at the back of a sloping shelf.

"Yes, I do feel sorry for her. I hope that she does have family around her." Jenny grabbed a handful of small packets of elastic bands and placed them into a compartment on the shelf underneath. "Did Dayna mention about the paper deliveries?"

"No. Have you got more then?"

"Well, one more. It's just that I need to deliver them in the morning and I was wondering how we were going to do it."

"Do you want me to do them?" said Tasha, as she added different sized brown envelope packs to the other end of the shelf.

"Would you mind?" Jenny added, "How would you be able to do them though, if you don't drive?"

"I've got a bike – I could use that."

"Well that's great, Tasha, but what if it's pouring down, like it was this morning."

"That's not a problem, I've got a wetsuit..."

"A what?" Jenny blasted out, before she burst into a ridiculous cackle. "I suppose you're going to tell me you've got flippers and a snorkel too."

Tasha looked at her oddly and nodded her head. "Yes. I have." She then returned to the stacking of the envelope packs, nonchalantly.

"Sorry... Tasha, I didn't mean to say that. You do make me laugh sometimes." Jenny placed a hand over her mouth to stifle a giggle, as a young Mum with a pushchair, entered the shop.

Leaving Tasha to finish filling the stationery shelves, Jenny went behind the counter and tried to gather her *compos mentis*, if she ever had one in the first place, and refrain from outbursts of giggling to herself.

After the young Mum had gone, Tasha came scuttling over to the counter. "I was joking about the wetsuit... well, I do have one but I meant that I could wear a waterproof suit. I've got a jacket and trousers."

"Look, Tasha, I really don't expect you to have to do a mini paper round each morning that you're here. It's just that if I did it, I'd have to leave you on your own in the shop. I'm not sure that I want to leave that responsibility with you." Jenny paused and then quickly added, "It's not that I don't think you're capable, Tasha..."

"No, I would much rather do the papers than stay in the shop on my own."

"Ok, well I am considering getting someone in to do the papers – problem is that the round isn't big enough to entice any youngsters to do it yet."

"I'm happy to do it for now then, Jenny."

"Great – thanks Tasha. Err... just out of curiosity... why do you have a wetsuit?"

"Oh, it's just one of my funny outfits," said Tasha, shyly and walked away as another two people entered the shop. And one of them was dear old Marj.

All at once there was a rush of people, mostly Mums with buggies, who filled the shop with chitter and chatter and their toddlers, whose squeals and cries resonated around the shelving units. Tasha looked across from the stationery shelves, with raised eyebrows.

Shrugging her shoulders, Jenny mouthed, "We're on a roll." She grinned widely and excitedly, then braced herself for the onslaught of customers, who were nearly all from the nursery.

As the first woman approached the counter, laden with milk, bread and several packets of sweets and crisps, she dumped the pile of items on the top and huffed as she withdrew her purse from her bag.

Two other Mums joined the growing queue and could be heard moaning about the unexpected rise in the nursery's fees.

Jenny tried to work as fast as she could on the till. She then collected the money, bagged the items and gave out any change due. The sudden influx of customers was a little unnerving and quite unexpected. As the queue began to stretch down the back aisle, Jenny politely greeted each person with a warm smile and a 'hello', knowing full well that all eyes were upon her.

"Tasha, could you come and help bag-up please," Jenny called out, fearing that the people at the back of the queue may become impatient. She was exhilarated by the number of people waiting to be served but had to remain professional and contain her excitement as one after another, they bought goods from her new shop.

Tasha joined Jenny behind the counter and quickly bagged up each item, once Jenny had keyed the amount into the till. Between them both, they soon had the queue under control, while yet more people entered the shop.

Out of the corner of her eye, Jenny just caught a glimpse of Marj, hobbling out of the shop, with a pack of turquoise toilet rolls tucked under her arm. Jenny shot another glance at her as she passed by the window. The odd thing was that Jenny hadn't served her. Marj had simply taken them.

"Did you see that?" whispered Jenny, between customers.

"What?" breathed Tasha, as another woman approached the counter.

"Marj... she just left the shop... she took some toilet rolls."

"No, I didn't see her," said Tasha and grinned, sheepishly. "She was in here a minute ago though."

"Hmm," muttered Jenny and continued to serve one customer after another as the surge of nursery Mums continued for another five minutes or so.

Jenny sighed and rested her chin on her hand. The rush of customers earlier in the afternoon had not equated to a massive increase in takings. She guessed that the bad weather, earlier, had something to do with it. The shop had been very quiet while the rain lashed against the window panes during the morning and it had been practically dead during the evening. Hopefully that would change as soon as the lights were fitted.

Thump...

Here we go again, thought Jenny as she rubbed her forehead hard and screwed her eyes up tight.

Thump, thump, thump, thump... thump, thump.

A moment later, one of the light panels at the front of the shop went out. *Great*, Jenny thought and flicked off her computer. She'd had enough for today and wanted to get home as quickly as possible.

Thump, thump, thump.

She grabbed her coat and bag and switched off the back lights. She was ten minutes ahead of herself.

Thump, thump.

Reaching the front of the shop, Jenny made a mental note of which light panel had gone out, set the alarm and switched the front lights off. She then followed the 'thumps' to the front door and left.

Thump, thump, thump.

Chapter 13

Peering into the freezer, notepad in hand, Jenny checked the contents. She shuffled the tubs of ice-cream and undamaged cheesecakes to the front of the unit, for easier access. The idea of putting up a sign, asking for assistance, had been a good one but she'd completely forgotten to do it yesterday. Having made the sign on her computer earlier, and printed it off, Jenny now stuck it above the chest freezer, on the back wall. The sign was bold and bright and she decided that it would suffice. Should anyone else end up inside the unit, it would be their own fault. Wouldn't it?

Checking her watch, Jenny noticed the minute hand had drifted past seven o'clock by two minutes. She wandered down the shop to the front door and turned the key in the lock. *Thump... thump... thump, thump, thump.* Jenny rolled her eyes and shook her head. What on earth was the man doing upstairs? She had a good mind to go and confront him, even if he was a bit peculiar. Maybe he was hopping – he did have a limp when she met him for the first time. Wasn't it all a bit extreme though? And why did it only happen early in the mornings and late in the evenings. That was something else that she had forgotten to do – ask the girls if they'd heard any thumping noises from above, during the day.

Drawn from her muse, Jenny listened to the rattle of one of the rings, attached to the underneath of the window, outside. She could see a little silvery-grey head of curls bobbing up and down outside and immediately, she knew it was Dolly – back for her daily bout of criticism and sneering.

"Morning Dolly," said Jenny chirpily. She was not going to be beaten down by a cantankerous old woman.

"Good morning dear. Am I the first person in this morning?"

"Err... yes you are – why do you ask?"

"I just wondered why you haven't put your paper display board out on the pavement yet."

"Oh, I didn't realise..."

"It's down there," said Dolly, peering, narrow-eyed and pointing down the first aisle. "Very dangerous – somebody could trip over it."

Jenny had already moved round the counter and was heading straight to the first aisle, "I've been open for approximately four minutes, Dolly. I would have moved it..."

"I only mentioned it, dear, because other folk may think you're shut if they can't see the newspaper board outside."

"Fair point," said Jenny as she picked up the board, carried it down the aisle, side-stepped around Dolly, and took it out through the front door.

Wilbur was sat patiently under the window and stared at Jenny, wide-eyed, as his little tail wagged frantically.

"So, Dolly, what can I get you? Do you need a paper?" asked Jenny as she returned through the door.

"Oh no, thank you... I'm going into town today. I like to get my main shopping on Fridays. I always pick my paper up at the supermarket."

"Oh, I see." Jenny didn't 'see' at all but she had to keep calm and grin through it. "So what brings you here this morning?"

"I popped in to see how you are doing, my dear. I do like to be supportive to the local stores."

"Really?" said Jenny, questioningly.

"Ooh yes indeed. So many independent stores are dying out these days, dear."

"Yes, I know." Jenny sighed. "Dolly, don't you think that you would help me by buying your paper here, at least?" Just as Jenny had asked the crucial question, Stuart (or his dog was called Stuart) walked in.

"Morning Dolly," he bellowed, before turning to smile and nod his head at Jenny.

"Good morning George, how are you?" said Dolly and at that instant, Jenny knew that the man's dog was called Stuart.

"I see we have rings to tie the dogs up," George exclaimed. "Darn quick service... and not something that our retail giants would ever consider doing. Well done to you."

Jenny smiled and nodded, "Thank you... and thank you for your support too."

Returning to her spot behind the counter, Jenny watched and listened as *J's Convenience Store,* slowly but surely, turned into an OAP, dog-walker's community centre, just as it had two days ago. The elderly residents of the area obviously didn't like rainy mornings, hence their absence yesterday... except for Dolly of course. There seemed to be no stopping *her.*

Tasha hadn't heard a thing and had given Jenny a rather peculiar look when she asked her about the strange noises, coming from the flat above.

Pondering over some of the unusual events of the last few days, Jenny sat in the seclusion of her office, while Tasha worked on the till. Today her dad and brother would be coming to fit the exterior lighting and Jenny wondered for a moment if the lights would really make a difference to the footfall in the evenings. She really hoped so.

A rap at the door brought Jenny back to the here and now. "Come in," she said, "you don't need to knock on the door, Tasha."

"I didn't know whether you'd be asleep or something," whispered Tasha, her head squeezed into the small opening she'd made. "There's a man here to see you. Do you want me to send him down?"

"Who is it?"

"Oh, I don't know... shall I go and ask him?"

"No, no – that's fine, tell him I'll be there in a minute."

Tasha grinned and mouthed 'ok' before closing the door.

Jenny heaved a sigh and pulled herself out of the chair. Her enthusiasm was waning and a steadily thriving irritation of her lacklustre attitude was really beginning to vex. She had no idea why she felt like this and may have expected these feelings to surface after maybe a month or so – but not after just a few days.

Walking up the aisle, towards the counter, she could see that Tasha was busy serving several people. Looking around the front of the shop, Jenny couldn't distinguish which man, if any, was waiting to talk to her. She halted by the end of the counter for a moment and watched Tasha use the till at quite a speed already, considering she'd only been using it for four days.

"Good morning," said a man's voice, directly behind Jenny.

Almost leaping into the air in fright, she turned sharply.

"Oh my goodness – you made me jump." Jenny held her hand to her chest. "Sneaking up behind me were you?"

"I've just been checking the contents of your freezer," said Aaron, smiling warmly. "Have you got any unusual, frozen meats for sale? Something like leg-of-old-lady or stocking-rump-steak?"

Jenny laughed and once again looked up into Aaron's eyes and was mesmerized. "No, nothing – it's been relatively boring in comparison, since you were here last."

"Ah, so no sign of that poor, old lady... err... what was her name?"

"Marj..."

"Oh yes, Marj. So you haven't seen her since?"

"Oh yes, she's been in. She is ok, if that's what you were wondering."

"Well that's good to know." Aaron let out a puff of air, signifying his relief.

"She came in yesterday – stole a pack of toilet rolls. I couldn't believe it."

"Oh, that's not good. Didn't you try and stop her?" Aaron seemed quite concerned.

"No, we were too busy at the time. She just walked out, quite innocently, while we had a rush on."

"Ah, I see," said Aaron. "Hopefully she'll be back and you can have a word with her. Anyway, I was just passing and thought I'd drop a card off to you."

"Oh, great – thanks." Jenny took the business card from Aaron and peered down at it. "You know, I thought you said your name was Frey the other day, but what with everything that happened, I forgot to ask you."

"What?" said Aaron, shuffling his feet from side to side.

"Do you know someone called Alex... Alex Frey?" Jenny twiddled the card in her hand, unable to tear her eyes away from his. They were like mystical, deep black holes and seemed to draw her in deeper and deeper, the more she stared into them.

Aaron laughed nervously, "Err, yes, I do know her," he replied, swaying from one foot to the other. "In fact, I know her pretty well – she's my mum."

"Oh, really – well, I don't know her that well, I just know *of* her. I mean, well, I used to work in the wholesalers. She was our biggest customer. She owns a shop – right?"

Aaron nodded his head, "Yes, she does. What a small world it is."

Jenny agreed with him, "Yes it is. I only know her to pass the time of day with. So I take it that your dad is Graham? Is it Graham – no Grant?"

"Yep, that's him." Aaron laughed again. "I can't go anywhere without someone knowing them."

The last customer had been served and Tasha looked across to Jenny, raised her eyebrows and smiled. "Shall I make a coffee Jenny?"

"Yes, that would be good, thanks, Tasha," Jenny grinned and then turned to Aaron. "Would you like a quick coffee? It's the least I can do after your help the other day."

"Sure, why not," said Aaron. "Maybe, if I'm here long enough, we could accost Marj when she comes in – start a toilet roll amnesty or something."

Both Aaron and Jenny laughed aloud again. This was becoming the norm for them.

Tasha walked off, oblivious to the in-house jokes, and headed down to the staff room with a dirty mug in hand.

"Oh no – son of Alex Frey – have you told your mum what happened here the other day?"

Aaron shook his head, "No I haven't... but that's not to say that I won't. Would she know who you are?"

"I'm not sure. I used to help her out sometimes when she needed a large quantity of stock. I helped her and your dad to load up their van a couple of times. I was the manager for several years, so I didn't often work on the checkouts." Jenny felt a little more relaxed now and as long as she didn't look too deep, she was sure that she wouldn't get sucked into those watery brown holes that were evenly spaced under Aaron's eyebrows. If she did, she feared that there would be no turning back. She'd be hooked.

The front door opened and Jenny instinctively edged round the counter. Stepping through the doorway was Dayna.

"Is it that time already?" said Jenny, glancing up at the clock on the wall. Momentarily, she couldn't understand how it had got to 11.55am so soon. Time certainly flew by, in the confines of the shop, and if she had been feeling melancholic earlier, it had certainly evaporated into a pool of excitement since Aaron had wished her a 'good morning'. Although there were only five minutes left, it definitely was a good morning now.

"Certainly is – you been busy then?" Dayna nodded to Aaron. "Hello again," she said and grinned. "Have we got another body in the freezer?"

Jenny rolled her eyes and tutted, "No, Day, Aaron came to drop a business card in," said Jenny, holding up the small, beautifully crafted, card in her hand, as if she needed to prove why Aaron was there.

Dayna smirked and then walked off to the staff room.

"How many people do you have working here?" asked Aaron.

"Only those two – can't afford any more at the moment."

"So have you finished now then?"

"No... oh no, Tasha finishes in two hours." Jenny added, "There is a cross-over period at this time. That way I get a two hour lunch break. Well, it's not even a break as such, as I use the time to do paperwork or go to the bank or the wholesalers, if I need to."

"Very busy then..."

"Yes, it's hard work – I practically live here." Jenny laughed off her last statement, knowing full well that she practically did and would do for some time to come.

Tasha called from the other end of the shop, "Where do you want these Jenny?"

"Do you want your coffee down in the office," said Jenny, looking into Aaron's eyes again, "We'd be out of the way of customers..."

"Yes sure."

"Well, that way, you can tell me all about these EPOS systems of yours and how they work," said Jenny, waving the card in the air.

Aaron nodded, "Yes, sure I can."

"Sorry Tasha, can you pop them in the office please," called Jenny. Glancing out of the window, to check that no one was coming in, she then beckoned to Aaron. "Follow me," she said, trying to hide her jangly nerves.

Deliberately, leaving the office door open, Jenny showed Aaron inside and offered her chair to him. "I'll just get another one from the staff room – be right back." As she passed Dayna, by the staffroom entrance, she raised her eyebrows and grinned widely. Dayna looked at her with a puzzled expression.
"Going to tell me all about the EPOS systems," whispered Jenny.
"Thought you couldn't afford one of those yet," Dayna whispered back.
"No, I can't but there's no harm in him telling me about it, is there?"
"Hmm..." Dayna smirked, "I know what you're up to."
"Day!" Jenny turned to make sure that no one was behind her, "I'm not up to anything."
"You fancy him..."
"Yes... and? So do you," said Jenny, in her defense.
"Enjoy your lunch break hun – see you laters." Dayna winked and then toddled off with a mug of coffee in her hand.
Returning to the office, Jenny plonked the stool down, lowered the seat and sat on it. "Sorry about that, I haven't had any visitors come to my office yet."
"No worries, are you sure you want me dipping into your lunch break like this?"
"Oh yes, it's not a problem at all – I've got two hours." Jenny picked up her mug of coffee and grinned. "I haven't, as of yet, managed to do anything I should be doing in my lunch breaks."
"Oh, ok. You must find it pretty hard running this place on your own – I'm assuming that you do it on your own?"
"Yes, I do... well, I've got my dad and my brother. They help me with the DIY and maintenance stuff – they're builders." As soon as

Jenny had said the words, she remembered that her dad and Jacob were coming this afternoon to fit the new lights outside. "Oh, that's just reminded me actually. I need to tell my dad – I've got a light out at the front of the shop."

"Handy to have family like that," said Aaron.

"Yes it is. I don't know what I'd do without them really."

"So... you don't have a partner, husband... or anyone like that, to help you run it?"

"Oh God – no. I've done this all by myself. Some people might think I'm mad, but..."

"But you're doing it anyway."

"Exactly," said Jenny, beginning to feel very comfortable talking to such a nice, charming, young man.

Aaron took a large swig of his coffee and looked at Jenny. "I've been thinking... I may have a proposition for you."

"Really?"

"Yes, well, two actually." Aaron grinned through perfectly white teeth.

"Ok... go on then."

"The first one is..." Aaron peered down at his shoes, "would you like to go for lunch, in the town?" His face turned slightly pink. "Then I could discuss the second one with you over a burger or something." Aaron met Jenny's eyes and waited, expectantly, for an answer.

"Sure, why not – sounds like a plan. Love burgers and I'm intrigued now."

Having told the girls that she was going out on an unexpected business lunch and she'd be back by two o'clock, Jenny left both Dayna and Tasha with bewildered expressions on their faces. She hopped into Aaron's very expensive looking *BMW*, waved to the girls, who were both peering out of the window perplexed, and headed off into town.

Sitting in the car together, the atmosphere had changed from the friendly, business-like meeting they'd had at the shop, to an awkward, 'Not sure what to talk about on our first date'. Of course, it wasn't a date but Jenny couldn't help feeling coy and a bit lost for words.

"So... where are we going?" she asked purposefully, as they travelled round the outskirts of the town, towards the harbor.

"I know just the place if you like burgers and that kind of thing – follow me."

Jenny giggled. "I can't exactly *not* follow you can I?"

Aaron shot a sideways glance and smirked. "Suppose you can't – so you'll have to sit there and wait until we arrive at our destination, madam."

Shaking her head from side to side, as a wide grin spread across her face, Jenny sighed contentedly. The stiff atmosphere was breaking up already. Why was she beginning to feel like she'd known Aaron forever?

Snax Bar was situated right on the waterfront, overlooking the harbour. The cloudless sky above reflected on the tiny, bobbing waves, in shades of dark blue and grey. The harbour was relatively peaceful, apart from the odd fishing boat passing by, or the ferry crossing over from the mainland.

"Do you want to eat in or out?" said Aaron as he parked the car opposite the large café.

"Out would be nice. It's a bit chilly but I really fancy the fresh air after being cooped up in the shop all day, every day."

"No problem," said Aaron as they crossed over the road and went in to *Snax Bar,* both feeling very hungry.

Ten minutes later, Jenny and Aaron found a table in the ferry gardens. They sat down in the warm sunshine and opened up their cartons.

"Never had one of these before," said Jenny, eyeing the pulled-pork and coleslaw, ciabatta roll. Her tummy rumbled as she picked it up and sank her teeth into it.

Aaron smiled at her, "They are very good. The lattes are great too." He took a sip from the drink and then grabbed his ciabatta roll and began to devour it, hungrily.

"So... what is the second proposition then?" asked Jenny, wiping her mouth discreetly.

"Well...." Aaron gulped a big piece of bun down, "I know that you said that you can't afford an EPOS system... but I've been thinking..."

"Yes..."

"I have put second-hand systems into shops before... for a quarter of the price..."

"I couldn't even afford a quarter of the price though."

"No, I appreciate that. I'm fully aware of your situation, having just set up your shop. You need to build up your customer base first."

Jenny nodded and then looked out across the harbour as a small boat drifted past. The sunlight sprinkled glistening dots on the frothy, turbulent water, behind the boat. Out to sea, as far as Jenny could see through the harbour's entrance, ripples of sunlit water undulated rhythmically. It was a beautifully, picturesque setting. Sitting here, with a charming and handsome man, Jenny suddenly felt despondent. Times like this would be few and far between, now that she had the shop. She didn't even have the weekends to look forward to. It was hitting her far sooner than she had ever thought, that her long hours at the shop were going to be for the long haul.

"Are you ok?"

"Yes... sorry, I was just gazing out at that lovely scene," she replied, pointing across the harbour.

"Thought you might like it here," said Aaron, gazing deep into Jenny's eyes with his own, almost lovingly smiling eyes. "Anyway, as I was saying, I'm taking out an old EPOS system from one of my customer's shops next Monday. So I was just wondering whether you would like me to fit it into yours."

"I couldn't afford it, Aaron. Not at all – I really appreciate your kind offer but how could I have it?"

"Well, like I said, I've been thinking about you..."

"Ooh... have you indeed." Jenny raised her eyebrows and grinned cheekily. "Sorry, I didn't mean that. I should be taking your proposition seriously – I am sorry."

"No problem." Aaron laughed, "Look, what I mean is... I would be happy to loan this system to you – call it a trial run?"

Jenny's eyes lit up. "Really? For how long?"

"As long as it takes. I could draw up a contract, let's say, for your first year of trading, so that you owe me nothing. If you like it after that, you could pay for it then. What do you think?"

"What do I think? I think it's a wonderful and very generous offer." Jenny looked up and across the harbour again but this time her irritability had vanished. "There's just one thing..."

"Ok, what's that?"

"Why would you be giving this system to me for nothing? Why would you want to do that?"

"To be honest with you, it would sit out in the back of my mum's store room, waiting for the remote possibility that someone would want to buy an old operating system. It's quite an outdated set-up and that's why my customer is upgrading to a newer one, he's had it for eight years or more."

"Oh, I see," Jenny replied, humbly.

"Don't get me wrong," said Aaron, wiping his mouth with a paper serviette, "it's a good system. Great in fact. I think it would be good for you – you know, with just starting out and all that."

Jenny thought for a moment, "You are so kind, Aaron. Wouldn't you be making a loss though? How long would it take to fit it? I mean, how can I pay you for your time?"

"Buy me a pulled-pork ciabatta," said Aaron, grinning cheekily.

"What now?"

Aaron shook his head, "No... on the days that I'm fitting your new EPOS system." Aaron winked.

A surge of bubbly excitement rushed through Jenny – not because she was going to get an EPOS system fitted but because Aaron had winked at her. She knew that she truly fancied him, for sure, which was not convenient at all, in her present circumstances. Feeling uncomfortable by her own admission, Jenny shuffled in her chair, gulped down the last piece of ciabatta and then picked up her latte and toyed with the lid of the cup. "So what do they actually do then? I know about some of it... we used similar systems in the warehouse."

"Thought you might ask that," said Aaron, pulling a small booklet from his jacket pocket. "Here's some bedtime reading for you."

"Oh, thanks." Jenny took the booklet from Aaron and their fingers touched... Instantly their eyes met... Immediately, Jenny's heart raced... Stupidly, the booklet fell from Jenny's hand, knocking the cup of latte over... Heroically, Aaron grabbed the lidded cup before it rolled to the floor... Knowingly, Jenny and Aaron gazed at each other... before bursting into a raucous laugh.

"Phew, that was close," said Aaron, placing the cup in front of Jenny. "Right, let me think... I'm taking the old system out of Ken's shop on Monday and then I'll be fitting the new one on Tuesday and Wednesday... it may go into Thursday too. How about next weekend? Are you around at the weekends?"

"I'll be around every weekend... I work seven days a week for the foreseeable future," said Jenny, pulling the corners of her mouth down, feigning sadness.

"Ah, poor you – it's really tough isn't it? I know... I've been there before too." Aaron mirrored Jenny's sad face. "So, does next weekend sound ok?"

"Yes, that would be great... and thank you so much for this, Aaron." Jenny thought for a moment and then she added, "Only problem at the weekends is that I wouldn't be able to take you out at lunchtime, for a bit of pulled-pork. There are only two of us working – it's not like during the week. I wanted to give the girls a day off each week, so the shifts are different. I couldn't expect them to work seven days a week as well."

"No, of course not. Well, not to worry – maybe we could do it during the week sometime. I'm pretty flexible – what with running my own business." Aaron propped his chin up on his hand. "So it's a done deal then – yes?"

Jenny nodded and smiled at him. "It's a deal," she replied. "And thank you, so much."

"Do you fancy some celebratory, billionaire's cheesecake?"

"Oh, go on then," said Jenny, peering down at her watch. "Let me get it."

"No – my call... that way you'll have to owe me cheesecake too." Aaron winked again and got up from his chair. "Be back in a minute."

As Jenny was mesmerized by the rippling waves out to sea, her phone began to ring, snapping her out of her blissful moment. Grabbing it from her bag, she noticed that it was an unknown number. "Hello," she said.

"Jen, your dad and Jacob are here. Where are you?"

"I'm down by the harbour – having lunch. Make them a nice cuppa, Day. I should be back in about half an hour."

"Your dad said that Calvin is coming to help too."

"Oh great! That's all I need. Why does he have to muscle-in on everything? It's bad enough that I have to go out for a coffee with him tomorrow. I wish I'd never agreed – it was only to get rid of him the other night... Actually..." she paused, thoughtfully. "I've just realised. I *can't* go out tomorrow anyway, can I?"

"I don't mind if you leave me for an hour, Jen..."

"Yes you do, Dayna – it's impossible! Right?"

"Oh, right. Yes – impossible."

There was a slight pause before Jenny added, "I hope he's not there when we get back."

"No, that could be a difficult one... You know what he'll think if he sees you getting out of some rich blokes car," said Dayna.

"Well, it's a business lunch," said Jenny, trying to convince herself of that remark. "And I'm single... so I can do whatever I want, whenever I want, wherever I want and with whoever I want."

"Absolutely," Dayna agreed. "Right, I'll go and make them a cuppa and tell them you'll be back soon."

"Thanks Day – hold the fort."

Dayna chuckled. "See you laters," she said, before ending the call.

Jenny looked across to the café and watched Aaron pick up two cartons and another two lidded cups. Slowly he wandered back to the table.

"Thought you'd like another latte," he said, placing the items on the table.

"Ah, thank you, Aaron. I've just had Dayna on the phone – my dad and brother have turned up to fit the lights outside."

"Do you need to get back then?"

"No, it's ok. I said I'll be back in half an hour or so."

"Right, let's get these cheesecakes eaten then. Best ever, you know," said Aaron, grinning as he held a forkful of cheesecake in the air and then devoured it. "Err... hmm," he said, struggling to eat the cake quickly, "don't forget to mention your light at the front of the shop."

Jenny stopped chewing and stared at Aaron in amazement. Struck by his retentiveness, she smiled at him and nodded.

Aaron looked deep into her eyes, before placing another piece of cheesecake to his lips. Opening his mouth slowly and provocatively, he inserted the cake.

Hot flush. Lust-overload. Jenny whipped her admiring gaze away and spluttered, "Err... yes, I will remember that, thanks. And thanks for reminding me – I'm amazed."

Aaron winked again, "You're amazed that I've listened to everything you've said?"

Jenny nodded, dumbfounded.

"I find you very interesting, Jenny Fartor."

Chapter 14

"Thank you for everything," said Jenny, "It's been really nice. I'll see you next weekend then."

"You've got my number on the card. Give me a call if anything changes and you can't do next Saturday."

"I'm sure it will be fine, thanks again, Aaron." Jenny smiled at him and then jumped out of the car. Behind her, Jacob and her dad were both up a pair of tall step ladders each.

They watched as Aaron drove away from the shop.

"Flash car – who's that?" asked Jacob, balancing at the top of the ladder while holding one end of a strip light.

"His name is Aaron, he's installing an EPOS system in there next week." Jenny pointed into the shop.

"How can you afford that?" asked Dad.

"Long story," said Jenny, grinning up at him. "I'll tell you later, Dad."

Strolling into the shop with a spring in her step, Jenny headed towards the staffroom, after shooting a quick glance at Dayna and Tasha, who were stood behind the till grinning, cheesily. As she reached the door, Calvin appeared. The scowl on his face brought Jenny's temporary euphoria to a grinding halt.

"Where've you been?" he grunted.

"What's it got to do with you, Calvin? And why the miserable face?"

"It's nothing, Jen... I just thought you were going to be here today."

"Well, I am aren't I?" Jenny raised her eyebrows and glared at Calvin. "What are you doing in here – I thought you were helping my dad?"

"I am, just needed a pee – is that ok with you?" Calvin sidestepped past Jenny.

"Calvin, what is your problem?"

"Nothing – gotta go – got work to do."

Jenny harrumphed, "Get on with it then..." and watched Calvin strut along the aisle to the front of the shop. *Freaky idiot*, she thought and then went into the staffroom and shut the door behind her. She needed a moment – just one moment to gather her thoughts.

"Right I'm going now, if that's ok," said Tasha, entering the staffroom and bringing Jenny back from her daydreaming.

"Oh – is it that time already. It's gone quick."

Tasha smirked and took her coat from the hook. "Did you have a nice lunch out?"

"Yes, it was really nice... and we're going to be having a new till system fitted next weekend, so I'm afraid you and Day will have to re-learn the till. It will be so much better though."

"That's fine, I'll wear my school-girl outfit and then you can teach me. See you tomorrow."

Jenny smiled awkwardly but couldn't bring herself to speak. She stared after her, as Tasha left the room, and then realised that her mouth had dropped open from sheer astonishment. Tasha was definitely a tad unusual.

Strolling down to the front of the shop, Jenny stopped by the counter and waited for Dayna to finish serving a young mum, who had an occupied pushchair in tow.

"You ok?" asked Dayna, turning her head sharply. The young mum took her change, stared across at Jenny, and then stuffed two magazines into a large handbag hanging over the handle bar of her three-wheeled buggy. "Thank you," said Dayna, as the young woman smiled and left.

Jenny moved round the counter to join her friend. "Yeah – good. We're going to have an EPOS system put in next weekend."

"Really, I thought you couldn't afford it?" Dayna remarked. "Oh, don't tell me – you're paying him in kindness are you?"

Jenny laughed. "No, of course not..."

"Err... You want me to pay him in kindness for you then?" Dayna pursed her lips, flicked a hip out to one side and perched a hand on it, while raising one eyebrow in a provocative way.

"No, Day, you wanton wench – it's not like that."

"Oh," said Dayna, disappointedly. "What then? How are you going to pay for it?"

"He's giving me a second hand one to trial, free of charge, for a year."

"He fancies you – I told you so."

"No he doesn't..." Jenny thought for a moment. "Well, even if he does... it's all going to be proper. He's drawing up a contract."

Dayna leant over closer and lowered her voice, "Well you want to be careful, Jen. Calvin had a right strop on his face when he realised you weren't here."

"Huh – tell me about it!" Jenny frowned and looked out of the window to where Calvin stood, holding on to her dad's ladder. "He bit my head off, when I came in."

"He's hoping you two will get back together, eventually. You must know that."

"He knows that there is no chance. I haven't gone through the last year of breaking up, selling the flat and dissecting our finances, just to rekindle the relationship." Jenny shook her head, despairingly.

"Well, I'd just be careful, Jen. He's obsessed with you. I honestly think you could kick him in the balls and he'd still come back for more."

Cringing at the thought, Jenny huffed loudly. "I just wish my dad wouldn't keep encouraging him. He makes it worse."

"Well why don't you talk to your dad then?"

"I have, Day, but he sees no wrong in anyone and thinks that I'm being too harsh on Calvin."

"Hmm," muttered Dayna, "it's tricky isn't it."

"It certainly is... and to make matters worse, I promised to go for a coffee with him tomorrow, thinking that both you and Tasha would be here. I forgot that we have a different set up at the weekends. So I need to tell him that I can't make it. I only agreed, so I could get rid of him the other night."

"I'll be fine if you want to go out anywhere tomorrow Jen. I'm not bothered about being here on my own for an hour."

"No!" Jenny screeched and then clapped her hand to her mouth. "Remember, Day, we need to both agree that it would *not* be ok for me to leave the premises – please."

"Ok, not a problem. Chill out babe," said Dayna, holding her hands up like she was just about to be shot.

"Sorry, I didn't mean to sound so stressy. I think I need a good night's sleep."

"You need something honey. You've got a tough time ahead – working seven days a week is no easy task."

"Yes, I know."

Patting her best friend on the shoulder, Jenny grinned and then left the counter to go outside and check out the new light fittings. "Wow, they are big aren't they?" she said, arching her neck to look up at the one strip light, already fitted. "I can't wait to see what it looks like tonight."

"Hopefully they won't light up the houses across the road," Dad laughed, and began to descend the ladder. "I'm going to put the switch behind the counter, is that ok love?"

"Yeah sure, whatever you say, Dad."

"I've got you a timer plug as well, that way you won't need to worry about forgetting to turn the lights on when it gets dark."

"You think of everything. I don't know what I'd do without you."

Passing his power drill to Calvin, Dad walked into the shop. "You're always saying that and you'd do just fine without me. Now, let me show you where I need to come inside with the cables."

Jenny followed him inside after shooting a cursory glare at Calvin – who probably mistook her brief attention as admiration.

A moment later, Marj appeared from nowhere, entered the shop and tottered off down the first aisle in her usual, merry way, followed by two other people.

It felt odd to have her dad behind the counter while there were people in the shop. "Are you going to serve a couple of customers while you're here, Dad?" asked Jenny, in jest.

"No, I am not," he replied, a horrified expression darting across his face. "I couldn't be doing with all that smiling and constantly saying please and thank you to everyone, all day long," he added, in a whisper.

"I know what you mean. It's hard sometimes – especially when you're feeling really fed up... and there's nothing worse than wearing a false grin all day. It gives me jaw ache."

The customers seemed to come in surges. One minute there were up to ten people or more in the shop, the next minute there were none and that seemed to go on most days. The quiet moments could last for up to an hour sometimes, which caused concern for Jenny – she needed a steady flow.

Standing at the back of the counter, she listened to her dad's recommendations and instructions. It was simple really, a small hole would be drilled through the top of the window frame and the cables would then run to the side of the cigarette gantry, where a switch would be placed. Dad had it all sorted out and the disruption to the shop would be minimal. There would be a brief moment where the electrical power to the counter area would need to be disconnected but that wouldn't be a huge problem, especially if it was during one of their quiet moments.

"Dad, while I've got you here, could you have a look at that light?" Jenny pointed up to the ceiling. "It went out yesterday. I thought they would last longer than that..."

"They should – maybe it's a dodgy one. I'll have a look when I'm done here."

"And Dad... do you have to keep asking Calvin to help you out?"

"Well, I didn't actually, Jen."

Jenny looked puzzled, "Why's he here then?"

"He called me and said he had the day off. He asked if I needed any help so I felt obliged to say that I was coming over here to do your lights and would he like to help. To be honest, I needed the extra hand anyway."

"Ok, fair enough," said Jenny and turned to see several people waiting to be served at the front of the counter. Dayna worked quickly and efficiently, always remembering her good manners and huge, toothy grins. "Do you want a cuppa, Dad?" Jenny whispered.

"Silly question," said Dad, winking his eye. "Right I'm going to have to make some noise soon, to get the cables through."

"No problem – do what you need to do. I'll make the tea."

Just as Jenny was about to leave the counter, she caught a glimpse of Marj through the window. She was standing outside, looking up the ladders with a pack of four, turquoise toilet rolls tucked under her arm. Jenny hadn't seen Dayna serve her and wondered for a moment whether she'd paid for them. Surely Marj wouldn't just take another pack of toilet rolls and walk nonchalantly out of the shop, in broad daylight – would she? On the other hand, Jenny hadn't been paying attention to who Dayna had been serving, as she chatted to her dad with her back turned to the till, so maybe Jenny was being too hasty to cast an accusing finger at the defenseless old lady. But Marj was definitely guilty of toilet roll pinching yesterday. Dayna was currently too busy to ask, so Jenny strolled off to make the tea and take a much needed, five minute, time-out.

Amazingly, one customer had complained about the noise that Jenny's dad had been making as he drilled through the window frame. More amazingly, Marj had eventually hobbled off with another unpaid, pack of toilet rolls, Jenny had discovered when she questioned Dayna later. Standing by the toiletries shelf, Jenny noticed that she had only two turquoise packs left. She made a mental note to get some more and also to confront Marj, the next time she came into the shop.

Calvin had come in to use the toilet again but Jenny suspected that his emptying-of-the-bladder frequency had more to do with checking up on her whereabouts. "Oh, Calvin – can I grab you for a sec," said Jenny, just as he passed her in the aisle.

"Grab me any time you like – you know that, Jen."

Jenny shot a distasteful glare at him, "It's about tomorrow... lunch... I can't go for a coffee. I forgot that the shifts are different over the weekends."

"Oh, great. When can you go then?"

"Well I don't know, Calvin. I don't really see the point of it..."

"Well that's nice – thanks!" Calvin leant against the shelving and stared deep into Jenny's eyes. "I only wanted to take you for a coffee to celebrate the opening of your shop. That's not a lot to ask."

"Yes I know Cal... it's just not convenient at the weekends." Jenny was so annoyed with her own feelings of quilt that she wanted to kick herself.

"During the week then?"

"Well... you work during the week, don't you?"

"I'm not working today," replied Calvin in his usual whinny, schoolboy voice. "We could have done it today but you were out gallivanting with some other bloke."

"Oh, don't even go there, Calvin. Is that why you were sulking earlier?"

"No it wasn't... and I wasn't sulking."

"Ok, I'm not arguing – this is ridiculous." Jenny snorted. "Why aren't you working today anyway?"

"Sick," replied Calvin.

"You don't look very sick to me."

"No, I've felt better as the day's gone on," said Calvin, sheepishly.

"Hmm... that's odd. Dad told me that you were going to help out, before today." Jenny lowered her voice and added, "Cal, why have you booked a day off sick, just to work with my dad?"

Calvin shrugged his shoulders and held his head down like a convicted man in a dock. "Wanted to help your dad and help you with the shop."

Jenny shook her head from side to side, "Calvin, you've got to stop this. You and I are over. Completely finished. Never again. You need to get on with your own life... and let me get on with mine. It's a nice thought but we can't stay the best of friends – it just won't work." Jenny cringed and held her breath as she waited for Calvin's normally, pathetic response.

"I can't help caring about you, Jen," he said, before slumping off with his hands tucked into his pockets.

Clenching her fists, Jenny screwed up her face and screamed inwardly. This was exactly why she had left Calvin in the first place – he was still a creepy little dork.

"The light at the front is working fine, love," said Dad, as he entered the back office and plonked himself down on the stool. "Just a loose connection."

"Really? I don't suppose it could have come loose by someone jumping about upstairs, could it?"

"It would have to be an elephant jumping about, Jen," Dad laughed. "They're pretty solid floors above."

"Well it doesn't sound very solid when he's jumping about upstairs. I hear the noise every morning and at night too."

Jenny's dad looked puzzled. "Kids?" he asked.

"Nope – I've met the weird man that lives upstairs. I don't think he has any kids. Well, I haven't seen him with any... not that I've seen him much at all. But he just doesn't strike me as being the type to have kids. I'm pretty sure he lives alone."

"Takes all sorts Jen," replied Dad, wisely.

"Hmm... it's just odd that I only hear the banging in the mornings and evenings. He's a very rude man too. I didn't like him much when I offered to help carry his bags the other day."

"Well, whatever he is, I'm sure that the light connection wasn't to do with him."

Smiling warmly, Jenny leant over and pecked her dad on the cheek. "What would I do without you to moan at?"

"Moan at someone else?"

"All done," said Jacob, poking his head in through the door. "I'm off now. Calvin's down the front, chatting to Dayna."

"Ok," replied Dad. "Thanks son, have a good weekend and I'll see you Monday."

"Yeah, thank you, Jay. I really appreciate what you've both done here," said Jenny, glancing from her brother to her dad. "And thank you for putting up with him." Jenny raised her eyebrows and directed her stare past Jacob, towards the front of the shop.

Jacob tutted and rolled his eyes. "No problem for me Sis – I expect he's more of a problem for you."

Grinning and nodding her head in agreement, Jenny smiled and then blew a kiss to Jacob. "See you soon," she said, just before he went. "See Dad – Jacob knows what a pain Calvin can be."

"I'm trying, love, I'm trying."

"Oh, we know you're very 'trying' Dad," Jenny replied before ruffling her dad's hair and laughing.

Back behind the counter, Jenny's dad showed her how to set the new timer for the exterior lighting. "I reckon you'll need them to come on at about five 'clock, for now. You'll have to adjust it again soon anyway, once the clocks go back."

"Ah, that's great. I can't wait for it to get dark now."

"Well, put them on before it gets dark, they are energy-saving lamps. They'll probably take a while to brighten up fully."

"Ok," replied Jenny, excitedly.

"And set the mornings too," said Dad. Moving away, from behind the counter, he looked up at the clock, "It's ten to five now, Jen. Not long to go."

"Do you want another cup of tea before you go? Then you can be here when they turn on."

Dad nodded and Calvin grunted a 'yes please'. Jenny hadn't actually asked Calvin if he wanted a drink but as always, he snuck in, unwanted.

"Ooh, another one? Count me in," said Dayna, before turning back to Calvin to finish telling him all about her new didgeridoo.

There was definitely a wintry nip in the air as Jenny, her dad and Calvin stood outside the shop and watched the dull, bluish hue of the lights slowly grow brighter, to a crisp white light, reflecting onto the large lettering. *J's Convenience Store* had come alive as dusk crept into darkness.

"Woohoo," screeched Jenny and beckoned through the window to Dayna.

Following the last customer out of the shop, Dayna joined the group to marvel over the shop's new nighttime appearance. "It looks even better than the daytime," said Dayna, gazing up in admiration. "You've done a great job, guys."

Calvin grinned smugly and Jenny's dad nodded his head. "There's no mistaking it now, Jen – you're definitely open in the evenings."

Jenny thanked her dad and even Calvin, for a job well done. She now awaited the surges of the daytime, to become late night, last minute rushes of the nighttime.

And they did indeed 'become'.

"Jen, before I get going – two things," said Dayna with a worried expression on her face.

"Yeah, what's up?"

"Well, I was thinking... are you going to be ok here, all on your own for another two hours after I've gone?"

"Yes, I'm sure I'll be fine. Wish I wasn't staying open until ten o'clock though, to be honest."

"It's very late to be open – and on your own as well."

"Yes, I know. I don't have much choice though. I can't afford to employ anyone else yet."

"No, I know that. Do you have to stay open so late though?" said Dayna, sounding genuinely concerned.

"Well, I've got to trial it and see if it's worth doing late nights on Fridays and Saturdays. I could be on to a good thing at the weekends. There are bound to be lots of people going over to the pub – they may pop in to buy something on their way."

"What like, cigarettes? You hardly make any profit on those, you told me."

"Yes, I know... like I said, it's just a trial and there's no need to worry, Day, that's why I got the personal alarm fitted under the counter," said Jenny, tapping the underneath of the counter top.

"Yeah but who is going to come to your rescue, should you need to use it? There's no one to come and help you."

"Have you heard how loud this thing is when it goes off?"

Dayna shook her head.

"No one will want to stay around here, hassling me, if that thing goes off – trust me."

"Ok, well I hope you'll be all right."

Jenny nodded and smiled at her friend, "So what's the other thing? You said two things…"

"I work from ten until eight tomorrow night don't I?"

"Yes…"

"Well, have you thought about how you are going to deliver the papers in the morning?"

"Oh shoot, no I haven't.

"I don't think the customers will appreciate getting their papers after ten o'clock, Jen."

"No, they were moaning a bit about having to wait until after eight o'clock." Jenny thought for a moment and then added, "What can I do, Day? I just didn't think about it…"

"Well it's a good job that I did then, isn't it?" Dayna grinned pompously. "I was thinking… what about if Xaylan does it for you at the weekends?"

"Xaylan?" Jenny remarked, trying to hide the shocked and horrified expression, creeping onto her face.

"Yes, I thought… well, maybe he could earn a little bit of pocket money."

"How would he get up here, Dayna?" Jenny was worried – worried that she may be just about to employ Xaylan, the child from hell.

"I could bring him up here."

"But the idea was that you have a lie-in on a Saturday, before your long shift."

"Ah, that doesn't worry me. I'd be more than happy to bring Xaylan up here – I could even run him round to do it."

"Well, if you're sure... I don't have any other options at the moment. He's too young to do a paper round officially, but I suppose we could work something out and give him a little pocket money for now."

"Ok, done deal."

Jenny thought for a moment. "Actually, I'd only need him on Saturday really. Tasha starts at eight on Sundays."

"Oh, I thought you didn't want to leave Tasha on her own in the shop."

"No I don't but I'm guessing that she could do it again..." Jenny pondered over her last statement and then retracted from it. "Well, ok, let's say that Xaylan does it on Sundays as well."

Dayna nodded her head and grinned. "He'll be pleased to earn a bit of pocket money, Jen."

"Yes but you won't get any rest will you?"

"Ah, I don't mind, honestly. It might make him realise that money doesn't grow on trees and that you have to work hard to get it."

"Hmm... well it can only be a temporary thing. He's just not old enough to do it legally. I'm guessing that, until we have enough newspaper customers to make up a decent round, we can't really advertise for a paperboy or girl anyway."

"No, you're probably right. So that's it then – Xaylan will be here at eight o'clock sharp, to collect the papers. I'll wait outside in the car. Does that sound like a plan?"

"Yes, it does... and thank you Dayna. Once again – and I feel like I've been saying this to everyone lately – I don't know what I would have done without you around to organize me and be my back-up brain."

"You would have probably screamed or even cried by now," said Dayna, winking an eye, before she walked off down to the staff room to collect her things.

"See you in the morning then," called Dayna as she opened the door. Then she left.

Jenny stood behind the counter listening to the lonely hum of the fridge units, while peering through the slits of the partially open blinds. A veil of bleak emptiness engulfed the road outside, the shop inside and Jenny's heart and mind, on all sides.

Thump, thump, thump... thump... thump.

Jenny almost leapt over the counter in her quest to get to the front door. She had to catch Dayna before she drove away...

"Just give me two minutes. I want you to hear this – just to prove that I'm not going mad," said Jenny, huffing and puffing.

The two women stood inside the front of the shop, tilted their heads towards the ceiling and listened.

Nothing.

"I do believe you, Jen. Why does the noise always happen when you're here on your own though?" Dayna was just as puzzled as her friend was. "Why don't you just go up there? Go and ask the man, what the hell is going on?"

Jenny was far more tactful than her colleague could ever be. "And say what?"

"Ask him what the hell he is jumping about for?"

"I don't know that he is jumping about, Day. It just sounds like that."

"Well go and ask him what the hell he is doing, then."

"You haven't met him – he's very stern-looking and unfriendly," replied Jenny, wishing that the noise would start again.

"Do you want me to go and have a word?" said Dayna in her, 'let me have a go at 'em' voice.

"No, if anyone is going to say anything – well, it should be me I guess. I'm the owner."

"Ok, so do you want me to wait down here then, while you go up there and confront him?"

Jenny shook her head, "No, I'll leave it for now. I will go up there and talk to him though – I promise." Smiling weakly, Jenny continued, "I just wanted you to hear it. You might have thought it was a different kind of sound. I just assumed it was a 'jumping' noise but it could be something completely different."

"Well it's obviously bothering you Jen, otherwise you wouldn't have come tearing out of the shop, to grab my attention, before I drove away."

Shrugging her shoulders, Jenny sighed, "I just want someone else to hear it... so that I know I'm not going barking mad."

"Haven't you always been barking mad?" said Dayna, in jest, "That's why we're mates isn't it?"

The shop's front door opened forcefully, causing both Jenny and Dayna to jump. In walked two burly men with practically identical bulging bellies.

"You gotta cash machine, love?" asked the older looking man with a bushy beard. "John said you might 'ave one."

"John?" said Jenny, "who's John?"

"Landlord – over there," the man pointed over his shoulder, with his thumb, "the pub."

"Oh, err... no I don't have one, sorry."

"Do cash-back then?"

"Err... I can do, if you're able to buy something," said Jenny, moving back around the counter. "Day, I'll see you in the morning. Don't worry about it – I'll record it if I have too." Jenny sniggered.

"Give us five a them *Hamlett* cigars, love," said the man, peering at Jenny, oddly. "I'll have 50 quid cash un all."

Dayna shuffled to the corner, where the window met the counter. She propped herself up against the windowsill and watched Jenny go through the transaction and pass over 50 pounds, in ten pound notes.

The second man moved closer to the counter and pointed up to the cigars on the top shelf. "Same for me please." He smiled warmly. "And 50," he said, passing over his debit card.

"Why didn't you go?" asked Jenny, glancing up at the clock. "It's twenty past eight, Day."

"I didn't want to leave you alone while those two men were in here."

"Well, I hope that there will be a lot more people in here before I shut at ten." Jenny tutted and rolled her eyes. "I shouldn't have called you back in here, I'm sorry."

"It's fine, don't worry. It's me who should worry... about you being here on your own..."

"Day, I will be fine – I'm sure. I have got the buzzer, don't forget." Jenny wasn't completely sure that she'd be fine but she had to give it a go. "No one will know that I'm on my own will they? They might think that there is someone else working out the back."

"Yeah, suppose so." Dayna shrugged and hooked the strap of her handbag back on her shoulder. "Well I'd better get going then, Xaylan will be wondering where I am – no, actually, Mum will be tearing her hair out by now and begging for respite." Dayna paused, "See you laters then – eight o'clock sharp."

Opening the fridge door, Jenny peered in the lit unit and shuffled some items around. A mass cull of fungal growth was required. She hadn't had a proper meal in a week and the items in her fridge had lain untouched. She slammed the door shut with her hip and headed straight to the sofa and slumped down heavily. Turning the television on, via the remote control, she mindlessly flicked through the channels. At 10.55pm there wasn't a great deal on, unless she wanted to watch an old western film or the sales channels. Jenny sighed and kicked her shoes off – she had to be up again at half past five, ready to leave for work at 6.15am. These late nights were going to be hard work but she hadn't realised just how tough it could be.

The takings in the shop had not been great past eight o'clock tonight. Previously suspecting that there may be a demand later in the evening, Jenny had been wrong, if tonight was anything to go by. Maybe she was being too hasty in her assumption and things would pick up over time. She hoped so. She didn't have too big a window of failure, before she would have to reconsider her options. Most of the customers who had come in after eight had wanted cash. When they discovered that there was no cash machine, they asked for cash-back, just like the first two men who'd asked. When Jenny's till had whittled down to just £20, she then had to refuse cash-back to another three people. This meant losing sales as well. Maybe she needed to hire a cash machine or she would have to make sure that she had an extra stash of money under the till's tray. Too many 'maybe' and 'possibly' equations entered her thoughts and gave Jenny a headache. Switching the TV off, she threw the remote on the sofa and went to bed. Maybe this, maybe that... possibly this, possibly that...

Only time would answer her questions, so Jenny tucked the quilt cover tightly over her head and went to sleep... and dreamt... and met up with Aaron, over a pulled pork ciabatta and a slice of billionaire's cheesecake.

Chapter 15

After the customary *'thumpty-thumps'* from the ceiling, Jenny opened the door to *J's convenience Store* with a weary hand and put the A-frame in its place. Although it was mid-way through October, a pair of House Martins were still shacked up in the eaves, above the shop. Obviously confused by the mild weather of late, the attractive, migrant breeders lifted Jenny from her glumness as they fluttered around. Just enough for her to smile, as Dolly came marching along the road.

"Good morning – what a beautiful autumn day it is, dear."

"Yes," replied Jenny, sniffing the crisp air, "it is lovely." Standing with her hands on her hips, Jenny watched as Dolly tied the dog's lead through and around one of the rings. "What brings you here today, Dolly?"

"I've come to get my paper, dear. Is there a problem with that?"

"No, no... not at all," said Jenny, trying not to show her absolute surprise and shock.

"I think you're doing a wonderful thing, dear." Dolly stood upright, arched her back, winced and then shuffled past Jenny, into the shop. "This will help your shop to thrive – other independent stores should take heed from your ideas."

"Sorry?" questioned Jenny, as she followed Dolly back through the door and closed it behind her.

"Offers, dear – your offers," said Dolly, before tottering off down the first aisle.

Just as Jenny opened her mouth to ask, 'what offers?' the door opened again and in walked two of the familiar dog-walking, *J's* community centre members. Every single morning, the clique of elderly gossipers had gathered in the shop to have a giggle and gab.

Moving round to her usual, early morning position, behind the counter, Jenny greeted each friendly face with a smile and a 'good morning'. From past experience, of just one week, Jenny knew that the aging tribe would be around for some time, gathering gusto and welcoming old and new members to their spot at the front of the shop. Jenny didn't mind too much really. The small assemblage was entertaining to say the least. The mainly male group made Jenny laugh, they made her other customers giggle, the time passed very quickly, Jenny felt less alone and the shop looked full and busy, every morning. Jenny realised that this was exactly the reason why she had wanted to run a shop of her own – customers were friends, friends were customers. But then again there were also the likes of Dolly and Marj – they were a law unto themselves.

Plonking a thick and heavy Saturday newspaper on the counter, Dolly placed a two-roll pack of white toilet rolls on the top. She held out two pound coins in her spindly fingers, ready to drop them into Jenny's hand.

"Err... that comes to £3.20 please, Dolly."

"£3.20, dear? I think you've got that wrong." Dolly turned to look at the remaining two members of the clique and grinned cheesily. Turning back round, she pointed to the small printed price at the top of the paper. "No, the paper is £2.00, dear – can't you see?"

"Yes, I know that. Those toilet rolls are £1.20 though, Dolly."

"I'm sure they are dear but I'm not paying for those, am I?" Dolly tutted and looked back at the men behind her.

Surprised by Dolly's odd remark, Jenny also looked over at the two men and shrugged her shoulders before Dolly turned around.

"Here," said Dolly, waving the two coins under Jenny's nose. "Here, take it."

"Dolly, the total price for the paper and the toilet rolls comes to £3.20."

"But they're free," screeched Dolly. "You're doing a free offer if I buy my paper here."

"Who told you that?" asked Jenny, fearing that Dolly was just about to burst into tears and tantrums.

"I said that I had come to get your offer dear... when I first came in. Don't you remember?"

"Yes, I do but I didn't get a chance to reply, Dolly, as someone else came in the shop at the time."

"Oh, so you're not doing any offers now then?"

"I haven't started any offers at all. I've only been open a week. Why do you think that I'm doing offers?"

"I've been conned," said Dolly, turning back to the two men. "She's made me waste my time coming here, when I could have gone straight to *KO Store*."

The two men looked at Dolly and both snapped their shoulders upwards and held out their hands as if asking for forgiveness from some divine being above.

"She's conning me," screeched Dolly, "I'm supposed to get these for free." Dolly grabbed hold of the toilet rolls and waved them in the air.

"No you're not, Dolly. They aren't free." Jenny cringed with embarrassment and shook her head at the two men. "Who told you they were free?"

"Brian and Joan told me. They said you were giving away free toilet rolls and that I would get a pack if I came in and bought my paper here."

"Well, I am really sorry Dolly – for a start I don't know who Brian and Joan are and secondly, I'm afraid to say that they have misinformed you."

"Dolly, just get the paper, love. You've obviously got it wrong. Poor girl's only been here a week – you'll frighten her off at this rate," said one of the men.

"Joan said that her neighbour has got some free toilet rolls from here. Why is it one rule for one and another for others?" Dolly frowned at Jenny with her small featured, prune-like face. "I won't bother with the paper then. I can get a much nicer service down the road. My face obviously doesn't fit."

Jenny wanted to slap the wrinkles out of Dolly's cheeks and had to stop herself from lurching over the counter and grabbing Dolly's scrawny neck. "I think I know where this has come from," Jenny huffed, desperately trying to please her customer but struggling to keep a smile on her face. The customer wasn't always right.

"Where?" Dolly puffed out her reddened cheeks embarrassedly.

"I think it must be Marj... I don't know if she lives next door to your friends but I did give her a pack of free toilet rolls the other day."

"See – I told you," said Dolly, twisting her head right round to glare at the men. She looked like the girl from *The Exorcist*. Straightening herself up, she brushed down her jade green raincoat and pushed up her grey curls. Turning back to Jenny, she snorted, "Why did she get free ones then?"

The two men behind Dolly looked uncomfortable. "Come on Doll – either get your paper here or go down to *KO*, it's not fair to keep pestering this lovely young lady," said the quieter one.

"Well?" With her hands now placed firmly on her hips, Dolly continued, "Why did that woman, Marj, get free ones then?"

"If you must know, I gave her free toilet rolls as a peace offering, after her little accident in here the other day."

"Oh my goodness, the old girl pissed her pants, did she? Hope you've moped up." Dolly placed her hands across her mouth, as soon as the words had left and the two men flicked their eyes around from one person to the other, embarrassedly, before they both burst in to a raucous guffaw.

Jenny gawped, disbelievingly, at Dolly. The Victorian, old lady's impetuous words had shocked her.

"No," said Jenny, and let out an unexpected bout of giggles. "She fell in my freezer..."

Those last five words were the funniest and they all snorted, sniggered and shrieked with the deepest of belly-laughs. Even Dolly, sniggered at the plight of a fellow pensioner's fate.

Dolly moved away from the counter as one, two, three people walked into the shop to get their weekend papers. Between the comings and goings of customers, Dolly, Jenny and the two men were exhausted by the absurd mirth bouncing around between them all. They just couldn't stop the laughter.

After the last person had walked out of the shop, carrying three papers and a receipt confirming their new paper delivery service, Jenny looked over to the three elderly extras in this farce and began to try and explain the misfortune of poor, old Marj.

It was of no use – no one could stay *compos mentis* for long enough to listen to the story.

"... So, I gave her the toilet rolls as way of saying sorry..."

"Got the papers?" said a little, grunting voice, from behind Jenny, making her jump.

Turning round, Jenny peered down at Xaylan's contorted, sleepy face. "Oh, where did you come from? I didn't see you come in."

"Door," mumbled Xaylan.

"Pardon?" replied Jenny.

Xaylan pointed to the door. "Came in there," he grunted. "Mum's outside."

"Oh, crumbs – I didn't realise that it was that time all ready," said Jenny, apologetically. "I haven't even got them ready yet. "Go and tell your mum, I'll be two minutes."

Xaylan sloped off with rounded shoulders and his head hung so low that he may have tripped over his nose, if he wasn't careful.

"I'll be back in a mo," said Jenny, scooting off to the piles of newspapers and grabbing the correct ones for the deliveries. She then looked at Dolly and said, "I'm just going to take these out to the car, hang on a minute."

Dayna shot a baffled glance at Jenny.

Jenny shook her head and mouthed, 'Sorry – yet again'.

Dayna tutted and mouthed back, 'Forget it – no worries', before heading off with her petulant son and several copies of the Saturday tabloids.

"Anyway..." said Jenny, attempting to finish her story, in her favour, "that's why she got them – the problem is that she now thinks she can have them free at any time. I'm just waiting to catch her, to let her know that she can't take them whenever she feels like it."

"I apologise to you, Jenny. My outburst of earlier was totally unacceptable," conceded Dolly, sounding genuinely humane for once.

"It's no problem – please don't worry about it."

"I'll take the paper but do you mind if I put the toilet rolls back?" said Dolly, holding out the two pound coins she'd kept in her hand for the duration.

"Of course you can," said Jenny jubilantly – she'd won the battle and hopefully gained a new customer and acquaintance out of the altercation – whether she liked it or not.

"Bloody miserable little sod he was this morning," said Dayna, approaching the counter with an envelope. "One of the customers, the man who couldn't talk properly, gave me this."

"Who was a miserable sod?" whispered Jenny, taking care not to be overheard by the people walking round the shop. There were some new faces in this morning – people who seemed pleasantly surprised by the shop's 'look and feel' and the range of items on sale. Jenny had a good feeling about today, although the morning had nearly got off to a wrong start.

"Xaylan." Dayna puffed out her cheeks and let go of a long sigh. "He doesn't want to do Sundays – only Saturdays."

"Oh dear, I didn't think he looked very happy this morning."

"No, you'd think that I'd chopped up his bloody game console, the way he was acting."

"Obviously doesn't like getting up early at the weekends," said Jenny, opening the envelope in her hand. "I really appreciate what you did though, Day. I was so wrapped up in other things this morning that I didn't even think about the papers until Xaylan turned up." Pulling the letter from the envelope, Jenny continued, "Go and make us a cuppa and I'll tell you all about Dolly's little explosion this morning."

Dayna nodded and grinned before strolling away, to the end of the shop.

Having read the letter from Rev. Arthur Brown, who was not the man who Dayna said couldn't talk properly, Jenny jotted the complicated schedule of works into the increasing newspaper deliveries book.

Rev. Brown was a new customer and he wanted an assortment of papers and magazines delivered to him each day, fortnight or monthly, respectively – and promptly. He had stated in his letter that he would venture down to the shop, during the following week, to pay up front. He had entrusted the letter with his neighbours, assuming that it would get picked up this morning – therefore, he expected a phone call, promptly, to confirm his subscriptions. *Huh,* Jenny thought, *he doesn't want much.*

"Well you can't knock it, Jen," said Dayna, looking back through the long-winded letter for a second time. "This is how you're going to start making the money."

"Hmm, it's a lot of faffing about. I'm going to have to get some sort of system in place, just so that we all know what we're doing with it."

It was a long day for both Jenny and Dayna. What with Jenny's 15 hour shift and Dayna's ten, the girls were both feeling weary by seven o'clock – and they still hadn't finished. They'd managed to snatch 15 or 20 minute breaks each, here and there, but they were constantly on the go for the rest of the time. Today was very busy in terms of the footfall and Jenny only hoped that the weekend's explosion of local residents would be reflected in the takings at the end of the day too.

"Another hour and you're finished, Day," said Jenny, patting her friend on the shoulder. "A day off tomorrow too."

"Yeah, I'll come and do the papers though – Xaylan or no Xaylan."

"I will make it up to you somehow, Dayna."

"Yeah, I know you will." Dayna picked up the counter notepad and flicked through the details. "So that's five new customers for papers today. Perhaps you should put a sign in the window, for a paperboy or girl, now."

"I was thinking that too," said Jenny, rubbing her brow and yawning.

"Bloody hell, how do you do it Jen – you've got three hours to go yet. You look tired out already."

Jenny nodded and smiled weakly, "Yes, worn out – we haven't even done a whole week yet."

"Once you've built up a good customer base though, you'll be able to employ someone else, won't you?"

"Yes, I do hope so. Today's been a good sign that things will get better, hasn't it?" said Jenny, hopefully. "We need every day to be like this."

"Makes the time go really quick, I suppose," said Dayna, "Right, I'll go and make a last cup of tea, before I'm finished."

The evening was a raving success, 'raving' being the operative word. Scantily clad groups of women, beer-swilling, big-bellied men and dreamy couples entered the shop for the first time and bought countless bottles of wine, crates of beer, liqueurs and snacks. Almost everyone asked if there was a cash machine and over half of them wanted cash-back with their purchases. Jenny had found herself in the same predicament as the previous evening and only just managed to scrape through to closing time, with barely a single note left in the till.

At around 8.15pm, once Dayna had left, a middle-aged woman entered the shop and went straight to the wine chiller, to peruse the manufacturer's offers of 'Buy one, get the second half price'. Jenny had pointed out, just this morning, that those offers were not her own but those of the manufacturers, when Dolly had been going off on one. But now the smart looking woman, wearing a fur-collar, beige coat and brown, knee-length boots, was the one and only person in the shop, showing an interest in the generous offers. She was also the one and only person to share in Jenny's twice-daily, thumping chorus. As the noises travelled across the ceiling, along their usual path, the woman looked up and appeared to follow the sound with her eyes. Glancing across to Jenny, behind the counter, she frowned.

"Happens all the time," called Jenny. "You're the first person to hear it though – maybe you could vouch for me that the noise does exist – just so that my colleagues don't think I'm going mad." Jenny laughed off the comment as the woman looked perplexed by her statement.

She grabbed two bottles of *Blossom Hill*, carried them over to the counter, carefully placed them on the top and took an old, over-filled purse from her expensive looking, brown handbag.

Peering up to the ceiling, the woman spoke softly and quietly, "Sounds like he's jumping about up there."

"He? Do you know him then?" Cringing at the thought of possibly having offended the woman or indeed the man upstairs, Jenny feigned a smile.

"Not really. I know *he* lives there though," she said, pointing above her head with a shaky finger. Her eyes narrowed, in what Jenny thought, was a look of antipathy.

"Oh, right... well, that'll be £12.00 please." The obvious animosity was unnerving and Jenny wished that she hadn't said anything.

"He's probably dragging around a dead body up there," said the woman, looking up, once again. "You want to stay well away from him." She brushed a straightened, blonde tress of hair, away from her face and avoided eye contact as she fumbled through her purse and produced the exact amount.

Before Jenny had a chance to ask the woman why she should stay away from him, a group of young women came in, giggling amongst themselves and preening their own hair, or someone else's in the reflections of their mobile phones. Jenny looked over and gave the usual courteous, welcome grin, before turning back to the woman and taking her money. As Jenny began to open her mouth, in response to the woman's last words, she suddenly left with her bottles of wine. Watching her walk across the road and into a house, further down, Jenny cursed. She had to find out what the woman had meant by her last comment. What did she know? Why would she think that he was dragging a dead body around the flat upstairs? A dead body would make a dragging sound, surely? Or was she joking?

It didn't sound like she was joking...

That's more like it, thought Jenny. She had counted the takings twice, just to make sure. The extra £540 did indeed reflect the amount of custom today. Locking the shop's front door, she peered up to the flat above. There were no lights on in the two front windows and Jenny wondered whether they were bedrooms or a lounge and kitchen at the front. She had no idea of the layout of the flats above. Momentarily, she wished she could be a House Martin – maybe from their position she would be able to see exactly what was going on in the flat above. She hadn't been able to get the woman's comments out of her head and a burning desire to investigate the strange noises was growing dangerously. But not at twenty past ten at night, it would have to wait. It would be too scary and probably, highly inappropriate to go knocking on someone's door so late in the evening, especially to ask if there was a dead person being dragged around the flat. Or worse still, being bounced around the flat.

Jenny shuddered, jumped into her car and headed home. She hoped that she may bump into Aaron again, when she went to bed – purely to share another ciabatta and another slice of cheesecake with him. In her dreams.

Chapter 16

Thump, thump, thump... thump... thump, thump... the noise sounded different this morning. Jenny was sure that she could hear a shuffling noise too – or was it just her imagination?

Arriving at the same time, Dayna and Tasha walked in and parted with a giggle. "Paper's ready?" asked Dayna, moving around the daily clique of retired, sociably-inspired, ladies and gents.

"Believe it or not... yes, they are. No Xaylan today then?"

"Don't even go there, Jen. In fact, let's forget that I ever suggested him."

"Oh dear, that doesn't sound good."

"No, it's not good – the little bugger stayed out past eight o'clock last night. Poor Mum had been pulling her hair out, phoning round everyone she could think of. It turns out that he was in next door's shed with his mate, Tristan – smoking a bloody cigarette that they stole from Tristan's dad."

"Oh no," said Jenny, feigning surprise. "Guess he's in a lot of trouble then."

"Yep – grounded – for a month." Dayna took the pile of papers from the end of the counter. "Told him that he's not doing this job either, he can't be trusted."

Jenny tutted, "Well maybe he'll learn his lesson now."

"Doubt it," replied Dayna. "I'll see you tomorrow. Hope your day goes nice and quick – early finish for you today - woohoo."

"Ooh yes – I'd forgotten about that. Yippee – six o'clock finish. That means that I can go home and have a bath," Jenny whispered, not wishing to share that information with the gathered group in front of her.

Dayna winked and left.

"Good morning," said Tasha, arriving behind the counter with two steaming mugs of tea in hands.

"Hi, did you have a nice day off yesterday?"

"Oh yes thank you. I went shopping with my mum. We bought a pole." Tasha smiled sweetly.

"A pole?" quizzed Jenny, "What sort of a pole? Don't tell me... for pole dancing." Jenny said in jest.

"Yes... our last one broke," replied Tasha, nonchalantly. "We've got a stronger one – mind you it was a lot more expensive."

For a moment, Jenny stared at Tasha, speechless. "Err... right, ok," she managed to say before she began flapping around like a caged bird, unable to think of anything else to say. Tasha's cool composure and innocent gaze made Jenny feel even more embarrassed. It wasn't the fact that Tasha and her mum did pole dancing, and Jenny had no doubt that it was done in the confines of their home (she hoped), and probably as a means of exercise (she prayed), but it was just the way that Tasha seemed to come out with these things, as if they were standard, everyday practice. After all, who doesn't have a wardrobe full of unusual costumes and uniforms and perform pole dancing with their mother?

The phone rang, giving Jenny the excuse she needed to leave. Snatching up the phone from under the counter, she walked off down to the end of the aisle. "Good morning, *J's Convenience Store.*"

"Hello Jen, love."

"Oh, hi Dad – how are you doing?"

"I had a confirmation email yesterday. The awning will be delivered next Saturday, between twelve and six o'clock – will that be ok?"

"Err, yes Dad, that'll be fine. Thanks."

"Have you got somewhere that you could put it? It's going to be quite big, I would imagine. We can't get over to fit it until Sunday."

"Oh crumbs – I forgot about that." Jenny tutted, "I'll have to put it in the stock room... and hope it doesn't get in the way. That man, Aaron, is coming to fit the new EPOS system next Saturday, too."

"Ah, yes... I suppose he's putting wiring in, is he?"

"I think so. Well... yes he will be won't he?" Jenny tutted again. "He'll be here all weekend, he said. Well, I'll just have to manage somehow, won't I?"

"Jen, if I had somewhere to put it, I'd hold on to it until Sunday but I'm full up with kitchen equipment."

"Yes I know. Sorry, it's just me panicking – everything's happening all at once."

"Don't panic, Jen, I'm sure it will be fine."

"Thanks Dad – I'm sure it will be fine too. I'll speak to you later – love you."

"Love you too, bye sweet."

Jenny took the phone back to the counter and placed it back on its base. "Huh, we've got all sorts going on here next weekend," she said.

Tasha turned to Jenny and grinned, "You look stressed, Jenny."

"I am." Jenny pulled an anguished face and grabbed bunches of her hair, pretending to pull them out. "I don't know why I feel stressed-out – must be in need of a good night's sleep again."

"You should try some pole-dancing," Tasha giggled, "it would chill you out. Good exercise too."

Instantly, Jenny's stress evaporated as a bewildered stare smothered her face. "I'll leave that to you Tasha – thanks all the same."

"We could start up pole-dancing lessons for the old folk around here... that would be funny."

"Err... no it would not."

"Oh, ok – I was only trying to make you laugh." Tasha frowned and lowered her long-lashed eyelids.

"You do make me laugh. I'm just not in the mood at the moment... not for pole-dancing... or anything else for that matter."

"Ok... no pole-dancing. Maybe later then?" Tasha grinned again.

"No – not later either." Forcing a smile, Jenny picked up her cooling mug of tea. "I'll be in the office if anyone needs me. I've got so much paperwork to catch up on."

The pile of papers in the office remained untouched after an hour. And then two hours. Surely it was all Aaron's fault that Jenny had been daydreaming and not done a single thing while lounging around in her office... well, in a strange sort of way it was. She hadn't been able to stop thinking about him. Glancing at the clock on the wall she noted that Tasha had been serving on the till, constantly, for several hours. Dragging herself up from her comfy chair, she opened the door and walked quickly up the aisle to the counter. "So sorry, Tasha. Please, go and get yourself a nice, long break," she said, just before another customer approached the till.

"Is it that time all ready?" Tasha sounded genuinely surprised.

"It's passed that time, I got so carried away with the paperwork. Go and get some time-out and bring some tea up when you're done."

Tasha nodded her pretty, young head and left the counter with her cold, untouched mug of tea, from earlier in the morning.

By late afternoon, Jenny had finally got her act together and was looking forward to an early finish. After two late nights, she was more than ready to get away early, go home, have a long soak in a hot bath and relax for the evening with a good book. Just as she picked up the final invoice to deal with, the counter's buzzer sounded and made her jump.

Several people milled around the aisle as Jenny walked hurriedly, up to the counter. "What's up?" she asked, puzzled to see that there was no one waiting to talk to her at the counter.

"I thought you'd want to know when Marj was in," whispered Tasha. "She's just gone down the other aisle. Have you spoken to her yet about the toilet rolls?"

"Ah, no I haven't and yes, I do want to speak to her. She hasn't been in much though... well, not that I've been aware of, anyway."

"Hope she remembers about the toilet rolls she's taken."

"Oh yes – now that's a point. If she doesn't remember anything, I can hardly accuse her of taking them."

"That's why I called you. You could maybe catch her in the act today."

"Good thinking Tasha – well done you."

Three people approached the counter, all at the same time. Two were laden with goods and another peered across the counter at the cigarette price list displayed on the gantry doors. Jenny wondered for a moment, whether the sudden surge of people coming into the shop was a deliberate act because they'd seen that *J's Convenience Store* was closing earlier on Sundays or whether the abundant footfall was a glimpse of good things to come. Jenny had no choice but to help Tasha with the forming queue, keeping an eye open for Marj, as she did.

The queue disappeared and Jenny realised that a great deal of diplomacy would be needed to confront Marj – the potential escapee with a turquoise bog-roll securely tucked under her arm. She did not want to cause a scene, should she have to accost Marj at the door, so she decided to go down the far aisle, meet up with her and politely aid her with her shopping. Leaving Tasha to do what she did best (assuming this was her best, as Jenny hadn't seen her pole-dance yet), Jenny casually walked over to the far aisle and glanced down it. No Marj. Hurrying down the end of the aisle, in pursuit, Jenny turned the corner. No Marj. Moving around two women at the end of the shop, Jenny slowed her pace, so as to appear as normal as possible as she got to the end of the other aisle. A cursory glance along the length of the aisle, while pretending to straighten items in the end freezer resulted in –no Marj. Jenny peered over her shoulder at the two women chatting by the bread shelf and then shot another glance up the aisle, in front. No Marj.

Catching Tasha's attention, between her serving the customers, Jenny shrugged her shoulders and held her hands out, whilst mouthing, 'Where is she?'

Tasha snapped a look up at the viewing mirror and then shrugged her shoulders too.

Back at the counter, Jenny waited patiently for the customers to be served and leave. "I didn't see her go, did you?"

"No," said Tasha, shaking her head and frowning. "I was serving a few customers but I kept a look out."

"Well she's gone and I don't know if she took any toilet rolls with her. Crafty-cat, she was too quick for me."

"Are you sure? I didn't even see her walk past the window." Tasha stood on tiptoes to see as far as she could through the viewing mirror. "She wouldn't have fallen right into the freezer, would she?"

Jenny laughed out loudly, "No, I've just been past the freezers – she'd have to be buried pretty deep for me to have missed her."

Astonishingly, Tasha burst into raucous, uncontrollable laughter and crossed her legs while doing so. She couldn't stop the horse-like neighing that was coming from her mouth.

"I'll take over for a minute," said Jenny, somewhat startled by her employee's sudden turn and the loudness of her peculiar laughter. "Do you need a glass of water?"

Tasha shook her head, "No..." she managed to splutter.

The two ladies who had been at the far end of the shop approached the counter and stared hard at what could only be described as a demented young girl – coughing and spluttering everywhere as she neighed and snorted.

"Please…" pleaded Jenny. "Please Ignore her – she's got a fit of the giggles, I'm afraid. Goodness knows what set her off."

As soon as Jenny had spoken, Tasha began to neigh even louder and left the counter with her legs tangled together in an attempt to walk and cross them at the same time.

The two, austere women, who appeared to be extremely unamused, huffed and mumbled under their breaths as they put their goods down on the counter and drew their purses from their bags.

Tasha had disappeared down the far aisle and could still be heard making the strangest of *hee-haw* sounds, somewhere near the pickles.

Once the sour-faced women had left the shop, Jenny peered up at the mirror and could see Tasha standing, cross-legged, by the toilet rolls, cupping both hands over her mouth.

Two more customers out of the way and Jenny sighed before calling out to Tasha. "All clear – you can come back now."

"I looked at the toilet rolls while I was down there," said Tasha, pulling the hem of her top down and straightening her hair. "I'm sure Marj must have taken one, there are two gaps on the shelf."

"Ok, well not to worry, we'll catch her next time. Fancy a cup of tea after all that laughing?"

"Yes please. I'm really thirsty now."

"I'm not surprised… I mean, the way you laughed, I'm amazed that you haven't got a sore throat."

Tasha's face turned pink, "Yes… my friends say that I sound like a donkey when I laugh."

"Really? I suppose it could be described like that." Jenny laughed aloud (very much *unlike* a donkey… or even a bog-standard horse). "I'll go and get that tea – you ok for a minute?"

Nodding her head, Tasha grinned sheepishly and then swapped places with Jenny, behind the counter.

Filling the kettle with water, Jenny placed it on its base and flicked it on. A discarded, half-filled glass of water stood on the worktop. Picking it up, she tipped the contents into the sink and placed the glass on the drainer, ready to be washed up. Although a very placid person normally, it did annoy her when people left drinks or other things lying around and it could have only been Tasha who had left the glass almost on the edge of the kitchen top. The kettle began to crackle and pop as it started to heat the water. Jenny reached for the tea canister, grabbed two tea-bags and popped them into two clean mugs. Then she spooned the sugar in and poured the milk, before slumping down onto the stool by the side of the door. Listening to the water bubbling inside the kettle, she closed her eyes and breathed a sigh of relief. Sundays were going to be her favourite day from now on – finishing at six o'clock would be heavenly.

The bubbling sound of the water, inside the kettle was mesmerizing... *bubble, bubble, pop, bubble...*

Then another watery sound added to the dulcet tones of the kettle. A whooshing, gushing, much louder noise. A flushing of water. A rustling.

Startled by the sudden interruption to her watery meditation, Jenny opened her eyes and bolted upright on the stool. The toilet, at the back of the staff room, had been flushed and a rustle of movement could be heard behind the closed door. Jenny's heart thumped heavily in her chest – there was someone in the toilet. Someone was using *her* toilet in *her* private staff room.

Fearing the worst, Jenny stood up and opened the staffroom door. She waited in the doorway. The kettle came to a boil and flicked off. Jenny glanced up the shop's first aisle. Unless Tasha looked in the mirror, she wouldn't be able to see Jenny from where she stood. With a shortened breath, Jenny watched and waited. The toilet door's interior lock turned. Jenny held her breath. Slowly, the door opened. Jenny gasped. Thoughts raced through her mind – what would she say? Who was in there? Should she tell them off for entering her staffroom? Should she have a go at them for using her toilet without asking? What should she say? What should she do? She waited, fearfully. The slow motion of the door turned Jenny's fears in to anger and then back to fear. "Hello?" she called out, too scared to enter the staffroom and venture towards the wash area and toilet for fear of an intruder, a burglar or a knife-wielding maniac (although they would hardly be using the toilets while breaking into a shop – would they?). "Excuse me –who is there?"

Silence.

"Oh for goodness sake," exclaimed Jenny, slapping a hand to her chest "What are you doing in there?"

As the little grey haired woman poked her head round the toilet door, Jenny slumped against the frame of the staffroom door. "You frightened the life out of me. What on earth were you doing?"

"I needed a piddle."

"I'm sure that you did but couldn't you have asked first?"

"Why do I need to ask to go for a wee?" Marj tottered away from the toilet door and climbed up onto a stool. "And where's my glass of water gone?"

Shaking her head, Jenny went back inside the staffroom and pointed to the glass on the drainer, "Is that yours then?"

Marj nodded her head, "Yes, just water thank you."

"Argh!" Gripping her head with both hands, Jenny glared despairingly at the defenseless old lady before snatching up the glass and filling it with cold water. "There... drink that and then you'll have to come out of here. This is our staffroom, Marj."

"Oh yes, I know it is..."

"Well it's private, Marj."

Marj grinned and took the glass from Jenny. "I expect you like it that way when you've got your husband in here."

"Pardon?"

After a large gulp of water, Marj wiped her lips with the sleeve of her coat and placed the glass on the edge of the worktop, where it had rested earlier.

"Sorry, Marj, what exactly do you mean by that? And I haven't got a husband, for the record." As soon as Jenny had finished speaking she realized what Marj had meant. "That man in here, the other day... he was not my husband."

"Oh, I see dear."

"Do you?" Jenny really wasn't sure if Marj saw or understood anything at all. "You're not supposed to be in here, Marj – it's private, staff only – it says so on the door."

"But I thought it was all right for me to come in here and have a glass of water. I'm sorry that I needed to use the toilet – is it *really* a problem?"

"Sheesh," exhaled Jenny, "Marj, it's not a problem to use our toilet..."

"What are you getting in a flap about then, my dear?"

Just as Jenny's head was about to explode, Tasha appeared at the doorway looking as perplexed as Marj was. "How did she get in here?" asked Tasha, pointing to Marj. "Sorry, I don't mean to sound rude but – how did you get in here?"

"Good heavens above, don't you start as well, young lady." Marj shuffled on the stool and placed her hands inside her coat pockets. "This good lady and her husband said I could come in, sit down and have a glass of water. What is wrong with you two fine, young ladies?"

Both Tasha and Jenny stared at each other disbelievingly, just before Tasha burst into horsey laughter again. Jenny could see the funny side to it but not quite enough to laugh and certainly not to start galloping around the shop neighing. "Look, Marj, I need to talk to you properly," said Jenny in desperation.

"You sound perfectly proper and normal to me, dear. I can hear you perfectly well. Although, your poor friend there sounds like a braying mule."

"Yes, she gets the giggles a lot... and yes, she does sound funny when she laughs... but that's not the issue here."

The door at the front of the shop opened and a cold draft tore down the aisle. Jenny turned and then tutted. "I'll be back in a minute," she said.

Passing by Tasha, whose discordant braying had intensified, Jenny tapped her on the shoulder and ushered her into the office. "I'll be back in a minute. Wait in here – don't want to upset anyone else." With that, Tasha's braying amplified and Jenny had no option but to close the office door quickly.

"Phew," sighed Jenny, under her breath, as she headed to the counter. *The customers always seem to arrive in surges and at the most inappropriate times*, she thought, as two more people walked in. Then another one.

It was growing dark outside as Jenny finished serving the last customer. A rough calculation, in her head, suggested that the last twenty minutes had been very productive for the shop's takings.

Tasha had stayed out of sight, hidden in the office and as for Marj... well, Jenny prayed that she was still in the staffroom, or at least *somewhere* in the shop. As long as she wasn't flailing about inside the freezer, everything would be ok. Wouldn't it?

Gone. Vanished, like before. But this time another pack of the familiar, turquoise toilet rolls had disappeared too and Jenny knew for a fact that she hadn't sold any in the last mini, retail-rush.

Tasha had morphed from a prized racing horse back to a reasonably normal, pole-dancing human being while Jenny had clock-watched, willing the hands to go faster around the dial. She'd had enough today – a bubble bath was calling her from a distant place of sanctuary and normality. Away from the insanity hovering around the shelving of *J's Convenience Store*.

"I don't know how I missed her," puzzled Jenny. "She's got her wits about her, you know."

"I'm sorry, it's all my fault." Tasha looked down sulkily. "If I hadn't been laughing so much, I could have served and then she wouldn't have got away again."

"What's done is done, Tasha. We'll stop her next time she comes in – without fail."

Warm bubbles wrapped around Jenny's shoulders as she sank further down, into the hot water. Closing her eyes, she ran the events of the day through her weary mind. She had to catch Marj and talk to her about a few things. She had to find out if Marj had any family and did they know about her condition? She had to get a paperboy… or girl. Jenny knew that she had to get more sleep too. The long weekend had taken its toll and she hadn't coped well, at times. She had to make sure that Tasha didn't get in to too many of her fits of giggles… or to rephrase it… *hee-haws*, either. Jenny had to knuckle down and get the paperwork sorted out more frequently. She had to take proper breaks, during the week, when there were three of them and she had to try and get that man, Aaron, out of her head. There was no time anymore for socializing, dating or anything else for that matter. The shop and the colourful characters it attracted, had to be her life completely, at least until it got off the ground and she could afford more staff. So many things she had to do and so many things she couldn't do, didn't want to do or shouldn't do. Do, do, do.

Thoughts drifted around her head aimlessly, floated away and then popped, along with the bubbles, as she lingered in the bath, dangerously drifting in and out of sleep. In and out of dreamy dreams. I do, I do, I do.

Chapter 17

The first boy hardly spoke and when a sound did pass his lips, it was no more than a grunt or a snort. His expressionless face couldn't rustle up a smile and he passed wind freely, noisily and potently.

The second had a vacant stare, apart from when he threw in a random cheesy grin here and there, but always at the wrong moment and he couldn't even read the name of the shop, let alone anything else.

Number three obviously smoked and by the red, veiny appearance of his eyes and lacklustre demeanour, Jenny wasn't so sure that it was only tobacco that he smoked at such a tender, young age.

A teenage girl, with over-sized breasts, was the fourth to arrive, on the second day. Giggly, dopey and caked in black mascara and a cheap foundation, which would have been more of a colour-match for a dusty camel, number four was far too vain and flirtatious in her manner.

The fifth one arrived late, blamed his school for keeping him in to do a detention, declared his hatred for all of his teachers and briefly mentioned what he'd like to do to them (which involved stones, bricks and car vandalism). He left the interview early.

Kicking off her shoes, Jenny sighed as she lifted her feet up to the desk and stretched back in her office chair. Maybe she should see the first boy again – perhaps he was so nervous that he didn't come across very well in his interview. His flatulence had been embarrassing, but then again, it wasn't as if he would be sat in the shop all day, so it might be possible to tolerate a short burst of farting, here and there. There was only one more boy to see and that wouldn't be until four o'clock tomorrow. Jenny needed someone quickly as the paper-round was growing by the day. Word had obviously got around that she was delivering newspapers and all of the elderly folk from the area were pouring in or phoning up, requesting papers, magazines and subscriptions. According to several residents, the other local newsagents, less than a mile away, provided a pretty poor service at a pretty expensive price. Many of Jenny's new customers had complained fervently about the service and were moving their custom to *J's Convenience Store*.

Dayna had been a star for the last two mornings. She'd delivered more and more papers without a hint of resentment. But then nothing could have compared to her infuriation, regarding her dear son, Xaylan, and his latest antics. And no one could even understand how he'd managed to perform such an animalistic act either. Dayna's treasured didgeridoo had been chewed. Tooth marks heavily engraved the outer edge of the mouthpiece. How Xaylan had succeeded in opening his mouth wide enough to clamp around the didgeridoo's circumference and then bite down hard on it, was anyone's guess – and no one could make a reasonable guess as to how he'd done it. When questioned, Xaylan's response had been, 'Dunno'.

Pondering over the paper-round, as she wiggled her toes on the desk top, Jenny came to the conclusion that she couldn't make an informed decision until the end of tomorrow. By the weekend, she would, hopefully, have a paperboy or girl joining the payroll, even if she did have to backtrack and employ one of the previous candidates.

A gentle rapping on the office door brought Jenny back from her muse. "Come in," she said, "I told you before, you don't have to knock Tash..."

Snatching her feet from the desktop, Jenny almost toppled off the chair in her hasty retreat to the floor. Fumbling and fretting, she attempted to pull her shoes on. "Err... sorry... I was just... err... well, tired feet, you know?"

"Please, don't mind me… and I know too well what it's like to have tired, aching feet." Aaron stepped inside the office. "The woman said to come down and knock the door," he added, pointing with his thumb, over his shoulder.

"Yes of course… err… no, that's fine." A red-hot flush coloured Jenny's face. "Sorry, I'm all over the place here, aren't I?" Retrieving a wedged thumb from the back of her shoe, Jenny looked up and met with those familiar eyes. "Can I get you a drink?"

"No," Aaron grinned, "I was passing and thought I'd drop in to check that you hadn't had a change of heart about the EPOS system. I can't stop."

"Ah, that's a shame. No, I'm good to go on Saturday, if that's still ok with you."

Aaron nodded. "I thought so and yes everything is still running to plan for Saturday." Leaning against the doorframe, he put his hands in his trouser pockets. "How are things going?"

"It's going ok. I probably look a wreck though. Been a bit tired lately – it's been harder going than I thought it would be." Jenny adjusted her hair and looked down at her chipped nails, before quickly clasping her hands together, in an attempt to conceal them.

"Yes, I remember my mum used to say how hard it was when she first started out." Aaron's casual stance and cool, calming voice were soothing. "That was well over 25 years ago."

"I can imagine. She's one of the most successful, independent retailers in the area. I'll get there one day," said Jenny, doubtfully. "I've got a few stories I could tell already though."

"Yes, I know. I could testify to one such tale," Aaron sniggered. "Seen any more of her?"

"Seen any more of her? She's our number one, most wanted villain at the moment."

Aaron frowned in puzzlement, "Villain? Why?"

"It's a long story…"

"Well maybe you could tell me over a couple of drinks one evening?" Aaron looked down at his shoes. "What do you think?"

"Yes, I'd like that... the only problem is – when?"

"Saturday?"

"I don't finish until ten on Saturday – and Fridays as well." Jenny sighed, "I don't have any free time at all really, that's the problem."

"How about Saturday lunch then?" Aaron peered up from his shoes. "We could go to lunch again, if you'd like?"

Shaking her head from side to side, Jenny replied, "It's no use, I don't have the two-hour cover at the weekends. It's just me and one of the girls on Saturdays and Sundays. I'm sure I've mentioned that before."

"Yes, you probably have – my head is always full of job-related junk. So, don't you ever get a day off?"

Jenny shook her head again and rolled her bottom lip down. "Nope.... I can't afford it yet."

"Ok, I could do next Monday, if you can?" Aaron smiled cheekily, "I have to keep my clients happy you know."

"It's a deal and yes, absolutely, you *will* have to keep me happy as your client. I can be very hard to please, you know."

Aaron laughed. "Ok, I'd better get going." Retrieving his phone from his trouser pocket, he added, "Got one more appointment today."

"Lucky you," Jenny replied, enviously.

"I'll be here about ten o'clock Saturday morning. I'll see you then.

"Ok, thanks Aaron," said Jenny, rising from her chair. "Enjoy your lie-in – I will have been up for five hours by ten o'clock on Saturday." She sighed and shrugged her shoulder. "Oh well, needs must."

"Indeed," replied Aaron. "One day, Jenny, one day..."

Propping herself up against the door frame, Jenny watched Aaron glide down the aisle and out of the shop. He didn't turn his head once as he left and she couldn't help but feel a little disappointed. Sighing to herself, she sauntered down to the counter where Tasha busily and efficiently served one customer after another. Grabbing the pad from under the counter, Jenny flicked through the contact details and delivery requirements of all the new newspaper and magazine customers. She was building up quite a sizeable paper-round which would require a responsible, switched-on teenager and certainly one that she could trust to get the job done. Unfortunately, she hadn't met that person yet.

The shop went quiet again as it always seemed to do after a sudden rush of people had come in, all at once. Jenny had wondered whether the surges of activity were due to certain programs finishing on the TV, or everyone in the vicinity having their meals at certain times of the day. There was definitely a pattern to the comings and goings at *J's Convenience Store* which had surprised her. She hadn't really thought about that sort of thing before. The footfall wasn't a steady trickle during the day. It was all or nothing and that went right through to the evening too.

Tasha huffed and shrugged her shoulders in an exaggerated way. "Tea?" she asked, peering at Jenny shyly.

"Great, thanks Tasha. Before you go… could I just remind you about using the buzzer if someone comes in for me."

"Ah, sorry Jenny, I had a queue and when he asked for you, I just pointed to your office and said you were down there."

"Hmm, it was a bit embarrassing when he opened the door. I thought it was you. I had my feet up on the desk, enjoying a slob-out moment."

"Oh no," replied Tasha, her face blushing. "I am sorry."

"Not to worry this time but please buzz me next time."

Tasha nodded her head fervently and scuttled off to the staff room to make tea… leaving Jenny alone with her daydreams.

As the late afternoon fell into darkness, Jenny twisted a blind rod and watched as the louvres of the first set of blinds tilted downwards. Then she paused and peered out of the remaining slit of window. The sour faced man from above the shop had just got out of a taxi, parked at the front. Jenny had a good mind to go and ask him about the constant banging and thumping but soon changed her mind when she realized that he appeared to be having some heated words with the taxi driver. Unable to make out exactly what was being said, Jenny sensed that the squabble was over the cost of the fare as the man was holding his wallet out and pointing to it. Spying through the tiny gap in the blinds, she was amused by the man's fervently flailing fists and raised voice. He banged his clenched hand onto the roof of the taxi and pushed the car, causing it to jerk from side to side. The taxi driver got out and put his hands up in the air, in what looked like an act of surrender. The driver tentatively moved around the car and approached the angered man, shaking his head from side to side, with his hands now clasped together in prayer. After a few more, less animated words, the man from upstairs turned sharply and hobbled off, leaving the taxi driver looking flummoxed. He got back in his car and a moment later, drove away.

Puzzled by the odd goings on outside, Jenny finished closing the rest of the blinds and then strolled down the shop to where Tasha was fronting the shelves. "That man from upstairs is pretty weird."

"Have you been up to see him yet?" asked Tasha, pulling milk cartons to the front of the fridge.

"No, I haven't. I don't really know what to say to him."

Tasha stopped, mid milk-pulling and turned to her. "Why don't you ask Dayna to go up there?"

"That's a definite no. I think it will take a lot more tact than Dayna would be prepared to give, from what I've just seen."

"Oh," Tasha looked surprised. "Why, what have you just seen?"

"Well, put it this way – I don't think the man would welcome a call from any of us and especially a complaint. I've just been watching him giving a taxi driver a telling off for some reason and at one point I thought he was going to overturn the car."

"Oh gosh. You might have to put up with that thumping noise that you hear then."

"Hmm, we'll see," replied Jenny, thoughtfully.

Thump, thump… thump, thump, thump… thump. Tutting to herself, Jenny rolled her eyes and then glanced up at the ceiling, ritualistically. It was almost like the man waited until Jenny had closed the shop, before he started banging about upstairs. It was the same in the mornings – the strange thumping noise had usually ended by the time Jenny opened the shop.

Counting out the coins, in her office, Jenny finished the cashing up in record time. However, things were really not going as well as she would have hoped and that was including finding someone to do the paper-round. The footfall and spend had to pick up at some point or she would be working the painfully long hours for a lot longer than she had originally anticipated.

Sighing heavily, Jenny checked the locks at the back of the shop, turned the lights off and went round to the staffroom. She had managed to get into a routine that ensured her swift departure from the eeriness of the shop at night time. As she approached the front, she noticed another light in the ceiling, had gone out. *It has to be that man upstairs*, she thought, grumpily. It would have to wait until the weekend now, when her dad came to fit the awning. Too tired to care, Jenny switched off the remaining lights, set the alarm and left the shop.

Chapter 18

His baby blonde hair swept across his unblemished face, like a wave of pure innocence. Cropped shorter around the back, his neatly cut hairstyle framed his handsome, adolescent features, admirably. He was every mother's dream, every young girl's sweetheart and Jenny's newest member to *J's Convenience Store*. Jordan Heel, well-mannered, well-spoken, intelligent and humorous. He had it all – and he now had the job too.

Jenny had warmed to Jordan's juvenile charm, almost immediately. At just 15 years old, she could see that this promising young man would go a long way in life, if he played his cards right. His infectious smile warmed her and his cheeky demeanor brought a frivolous freshness into the shop.

Dayna had swooned at the sheer delight of such a lovable youngster being 'on the team', as she put it, and the relief on her face was apparent – she wouldn't have to do the papers anymore. Jordan was more than happy and willing to start on Friday.

Wanna do lunch on Friday? Got afternoon off. Jenny cringed as she read the message on her mobile phone. If she didn't reply to it, she'd be guaranteed to get a phone call within the next 30 minutes.

Thanks for the offer Calvin, but I'm going to decline. Got a busy weekend ahead.

Jenny held onto her phone and waited for the aftermath. It would either be, utter rejection syndrome or a pathetic, uppity response.

Surprisingly, Calvin's reply was short and to the point. *Your loss.*

The buzzer rang and Jenny jumped from her office chair, patted down her hair and straightened up her blouse. Dayna obviously needed her for something. Usually, Dayna was more than capable of dealing with any situation so Jenny guessed that someone was in the shop to see her.

As Jenny stepped out of the office door, she almost bumped right into Marj. "Oh, hello Marj." Jenny peered up the aisle to see if Marj was the reason for the buzzer. Dayna pointed a finger, discreetly, in the direction of Marj, indicating that the dear old lady was, in fact, the reason for Dayna's call. "Marj," said Jenny, gingerly, "could I have a quick word with you?"

"Oh, hello dear…yes of course you can."

"Would you like to come through to my office?"

"Yes dear. Do you think I could have a glass of water, I'm very thirsty – I've just got back from the town?"

"Yes, of course. I'll get you one." Jenny showed Marj through to the office and offered her own chair. "Sit here for a moment and I'll get you some water."

Marj plonked herself down with a huff and a puff and immediately reached for the mouse, almost instinctively. "Ooh, I like playing with these things. My daughter has a computer like this."

"Well please don't play with mine, Marj – it has all my important accounts and spreadsheets for the shop." Jenny placed her hands on her hips and frowned, "You have a daughter?"

"Pardon, my dear?"

"You just said that you have a daughter."

"Could I have that glass of water please, dear?" Marj clutched at her throat and poked her tongue out like a child would, indicating her dire need for a drink.

Rolling her eyes, Jenny turned to go. "Marj, please wait here for a minute, I do need to speak to you – it's very important."

"What do you need to speak to me about, dear? Ooh… I'm so parched."

Jenny sighed, "Ok, Marj – wait there – I'll get your water." Rushing round to the staff room, Jenny grabbed a glass from the kitchen cupboard just as the shop's phone began to ring. The dual ring tone stopped abruptly and Jenny assumed that Dayna had taken the call at the other end of the shop. Taking a deep breath to calm her nerves, she ran the cold water tap for a moment and then filled the glass. As she walked out of the staffroom an elderly man stopped her.

"Excuse me... umm, sorry, do you work here?"

"Yes, I do," said Jenny, impatiently.

"Good, good... then maybe you could help me." The man took hold of Jenny's upper arm and grinned scarily as his lips sunk deep into his toothless mouth. "My wife would like some pegs – do you have any?"

Jenny smiled awkwardly, "Yes, we have some small bags of about 20 pegs I think. They're hanging up, half way along that aisle – near the rubber gloves," said Jenny, pointing to the first aisle.

"I don't see very well and I've left my glasses at home. Could you help me find them?"

Standing outside the staffroom with a glass in one hand and a freaky old man, with a pungent smell of fried onions, attached to her arm, Jenny pulled herself up on tiptoes to see over the shelving units in a desperate attempt to get Dayna's attention.

Dayna was chatting merrily to a couple of women at the counter, oblivious to the goings on at the end of the shop.

"Excuse me... it's for you." Marj's squeaky little voice came from behind Jenny.

"Sorry?" Jenny turned around sharply, almost catapulting the old man from her arm, and stared at Marj, disbelievingly.

"The phone – it's your husband." Marj beamed a devilish smile and held the phone out to Jenny.

"Could you direct me to the pegs please," reiterated the old man. "I only want a bag of pegs."

The word 'husband' sent a flutter through her stomach. Snatching the phone from Marj, Jenny glared at her and then held the phone to her mouth. "Hang on one minute Aaron – I'll be right back." Reaching into the staffroom, Jenny placed the phone on the kitchen worktop and swiftly closed the door. "I'll show you where the pegs are, Sir," said Jenny, as she shot a menacing stare at Marj.

The old man was more than happy with his bag of pegs and was escorted, as quickly as possible, to the counter to pay for them. Jenny tutted and shook her head at Dayna. "Phone call," she said, holding her thumb and little finger up to her ear and mouth, "keep Marj in here – I'll be back in a minute."

Tearing back down the aisle, Jenny reached the staffroom door and grabbed the handle. As she opened the door, Marj came out from the office, to her left. "Don't worry about the drink of water, dear. I really must be going."

"No – wait a minute – please." Jenny grabbed the phone, "Hi Aaron, I'm so sorry about that. Could I phone you back in a minute?"

"Sorry but I'm not Aaron," came a man's voice, before he sniggered, "and I'm certainly not your husband or at least, I don't think I am… unless, of course, you roped me into it when I was slightly inebriated last weekend." The man let out a cheeky chuckle.

Jenny froze.

"It's *Bob's Bits & Bobs*. Just a courtesy call madam."

"Oh," sighed Jenny, rubbing her brow, "I do apologize for the mix up." Falling in to the staffroom, as Marj trotted away, up the second aisle, Jenny slumped down on the stool nearest the door. "Thanks for calling today, I was hoping that you may be able to send a rep in to see me."

"Yes, certainly. Will you be the contact for any orders?"

"Yes, I will."

"Could I take your name?"

"Err… yes, Jenny… Jenny Fartor."

"Thank you, and are you the manager of the shop?"

"Err... yes, you could call me that, I suppose – I own it."

"Oh sorry, Mrs Fartor, I have the proprietor's name as Margery Daw?"

"Who?" Jenny paused momentarily. Wide-eyed, she gulped back a rising frustration. "Did you say Margery Daw?"

"Yes, the lady I was talking to a minute ago. Dare I say, the older lady?"

"She is not the proprietor, I can assure you."

Ok, there seems to be a slight mix-up. The other woman told me that she was the owner."

"Well I'm afraid that she is not the owner – she's nothing to do with this shop. I don't even know why she answered the blood... the blinking phone. If you check the listings you will see that I own *J's Convenience Store*. And I'm a Miss not a Mrs."

"Ok, Miss Fartor, I can tell that there has been some confusion here. I'll remove Margery Daw's name."

"Thank you... and I think that Margery Daw has been playing on her spurious see-saw for far too long."

"Sorry?"

"Never mind – when will a rep be coming out?"

"I'll get one out to you next week. Should be Tuesday – is that ok?"

"That's fine – thank you." Jenny heaved a sigh of relief, "And I apologise for the confusion."

The man laughed, "Not a problem. I get what you mean now about the see-saw."

"Hmm, well thank you for calling."

"You're welcome – oh and please let me know if Johnny gets a new master, won't you."

"Pardon?" Jenny frowned and then began to smile as it dawned on her. "Oh very funny, thanks. Bye."

"Goodbye."

"I tried to keep her in here Jen," said Dayna, "Apart from leaping over the counter, knocking a few customers out of the way and diving on her to wrestle her tiny frame to the ground, there wasn't much else I could do."

Jenny nodded in agreement, "I know. Wish I hadn't got so tied up at the back of the shop."

"And I haven't got a clue how that old man even found our shop, let alone walk through the door without bumping in to anything." Dayna cringed. "He couldn't see a thing and threw the entire contents of his wallet on the counter, for me to count out." Screwing her nose up, Dayna shivered. "Ugh – it was disgusting, Jen. He had bits of sticky fluff and crusty stuff mixed up with all his pennies. I wanted to throw up."

"Ewww, that's gross."

"Yeah and I had to separate the greasy money from the grotesque, hairy bits to count it out."

"Oh no," Jenny heaved, "think I'm going to be sick."

"You haven't heard the worst bit yet..."

"Do I want to know?"

"Probably not but I'm going to tell you anyway, as you're my best friend and we share everything."

"Go on then." Jenny wrapped her arms around her waist and braced herself.

"Well, the two customers behind him were watching everything. I was so embarrassed, Jen." Dayna feigned a gag and then continued, "I had to put all of his money back in his wallet..."

"Yes..."

"And then he left and all the sticky, scabby bits were still on the counter top."

"Ugh, hope he doesn't come in again," said Jenny as a queasy ball stuck in her throat.

"I had to scrape it all off the counter with a piece of card while the customers watched."

"Think I'm going to throw up now," said Jenny, clutching her throat. "Where is it?" Jenny scoured the floor, around her feet.

"Well I couldn't throw it on the floor could I? The customers were watching me."

"No, of course not – how awful."

"I put it all in your coffee mug – you'll have to give it a good scrub later, when you've emptied it."

Jenny glared, open-mouthed. "What?"

"You should be able to scrape it out with a spoon and then you could disinfect it."

Dayna's straight face infuriated Jenny. "I hope you're freaking-well joking, Day."

"It's quite sticky stuff but it should come out with a spoon."

"Throw it."

Dayna's deadpan expression began to break and she burst in to a resounding cackle. "I'm teasing you, Jen."

"Where is it then?"

"In the bin," Dayna blurted out, before grabbing the waste paper bin and holding it under Jenny's nose.

Backing away, Jenny held her hands up. "Ugh, get rid of it."

Dayna scurried away, clutching the bin at arm's length, laughing raucously.

Blinking away the sting of her smarting eyes, Jenny breathed in deeply. She was *not* going to cry, even though the rampage of erratic, negative thoughts, jittering around in her head, would have decided differently. *Get a grip Jenny Fartor, you're just over-tired.*

A few minutes later, Dayna returned with an empty bin. "You ok?"

"Yes – I'm just frustrated by that bloody woman, Marj..." Jenny gave Dayna a brief run-down of her experiences at the end of the shop. "I'm sorry I had to dump that old man on you but I was worried that she would get hold of the phone again."

"We'll catch her next time. I will jump on her if I have to and pin her down until there are no customers in the shop. Then we'll sort her out."

"I don't think we need to be quite that rough with her. She's pretty cunning though."

"Why don't you search her name in the directory, online? If we could find out where she lives, one of us could go round to her house and talk to her. Or try and find out more about her daughter." Dayna had her detective head on and would enjoy nothing more than to go 'seek and find'.

"Yeah, I could do. Do you think her name is really Margery Daw then?"

"Well that's what she said – you've got nothing else to go on, Jen."

"No, I suppose not."

"Ask some of the locals, they might know," said Dayna, wisely.

"Good idea. I'll ask them in the morning, when they have their community centre meeting in here."

Dayna rolled her eyes and tutted. "They don't buy any more than a paper – bloody cheek if you ask me. You'll be making them teas and coffees soon."

"They make the shop look busy in the mornings and they keep me company for an hour," replied Jenny, in her defense.

"They make it look busy for who?" Dayna shifted to her 'protect and preserve *J's Convenience Store,*' mode, "There's hardly anyone who walks up and down this road, apart from the nursery staff and parents. Oh... and the community centre dog walkers."

"I know... I'm hoping that 'word of mouth' will get us more customers."

"Get that paperboy to deliver some leaflets to advertise."

"That would cost more money – I wouldn't expect him to do it for nothing."

"You need to do something, Jen. You look so tired all the time now... I know you were expecting to work a lot of hours for a while but I think the sooner you can afford someone else to work here, the better."

Of course, Dayna was right. However, Jenny hadn't expected to feel so worn out, in such a short amount of time. Maybe more advertising was the answer – well, of course it was. Jenny had to do something about it – she knew that.

Chapter 19

The man upstairs sounded like he'd beaten Jenny to it this morning. *Thump... thump, thump.* Following the noise down the length of the shop, Jenny flicked on the lights as she went. She had to be a little more prepared in the mornings now that the new paperboy was delivering the papers before he went to school. Glancing at her watch, she noted that she had 25 minutes to get the papers sorted out, stacked on the shelves and then pick out the ones for today's delivery, before she had to open up.

Thump, thump, thump, thump, thump... back along the whole length of the shop, to the front door. Shaking her head, Jenny rolled her eyes and mumbled expletives, under her breath. The way she was feeling today, she had a good mind to go upstairs and thump the man – for thumping. After a restless night, she was in no mood to be dealing with the likes of the surly man above, or even Marj for that matter. Today she was going to keep herself busy. She planned to create an A6 sized advertisement, which she would print off herself, by the hundreds if need be. And at lunchtime she would nip out to get some more ink. Mission no. 1 commence.

Dreamy Jordan arrived promptly, at 6.40am. With a beaming, rosy-cheeked face, he studied the delivery addresses, checked the whereabouts of unknown streets on his *iPhone* and then looked up and grinned. "Can you give me your number?"

"Yes, sure. It would have been on the paperwork I gave you yesterday."

"I know but I forgot to put it in my phone," replied Jordan, with a cheeky, endearing grin.

Jenny smiled warmly and recited the number as Jordan entered it into his phone.

"Thanks. If I get any problems, I'll call you."

"Great, thank you Jordan."

Thump, thump... thump, thump.

Jordan looked up to the ceiling and frowned.

"I think you're only the second person who has heard that."

"Is someone jumping upstairs?" asked Jordan, innocently.

"Yes, it happens every single morning though – and every night."

"Strange."

"Hmm, very." Jenny smiled again. There was a calming aura about Jordan and his boyish looks were charming. "Anyway, you'd better get going – don't want to be late for school."

Jordan chuckled, "No, can't be late, I've got double maths – love maths. See you tomorrow."

Jenny walked Jordan to the door and locked it behind him. She had another 20 minutes before the shop opened and she was going to make full use of it by making herself a mug of milky coffee and toasting a couple of crumpets, taken from the bread shelf.

Watching Dolly tie Wilbur to a ring outside, Jenny thought about her second mission of the day. She had to find out where Marj lived. A brief scour of the internet's directories hadn't come up with anything about a Margery or Marjorie or Marj Daw, who may live in Farehelm... or anywhere else for that matter. It seemed that dear old Marj could either be lying about her name, believe that she was actually Margery Daw or possibly have eluded all internet directories, somehow.

"Good morning," chirped Dolly, as she trotted through the door. "Lovely morning, isn't it?"

"Yes, it is." Jenny peered out of the window again at the sunlit road. "Cold though."

"We've done well this year, what with the Indian summer. The leaves are changing now though. Winter is on its way."

Nodding her head, Jenny smiled and leant over the counter. She liked the regular, morning chitchats with the older folk. Talking about the weather, the news and any of the local community issues allowed Jenny to forget about her long lists of jobs to do and it kept her amused. 'Miss Lonesome' didn't have a chance to rear her ugly head when Dolly and the others were in the shop.

"Dolly, do you know that woman, Marj, who comes in the shop?" Jenny asked as Dolly stepped towards the counter with her paper in her hand.

"Marj?"

"Yes, the little, grey-haired woman. She's Irish – or at least she has a slight Irish accent."

Dolly thought for a moment. "Don't think I do," she said, shaking her head from side to side.

"I'm sure she's been in here before, when you've been here."

Rolling her bottom lip down, Dolly continued to shake her head.

"Who was it that told you about the toilet rolls?"

"Oh, you mean the free... but not free ones?"

"Yes." Jenny held her breath, hoping there would not be another commotion over the toilet roll issue.

"It was my friend, up the road."

"Maybe your friend knows Marj then?"

"I don't know. I'll ask her. I think I know the woman you're talking about though. I remember now."

"Really?" Jenny's eyes lit up in hopefulness.

"Yes dear, I think she lives near my friend, up at the top of Millen Road somewhere."

"It would be good if you could find out for me. I need her name and address if possible."

"Why do you want to know?" asked Dolly, wearing a puzzled frown on her powdered face.

"Err... it's a long story really... I'm hoping I might be able to contact her daughter. I want to help her out if I can."

"Why does she need help?" Dolly leant against the counter. "Is this the one who had an accident? What has she done now? Pooped herself?" Dolly let out a squeaky giggle before daintily placing a withered hand across her mouth.

"Err... it's not for me to say, Dolly. I shouldn't really discuss other customers with you." Jenny tried to back-track. "I care about people and just want to make sure that she's ok, living on her own and all that."

"Oh, I see. Very community-spirited of you, dear."

Jenny smiled and nodded, "I do try to do my bit for the community." *After all, my shop has become the heart of the community... and you're the chairperson of the clicky community centre,* thought Jenny, but decided not to repeat it.

Poor Wilbur was beginning to shiver and whine outside, by the time Dolly had finished gossiping to her early morning group. Nobody knew where Marj lived or whether her surname was, in fact, Daw. A couple of the men knew of her but hadn't really spoken to her in length, apart from to pass the time of day and say 'good morning'. So it appeared that dear, old Marj was as elusive as ever.

Punctual as always, Dayna breezed through the door at eight o'clock. The pointed heels of her red shoes clicked on the floor as she glided across the shop. Dressed in a short, pink, shift dress, a lemon, bolero jacket and carrying an oversized, lime green handbag, Dayna looked her usual self – a flamboyant, Caribbean carnival queen. However, it was not her normal attire for working at the shop. "Did you get my message, Jen?"

Jenny shook her head. "No."

"I sent you a text an hour ago."

"Oh, I haven't looked – sorry."

"Anyway, I got an appointment for half nine – hope that's ok."

"Appointment for what?" Jenny wondered if Dayna actually had an appointment to join a carnival, by the way she was dressed.

"The dentist. We shouldn't be too long. I'll pick Xaylan up from school and get straight down there." Slinging her bag under the counter, Dayna perched her bottom on the stool, behind the till. "Really hope it won't be a problem, Jen."

"No, it's fine. What's up with Xaylan then?" asked Jenny, still musing over Dayna's colourful display of cloth.

"He's got a cracked tooth."

"Oh dear, how did he do that?"

"Well, how do you think, Jen?" Dayna tutted and rolled her eyes. "He did it on the didge – obviously. He didn't tell me until last night though."

"Oh no. Hopefully he won't do that again then, will he?"

"He wasn't going to tell me but I knew something was wrong when he wouldn't eat all of his tea at Mum's. Then he was sulking around, not talking much."

"So why have you tarted yourself up just to take Xaylan to the dentist?"

"Have you seen the dentist at the health centre? He's American," said Dayna, with a glint in her eye.

Dayna had a penchant for American men and Jenny feared that this poor dentist may have far more to deal with than just looking into a young boy's mouth.

"Also, I've come up with an idea to help push up those sales."

"What? You're going to parade around as a carnival queen?"

"No, stupid."

"Let's call Tasha, she could turn up in all sorts of fancy dress costumes," said Jenny, sarcastically.

"Shut up for a minute and I'll tell you," said Dayna.

Jenny held her hand up. "Hang on – if you're leaving in an hour or so, we'll have a coffee now. I'll go and make one, then you can tell me." Turning to leave the counter, Jenny added, "And if you see Marj, take your heels off, hitch your dress up and chase after her."

Hitching her dress up in jest, Dayna failed to notice the two elderly women walking in to the shop. The sheer horror in their greying eyes was a picture of hilarity.

Leaving swiftly, Jenny hurried down the end of the shop, sniggering under her breath, while Dayna feigned shyness and tried to explain away her actions as, 'just a bit of a joke between friends'.

Placing two mugs of coffee under the counter, Jenny waited for Dayna to finish serving a middle-aged man. Flirtatious in her manner, Dayna was always the same. She took on a whole new personality when wearing her heels.

Jenny almost pitied the 'American dentist'. He really didn't know what he had in store for himself today.

As the middle-aged, office-type, man left the shop, he turned his head and smiled, admiringly, at Dayna.

"So, what's your idea then?" asked Jenny, inquisitively.

"Some of the parents, from school, are coming up here later."

"Oh, really? Why?"

"Well, we were talking in the playground this morning and we've all come up with a plan."

"Ok..."

"They're bringing their kids up here and are going to wear bright clothes... and bring big shopping bags."

Jenny looked puzzled, "Why?"

"Don't you get it, Jen?" Dayna held her hands out to her sides. "When the parents from the nursery and the people on the buses, see how packed out and busy we are, they're going to wonder what is going on in here. The girls are going to stand around outside, chatting, as well."

"Whose idea was this?"

"It was a group decision really." Dayna dropped her hands down and rested them on her hips. Flicking one hip out to the side and resting her weight on one leg, Dayna's stance was one of determination.

"Why would the parents want to waste their time coming up here, Dayna? What's in it for them?"

"Aah... well...."

"Well what, Day?"

"Well... I told them that they could get a free newspaper and chocolate bars for their kids, if they will do it." Dayna switched hips and rested on the other side.

"Oh did you. And who's going to pay for all of this?"

"I will, of course." Snatching her hands from her sides, Dayna folded her arms, willfully.

"How many are coming?"

"About 20... and all their kids."

"Blimey, Day – so that's at least 40 people – possibly more," said Jenny, thoughtfully.

"Yeah – good init?" Grinning like a teenager with a selfie-stick, Dayna continued, "We're all coming up at about four o'clock so I'll have to warn Tasha, otherwise she might have a panic attack."

"So, let me get this straight – you're coming back this afternoon then?"

"Yes, of course. Why do you think I've got all this on today?" said Dayna, looking down at her shoes.

"Err... for the dentist?"

"Well, yeah... that as well."

"Day, in all honesty, I do not expect you to fork out money to try and get us more business. That's supposed to be my job." Jenny attempted a mental calculation. "It could cost you £80 or more, depending on the paper and chocolate bar."

"I told them all that it's only the local paper that they'll get for free and the kids can have the 10p Choco bar. So I reckon it'll be about 20 to £30."

"Ok," said Jenny, thoughtfully. "I'll cover the cost this time but in future, please talk to me about it first."

"You don't have to fork out for it, Jen. This was my idea – I'll pay up for it."

"No – it's fine – at least you've got the gumption and forethought to go ahead and arrange something... and consider the costs too. No, I'll pay."

Dayna nodded and looked at her watch. "I will have to leave soon. I've got to pick Xaylan up and get down to the Health Centre. I won't be too long and I can make it up to you this afternoon. How about we share the cost though? I didn't expect you to pay for my idea."

"It's fine, really. I can lose a bit of the costs in wastage. Just let me know next time you have an idea like this. I'd already decided to make up an advertising leaflet today anyway. I'm going into town at lunchtime to get some more ink."

"Consider it a no-brainer, Jen, I'll let you know in future. Who's going to deliver the leaflets then?"

"I haven't thought about that yet – maybe I will, at some point. Don't know when though." Jenny shrugged and rolled her bottom lip down. "I'll think of something."

"Already thought of something," said Dayna, grinning devilishly, "haven't got time for that now though."

"I dread to think," said Jenny. "Go on then, if you want to go now..." Placing her hands on Dayna's shoulders, Jenny guided her around the counter and gently slapped her on the bottom. "Off you go... see you later you little floozy."

"Give me an hour and a half – tops!" said Dayna as she hooked her super-sized bag over her shoulder and tottered to the door.

"And yep –you're right – given half the chance, I will be a little floozy."

"He's going to crown it," said Dayna, pointing to her own teeth, as she approached the counter. The woman, standing at the counter, turned, looked Dayna up and down and then walked away with a snooty air about her. "Thank you – come again," called Dayna, sarcastically, as the young woman exited the shop.

"Who's 'he'?" Jenny peered through squinted, suspicious eyes. "The American, you mean?"

"Umm... he's gorgeous, Jen." Stepping behind the counter, Dayna kicked off her heels and slipped a pair of dolly shoes on. "My feet are killing me."

"Not surprised. So, when is Xaylan having the crown done?"

"He's got a temporary one on now. Can't believe they did it so quick." Dayna slipped her thin, bolero jacket off and pulled a thick jumper from her bag.

"What else have you got in there?" asked Jenny, peeping inside the cavernous, canvas bag. "Slippers? Pyjamas?"

"It's cold today, Jen."

"I know – I'm surprised you're dressed like that... No, actually, I'm not surprised."

"I've got to take him back next Thursday afternoon, so I won't miss any more time at work."

"Ok, that's great."

"After that, it'll be a couple of weeks before he gets the permanent one. Will said that Xaylan must have bitten the didge incredibly hard to cause so much damage. Not to mention the damage to my didge."

"Will? Who's Will?"

"Doctor Davey – the dentist. His name is Will."

"Blimey, Day, you don't waste much time, do you?"

"What do you mean?"

"You know the dentist by his first name after one visit?"

"We were having a bit of a giggle about my didge. I told him what I did when I first bought it. He thought I was really funny."

"I bet he did."

"I've seen him once before. When I had my checkup he was in the reception office, talking to one of the women there."

"Don't tell me, you fell in love with him, first sight," said Jenny, more inquisitive now.

"Yes, I did."

"You've never mentioned him to me before."

"What was the point – didn't think that someone like him would be interested in me."

"Don't put yourself down, Day. You're as good as anyone else."

"Yes I know and I'm working on it now."

"On what?"

"On Will, of course." Dayna pulled the jumper over her head and then lifted her long, dark curls out from her neck. "He fancies me – I can tell."

Tasha was raring to go when the time approached four. Unusually excitable, she paced up and down the aisles, moving this and straightening that. "Do you think it'll work?" Tasha asked, as she returned to the counter.

"Hope so," replied Jenny, unsure whether it would help or hinder her efforts to gain customers. "Might frighten everyone away."

"No... I don't think it will frighten people away. They'll be curious as to what is going on in here."

"Hmm," muttered Jenny, "hope you're right."

Dayna was the first to walk through the door. Followed by one, two, three...

Twelve women, seven pushchairs, eight children, around Xaylan's age (including Xaylan) and approximately 15 younger children, were in the shop, according to Jenny's last head count. It was packed and the two men who were already inside, looked decidedly worried by the surge of noisy children, crying babies and chattering, gossipy mums. Fighting their way to the counter, while Dayna was attempting to introduce every single mum to Jenny and Tasha, who were stood behind the counter in a daze, the two men paid for their goods and left swiftly. It was pandemonium.

As previously instructed by Dayna, each of the mums and her small tribe of followers, walked around the shop, picking items up, looking at things and generally appearing to be shopping. They all carried large shopping bags on their shoulders and one woman had a huge holdall. She looked like she should have been perusing the aisles in an airport shop, before flying off for a month's holiday. Her empty holdall was a ridiculous size.

From time to time, Dayna strutted her stuff outside the shop, along with a couple of her friends. Swinging her lime-green bag and clicking her heels on the pavement, Dayna stopped, peered in the window and pointed. Her exaggerated movements were comical, to say the least. As a bus rolled by, Dayna took a newspaper from her bag, opened it up and pretended to read it. Luckily for her, the late afternoon sun was beaming down on *J's Convenience Store*, creating a warm glow around the hive of activity.

"There should be some more yet," said Dayna, grinning from ear to ear, as she returned inside. "Haven't you noticed outside?"

"Yes, passers-by looking in you mean – and looking at you, inquisitively?"

"And the bus – did you see that go past?"

"No," replied Jenny, piling up more Choco bars on the counter.

"There were loads of kids on there, they were all looking in." Dayna puffed her chest out and put on her conceited look, by smiling tight lipped and squinting her eyes.

"Don't they normally look in anyway?"

"Yeah but curiosity will get the better of them today, so they will get off the bus and walk this way, instead of the other."

"Ok, we'll see. I do hope you're right." Jenny really did hope that her friend was right. She'd gone to a lot of trouble.

The door opened and Andrea Douglass, from the nursery, walked in. Halting in her stride, she looked down the first aisle and then across to the small crowd, gathered by the counter. With a puzzled expression she moved across the front end of the shop and proceeded down the second aisle. Weaving her way through the bodies, Andrea collected two large cartons of milk and made her way back to the counter. "Blimey, you're busy," she said, plonking the milk on the counter. "Where have all these people come from?"

"They're Dayna's friends," Jenny replied. "More milk? Didn't we give you enough in your order this morning?"

"Yes – we've got our AGM this evening and then the owner has organized a big dinner for everyone."

"Oh, I see." Jenny keyed the amount in the till and then looked up, "Do you want them added to your bill?"

"No, I'll pay for them separately. It's a different account." Andrea looked back along the second aisle, "So why are all of her friends in here then?"

"Between you and me, Dayna thought that if the shop looked busier, it would encourage more people to come in."

"I'd say that it would have the opposite effect, folk around here can't be bothered with fighting their way through crowds or waiting in queues to be served. You might have just gone and shot yourself in the foot, as they would say."

"Oh dear, do you think so?"

"Hmm," muttered Andrea. Grabbing the milk from the counter with both hands, she turned to leave. "I'm sure I've said it before – you'll be hard pushed to make a living around here. No one else has managed it yet – except us, of course. And that's had a lot to do with me," she said, pompously, before gliding out of the shop with a smug look on her face.

Jenny and Tasha looked at each other, stunned by Andrea's lack of tact and her negative prediction.

"Just ignore her, Jenny. She's obviously jealous because you own your shop and she's just the manager of the nursery."

"Hmm... I do wish it was this busy all of the time though." Through the mirror, Jenny watched Dayna and her friends, walking around and talking about the products they held in their hands. Dayna's enthusiasm was infectious.

"It will be, give it time. My mum is coming in at the weekend to have a look around."

"That's nice... tell her to bring about 50 friends with her then." Jenny feigned a light-hearted laugh but really wasn't feeling it.

Fifteen mums, in total, had visited the shop. The sales had rocketed as the average spend, by Jenny's calculation, was peaking at around £12 per head. Elated by its success, Jenny had happily given every child a Choco bar and the mums got their local newspaper for free, as previously arranged. A couple of the mums had even said that they would try and get up at least once a week but Jenny didn't hold out much hope – after all, why would they come all this way?

Two hours had passed. Dayna, Xaylan and his temporary crown had left and Jenny was exhausted. If her shop ever got this busy, she would definitely employ another person. Time would tell and although the initial sales figures had been far short of what she had been expecting for the new shop, she still had hope for the future. This afternoon had been more like it.

But, when everything returned to the norm, there wasn't a rush of kids from the buses or an influx of curious passers-by or indeed, any sort of countable increase to the footfall. Jenny pondered over the expected impact of Dayna's unusual idea and came to the conclusion that there was nothing to draw from the conclusion. It hadn't worked, in the long run.

One car, two cars, three cars and then some more. At half past seven Millen Road was beginning to look like a jumbo car park. Cars, vans and the odd motorbike lined the road, on both sides, nose to tail. Then the parking bays began to fill, then the side road became cluttered. Upon inspection, Jenny noted that the car park at the rear of the shops was also, dangerously full. Like the *Road Block* game, Jenny tried to figure out just how everyone was going to get out of the small parking area without hitting anyone else. It was car chaos.

"I've just realised what it is," Jenny thought out loud. "For a minute there I thought they might all be coming here – huh – no such luck. They're all going to the nursery, it's their AGM tonight. They've got some dinner event going on too."

"What's that?" asked Tasha. "What's an AGM?"

"Annual General Meeting. Andrea said that it was tonight." Jenny peered through the blinds again. "Didn't realise there would be so many cars though. Look – they're parked in my bays as well."

Tasha peeped out of the window. "They shouldn't park there should they?"

"No they shouldn't... those are my bays. Bloody cheek... and I bet they don't even come in here to buy anything."

Tasha moved away from the window. "Are you going to say anything?"

"Well it's a bit late now, they've already gone into the nursery."

"Ooh," replied Tasha. "I'll carry on with facing-up, shall I?"

"Yes, thanks Tasha. I don't expect we'll be busy now… certainly not with any customers who might have driven here."

J's Convenience Store didn't see more than eight people before close and Jenny couldn't help thinking that the congestion had something to do with it. Dayna's efforts, earlier in the day had been fruitless after the evening's takings of less than twenty pounds.

Whichever way she tried, Jenny was not going to squeeze her car through the gap without taking either her own or someone else's wing mirror off. The other options were, to go to the nursery and find out who the car belonged to or move all of the commercial bins out of the way.

After an exhausting, mind-numbing day, she really didn't fancy the idea of going to the nursery, explaining her predicament and waiting until they found the owner of the car. It was past 10.30pm and the growing thump in her head had been singing in unison with the nightly *thumps* from above, earlier. No, she would move the bins out of the way, pull over somewhere – she didn't know where – and then pull the 1100 litre bins back to their places.

The first two bins were full as the fortnightly rubbish disposal was due tomorrow. *'Typical'*, thought Jenny as she pulled and heaved a heavy container down the pathway and parked it alongside her shop. The next two bins, which belonged to the nursery, were overflowing with rubbish bags. Building up a sweat, Jenny just managed to inch the first stinking container away from the car park and down to the side of the shop. With aching legs, she returned to the last bin.

"Oi!" A man's voice hollered from the flats above. "What you doing?"

Jenny looked up to see the man who lived above her shop. Hanging out from a back window, he scowled, threateningly, at her.

"I'm sorry but I can't get my car out. I'll put them back in a minute."

"Don't make so much noise about it then," shouted the obnoxious man.

"I do apologise," replied Jenny, sheepishly.

"Some of us are trying to sleep, you know." The man glared down at Jenny and then pulled his head in and slammed his window shut.

By the time Jenny had moved all four bins, the pavement was inaccessible. She hoped and prayed that the AGM/dinner event wouldn't finish now as the people would have to walk in the middle of the road to get round to the car park.

In hindsight, Jenny decided that it would have been easier to track down the culprit of the parked car as she climbed into her own and turned the engine on. Fearing that the man upstairs would come down and start shouting his mouth off again, Jenny swiftly exited the carpark, drove down the road and halted at the end. There just wasn't anywhere to park, at all. Turning left, she went along to the next road and drove up it, looking for a big enough space to park her faithful old jeep.

Wrapping the belt of her coat tightly around her, Jenny tied a knot and tugged at it hard. The cold, autumn air whipped across her face as she speedily made her way back to the shop, two blocks away. Glancing at her watch, she cursed. The time was approaching eleven o'clock. She still had to put the bins back, as quietly as she could, and then walk back to her car. By the time she got home it would be getting near to midnight. It would be a case of straight to bed and then straight back to work again in the morning.

With a full bin in tow, Jenny stared, horrified, at the sight in front of her eyes. A small blue car had squeezed into the bin area. She'd been gone ten minutes and now someone had parked right where she needed to get to. '*Argh!*' screeched Jenny, under her breath. As her ever worsening headache impaired her judgement, she attempted to pull the cumbersome bin, with all her might, through the gap between two parked cars.

Crack!

The right-hand wing mirror hung by a wire, down the side of the blue car's door. Jenny's heart skipped a beat as she realised what had happened. Not daring to pull the bin any further through the gap, she reversed her actions and pushed it back along the pavement. Tears pricked at her eyes. Why hadn't she gone into the nursery in the first place? A vision of Aaron entered her mind but he wasn't being sympathetic, he was laughing his head off. Once again, she had been rather foolish.

Returning to the damaged car, Jenny crouched down to see if she could repair it. Suddenly, she froze as she listened intently – there were people coming towards her.

As the voices drew closer, Jenny could hear odd words of the conversation, between two people. 'Meeting'… 'Bloody cheek'… 'Nursery'… 'Nice meal'.

"Bloody hell. You – you stupid girl – you made me jump," said a tall young woman, dressed in a long black coat and carrying a large, shiny briefcase. The man beside her looked frail in comparison, his weak and delicate stance highlighted by the formidable woman towering above him. "What the hell are you doing down there?"

"Oh gosh, I'm so sorry… is this… err… your car?" asked Jenny as the woman twirled a set of keys around her finger. Rising from her crouched position, Jenny held the wing mirror in one hand, still attached to the car by a wire.

"What the bloody hell are you doing?" The woman's heavily mascaraed eyes glared down into Jenny's and tore strips from her soul.

"Look, I am so sorry… I had a bit of an acc…"

"You've snapped my wing mirror off." The woman stepped closer, towering over Jenny. "Tom, call the police."

"I don't think there's any need to call the police, Tracey."

"Look, I will pay for the damage to your car – I am truly sorry," Jenny spluttered, pleadingly.

"Where's your car then?" the surly woman demanded. "Watch her Tom – she's liable to do a runner."

"I hit it with that wheelie bin," replied Jenny, pointing to the container behind them.

"Oh." The woman feigned an insane laugh, 'Ha, ha, ha!' "So you're going to tell me that it was the bins fault, are you? Tom call the police – now!"

"No, I'm not – it's entirely my fault and I'm more than happy to pay for the repair."

"Calm down," said the meek and mild man, beside her. "We'll take her details and send her the bill, it's simple."

"Yes, well don't let her fob you off with a name like Rusty Clutter, will you Tom? You've been fobbed off before – you brainless idiot." The woman's disparaging remarks were unnerving.

The man, called Tom, shook his head and pulled a small notepad from an inside pocket of his smart suit jacket. "Your name?"

"My name is Jenny Fartor"

"Can you spell that?" asked the man, meekly.

"F A R T O R."

The woman peered down at Tom's notepad. "She's taking the piss – that says 'farter', Tom. For goodness sake – can't you see? Call the police!"

"I can assure you that I am being serious. My name is Fartor – it's pronounced Fa-toar. I know it looks like something different but it is Fa-toar. I own the shop here. If you'd both like to come inside I can prove who I am."

Tom nodded his head and looked up at the woman beside him for approval. "Come on Tracey it's cold out here."

"Ok," said the woman, sternly. "Hurry up about it – I want to get home."

Turning round the corner, the man and woman waited at the door, while Jenny unlocked it.

Pouring out from the nursery, the people from the AGM event had finally finished their meeting and meal. Swiftly piling into cars parked along the way, up the side road and round the back, the nursery people were gone within minutes. Millen Road turned back into the sleepy suburb it had been before.

Another ten minutes passed and then Jenny was locking her shop door again. The odd couple had agreed to pop the repair bill into the shop by next week and then they had left without so much as a thank you or goodbye. With frazzled nerves, Jenny walked the short journey back to her car and drove home. The four wheelie bins remained on the pavement, where Jenny had left them. After the day she'd had, she did not want the man upstairs moaning at her again or worse still, coming down the stairs. It would have been a foregone conclusion – Jenny would have lumped him one, if he had.

Chapter 20

J's shop
To the shop,
I am not happy about all the noise
and commotion. It went on all afternoon
and the evening was flaming stupid. What is
going on in your shop? I do not want to have to
listen to cars revving their engines at the
back of the building, half way through
the bloody night, or look out of my
windows to see hundreds of cars parked
out the front and up the side street.
As for the bins, well what the flaming
hell do you think you're playing at?
Also, I think there are too many children
using your shop, the noise is terrible.
Please consider the residents here as
we were here before you were. If you don't
I will be contacting the council.
Are you some kind of a weirdo?
What's with all the hanging around
the bins and cars in the middle of the night?
Sort it out!
From D upstairs.

Jenny slapped the crinkled note on to her desk and made a deep throaty growl, '*Grrr*'.

Thump... thump, thump... thump, thump, thump...

Her overly tired, stinging eyes welled up and two single tears fell onto her cheeks – *do not cry, Jenny Fartor, you're better than this* – she tried to convince herself. Wiping the droplets away from her face, she slumped down into her chair and read the note again. This time there were no tears, just a bubble-bursting unrest, in the pit of her stomach.

The papers weren't ready when young Jordan arrived.

"No problem, I'll help you do them quick," he said.

"I'm so sorry, Jordan, I've had a lot of extra work to do this morning." Jenny recalled her morning task of dragging the four bins back into their rightful places, as quietly as she possibly could. She'd left for work half an hour earlier, in order to remove the bins from the pavement. Then she'd found the note on the doormat and things had gone downhill from there.

Jenny wished that life could be filled with lots of Jordans – beautiful, calm and simple. His disposition brought sunshine into the shop and into Jenny's shattered dreams. Her new business was taking a lot more out of her than she could have ever imagined. But it wasn't the shop that was the problem – it was the customers, or some of them at least. And one local resident in particular.

Holding the bag open, while Jordan pushed the papers inside, Jenny worried. "I hope this won't make you late for anything else you might have planned."

"Nope, it's ok. It didn't take me that long yesterday."

"Oh, that's good, although there are more at the weekends and the bags a lot heavier."

"No worries. Oh, I was going to ask you if I can deliver the weekend papers later. I was thinking eight o'clock?"

"Oh yes, of course. That's fine. You should have come in at eight today – I might have been ready by then." Jenny smiled weakly.

"No, I wanted to check it was ok first," replied Jordan.

"Ah, bless you. Very conscientious – very admirable, Jordan."

"Thanks." Jordan grinned, displaying a perfect row of beautifully white, young teeth. "Cool – I'll see you at eight tomorrow then."

Crossing paths, Dolly walked in as Jordan went out. Jenny never thought that she would be so pleased to see a familiar, friendly face, like Dolly's. "Morning Dolly, how are you today?"

"Very well, my dear. Was that your new delivery boy?"

"Yes, Jordan – started a couple of days ago."

"He's leaving it late isn't he?"

"No, well... it's my fault really. I wasn't ready for him today."

"You need to be ready for your paperboys, dear. Can't keep these young lads hanging around."

"I'm well aware of that, Dolly."

Although Dolly was being her normal, to the point, say it how it is, self, Jenny was glad of the company, to take her mind off the other matters that were troubling her so much now.

Soon enough, the community centre crew arrived and there wasn't a single moment to think about anything else. Hopefully they would hang around long enough until Dayna arrived, at which point, Jenny was going to give herself permission to fall apart.

Just before ten o'clock, Jenny had a sudden urge to cry again. She had just remembered who and what was coming today and what would be happening. Aaron... and the awning! She'd been so wrapped up in her own self-destruction, by reading and re-reading the crumply note all morning. She hadn't been able to think past the moment when she imagined herself going up the flight of stairs at the back of the shop, knocking on the man's door and planting her fist in the grumpy git's face. Although it would never happen as Jenny imagined it, because she was far too professional and moral and certainly not brave, at all. However, the thought of shutting the man up for good had been a satisfying muse.

Hello Jenny, I'm running late today. Hold up at the other shop. Hope to get there by lunchtime. Aaron Frey.

Butterflies fluttered in her stomach as she replied to the text message. *Not a problem Aaron. Thanks for letting me know. Jen*

Dayna arrived, on time as usual, wearing a more suitable attire, compared to her efforts of yesterday. "You alright?" she asked, the moment she walked in. Her intuitive and instinctive capabilities to suss her friend out, at any given moment, were second to none.

"Yeah..."

"No you're not – what's up?"

"Make us both a milky coffee, Day, and I'll explain all."

"O...k..." muttered Dayna, staring deep into Jenny's eyes. "Want crumpets as well?"

Jenny nodded her head and then peered up to the ceiling, blinking away the wetness.

"Be back in a flash, Jen," Dayna said and then shot off down the aisle to the staffroom, grabbing a pack of crumpets on her way.

"So, that's what's been happening so far..."

"Wonder who she is?" Dayna frowned. "Got any idea how much the bill will be?"

"No, haven't got a clue. Dad will be here tomorrow, I'll ask him."

"You poor thing, nothing seems to be going right for you at the moment." Dayna slung an arm around Jenny's shoulder.

"I haven't finished yet..." Pulling the crumpled note from her pocket, Jenny passed it over. "This had been pushed through the letter box when I got here this morning."

With a more than curious expression, Dayna opened the fold of paper and started to read. Slowly her features began to change. She frowned, her eyes glared, her mouth dropped open.

Watching Dayna's eyes dart up and down the length of the note, Jenny knew that she was reading it again and again. "What do you think of that?"

Dayna looked up, said nothing and peered down at the note again.

Jenny could almost smell the rage seeping from Dayna's skin, "He thinks I'm a weirdo."

"I'm going up there... freaking old codger... who does he think he is?" Dayna looked at the note again.

"No you're not, Day. I will deal with this."

"You're too diplomatic – he needs putting in his place."

"I totally agree with you, however, that's not the way to deal with it." Jenny took the note from her infuriated friend. "When I feel calmer, I will go up and see him... try and sort it out amicably."

"If I see him, I'll bloody well sort him out."

"Look, I don't want this situation getting any worse – we can't afford to have any trouble around here."

Huffing and puffing, Dayna paced up and down behind the counter, "It pees me off, Jen."

"I knew it would. We do need to be professional and play it cool though."

"He can't call you a weirdo and get away with it."

Dayna's agitated state was beginning to concern Jenny. She knew what Dayna was capable of when she was enraged. There had been times throughout their lives when Jenny had found herself in some sticky situations. Peeling her best friend off of some poor person, male or female, had been a regular affair in their younger days. Dayna's motto had always been, 'Treat me right, we won't fight. Treat me wrong, you'll see me strong'.

"It's not worth the agro, Day. No, he can't go around calling me names but, for the sake of the shop, I'll try and resolve this amicably."

Clenching her hands into fists, Dayna squeezed them tightly. "Arg!" she spurted out and then shook the tightness out from her hands. "Ok, you win – I will control myself. I just hope that he does not come in this shop – ever!"

"Well he hasn't been so far and he only lives upstairs."

"Yeah, probably too frightened to. I bet he knows that he is annoying you by banging about up there, every morning."

"And the evening," added Jenny.

"Grr..." uttered Dayna, "Right... keep calm, keep calm... another coffee, Jen?"

"Absolutely. We've got a lot on today."

"Oh yes – I forgot about that. Aaron isn't it?" Dayna tilted her head to one side and fluttered her eyelashes. "He's coming today, isn't he?"

"Yes and the awning's being delivered."

"Well that will cheer you up – Aaron, I mean... not the awning. Well... the awning might cheer you up too." Dayna laughed, grabbed the mugs and plates from under the counter and headed off to the staffroom. "I'm over it now – no worries," she called back, before disappearing round the end of the aisle.

It was heavy work, moving pack after pack of fizzy drinks cans. Each pack contained 24 cans and by the ninth pack, the burning pain in Jenny's lower back, was unbearable. The fact that she had hauled the bins around last night and again this morning, really hadn't helped matters. Straightening her spine up, she placed her hands on her hips and stretched back, trying to ease the pain.

"I'll do the next lot," said Dayna, "there aren't any customers at the moment."

"Thanks, Day, they're heavy though – mind your back."

"Squat – that's what you need to do when picking up heavy things. You've been doing it wrong – you should have known that, Jen. Health and safety and all that rubbish."

"Hmm... I'll serve if anyone comes in – my back is killing me at the moment."

"Is it going to fit in here?" asked Dayna, grabbing a pack of cans and shuffling it round the corner.

"Hope so, can't keep it out there in the shop."

Dayna glanced out of the office door. "Yeah, it will, I reckon."

And it did. Between the two of them, Jenny and Dayna managed to drag the large awning box, along the end of the shop, through the office and to the back of the store room. And they did it all in between several customers.

The front door opened again, Jenny let go of the box and put her hand up. "I'll do it. You make us another cuppa."

Reaching the front of the shop, feeling hot and sweaty from the recent removals, Jenny halted mid-stride. "Oh... hi, Aaron."

Standing near the counter, Aaron's inviting smile and gorgeous big eyes, melted away any remnants of pain or sorrow that Jenny had endured over the last 16 hours.

"Really sorry I'm so late, Jenny."

"Not a problem. We're just having a cuppa, do you want one?"

"Yes, that's great. Coffee, two sugars. I'll start bringing all of the gear in."

"Do you need a hand?"

"No, there's not too much, at the moment." Aaron smiled again, "I'll get all of the nitty-gritty stuff, like the wiring, done today. Then I'll be back tomorrow to fit the till... or tills... and set up the computer."

"Tills? Are there more than one then?"

"I was going to ask if you wanted two. I've got a spare one."

"Hmm... the way things are going here, I doubt I'd need two," said Jenny, feeling the burn in her back continue to rage on, despite her giddy feelings of infatuation.

"Well we can sort all of that out tomorrow. Don't need to worry about it at the moment. I'll rig you up for two – that way, the second one is there if you need it." Aaron moved backwards, towards the door and reached for the handle. "Right, I'll go and get the stuff in."

"Wait!" Through the glass of the door, Jenny caught a glimpse of Marj. She'd approached the door, looked through the glass at Aaron and then turned sharply and walked away.

Startled by Jenny's sudden, loud burst, Aaron frowned. "What?"

Hurtling towards Aaron, Jenny thrust herself at the door and snatched the handle as Aaron whipped his hand away, in shock. "Got to stop her..."

Tearing the door open, Jenny knocked Aaron to one side and flung herself through the doorway...

Smack!

"Arg..."

The towering figure of a woman, who was just about to walk through the door, lost her footing as Jenny flew out and landed on her. She staggered back as Jenny's momentum carried them both towards the edge of the pavement. Twisting her ankle on the edge of the kurb, the bewildered woman tumbled down to the ground with a heavy thud. Jenny just managed to save herself from falling right on top of her and directed her fall to straddle over the top of the woman's head and onto the road behind. Turning round, Jenny looked in horror to see the woman sat on the ground, in a confused heap, breathing heavily.

"Oh my goodness... are you ok?" asked Jenny, shakily. Bending down, she peered at the lady's face. "Oh my God... no... I am so sorry." Jenny stared, disbelievingly. "I am truly sorry. Oh no."

The woman said nothing. Obviously shocked and dazed, she sat motionless, with her hands resting back, on the edge of the pavement. Her pale complexion and wide stare were scarily worrying.

Tearing out of the door, Aaron approached the woman and crouched down beside her. "Can you get up?" Glancing up at Jenny, with an odd look of mistrust in his eyes, Aaron added, "Please, can we help you get up? Come in to the shop, madam." Sliding his arm underneath the woman's, Aaron beckoned to Jenny to do the same on the other side.

Crouching over, Jenny's back ripped and the intense pain surged along the length of her spine. Despite the acute spasms, she managed to help Aaron lift the woman to her feet.

"Ooh," cried the woman, in distress. "My coccyx..."

Shooting a fierce stare down the length of Millen Road, Jenny spotted Marj, scuttling away in the distance.

Holding both hands to her mouth, Dayna stood in the shop's doorway, wide-eyed and dumbstruck.

The window of the flat above squeaked and flung open. Poking his head out of the opening, the man upstairs grunted. "Bloody hell... what have you done now? Are you some sort of a psycho?"

Dayna moved out to the pavement and glared up at the man. "I'd keep your nose out of it, if I were you."

"Ooh... argh... my coccyx," moaned the woman.

Slowly, Aaron and Jenny eased the tall woman, past Dayna, and into the shop.

The man upstairs spat a globule of saliva, which landed on the pavement just to the side of Dayna's feet. "Oh... sorry about that. Didn't mean to spit on you." He laughed wickedly. "Accidental dribble," he added scornfully, before pulling his head back in and slamming the window shut.

Scowling up at the flat above, Dayna muttered some expletives and then glanced down at the oozy patch on the pavement. Turning round, fists clenched tightly, she drew in a deep breath and walked back into the shop.

Both Aaron and Jenny were guiding the woman down to the end of the shop. Catching up to them, Dayna whipped in front of them and opened the staffroom door. Reaching for a stool, she offered it to the woman. "Here, sit down," she said as the woman shakily entered the staffroom.

"I can't sit down – I've smashed my coccyx, love," said the woman.

"Tracey – right?" said Jenny, nervously. "Your name's Tracey? I am so terribly sorry."

The woman glared, disdainfully at her attacker. "Where's your phone – I need a phone."

"A phone? Why do you need a phone?" asked Jenny, looking to Dayna and then Aaron.

"I'll get it," said Dayna as the door opened. Peering up the shop, she saw that two people had walked in. "I mean, I'll serve the customers." Dayna looked despairingly at her friend. "You need to get her a phone, Jenny…" Then Dayna shot off to the front of the shop.

"Where's the phone?" asked Tracey, angrily. "I want to make a phone call - now. I need an ambulance. My coccyx. You've smashed my coccyx." Her voice grew louder and louder.

Jenny nodded, nervously and scurried through to the office, leaving poor Aaron with the disgruntled, vociferous woman.

Snatching the phone from Jenny's hand, Tracey proceeded to dial a number. She held the phone to her ear and waited.

With a pleading gaze, Jenny mouthed, 'I'm so sorry', to Aaron and felt the all too familiar sting in her eyes.

"Tom!"

Tracey listened intently, as a determined scowl creased her face. "Tom – get up to that shop, by the nursery – I've been attacked."

A lump caught in Jenny's throat and she gulped, hard. Staring deep in to Aaron's eyes for support and reassurance, Jenny swallowed again. "Excuse me... you haven't been attacked."

"Yes – just get here quick, Tom." Tracey pressed the 'end call' button and practically threw the phone back at Jenny, who just managed to catch it. "What did you call that..." said Tracey, pointing towards the shop's entrance, "...if it wasn't an unprovoked, out and out attack."

"I... I didn't..."

"Look, I think this has been a terrible accident. I know that Jenny wouldn't have meant you any harm. She saw someone, whom she needed to speak to and very carelessly ran out of the shop." Aaron's calming voice of authority was enough to turn Tracey's hard stare to a softer, more approachable gaze. "Is Tom your husband?" Aaron enquired, respectfully.

Tracey nodded.

With one hand clutched around her waist and the other one, over her mouth, Jenny said nothing. The urge to burst into tears was overwhelming. She had to keep it together somehow. Watching the interaction between Aaron and Tracey, she sensed an 'out of body' experience. Like watching a film on the television, Jenny listened to the dialogue and viewed the scene before her, as if she could turn if off at any given moment and return to the normality of her life. This really couldn't be happening...

The sound of the shop's door opening, several times, didn't perturb Jenny's day-dreaming. The sight of Aaron comforting Tracey, while they waited for Tom to arrive was soothing, in fact. The reality of the situation had floated away as Jenny sunk further into disbelief. The scene unfolding in front of her was dramatically good to watch... as long as she didn't have to be involved in it...

"Jen!" the sound of her name being called loudly, brought Jenny to her senses. Turning round, she peered up the shop. Dayna stood at the other end of the aisle, beckoning to her frantically. "Jen, come up here, quick."

The urgency in Dayna's voice was instantly recognizable. Something was wrong. "I'll be back in a minute, Aaron. Will you be ok?"

"Will *he* be ok? Are you serious? I've broken my coccyx and you're asking *him* if he's ok..."

Aaron nodded and shot a faint smile at Jenny. "Can I get you a glass of water, Tracey?" he asked, politely.

Jenny arrived at the front of the shop as they walked in, through the door.

Two policemen stood side by side and scoured the shop with discerning eyes. The expressionless look on their faces suggested that they were not looking for a pint of milk.

"Can I help you?" asked Jenny, nervously, while shooting a cursory glance across to Dayna.

"Looking for the owner of this shop, Miss," replied the stockier policeman.

"I am the owner." Jenny held her breath...

"We've had a report that there has been an incident here, Miss."

"Yes... well... more like an accident, rather than an incident, officer," Dayna called out, from behind the counter. "I think you've been slightly misled, Sir."

"We'll be the judge of that," said the other policeman.

"It's that man upstairs, Jen – he spat at me, from his window. It's him that's done this, I tell you."

Jenny glared at her friend with a historically recognisable, *'shut your freaking mouth, Dayna, just for one minute'*, stare.

The door opened again and the two policemen turned around spontaneously.

With a worried expression across his pointy face, tiny Tom walked in. "Where's my wife?" he squeaked, loudly.

"I'm down here," came the shrill voice of Tracey. "Tom – I'm here!"

Passing the policemen, Tom looked across at Jenny and smiled sheepishly, before disappearing down the first aisle.

"Is there somewhere we could go for a talk?" asked the first policeman.

"Err... yes... my office," replied Jenny. "Would you follow me?" She walked off down the second aisle, followed by the two police officers.

"Take me to the hospital, Tom" hollered Tracey, as Jenny and the policemen went into the office.

"Who is that?" asked the second policeman.

"That's the lady who I accidentally knocked on the floor," replied Jenny.

"I'll go and talk to her," said the first officer.

"I need to go to the hospital, Tom. I'm not kidding you – I've cracked my coccyx. I've been attacked."

Tracey's voice was growing louder and Jenny cringed at every word she uttered.

"Are you sure, sugarplum? We'll get you checked out first. You may just have a bruised bottom," said Tom.

"Don't call me sugarplum. Get me to the hospital, Tom. I'm telling you – my coccyx is cracked! I know a cracked coccyx when I've got one. That woman is a maniac – she should be locked up. First my car... and... and... now me. Get those policemen to lock her away, Tom."

Pulling a notebook and pen from his pocket, the second policeman leaned on the door frame. "Ok, I need to know what has happened here. Can you start from the beginning?"

"Well..." said Jenny, "it's my fault – yes, I admit that, one hundred percent – but it's all been a terrible accident."

"Carry on," said the officer, as he began jotting notes down. A half smile was slowly spreading across his face as he tried to listen to Jenny, while Tracey gave an overwrought, long-winded account of her physical assault, in the room next door.

"Tom – listen to me. I don't care what anyone says or thinks – I've got a broken coccyx – it's not just any old sore or bruised bottom. We should sue her, Tom. Constable – arrest her – she cracked my coccyx. She attacked me for no reason." There was a momentary pause before she continued. "And... and she maliciously damaged my car last night, as well. She needs locking up."

Escorting Tracey out of the shop, Tom and Aaron helped her to hobble to Tom's car. Complaining all the way and causing such a raucous commotion, Tracey's exit from Millen Road was highly dramatised.

The two policemen left, satisfied that they had enough information to draw a conclusion that the incident was indeed, an accident. A report would be made and both Jenny and Mrs Tracey Gubbins would receive a copy. However, if Mrs Gubbins wished to pursue matters further, the report would help with any claim for compensation she wished to make for the injuries she may have received.

Slumped behind the counter, Jenny sat on a stool, staring mindlessly out of the window.

Upon Aaron's return from the depositing of Mrs Gubbins and her sore bottom, Dayna brought three mugs of coffee to the counter.

"Blimey, there's never a dull moment in here, Jenny," said Aaron, rubbing his forehead. Glancing up at the clock, he added, "what time do you close tonight?"

"Why? Jenny asked, flatly.

"Well, I was thinking about getting this job done but it depends how long I've got."

Peering up at the clock, Jenny noted the time. Over an hour had passed and Aaron hadn't been able to start anything yet. "Look, if it's too much today… after what I've just put you through… well, I'm happy to leave it for another day. I'm really sorry Aaron."

"Jenny, I have no issue with staying here longer. If it takes me half the night, I'm happy to do that."

Resisting the urge to burst into tears, Jenny picked up her mug of coffee and slurped it. "I just don't know what to say, Aaron. I'll leave it for you to decide. I'm here until ten tonight."

"Then I'll make a start." Aaron took a sip of his coffee and placed his mug on the windowsill, behind the till. "I'll get the gear in… if it's safe to do so now. Joking!"

"Ok," replied Jenny, without raising as much as a smirk. "And I do apologise for everything, Aaron – really, I do."

"It's not a problem. Can I just ask though… is it like this every day, in your shop?"

Dayna jumped in quick, "No, it only seems to happen when you're here, it must be all your fault that these bad things keep happening." Dayna let out a tiny titter. "Only kidding," she added.

"Very funny," said Aaron and walked out of the shop, grinning.

Jenny forced a smile and picked the envelope up, which had been laying on the counter since Tom and Tracey had left.

"Have you looked at it yet?"

Shaking her head, Jenny replied, nonchalantly, "Nope."

"They got their car looked at pretty quick, if you ask me. Have a look how much it is."

"I daren't after the luck I've been having lately."

"It's not going to be that much, just to repair a wing mirror."

Hooking a finger into one end of the sealed envelope, Jenny ripped it open. She pulled the headed piece of paper out and unfolded it. She stared at the garage's report. She blinked. She looked over the piece of paper again. She blinked again. Thrusting the report towards Dayna, Jenny stood up and adjusted her top. "I'm going to the toilet. I'll be back in a minute."

The tall, step-ladders were in, propped up against the magazine rack. Rolls of cable and other peculiar looking objects, were piled neatly, at the end of the counter. Aaron's toolbox sat on the floor, behind the counter and Aaron was leant on the till, finishing his coffee and talking to Dayna.

Jenny had been gone for ten minutes. She had not wanted her friend or Aaron to see her cry.

"You ok?" asked Dayna softly, as Jenny approached the counter and gave a wavering smile.

"Yes, just needed some time-out…"

"I've told Aaron everything – hope you didn't mind, Jen. He now understands why you flew out of the door to try and catch Marj."

"Ah good. I was going to explain everything to you sooner or later, Aaron."

"I'm sure you would have, in time." Aaron continued, "I hear that you have had an encounter with that obnoxious woman, Tracey, before?"

"Yes, last night."

Aaron nodded his head, sympathetically. "Yes, Dayna just told me. I think she's trying to con you with that bill, Jenny."

"Do you think so?"

"Yes, it's a ridiculous price. Did you see any scratches on the driver's door last night?"

"I didn't really look, to be honest. It was dark."

"Well, I would say that you should get a second opinion. £235 is a lot of money to pay when all you did was knock her wing mirror off. Even if there is a small scratch and she needs a new mirror, you can get it done a lot cheaper than that." Aaron stood upright and folded his arms. "Don't let them take the mick, Jenny. If there's anything that I can do to help, let me know."

"I will, thanks Aaron." Jenny sensed the warmth, genuine concern and desire to help, radiating from Aaron's heart. Deep down, she knew that the feelings of attraction were mutual. If only she had time in her life to give it a go...

Chapter 21

With dexterity and an aptitude to work conscientiously around the customers using the shop, Aaron plowed through the task of running cables from one length of the building to the other. Pulling the cables through the ceiling void, he politely waited for people to do their shopping before he moved his step-ladder along to the next part of the ceiling. After a couple of hours of taking ceiling tiles down, putting them back, running cables neatly around the walls where the joists prevented access above, Aaron came down from the ladder and stood with his hands on his hips, staring down the length of the shop. "Right, that's the first bit done. Need to fit the sockets next." Looking at the clock on the wall, he added, "Just a loose fitting on that light, Jenny. I've pushed it back in for you. Now then, anyone hungry?"

Dayna's eyes lit up. "Starving – what do you fancy? We could cook up something, in the microwave."

"I was thinking more along the lines of a take-away. What do you think, Jenny?"

"Yes, that sounds good... and thanks for doing the light. I'm sure it's because of that man upstairs jumping around every day." Jenny's mood had lifted during the afternoon and the three of them had enjoyed a bit of banter and a few giggles. She'd been impressed by Aaron's friendly, fun nature with the customers. And almost every one of the shoppers had stopped to ask him what he was doing and then have a chat with him. He'd been up and down his ladder far more times than he had needed to but out of politeness, he'd come down from the ceiling space to talk to them. Jenny was sure that he could have done the job in half the time, if it hadn't been for the countless, trivial conversations. Not that she was timing him – he could stay and chat to people all day long as far as she was concerned.

"Chinese? Indian? Plain old fish and chips?"

"I'm not fussed," replied Jenny.

"Well if someone's got to choose – I go with Chinese," called Dayna, from behind the counter.

"Ok," said Aaron, dusting his hands off. "I'll go and get it and it's on me too."

Dayna looked over to Jenny and raised her eyebrows, then she called out, "Cool, thanks Aaron."

"Yes, thank you," repeated Jenny. "You really don't have to pay for it though."

"Yes I do... got to keep the client happy." Chuckling to himself, Aaron went through to the staffroom to wash his hands.

"I'm hardly a client if you're doing all of this work for nothing, Aaron. I just hope that it is going to pay off within a year," said Jenny, following him into the staffroom and leaning on the doorframe while she watched him wash his hands.

"It will pay off, trust me – I'm an expert in these things." Aaron turned and smiled sweetly.

"And why are you an expert?" Jenny asked, lightheartedly.

"Just am... I can tell." Winking a thick lashed eye, he shook the water from his hands and grabbed a towel. "Look, seriously, don't worry about it, Jenny. You've got enough to think about at the moment. Like I've said before, if you weren't making use of this system, it would be sat in my garage or my mum's store room, rusting away. Whatever happens in a year's time – we'll deal with it then."

Jenny refrained from melting into a haze of passionate longing down the edge of the door frame, and simply nodded. "Ok... and I am really grateful, Aaron."

"I know. Right, I'm off. I'll be back with your dinner soon, madam."

Moving out of the way to let Aaron through, Jenny watched him as he walked up the aisle and out of the door. Then all of her troubles trickled back into her head, one by one.

Between the pair of them, Jenny and Dayna had managed to eat a delicious assortment of Chinese cuisine while taking it in turns to hurry up the aisle and serve any customers. Aaron had sat on a stool in the staffroom and consumed as much food as the other two put together. *Where did he put it all*, Jenny had wondered? His sleek frame did a perfect job of disguising his man-sized appetite.

By seven o'clock Aaron had finished fitting the two sockets. "Ok, I'm off now, Jenny."

"What time are you back tomorrow?"

"Err… as soon as I can. In the morning sometime. Is that ok?"

"Yes, fine. My dad and brother will be here tomorrow. I hope they won't get in your way. They're fitting that," said Jenny, pointing to the big box behind her.

"Ah yes – your awning. It'll look cool when it's finished, eh?"

Jenny nodded her head and smiled. "Yes, I feel like the shop is really coming along nicely – just need to sort out a few of the existing customers and local residents, get some more people using the shop and then employ another assistant."

"It'll come soon enough. You haven't exactly got a lot of competition around here. It's just a case of letting people know you're here."

"Yes, I know. I'm on it," said Jenny, remembering her mission to print off some flyers – which she hadn't got around to yet.

"Good. Ok, I'll see you in the morning. Keep your chin up and sort that bill out." Aaron winked and then left.

"So, when are you going upstairs to have a word with that man?" asked Dayna.

"I'll leave it until Monday lunchtime, when you and Tasha are both here." Jenny thought for a moment. "No... actually, it'll have to be Tuesday."

"Why?"

"I think Aaron said that we were going out for lunch on Monday."

"Are you dating him?" asked Dayna, wide-eyed.

"No, Day. Not at all. He mentioned it last week. He may not even remember or he might even change his mind before Monday... it's purely business anyway."

"Hmm... he fancies the pants off you. It's so obvious. It'll lead to more if you let it."

"No, I don't have time anymore, Day. I can't even manage to find time for myself – let alone anyone else. It's not going to happen, unfortunately... and I could hardly say to him, 'Ooh, I really like you but could you wait a year or two and then maybe we could date'."

Dayna laughed. "You could try – if he wants you badly enough, he'll wait."

"Yeah right," replied Jenny, despondently. "Gosh, look at the time, it's gone so quick today. You'd better get going."

"It's gone quick because you've had Aaron to chat to. He's taken your mind off things. I hope you won't start moping around when I've gone, Jen."

"No. Why would I do that?"

"Don't go reading that note again – I know what you're like."

"No, I won't. I promise."

Dayna had just missed the nightly 'thumps', dancing across the ceiling, and they appeared louder tonight, almost like they were 'revenge thumps'. An absence of people in the shop meant that the noises were purely for Jenny's ears. The vexatious sound was beginning to soak into her head, swim around her brain and swill out her usual buoyant, bubbly approach to life.

The last two hours of the day were the longest. Jenny opened the note and browsed through the contents. She wasn't really reading it – more like a cursory glance or just taking a quick gander. Ok, she was reading it again, despite her promise. She picked up the other sheet of paper, from the repair garage, and scanned the itemized bill. Then she moped around for the last hour, wearing a false smile for every person who walked in the shop, just as Dayna said she would.

After another restless night, the morning thumps grated and ground-down Jenny's nerves. Today, there would be lots of things going on, what with Aaron returning to install the till and set up the computer and Jenny's dad and brother fitting the awning. Her dad would know what to do about everything. He would be able to give her the best advice. He would know how to deal with all of the mess. Her dad would tell her to stay positive and that these were just the small hiccups in life that everyone had to deal with, from time to time and she would have to smile her way through them. He had become very philosophical since Jenny's mum had died.

Jenny's dad and Jacob arrived a few minutes after Tasha had walked through the door. "Morning Dad," called Jenny. "Alright bruv?"

The two men looked at each other with puzzled expressions.

Jacob said nothing which was the norm for an early Sunday morning, or any morning.

"Morning love – you sound cheerful," replied Dad.

Jenny tutted and rolled her eyes upward. "You wouldn't believe the week I've had. It's a case of keep smiling or lay down and die."

"Oh dear, get the kettle on and you can tell me all about it."

"I'll do it," said Tasha, removing her coat and hanging it on a peg in the staffroom.

"So, what sort of week have you had, Jen?" asked Dad, leaning on the counter top.

In between customers, Jenny began to tell them about her eventful week...

Handing the note over, Jenny watched the faces of her dad and brother as they read it together. Then she gave Jacob the repair bill. The two of them scrutinized the pieces of paper in their hands, peered at each other with deadpan faces and then looked at Jenny.

"Bloody hell – you've got some strange people living around here," said Jacob, staring down at the bill in his hand. "And don't think you're paying this for one minute." Jacob tossed the sheet of paper onto the counter and thumped his fist on top of it. "I'll contact these people and tell 'em I'm acting on your behalf. You're not paying this, Jen."

Surprised by her brother's animated reaction, Jenny nodded in agreement. "I could handle it myself, Jay, but I just don't have a lot of spare time to go chasing up people at repair garages."

"No, it'll be dealt with. I've used them before. I know one of the blokes there. I'll sort this out – bloody taking the piss if you ask me," said Jacob and then turned swiftly to make sure that no one was in the shop and had heard his ill-chosen words.

Young Tasha stood at the end of the counter, dumbstruck. Listening to every word, her bewildered expression suggested that she couldn't believe that so much had happened, while she'd been having one day off work.

"Right," Jenny's dad interrupted, "let's get this awning fitted. I think that ten past nine is a reasonable time to start – what do you think, Jen?"

"Yes, go for it Dad. He can complain all he likes, upstairs."

"Worst thing is… you're fitting the awning directly below his flat," said Tasha, a worried expression creeping on to her face.

"That's a point," replied Jenny. "How much noise are you going to be making?"

"We've got to get it out of the box yet," said Dad. "And read the instructions – I may not even have everything that we'll need, love."

Tasha's wide-eyed stare began to soften. "Isn't it supposed to be 'no noise before ten o'clock on Sundays'?"

"Well there probably won't be any before ten – especially if you're going to be making another one of those nice cups of tea," said Dad, handing his empty mug to her and winking.

"And he doesn't have a leg to stand on anyway. He makes enough noise of his own, whatever day of the week it is," Jenny added.

"Is it safe to come in?" asked Aaron, poking his beaming face around the door.

Jenny looked up and chuckled as a warm, swirly feeling, filled her whole being. "Think so," she replied. "Quick – get in while you can."

Aaron peered left, then right with narrowed eyes. Crouching over, he stepped tentatively into the shop, swiveling his head from left to right repeatedly, as if he were in the throes of a commando attack.

Chuckling like a little girl, Jenny watched as he made his way towards the counter. She couldn't remember the last time she had felt like this. "You do make me laugh," she spurted.

"Now…" Without warning, Aaron's voice changed to a serious tone, "if I'm not mistaken, there's a rather odd looking, long metal object lying on the pavement outside…"

Jenny smiled. Tasha stared, in amazement.

"I have reason to believe that you may be constructing a two-person, oscillating vehicle for the sole purpose of enticing valued customers to your premises, Madam."

Shaking her head, Jenny frowned. "What?"

"Either – you are erecting an awning of some description, Madam, or as I suspect, you are building a see-saw."

Jenny stared blankly for a moment.

"Is that a see-saw you're building? It's all becoming clearer, Madam. Your intention is entrapment, is it not?"

Jenny burst in to a raucous laugh. "To catch Margery Daw..." she shrieked.

Aaron and Jenny had a fit of the giggles. When a customer entered the shop, the raucous pair had to head off towards the staffroom, leaving a bemused Tasha standing behind the counter.

"What are you two laughing at?" asked Dad, from the back of the office.

Jacob was crouched on the floor behind his dad, examining the contents of the large box.

"Oh, it's just Margery Daw... and her seesaw," replied Jenny, peering round the door with watery eyes. "You've met Aaron before, haven't you?"

Jacob looked up. With a mischievous glint in his eye, he grinned. "Yeah – hello mate."

Peering over Jenny's shoulder, Aaron smiled. "Hello. Please, give me a shout if you need any help with the fixings out the front. Looks a pretty cumbersome piece of kit."

Jenny raised her eyebrows and smiled as a cold shiver ran down her back.

"Thank you, we may just take you up on that offer." Dad looked at Jenny. "I don't think Calvin will make it today. He's got a hangover – silly bugger." Turning back to Aaron, Dad continued. "Has our Jen had you working hard, this weekend?" he asked, brushing a dusty cobweb from his sleeve.

"Slave driver," replied Aaron and laughed.

Jenny cringed at the mention of Calvin. Why did her dad insist on including that total loser in everything?

"Right," said Jenny, clapping her hands together. "I'm making Aaron a drink – anyone else want one?"

"Have you got two brothers?" asked Aaron, as he watched Dad and Jacob carry parts of the awning to the front of the shop.

"No... no.... only the one."

"Ah, ok. Who's the one with the hangover?"

"Oh, that's just Calvin... he... err... he works with my dad sometimes... you know, helps him out."

Aaron nodded his head. "Were you all right about me offering to help them if they need me to?"

"Yes – sure. It's really kind of you, Aaron. Thanks."

Aaron grinned. "I've brought the two tills with me today. If you're going to have the two, it'll be easier to fit both of them at the same time. Then I can set the program to recognise both tills." Aaron paused, in thought. "What about doing your newspaper delivery accounts on the second till? I could set it up and run through the program to show you how to do it."

"Now that's a good idea," said Jenny. "At the moment we've got a cash box under the till to put payments in. Then I write out a duplicated receipt. Would I be able to give them a receipt from the till?"

"Absolutely," said Aaron. "Leave it with me. It'll probably take me most of today to fit the tills and set the program up but I can come back pretty much any time at the moment, to go through things with you."

"Thanks Aaron – you're a star."

Aaron laughed. "Are we still on for lunch tomorrow?"

"Ooh... yes. I forgot about that," Jenny lied. "Between 12 and 2 is good for me."

"Yep – I'll be here at 12." Aaron gazed into Jenny's eyes, thoughtfully. "Right... I'll get the gear in and then make a start when I've drunk that tea you're making me."

"Oh, sorry, I forgot."

"Thought you had – the kettle boiled five minutes ago." Aaron smiled and left.

Pathetically swoony, Jenny watched the contours of Aaron's behind undulating, as he walked up the shop. She flicked the kettle back on and began making tea for everyone. She sensed that it was going to be a good day and even more so because it was early close on Sundays. Finishing at six o'clock in the evening was becoming the highlight of the week.

Chapter 22

The awning was up by four o'clock. It looked beautiful. Turquoise blue and green stripes complimented the *J's Convenience Store* sign, perfectly. The remote control awning extended and retracted, silently and effortlessly. Dad had reported, late morning, that the man in the flat above had stuck his head out of the window and growled something incomprehensible, when he and Jacob were drilling the walls. Dad had shouted an apology and assured the man that he would be no more than ten minutes making the noise. The man growled something about making a complaint to the council and then slammed his window shut.

It had been difficult to serve customers effectively, during the afternoon. However, Tasha's patient and friendly nature had ensured that there were no disgruntled customers as Aaron switched the tills around. Leaving the old till working and situated peculiarly, in the centre of the counter, Aaron placed the other two into position, ready for the switchover later. One customer after another, quizzed, questioned or commented on the number of tills on the counter. Why were there three of them? Time and time again, Tasha explained that they were not expecting a deluge of custom to the shop and that it was purely a temporary set up, while the new tills were being installed.

Jenny had helped Aaron with the installation. Creating passwords, restarting the computer and beginning the arduous task of inputting data and scanning the barcode of every single item she sold in the shop. It was going to take a week to complete the task, as Aaron had previously warned her, but it would all be worth it in the end. Starting with the products that were sold the most often, Jenny had completed over a hundred items by the time the awning was finished.

The shop had been busier than normal. Jenny suspected that the activity outside had drawn curious passers-by to come inside and have a look around. Both Jenny and Tasha had noted that there were a lot of new faces on the scene.

"It's amazing! Thank you – both of you." Jenny peered up at the awning and pressed the retract button on the remote control again. "I hope it's really sunny tomorrow. Then we can have it out all day."

Dad smiled, "Yep – it's very nice, Jen."

Jacob nodded his head and looked at his watch. "Come on then, dinner will be ready soon."

"Load the tools up then boy," said Dad, in jest. "I'm getting a roast dinner tonight – not bad eh?"

"Can't remember the last time I had a roast dinner," said Jenny, dolefully.

"Well, why don't you come to me one Sunday evening? We can cook something up together."

"I will Dad- thanks." Jenny flung her arms around him and kissed his cheek. When Jacob returned from the van, she did the same to him.

"Ok, ok. That's enough," said Jacob, wiping his cheek in disgust.

Jenny laughed. "See you both soon –yeah?"

Dad and Jacob nodded and smiled, simultaneously, like they were twins.

"I'll call you as soon as I've been to the garage – let you know what they say," said Jacob, as he walked away.

"Yes and thanks big bruv."

"Do I get that when *I've* finished?" asked Aaron, in a hushed voice, as Jenny returned inside.

"What?"

"That treatment – do I get it when I've finished this job?" Aaron was behind the counter, programming the second till and Jenny could just see the top of Tasha's head, down by the milk fridge.

"What? Do you mean the goodbye I just gave my dad?" Jenny whispered.

Aaron nodded. "Yeah."

Jenny's face flushed. "You mean the kiss goodbye?"

"Well, I was thinking more along the lines of both. The hug as well." Aaron smirked. "I don't want to be short changed with just a kiss on the cheek."

The heat in Jenny's face began to burn. She smiled, bashfully. "Of course – everyone gets a thank-you like that from me."

"I'll hold you to that," said Aaron and laughed.

With her heart jumping up and down in her chest, Jenny replied casually, "Ok," before scooting off down the aisle to join Tasha at the fridge.

Feeling nervous and excitable about Tasha's departure at five o'clock, Jenny said goodbye and watched her walk out of the shop. Aaron was down in the office completing the installation of the EPOS system. The new tills looked like brand new ones but as Aaron had already told her, he had spent a lot of time cleaning them. When the shop closed at six, the old till would be removed and the new ones would come alive. Aaron had explained that it would be easier to do the initial 'hook-up' once the shop was closed. That way, any problems that may arise, could be dealt with without the worry of inconveniencing customers.

The fact that Aaron was still in the shop and would be until close gave Jenny butterflies in her stomach and a racy heart. The atmosphere between them had changed dramatically since Aaron's suggestion, earlier. The inside of Jenny's mouth salivated, wildly, and she found it difficult to talk to customers without first gulping. She wanted him. She knew, for sure, he wanted her.

Turning the 'open' sign round, Jenny locked the front door and switched off the front set of interior lights. The half lit shop didn't feel quite so eerie tonight, in contrast it seemed to glow romantically, causing Jenny to shudder. The time had come to cash up the old till and start up the new ones. Excitedly, Jenny watched in anticipation as Aaron turned the key on the first till. After a few bleeps, it sprang to life. A blue display screen shone brightly, lighting up Aaron's handsome face. He then turned to the other till and repeated the process.

"Right, they're on. Come round here and I'll show you how to turn them on," said Aaron, a satisfied grin beaming across his face.

Moving round the counter, Jenny's heart skipped. She stepped closer to Aaron and could feel the heat emanating from his body. "Go on then," she said, softly.

Aaron looked down at her, by his side, and then quickly snatched his gaze away. "Right... so... you put the key in and turn it three times, to here," said Aaron, marking the position with his finger.

"Ok," replied Jenny. The thumping in her chest and an excessively wet mouth, caused her to swallow hard.

"Then this screen will appear," Aaron continued, pointing to the wording on the small screen.

"Right..."

"You'll then have a menu of options to choose from."

Jenny leant over the till to look closer.

"To use the till in normal mode, tab down to here," said Aaron, tapping the cursor down the list of options.

"Ok – that seems quite straight forward."

"Well that's pretty much it for the till. That will get you up and running tomorrow morning." Aaron glanced down at Jenny and smiled. "I need to show you a few things on the computer, which you will need to know, and then I can come back a couple of times to train you up on the more detailed things. Is that ok?"

"Sounds great. I can't thank you enough for this, Aaron."

"Yes you can... I mean..." Aaron paused, thoughtfully. "Why don't you... come out for a meal with me tonight? When you've finished up here."

"I thought we were doing that tomorrow."

"We could do both."

Jenny looked down at her jeans and dusty dolly shoes. "I can't go out for an evening meal dressed like this."

"So go home, get changed, slip me your address and I'll pick you up around eight. What do you say?" Aaron beamed.

Jenny gulped. "Err... right... ok. Yes, why not." Jenny knew that the other option was a frozen meal-for-one. "Can't be a late one though – I have to get up at five."

"I promise it won't be late. Write your address down for me... and while we're at it... do you want to give me your mobile number?"

"You've got it already – remember – you texted me?"

"Ah, yes, ok – just your address then."

Jenny nodded. "Yes, sure." Fumbling around under the counter for a scrap of paper, she took a pen and then shakily, scribbled down her address. "Here," she said, shyly. "Do you know the area?"

"I soon will." Aaron winked and then led the way to the office. "Come on, let's get the computer lesson out of the way."

"Coming Sir," said Jenny and giggled, nervously.

The computer lesson ran smoothly. Jenny had enough knowledge of EPOS systems to get through the basics. However, there was an awful lot that she didn't know, but with Aaron's help, over time, she would grasp the workings of her new operating system.

By 6.45pm, Aaron had finished the computer run-through, removed the old till from the counter and gathered his tools together. "Right, I'm all done. Can I do anything to help you get out of here quicker?"

"Oh, thanks – you could put the newspaper bundles out the back for me. There's a cupboard by the back door."

"No problem – I'm on it."

Aaron trotted off with a spring in his step. Excitement filled the air with anticipation. Was tonight's meal going to be a date? Or was it purely business again? No, there was too much sexual energy buzzing around. Jenny could feel it. She could sense it. She knew it.

"Thank you for everything you've done this weekend, Aaron," said Jenny, as she slipped her coat on and picked up her bag. Stretching up closer to him, she pecked his cheek quickly.

Turning to her in surprise, Aaron smiled and chuckled under his breath. "That's only half of it."

Jenny looked down, coyly. "Oh yes – a hug, you mean."

Opening his arms wide, Aaron invited her in.

Jenny moved closer and put her arms around his waist. Melting into the charged aura surrounding him, Jenny hugged his waist. Two long arms wrapped themselves around her shoulders and pulled her in closer. Looking up, Jenny met Aaron's gaze. They stared. Aaron's head lowered to hers. Their lips met briefly. Jenny swallowed hard. Their lips met again. Opening her mouth, she let him in. There was no use trying to stop it.

A minute later they drew apart. Speechless, breathing heavily and flushed with a sensual energy, the pair gazed into each other's eyes.

Jenny rubbed her hand across her mouth. "Err... gosh. Shall we go?"

"Sorry... I... err... wasn't expecting that to happen. Are you ok?"

Jenny nodded.

"Ok, think we had better go." Aaron put his hand up to his mouth. "I'll pick you up at eight." Bending down, he briefly kissed her on the cheek. Then he left.

Absent-mindedly, Jenny went through the shop, turning switches off. She set the alarm and walked out of the door. *J's convenience Store* had been revamped today and Jenny's faith in '*All good things come to those who wait*', had been renewed.

At 7.55pm, Jenny waited nervously. Pacing up and down the hallway, she willed the buzzer to sound. A queasy sensation filled her throat. Dressed in a knee length black skirt, a tight fitting, red polo-neck jumper and black high heels, Jenny's attire was conservative, yet attractive. She had relived the kiss, constantly, on her way home, while she was showering, while she was dressing, while she was waiting. She couldn't get it out of her head. It had been amazing. It had been magical. It had been the clichéd best kiss she'd ever had.

The buzzer rang at 8.03pm. Jenny flew down the stairs, as quick as her heels would allow –which wasn't fast at all. Breathless, she reached the main door and opened it. "Hi – I'm just about done."

"Come on then. I know just the place to go... and you look stunning, I have to say."

Pulling into the Shipmakers carpark, Aaron parked up and they both climbed out of the car. "Have you been here before?" asked Aaron.

"No, I haven't – looks nice."

"Good food." Aaron offered his arm, as support, and led her in.

"So," said Jenny, as they sat at the table, waiting for their meal to arrive, "tell me a bit more about you."

"What do you want to know?"

"Err... let's start with inside leg measurement and move through to age, height etc. You know, the usual kind of stuff." Jenny giggled.

"Not sure about the inside leg, maybe you could measure that for me sometime," said Aaron, jokingly. "I'm joking. I'm 29, over 6ft tall and very hungry."

"Me too... well, hungry I mean." Jenny giggled again. "I'm nowhere near 6ft, I don't have a clue about my inside leg measurement either, I'm guessing it's not as long as yours, I'm 28 and I own a shop and have some rather unusual customers and neighbours."

"I can vouch for that." Aaron laughed. "Ok, sorted. That's the getting to know each other bit, out of the way." Aaron laughed again. "So when am I moving in?"

Jenny knew that the comedic nature of their light conversation masked a desire in both of them. How could she ever have time for this though? Apart from Sundays, there was no other time that she'd be free to enjoy a relationship with him... unless she gave up sleeping at night.

"So where do you live?" asked Jenny, eating her meal gracefully, although she wanted to shovel it down as quickly as possible, she was so hungry.

"I live at home with my parents still." Aaron held a piece of steak on his fork. "Yep – I know, it sounds weird at my age. I'm waiting for the right house to come along."

"The right house? What are you looking for?"

"Maybe a four bed, in a small village somewhere. I would like a fair bit of ground around it too."

"Blimey – you're talking big money then."

"Possibly. I've looked at a couple of places already."

"Oh and dare I ask how much they were?" Jenny was intrigued.

"Around the four mark."

"Four? Do you mean four hundred thousand?"

"Yeah – can't really go any more than four fifty though. And five would be really pushing it." Aaron smiled.

Jenny managed to hold her jaw closed but her eyes were as wide as saucers. "That would be some mortgage," she laughed.

"Well, I'd put down a substantial deposit. Maybe a hundred grand."

Just as the involuntary action of her jaw fell open, Jenny snapped it back and proceeded to shove a fork full of chips into her mouth. "Mmm... a lot of money... mmm... this meal..." mumbled Jenny, covering her mouth with a hand, "...is so good."

Aaron smiled, warmly. "I come here quite often."

"Oh, do you," she replied, trying to swallow the last lump of chip, which seemed to be getting stuck in her throat. "It's a lovely... place... very posh." Managing to refrain from choking on the chip, Jenny continued. "So... what about girlfriends? Please, tell me if I'm being too nosey, Aaron."

"No, it's cool. I've had a few, in my time. Nothing serious though." Aaron shuffled in his seat. "My mum always says that my problem is that I only have a relationship with business. She thinks that I don't have time for any other relationships."

"And is she right?"

"Yeah, I think so. Up until now..."

"What's changed now?" This time Jenny shuffled in her seat, trying to brace herself for anymore shocks.

"Getting older. Time to move into my own place. The businesses are going well so I don't need to spend so much time on them." Aaron placed his knife and fork neatly on his plate and stretched back in the chair.

"Businesses? How many have you got?"

"Three."

Jenny stared, wide-eyed, and tried to swallow the last few peas in her mouth. She placed the cutlery neatly on her plate and gulped awkwardly as the little peas slid down her throat. "So... err... what else do you do?" Aaron was becoming more intriguing by the second.

"I've got a team of lorry drivers, who transport antique furniture around the UK and we've recently gone into Europe."

"Wow – I would never have guessed that there was so much to you, Aaron."

Aaron laughed the comment off. "I also own several gaming sites and servers around the world."

Jenny didn't really get that bit but it didn't matter. There was so much more to Aaron, than what met the eye. "Gosh, I'm speechless. You're a real entrepreneur then?"

Aaron laughed. "Yes, suppose you could call me that."

Suddenly, Jenny understood why Aaron had been so generous in giving her the EPOS system to try out for a year. He possibly had so much money that he didn't know what to do with it.

"So, apart from buying yourself a mansion..." Jenny giggled, "...what other plans do you have for the future?"

Aaron smiled. "Settle down, buy the house and live happily ever after."

"Four bedrooms? Take it you want a house full of kids too."

"Absolutely – the more the merrier."

"Wow – big ambitions," replied Jenny.

"Yep... a bit like you really."

"Sorry?"

"You're ambitious too. Look at the big shop you have."

"Yes, I know," said Jenny, feeling miserable, all of a sudden. "It's a real struggle at the moment though... in all sorts of ways."

"It will be at first. Things will change."

"Thanks for the vote of confidence. I hope you're right."

Winking an eye, Aaron picked up the menu and looked at it. "I'm usually right. Fancy a dessert?"

"Yes – let's do it."

On the way back to Jenny's flat, she mulled over the idea of inviting Aaron in for the proverbial 'coffee'. It's was almost ten o'clock –she had to be up at five. To hell with it, she was going to invite him in and put the word 'quick' before the 'coffee'. And the flat was pretty tidy as she was hardly ever there, so her decision was final.

"Do you want to come up for a quick coffee?" asked Jenny, shyly. "It'll have to be a quick one as I'm up at five."

Aaron turned the car's engine off. "A quick one – why not." He looked at Jenny and smirked.

"Not that sort of quick one." Jenny laughed and flicked her hand at his arm. "Come on then."

The coffee was the longest drink that Jenny had ever had. An hour had passed and she had noted the time. Then another half an hour passed and Jenny noted the time again.

After almost two hours of talking about everything from Aaron's mum, Alex Frey, the 'Independent's Giant' to Calvin, who was in fact, Jenny's x-boyfriend, Jenny breathed a sigh and looked at her watch again. "Have you seen the time? I've got to get up in five hours."

"I was just thinking the same thing." Aaron stood up. "I'm going now. I'll come and get you at 12... in fact..." Aaron looked at his watch too, "...in 12 hours' time, precisely."

Jenny rose to her feet. "Are you sure?"

"Yes," said Aaron and stepped closer. "I'm very sure." Sweeping his arm around her waist, he pulled her towards him. "Couldn't be surer..."

They kissed. Passionately. Jenny's pulse rate could have burst her veins. They stood in an embrace for a long time.

"I'm going," breathed Aaron, pulling away. Holding her hands in his, he gazed into Jenny's eyes. "I'll see you tomorrow. Goodnight."

He left swiftly and silently, disappearing into the darkness.

Jenny climbed into bed, untouched, except for her lips, wanting and wishing to be touched again. To be taken.

Chapter 23

Jenny turned the key three times, just as Aaron had said. Bleep went the till and after a few more sounds, a blue light glowed from the small screen. Following the ceiling thumps back down to the end of the shop, Jenny turned the computer on, which she hoped would automatically activate the EPOS program – *7.06am Monday 2nd November. J's Convenience Store – Active.* Just as Aaron had told her, the system kicked in to action immediately. A small icon of a building flickered in the taskbar. Jumping up, Jenny went to the bundles of newspapers on the floor, and began to sort them on to the shelves and make a separate pile for Jordan to deliver.

The early sun, just peeping above the rooftops, lit up Millen Road with an orange glow. It was a beautiful autumn morning. Jordan had collected his papers and disappeared as quickly as he'd arrived. Unlocking the front door earlier than normal, Jenny turned the door sign to 'open' and went down to the staffroom to collect her mug of coffee, with a spring in her step.

She had no Monday morning blues and the thumping noise hadn't bothered her in the slightest. The only thing that had dampened Jenny's morning was the thought that it was Tasha's shift first on Mondays. She would have to wait until the afternoon to have a good old natter with her dear friend, and right now, she needed it. She couldn't wait to tell Dayna what had happened. She couldn't wait to shock the life out of her. But it would have to wait. Until she got back from lunch. Lunch with an amazingly gorgeous, kind and generous, entrepreneurial, rich man. Jenny shook her head and tutted – the 'rich' bit had nothing to do with it. She did not want Dayna getting the wrong idea. Jenny decided she would leave that bit out. It could come later. As a bonus.

Tasha arrived promptly, signed a 'T' shape with two fingers to Jenny, who was serving a customer, and then went down to the staffroom.

"That Aaron fella is nice, isn't he?" said Tasha, carefully placing two mugs of tea under the counter. "He's quite funny."

"Err... yes, he is. Talking of which, I need to show you how to use this. Dead simple really," said Jenny, placing a hand on the main till. "That one," she added, pointing to the till next to Tasha, "will be for newspaper delivery payments only. Just for now, anyway."

"Ok," replied Tasha, with interest.

Jenny ran through the operation of the two tills and stood and watched Tasha serve a customer with ease. "Told you it was easy," said Jenny, smiling at just how much easier these tills were. "If you get an item that doesn't scan, just ring it through in the old way using these keys here." Jenny pointed out the six, categorised keys on the far right. "And if you're not sure – use the 'miscellaneous' key. I'm in the process of getting every single item in this shop put on the system. It'll take some time though, so bear with me."

Tasha nodded her head and grinned. "Think I've got it now. They're nice aren't they," she said, wiping her hand across the top of the till, admiringly.

"Yes, they're fab. Going to make my life a lot easier with the cashing up, stock-taking and accounts."

"Cool – you'll soon have more staff working for you, Jenny. Then you can use both tills."

"Tills don't make money on their own – I need more customers before more staff." Jenny laughed.

"Well, when you've got more customers... I know someone... well, my friend is looking for a part-time job. She's at college." Tasha's cheeks flushed bright red. "That's if you'll be interested." Tasha shrugged her shoulders and looked down at the floor, bashfully.

"I'll bear that in mind, Tasha, thank-you." There was a moment of awkwardness before Jenny added, "What's her name? I'll jot it in my diary for later."

Tasha looked up in amazement. "Really?"

"I'm not promising anything, but who knows what the future holds."

"Her name is Jane – Jane Thornton. She's a really nice girl. You'd like her." Tasha's dark eyes stared, hopefully.

"Ok, well like I said, there's nothing at the moment."

Nodding her head, Tasha smiled and then moved away from the counter. "Thanks Jenny. I'll go and do the nursery order now."

"Great and could you serve in between. I need to get as many items scanned on to the system as possible."

"Yes, of course."

One hundred and thirty six products later, Jenny stretched back in her office chair and yawned. It was mind-numbing work, collecting a basket of items, carrying them through to the office, scanning each one, inputting the related data and then putting the products back on the shelves.

Tasha poked her head around the office door. "The nursery haven't picked up their order yet."

"Really?" said Jenny, looking at her watch. "They've normally got it by now."

"That's what I thought."

"I'll nip along there – see if they're going to pick it up soon, otherwise we'll have to put the milk back in the fridge. Will you be ok for five minutes on your own?"

"We've got their phone number," Tasha replied, holding the address book from the counter in her hand. "Shall I call them?"

"Oh, ok. Do that and I'll man the till." Jenny levered herself out of the cosy chair. "I could do with a break from this, before I end up with permanent goggle-eyes – too much computer work."

"Which phone shall I use?" asked Tasha, looking into the office.

"Use this one." Jenny pointed to the phone on her desk, "You can sit there – it's not a sacred seat, you know. Look, I've kept it warm for you."

Tasha giggled and sat down.

Jenny went off to the front of the shop and peered out of the windows. It looked like a summer's day out there. If the weather stayed the same, she would try out the awning for the afternoon.

Watching a shabby looking woman walk past the window, Jenny noticed her dirty, long blonde hair, tied up in a ponytail, flicking from side to side as she stomped past. She looked up at what Jenny assumed was the shop's sign and then paused at the door. Tapping her wellington boots on the side of the building, she first peered up and down the road and then she opened the door. She wafted in, literally. In fact, the smell wafted in first, before she'd stepped over the threshold.

The foul smell of a farmyard, baking in the hot sun, filled the front of the shop instantly. The middle-aged woman stood, legs astride, with her hands tucked into two breast pockets in her khaki green, wax jacket. Her knee-high boots were encrusted in varying colours of orangey, brown mud. She looked down the shop and then turned her weather-hardened face towards Jenny.

"Would it be possible to speak to the manager please?"

Surprised by the unexpected tone of the woman's voice, which did not match her appearance at all, Jenny replied. "Can I ask why?"

"I would just like to have a confidential chat with the manager, please." The woman approached the counter with a wide stride and looked pleadingly at Jenny.

"Well, I am the owner. How can I help you?"

The woman scanned the shop and then stared out of the window. "Oh, ok. Well... it's my mum..."

"Sorry?"

"My mum – you know her."

"Do I?" Jenny held a hand up to her nose and mouth in a vain attempt to get a moment's respite from the putrid stink.

"Yes, I think so."

The front door opened and in walked two elderly women. They smiled at Jenny and then continued down the first aisle, nattering amongst themselves, oblivious to the stench emanating from the woman's clothing.

Tasha appeared at the counter, looking jittery.

The smelly woman coughed. "Could I talk to you privately?"

"Of course, that's no problem." Jenny looked across at Tasha's worried expression. "Will you be ok for a minute? I'm going to take this lady to the office." Jenny frowned. "Everything ok?"

Tasha shook her head. "You go – I'll tell you in a minute."

Puzzled by Tasha's fretful appearance and the filthy woman's request, Jenny led the way to her office.

"Come in," said Jenny, knowing full well that if she shut the office door, she would be overcome by the fumes exuding from the woman's boots.

The woman closed the office door and sat down on the small fold-up chair offered to her.

"Right," gulped Jenny, "your mum..."

"Yes, Marjorie."

"Oh – Marj." Jenny's eyes widened. "Yes, I know Marj. Quite a character."

"Yes, she is... that's why I'm here."

"Ok," said Jenny, intrigued by the woman's appearance and the over-powering smell.

"You'll have to excuse me," said the woman, "I've been mucking out my horses this morning."

"Oh... I see," said Jenny. "I have to say – I did wonder what you did for a living. I mean, dressed like you are." Jenny smiled and diverted her gaze away from the woman's fetid boots. "Looks like you've been rolling in it..." Jenny smacked a hand to her mouth as soon as the words had left. "Sorry, I didn't mean that – just not used to seeing people that work with horses."

"It's ok. I am a bit of a mess. I do apologise. I was passing and thought I'd nip in quickly." The woman looked down at her boots. "I tapped most of it off, before I came in."

"Yes, I know. I saw you." Jenny was beginning to warm to the woman, even with the smell.

"We've been digging out part of the perimeter of the field we use. New fences going in. Guess I've got a bit clogged up with mud and horse-shit today."

Jenny let out a short burst of laughter and then composed herself, so as to look professional. "So, about your mum, how can I help you?"

"Well, I've had problems like this before. She has recently been diagnosed with the early onset of Alzheimer's."

"Ok," Jenny looked down, respectfully. "We had worried that that might be the case. She's been using the shop quite a lot since we opened and there have been a couple of times that we've had a slight problem with her."

"Oh, what sort of problems?"

"Well, she gets a little muddled sometimes. It's like the toilet rolls – she thinks that they are free."

"Ah, I was going to talk to you about toilet rolls. She has so many packs stuffed down by the side of her toilet." The woman leant back in the chair, looking far more relaxed. "She told me that you gave them to her for free. I take it that's not true then?"

"Somehow, I knew you were going to say that." Jenny huffed. "No, it's not true. I'm afraid that your mum has got very muddled about the toilet rolls."

"Thought as much."

"I've been trying to catch up with her each time she comes in, but I haven't managed to talk to her yet. Something else always seems to come up." The overripe manure smell had become less offensive. Jenny wondered if she was just getting used to it. She was beginning to like this odd-looking woman whose grubby wax jacket seemed to crinkle and crunch, every time she moved or spoke.

"She's crafty."

"Crafty?" Jenny frowned. "What do you mean?"

"She's like a cunning cat." The woman crossed one heavily laden leg, over the other, resulting in a small lump of grassy mud falling from her boot. Peering down, she picked up the piece of earth. "Oh, sorry – I'm drying out a bit." Popping the mud into her pocket, she continued. "Mum's playing on the diagnosis."

Intrigued, Jenny leant over the side of her desk and propped up her chin with a hand. "How do you mean?"

"Well, she's always been the same but now she's had the news from her doctor, she's got worse."

"Sorry, I don't understand what you mean. Got worse?"

"Yes –she's having us all on. She's pretending that she doesn't know what she's doing." The woman paused for a moment. "But most of the time she does know." The woman looked up with watery eyes. "I just don't know what to do with her..." Pulling a tissue from her pocket, the little cluster of dried soil flew out and landed on the floor in front of Jenny's feet. The woman blew her nose, noisily, folded the damp tissue over and shoved it back in her pocket.

Reaching down, Jenny cringed as she picked up the nugget of mud and immediately threw it in the waste paper bin, under her desk. "Look – I can see that this is a real problem for you but I'm not sure what I can do to help."

"Please... do not let her buy into your shop."

"What?" Jenny threw herself back in her chair, picked a pen up from the desk and began chewing the end of it.

"Tell me it's not true..."

"I'm sure it's not true."

"Has she told you how much money she has in the bank?"

"No – not at all." Jenny's heart began to beat a little faster. Was she going to be accused of stealing Marj's money?

"Well, she's told me that you've been open only a few weeks..."

"Yes, that's right. I have."

"She said that you're struggling. You don't have enough customers."

"Well..." Jenny shuffled in her seat, uncomfortably. "Yes. That is true as well. I'm not sure how your mum knows that though."

"That's what I mean – she's actually very clever. I fear that this Alzheimer's will assist her in being quite dangerous. She's like a little *Gangster Granny.*"

"Really?" Jenny wondered just how dangerous an old lady, who was losing her marbles, could really be. "How do you mean?"

"She said that you allow her to use your staffroom..."

"Well, no actually. That's all a mix up too."

"And you've asked her to answer the phone for you..."

"Again, that is all a bit of a muddle." Jenny rolled her eyes. "I'm beginning to see what you mean about your mum. We were busy one day and the phone rang... I did not ask your mum to answer it. I'm afraid that she took it upon herself to answer my phone. Ok... she was in here at the time... but that was only because I needed to talk to her about the toilet rolls."

The woman nodded her head agreeably. "I see..."

"I do hope so. Look, I am more than happy to do anything I can to help you out. I think your mum is a dear old lady… and I have to say… you've got to see the funny side to this – she's quite a character, isn't she?"

The woman harrumphed. "She also told me that your husband wants her to help run the shop."

"Ok – I'm getting it," said Jenny, holding her hands up. "Firstly, can I assure you that I do not have a husband. Secondly, I have never asked her to do any sort of job in this shop… and thirdly, we do not allow anyone, who is not a member of staff, to go into our staffroom."

"Ok, so why has my mum been to the bank to organize the withdrawal of £15,000 in just over a week's time?"

Jenny's mouth dropped open. "I have absolutely no idea."

The likeability of this woman was faltering. It seemed to Jenny, that one minute she was forewarning her and the next she was accusing her. "Why do *you* think?" asked Jenny, tentatively.

"The man who you claim, is not your husband. Is he called Aaron?"

"Yes…"

"Well he has asked my mum to buy into the shop – to help get you off the ground."

Stunned, Jenny sat silently for a moment. "I can't believe that that could be true."

"I've been to the bank and checked. She has arranged for the withdrawal, in cash, next Wednesday. The manager, who I have come to know well, said that she is buying a share of a shop. He tried to stop her arranging it but at the end of the day, it's her money and she can do whatever she wants with it – well, up until now."

"Oh my God… I don't believe this."

"Is there something going on behind your back that you don't know about?"

Jenny thought about it for a moment. *No, there is no way that this could be happening – is there?* "Look, to be honest with you, I hardly know Aaron. I met him a couple of weeks ago and your mum has got it into her head that he is my husband. I just don't know what to say about all of this." Jenny rubbed her hand across her forehead and sighed.

"Why is this man hanging around your shop then?"

"He's not," Jenny replied, suddenly feeling guilty that he would be turning up soon to take her to lunch. Thoughts drifted in to her head... the kisses... the cuddles... the beautiful passion of it all. Had she been misled? "Look, he has fitted a couple of new tills for me, that's all." Jenny remembered how Aaron had been left in the staffroom with Marj once, but she couldn't think of any other time that this supposed business deal could have happened. It had to be a lie... didn't it? "Like you keep telling me, your mum has Alzheimer's, could this just be in her head?"

"I'm not sure. She's adamant that she is buying part of this shop. Usually there is a glint in her eye that tells me if she is pulling a fast one – like with the toilet rolls – I can tell that she is playing on that."

"Really? Well...I just don't know what to say. As far as I am concerned, none of this is true and I would certainly *not* be taking any money from your mum for this shop." Jenny fought off the compelling urge to run out of the shop screaming wildly, all the way down Millen Road. A bubbling in her stomach was eagerly waiting to surface as tears. It was all becoming too much. Jenny's tone lowered. "I'll talk to Aaron about this today. He'll be in later." Jenny looked down at her watch... Aaron would be here in less than half an hour. She had to get rid of this woman before he arrived. Whatever might have gone on or not gone on, Jenny wanted to get out – she needed some fresh air. Even if it was with a villainous man. He couldn't be though, surely. She needed to talk to him, away from the shop.

"I'm applying to the court for 'Power of Attorney'. Mum's just going to get worse." The woman grabbed her tissue again and wiped under her nose. "Until that's in place, can we exchange contact details? She's fixated with this shop and also with that man, Aaron."

"Yes, of course we can. If there is anything that I can do further, please let me know." Jenny took a notepad from her desk and used the half-chewed pen which had suffered most of her anguish, during the conversation. "I'll give you a call later and let you know what Aaron says, too," she added.

The woman nodded and gave a weak smile before reciting her name and phone number.

"Thank you for coming in today," said Jenny. "I will give you a call later." Opening the front door, courteously, Jenny said goodbye and stood in the doorway, absorbing the warm rays of sunshine. There were ten minutes left before both Aaron and Dayna turned up. She just had to hang on until then.

"Are you ok?" asked Tasha. "You look like you've seen a ghost."

"Yes... I will be when I get my lunch break."

Tasha puffed out a chuckle. "Thought the smell from that woman had made you sick... by the look of you."

"It nearly did. You get used to it though." Jenny moved away from the door as a man walked towards the shop. As she approached the counter, she looked down at the empty nursery crate. "They've been then?"

"Oh... no. I've put all of the stuff back, Jenny. I was going to tell you about that but that muddy woman was here."

"Why haven't they collected it?"

Tasha looked down. "They've cancelled it."

"Oh, why's that? They're open today, aren't they?"

Tasha nodded and continued to look at the floor, intensely.

"Tasha, what's going on?" Jenny's pulse began to race again. *Now what?*

"They've... well... err... they've cancelled the order completely."

"Why?" Jenny's eyes glared but she tried desperately not to direct them at Tasha. "Why have they cancelled?"

The man who had been walking towards the shop, came in.

Tasha lowered her voice. "Andrea said that her boss has told her not to order from here anymore."

"Why?" The option to run down the road screaming, like a raving lunatic, was looking more favourable, by the second.

"Andrea said that you attacked her boss..."

"What?" Jenny gawked. "Her boss?" She paused. "That woman – the tall one – Tracey?"

Tasha nodded her head with each word that Jenny spluttered out.

"I don't frigging well believe it..." Placing a hand to her mouth, Jenny turned round and looked for the man who was in the shop.

At the far end of the aisle, the man was perusing the information on the back of a frozen 'Meal for One' box.

"What exactly did she say?"

Tasha looked worried, "Andrea was... err... well... she was quite nasty..."

"Yes, go on."

"She said that her boss had told her you were..."

"Tasha, please, just come out with it and tell me exactly what she said." Jenny fidgeted from one foot to the other.

"She said that you're a psychotic, money-grabbing, bitch."

Jenny's heart sank. Tears pricked. The time was approaching 12 o'clock. She had to get out. Get away. Before she burst. Before she broke. "That's over £300 a week we've lost." Drawing a deep breath, she let out a huge sigh. "This all stems from that bloody woman, Marj."

Tasha began to chew on her nails.

Looking up at the clock again, Jenny willed the small hand to move faster. "I'm going out for lunch in a minute, can you open the awning please? The remote is under there," said Jenny pointing a finger, under the counter. "I'll go and get my coat..."

Half way down the aisle, Jenny heard the front door open behind her. It was Dayna. Jenny couldn't look her in the eye for more than a second or two. That would have been the end of her steadfast persona. "I'm going out for lunch, Day. I'll be back at two," she shouted along the aisle. Snatching her coat from the staffroom, Jenny proceeded back up the shop. Dayna stood by the counter, looking perplexed. Jenny darted her eyes towards Tasha. "Can you run through the till with Dayna, please? I really need to go."

Tasha nodded and smiled cheerlessly.

"I'll see you both later," said Jenny, before scooting out of the front door.

Darting round the corner of the shop, out of sight of the girls, Jenny watched Aaron's car pull into the side road, right on time. Waving her hand, she flagged him down, opened the passenger door and jumped in. "Let's go – please."

Aaron looked at her with a startled expression.

"Please – get me out of here – quick!"

Chapter 24

Aaron's shocked expression made Jenny laugh. She laughed some more. And some more. She laughed uncontrollably. Then she cried.

Driving away, Aaron's abilities to control the car, peer curiously at Jenny, cup her hand in his and keep calm, were admirable. The look on his face told a different story. Speechless, he frowned in puzzlement. Thrown completely by Jenny's sudden outburst of tears, Aaron could only look on as he steered the car away.

"I'm sorry," Jenny sniffled. "Have you got a tissue?"

Aaron pointed to the glove compartment. "There might be some in there."

Opening the door, Jenny searched around but found nothing. She sniffed and then wiped her nose on her sleeve. "You must think I do this all the time."

"Do what?" asked Aaron, driving along slower than the road would dictate.

"Every time I see you... well, something happens, doesn't it."

"Something else has happened?"

"Everything has happened... I think I'm losing it."

"No you're not. We've got two hours haven't we?"

"Yeah," Jenny replied nonchalantly. Wiping the tears from her face, she took a deep breath and let it out slowly, through pursed lips.

"We'll talk it all through... that's if you want to tell me."

"Ok."

"Do you want to go to the café by the harbour again?"

"Yes." Jenny sighed, "That would be nice." Sniffing again, she managed to grasp her composure. "Just get me way from this crazy place."

Pressing his foot on the pedal, Aaron sped up and swiftly left Millen Road and its residents behind.

The glistening sun lit up the picturesque view of the harbour and the sea beyond, just as it had the first time she was here. And every time she'd been here in her dreams. Jenny was calmed by the serenity of it all. This was just what she needed right now. Although it was a bit too chilly to sit outside today, the view from inside was just as spectacular.

Aaron stood at the counter ordering two pulled pork ciabattas and two large choco lattes.

Peering out of the window, Jenny felt the tears prick at her eyes again. She couldn't cry again. Not now.

"Right, what's been going on then?" asked Aaron, joining her at the table. "You said something about Marj and the nursery but it was all a bit jumbled up." Aaron smiled warmly and took one of Jenny's hands. "I want to help you. I care about you... and your shop."

The last three words made Jenny sit up straight, *'and your shop'*. *Was it true, what Marj's daughter had told her?* "How much do you care about my shop?" she asked, suspiciously.

"What do you mean?" Aaron looked stumped.

"Well... how much do you care about it? What does it mean to you?"

"I'm not sure where you're going with this, Jenny. I care enough to want you to succeed – if that's what you mean?"

"And what would you do to ensure that I succeed?" Jenny replied, bluntly.

Aaron let go of Jenny's hand and leant back in his chair. "Jenny, could you tell me what has happened this morning?" He moved forward and propped his chin up on the table. "There's something you're not telling me."

"I'm just asking a simple question. What would you do to ensure that I succeed?"

"Ok, I'll be honest..." Aaron hesitated. "The way I feel about you right now, I'd probably do anything within my power to make sure that you succeed..."

"Like what?"

"Well, like fit an EPOS system into your shop... for free." Aaron sat up straight. The frown on his face suggested that he was a little peeved by Jenny's abrupt questioning.

"Anything else?"

"Can't think of anything yet," Aaron replied.

"What about money?"

"What about it?"

"Would you invest money in my shop?"

"Whoa – steady on," Aaron let out a short laugh. "Is that a theoretical question or a request?"

"Or anyone else's money, for that matter?"

"You've lost me." Aaron stretched his arms across the table and beckoned her to give him her hand. "Just tell me what's happened today."

Her hands cupped inside Aaron's, Jenny's eyes filled up again. "It's all madness... Everyone's crazy." Tears began to fall from her cheeks.

"Tell me everything – I want to help you," said Aaron, softly. He squeezed her hands, gently, and then offered her a serviette. "We've got over an hour and a half. Take your time."

"It's Marj – she's the cause of everything. I know she's just a little old lady but she's caused so much trouble." Jenny sniffed and took the serviette.

"I'm all ears... carry on..."

The meal and the 'off-loading' had made Jenny feel so much better. Aaron had sat listening, intently and had appeared somewhat stunned by her revelations.

"And you say that you have the woman's phone number?"

Jenny nodded her head.

"Could I give her a call?" Aaron paused. "Just to reassure her… you can listen in on the conversation if you'd like."

Jenny nodded again. She was too exhausted to speak and her jaw was clamped shut and propped up by her hands anyway.

"And your shop will take off, eventually. Three hundred pounds lost from the nursery, will seem like nothing in a few months' time."

Nodding her head repeatedly, Jenny wished that she didn't have to go back to work. It was cosy in the café, sitting opposite Aaron and gazing into his eyes. She had to return though. Tasha would want to leave at two o'clock.

"Come on – we'd better get you back to the shop. I'll make that phone call when we get back."

How could she have ever doubted Aaron? Maybe she was going insane. Perhaps she was more tired than she thought. Possibly, she needed a break from the shop already. What a wimp she was turning into.

Tasha left after asking if Jenny was ok.

Jenny had assured her that she was fine and also commented on the delightful appearance of the awning. She had thanked Tasha for 'taking over' at a moments notice, as well.

Dayna had been stuck behind the counter, with one customer after another. The urgency in her eyes looked painful. Jenny knew that she had been told everything but Dayna would be desperate to get it 'from the horse's mouth', as she always liked to quote, when she was homing in on the latest gossip.

"Hello... is that Trudy? Trudy Grange?" Aaron sounded very professional on the phone. "My name is Aaron Frey." Aaron looked up and winked at Jenny. "Aaron... Aaron Frey." Rubbing his forehead, he continued. "You may not know me by my last name. I am Aaron –from *J's Convenience Store.*"

Jenny signed a 'T' and Aaron nodded eagerly.

"No, I don't work at the shop. I have carried out some work here though. And I have met your mum, Marj, quite by accident, when I've been in the shop."

From the staffroom, Jenny could just hear Aaron's voice, through the small adjoining window.

"Yes, she has told me everything. I can assure you that the whole story is complete fabrication, madam."

While the kettle boiled, Jenny heard only snippets of the, longer than expected, conversation that Aaron was having. She made tea for three and carried one up to Dayna, who was still itching to know everything.

"You ok," mouthed Dayna, in between serving two people.

Jenny nodded and smiled. "I'll talk to you soon. Aaron's on the phone at the moment. I'm going back to the office."

"Ok," she whispered. "Make sure you do."

As Jenny arrived at the office door, Aaron had just replaced the receiver. He puffed out his cheeks and stretched back in the chair. "I'm not sure that she is convinced, you know," he said, clasping his hands together at the back of his head.

"Oh dear – why?"

"Well, she seems to think that you and I are in this together."

Jenny tutted. "So what do we do about that?"

"I'm not sure that there is anything we can do about it." A wry smile crept across Aaron's face. "I would say... whatever you do Jenny... just don't take any money from Marj. Like £15,000... even if she wants it in toilet rolls."

Jenny burst into laughter and almost cried again. "You're so funny. Not!" Then she laughed some more. Almost hysterically.

Gulping down the last of his tea, Aaron stood up. "So, I'll come back at eight and run through the cashing up process with you."

"Are you sure that you don't mind coming back so late?"

"Part of the job," said Aaron, pecking Jenny on the cheek. "Come out for dinner with me, afterwards."

"You'll be getting sick of the sight of me soon," Jenny joked.

"No I won't." Aaron looked her up and down. "And you're fine dressed like that. We'll go straight from here – yes?"

"Ok, if you're sure."

"I'm sure," replied Aaron. "I'll see you later."

"You're going to ask me to start at the beginning – I know it."

"Uh-huh," breathed Dayna, nodding her head, slowly.

"Well, we haven't got all day. What do you know already?"

"All of it, I think." Dayna shook her head. "It's crazy around here. What have we got ourselves in to, Jen? Or should I say – what have *you* got yourself in to?"

"You know, when I got this shop… I knew that it would be hard work and I'd struggle with tiredness… but this is a level up from that. I didn't for one minute, expect the sort of problems I'm getting now."

"No, I know. I can't believe what Andrea said about you…"

"Well, to be fair, I think that came from Tracey – the boss."

"Hmm…"

"There is something that you don't know though…"

"What?" Dayna's eyes lit up. She was hearing it (whatever 'it' was) straight from 'the horse's mouth' now.

"I've been, err… sort of seeing Aaron." Jenny's face beamed.

"You have?"

"Hmm."

"In what sense? Do you mean you're dating him? I thought you said you weren't dating him. You said it was purely business." Dayna bit her bottom lip. "Have you slept with him?"

"No – just seeing him, really."

"Well I know that you've been 'seeing him', as you say. So what do you mean if you're not dating him?"

"Well..." Jenny gazed out of the window. "We've kissed."

"Blimey – have you?"

Jenny nodded and smiled.

"So. Along with going out for lunch and the fact that you've kissed him – you must be dating him." Dayna clapped her hands together. "What's he like?" she asked excitedly.

"You know what he's like..."

"I don't know what he's like – I haven't kissed him, Jen. I mean, what was *it* like?"

"Dreamy," Jenny grinned. "He's lovely."

"Knew he fancied you."

"Don't know how I'm ever going to fit him in though..."

Dayna frowned. "Why? How big is his old todger for heaven's sake?"

"Dayna!" Jenny slapped her friend around the arm and laughed out loud. "You know what I meant."

"You said you can't fit him in – I assumed you'd had a feel, what with kissing him. It does arouse them you know."

Jenny couldn't say anything due to her fit of giggles. Dayna then joined in.

"You crack me up sometimes," spluttered Jenny. "I wouldn't know about that, I never went there."

"Are you going to?" Dayna asked, in between gasps and chuckles.

"I don't know. I haven't planned that far ahead. We've kissed a couple of times and that is it." Jenny gently poked her bestie in the side. Dayna was just the tonic she needed. "I don't know how I could squeeze him in though, to be honest."

"There you go again – rattling on about the size of his man-bits."

Shaking her head and giggling, Jenny placed a finger to her lips as a woman pushed the front door open.

Dayna burst into a raucous roar and immediately slapped her hand over her mouth. "I'm so sorry," she mumbled through her fingers.

"Got the giggles," said Jenny, apologetically, to the surprised looking woman. "Go and make drinks," Jenny whispered. "Now."

Dayna scurried away, still clutching her mouth and making muffled chuckling noises.

"Jen!" Dayna called from the far end of the empty shop. "Jacob's on the phone."

Jenny raced down the aisle, suddenly recalling the conversation she'd had with him yesterday. Taking the phone from Dayna, she said, "Hello."

"Jen, I've spoken to Rob at the garage. He said that they can't do anything about the bill – well, I didn't think they could, but he did say that the woman had stated clearly that she wanted the 'full-works' to get her car back to normal."

"Ok..." Jenny rolled her eyes.

"Rob said that she could have had it done a lot cheaper but she insisted on a brand new wing mirror and a re-spray of the whole door. They could have rubbed the tiny scratch out – according to Rob. And refitted the mirror."

"Great."

"You should contact your insurance company, Jen. She's making this claim privately but your insurance would sort it out fairly."

"And charge me for it... and I'd lose my no-claims. I've got nine years on that."

"Well, it's up to you, Sis. Alternatively, take her to a small claims court – fight it out there. Could cost you even more though," Jacob warned.

Jenny sighed. "Ok, thanks, Jay. I do appreciate you going over there for me. I'll have to think about it."

"Don't leave it too long – especially if you're going to claim on the insurance."

"No, I won't. What a bloody mess this is," admitted Jenny.

"Yep – teach you to not go hauling heavy bins around in the middle of the night." Jacob tittered.

"Tell me about it... turns out, she's the owner of the nursery. They've now cancelled their daily order with me because they think I'm some psychotic maniac."

"Seriously?"

"Seriously," echoed Jenny. "I've lost over £300 a week now. I know it was my stupid fault to go flying out of the shop at breakneck speed... but it seems that things go from bad to worse around here."

"Sounds like it, Sis. Maybe it's not you that's a psychotic maniac – it's them."

"I am wondering."

"You've landed yourself in a right weird community there, haven't you?" Jacob sounded sympathetic.

"It appears so. I'll work it out though. You know me – never give up on a dream."

"You said it, Sis." Jacob sighed. "Let me know what happens with the car. And call me if you need me to do anything else."

"I will. Thanks, Jay. You're my favourite brother."

"Yeah of course – your only brother – thanks for that." Jacob laughed down the phone. "Catch you later."

"Jen, I meant to say to you earlier…" Dayna peered out of the window and watched one of the parents from the nursery, wrestle her toddler into the back of a car. "We noticed – as in me and Tasha – that none of the nursery staff came in to get their lunch today."

"That explains why the till doesn't look as full as normal then," said Jenny, dejectedly.

"One of them – the one with the big, orange hair?"

"Yes, I know…"

"Well she walked right past the shop with a *KO Store* carrier bag. She was deliberately swinging it as she went past and she had her nose stuck up in the air."

"Nothing I can do about it…"

"I wanted to go out there and punch her nose further up her face… lairy cow."

"That would just confirm the psychotic maniac accusation. But it would be even worse… everyone would think that we had two psychopaths in here."

"Yeah well… she better not cross my path with that attitude though." Dayna watched the woman with the toddler, drive away. "I'm still peed off with the old git upstairs and if I see him… well… he's gonna get it. Spitting at me – dirty bugger."

"All right, Day, calm down." Jenny worried for Dayna when she was in fighting-talk mode. "We'll get through this, I'm sure. I still have faith that we *can* make it work here."

"Too right, and all the more so since this has happened."

"Hi… Aa…ron," said Dayna, foxily. "Jen's down there." Pointing towards the fridges, Dayna smirked. Before Aaron had moved from the doorway, Dayna called down the aisle, in her most sultry of voices. "Jen…ny! Aa…ron is here."

A tinge of red flushed Aaron's cheeks as he smiled and nodded at Dayna.

Watching his every move, Dayna continued to tie up the paper bundles. "You two off out tonight then?" she called after him.

Aaron turned and grinned.

Jenny looked up and nodded.

"Hope you have a nice time," said Dayna. "Jen, I'm off in a minute. Want me to put these out the back?"

"I can do that for you," said Aaron, drawing his hands out from his pockets and walking back to the counter.

"Ooh... gentleman as well."

Aaron laughed, embarrassedly. He collected several bundles from the counter and headed off to the office.

Jenny placed the dairy order-pad on the side of the fridge. "Shut up, Day," she whispered. "We're not teenagers."

"All right – just having a little joke," she replied, holding her palms up. "He's sweet. I was only playing."

"He's here to show me how to cash up on these new tills." Jenny turned to make sure that Aaron wasn't behind her.

"So you're not going anywhere with him, after?"

"Well... yes. Just for a meal. He insisted. After the day I've had, I don't fancy going home to sit in my flat and stew."

"Take him home with you... you could cook up a steamy stew together." Dayna giggled.

"Shut up. Time you went home yourself. See you tomorrow." Jenny's relationship with Dayna was strong enough to take the odd bit of banter or in Dayna's case, the odd telling-off. "Go on – clear off." Jenny winked at her dearest friend and shoved her towards the staffroom. "Goodbye, Dayna."

Jotting down each step in the process of cashing up and recording the day's takings, Jenny was baffled by the complexity of the 'reporting' process. "Glad I've written it all down. I'd never remember all of that."

"That's why I said take notes. I haven't got a spare manual to give you at the moment. It does tell you everything on here but I think it's easier to show you."

"Hmm..."

"But look at what you have now..." said Aaron, as he brought up a new page.

"Wow – it's got everything there."

"Yep. Good enough for the taxman. This one page can be used for pretty much all of your accounting."

"Gosh – it looks so much clearer now."

"Wait until you see the stock control sheets..." Aaron looked at his watch. "But shall we do that later in the week?"

"Yes, sure."

"Let's go and get dinner – I'm starving." Aaron stood up and stretched his legs. "I'm away for a couple of days, from tomorrow. I could come in on Friday and go through the stock control with you."

"Yes. Ok..." Jenny registered Aaron's last words. "...Off anywhere nice?" she asked, falteringly.

"Business trip, nothing exciting. Germany. I'll be home Friday morning so I could come back that afternoon."

Jenny nodded. "Yes, I'll book you into my diary," she half giggled.

"Come on then, let's go. I'll follow you back to your place and then we can go in my car."

"Chauffer driven – that's what I like," replied Jenny, in jest.

Aaron looked up to the ceiling as the thumps started. They were a little later than normal. "See what you mean about that," he said, following the trail of sound along the shop. "Come on, let's see if we can beat him to the front of the shop." Taking hold of Jenny's hand, he pulled her along the aisle at a fast pace. They laughed like a pair of kids, racing around a playground.

The evening had flown past but then it was almost nine o'clock when they arrived at the quaint, little village restaurant. Jenny commented several times on the tranquility of the large, cottage-style building and the quiet laid back feel of it. It was her kind of place.

Following the delicious meal, consisting of rib-eye steaks, French fries and peas, both Jenny and Aaron set about devouring a share-size, Knickerbocker Glory. The evening had been swift but sweet. Much small talk and dreamy glances across the table had made for a romantic evening.

Back at Jenny's flat, they had arrived at the 'Do you want to come in for a coffee' moment. Jenny glanced at the clock on the dashboard. Another late night. If she invited him in, they could be there until the early hours. What the heck – she would invite him in anyway.

"Do you want a quick coffee?" Jenny asked, softly.

Aaron looked across at her with his dark eyes. "Jenny, I would love nothing more than to come in for a coffee... but... I have to be at Gatwick by six thirty."

Jenny's heart sank, she'd geared herself up for this. "Oh really? Guess you'll have to leave about half four then?"

"Yes, something like that." Aaron slid his arm behind Jenny's shoulders. "Wish I didn't have to go. Would much rather stay for a coffee." Leaning over the gear stick, he kissed her gently on the lips. Then again. Softer. Slower.

"I've got to go," breathed Aaron. "Any more of this and I'll be coming in for coffee..."

"I really have to go…" Aaron sat up straight and tugged at his dishevelled shirt. "If I don't go, I'll be coming in for *more* than just coffee." He smiled and looked deep in to Jenny's eyes. "I'm joking."

Jenny stood by the front door and waved as Aaron glided away in his sleek, black *BMW*. She would miss him. She hardly knew him. But she would still miss him.

Chapter 25

J's shop
Did you get permission for that?
Don't think you're keeping that disgusting looking, bit of cloth sticking out all the time. I'm contacting the council this week. This is out of order.
I can't see the pavement outside my flipping window. How dare you!
As for the work your builders did on Sunday – it woke me up. Shouldn't builders have a day off on Sundays? Obviously, not your builders! You have no care or consideration for anyone but yourself.
You'll be hearing from the council soon.
From D upstairs.

He's got a bloody nerve, thought Jenny. Tossing the note under the counter, she strolled down the shop, flicking fridge lights on, as she went. She would pay 'D upstairs' a visit today. Once Tasha and Dayna were covering lunch, she would go up there and have a quiet word with the man. Jenny was calm, for some strange reason. The note hadn't fazed her in the slightest. She was empowered by the thought of seeing Aaron again on Friday. She could and she would sort out every little niggle that had started to turn her lifelong dream of owning her own shop, into a living, breathing nightmare. Aaron had breathed a new sense of worth into her, she had inhaled a new determination to deal with all that is, or was, wrong in her life. And that included Calvin, should he cause any problems once he got a sniff about her new, blossoming relationship. Today was 'Go Jenny!' day.

'Go Jenny!' day lasted for 45 minutes, in fact, right up until Dolly walked into the shop.

"It's not in keeping with the rest of the block, is it?" she said, pointing to the top of the window.

"The awning you mean?" Jenny replied, averting her glare away from Dolly's powder-puff face.

"No one else has one of those along here. It looks out of place."

"Well I thought it looked very nice, Dolly. Have you seen it when it's extended?"

"No." Dolly picked up her paper and hobbled across the floor. "Wilbur didn't like it. He was looking up at it as we came along. I thought he was going to start barking at it."

"Ok... if Wilbur doesn't like it... then I guess it will have to come down."

"Oh, don't be silly, dear. You can't take it down now – just because my dog doesn't like it. You'll leave horrible, big holes in the walls... and then it will really look unsightly."

"So what do you suggest, Dolly?" Jenny thought for a moment. "Hang on a minute – didn't you come in yesterday morning?"

"Yes. You know I did."

"Well it was there yesterday. Why didn't Wilbur worry about it then?"

"We were in a rush yesterday, dear. Church choir practice."

"You hung around here long enough," replied Jenny, abruptly. "You – or should I say, Wilbur, must have noticed it then."

"Yes I... we err... did, dear. I didn't have the time to mention it to you."

"Dolly, I get the distinct impression that you like a good tittle-tattle and a good old-fashioned moan." Too late – Jenny couldn't retract the words. All she could do was wait for the aftermath and by the expression on Dolly's face... it was going to be bad.

"I beg your pardon!"

"Sorry, Dolly. I'm just sick and tired of people sticking their nose in where it's not wanted." Jenny heaved a sigh. "I don't mean to dig at you... I've had a lot of problems to deal with lately."

"I've never been so insulted in all of my life." Dolly snatched her paper from the counter. "All I was saying was, the residents around here, may not like the new look of your shop. It sticks out from the rest."

"Look, I do apologise, Dolly. I've been stressed out and over-tired... and as for the residents... well, there are some very odd characters around here and I don't particularly value their opinion much anyway."

Dolly's mouth fell open. "And what do you mean by that?"

"Nothing that concerns you – I can assure you. You're probably one of the regulars that keeps me sane," Jenny lied. She had to lie. She didn't want to risk losing Dolly or any of the other dog-walking members of her little, in-house community centre. Dolly's gossipy potential could be capable of destroying all of that.

Dolly huffed. "You should have thought about all of that, my dear, before you took on the heavy burden of running your own shop... on your own... and at such a young, inexperienced age."

"Believe it or not but I am very experienced in the retail trade, Dolly." Jenny curbed the desire to tell her where to go.

"You can't have that much experience, dear, you're still a baby." Dolly sneered. "Now, when you get to my age," she continued, while waving a crooked finger in the air, "then you will have many, many years of experience."

"Ok, Dolly. Well, thanks for giving me your point of view. However, I do need the awning up there as the sun pours in through the windows, and it can get very hot. I've got a lot of chocolate here that could melt."

"If you'd been a little more experienced in these things, dear, you might have considered air conditioning."

"Can't afford it."

"So that's where experience comes in," said Dolly, placing one hand on a hip.

"Not sure how experience could afford me air-con."

"Experience is time. Time is money. Isn't that what they say?"

"No... well, yes – that is what they say, Dolly, but it doesn't mean that you get money from time – it's the opposite, in fact."

Dolly huffed, lifted her coat sleeve and peered at her watch. "Well I don't have any more time to waste. I've got choir practice this morning which, incidentally, doesn't cost me any money. Goodbye." Tucking the paper under her arm, Dolly left the shop, untied Wilbur and waddled off down the road.

Wanna meet for lunch today, I'm in your area?

Jenny tutted, and then typed a reply. *Thanks Calvin but I'm busy. Let's move on from here, please. I haven't got time for this.*

Just being friendly! You're so uncool these days – get a grip, Jen.

Dayna flew in the door at one minute past eight. "Sorry I'm late – bloody Xaylan – he's a pain to get up in the mornings."

"You're hardly late, Day. It's not a problem, at all."

Dayna raced off down the first aisle, to the staffroom. Moments later she returned, puffing and panting.

"You in a rush to go somewhere today?" asked Jenny, laughing at her friend. "And where's our tea and crumpets? Jenny frowned at the apparent urgency in Dayna's face.

"Yeah, will do, in a minute." Dayna walked behind the counter. "Have a good night, last night?" she whispered.

"Why are you whispering? There's no one in here."

Dayna grinned. "You never know in this place. Could be hidden microphones and cameras..."

"What?"

"Well, it's the psycho-shop in psycho-land isn't it?" Dayna sneered. "Probably got surveillance cameras on every street corner around here – to make sure that no one acts normal."

Jenny laughed. "For your information, I had a really nice evening. Went to a lovely restaurant, out in the sticks somewhere."

"And?"

"And then he drove me home."

"And?" Dayna leant closer. "And then?"

"And then he drove away and I went to bed."

"What – on your own?"

"On my own." Jenny shrugged. "Just me and teddy." Rolling her bottom lip, she fluttered her eyelashes, trying to look sad.

"Seriously? No way." Dayna frowned. "No sex then?"

"None." Jenny paused. "It's not like that. He's kissed me a couple of times – that's it."

"Don't you want to?"

"Hasn't crossed my mind." Jenny lied, for the second time in less than an hour.

Dayna peered, with narrowed eyes, into Jenny's eyes. "Thought you fancied him..."

"I do. It's just not that easy, Day. I don't get a lot of spare time, as you well know, and now he's gone off to Germany for the rest of the week." Jenny looked down. "I don't see it going very far, very quickly at all."

"Well you've got to work at it, Jen. He seems like a nice fella – don't let him slip."

"I won't... but I did say to you, only the other day, it's near on impossible for me to have a proper relationship at the moment."

"Nothing's impossible," said Dayna, grinning, as she passed by Jenny and left the counter. "Work at it – find time – don't sleep. Get some crumpet in your life... and in the meantime, I'll put the crumpets on."

Just ten minutes after Tasha had arrived, Jenny put her coat on and drew in a deep breath. "Right, I'm going up there," she said with conviction.

"Are we doing this?" asked Tasha, holding up the awning's remote control and smiling sarcastically. She had just read the latest note.

"If it wasn't so gloomy, I would have said yes – absolutely."

The awning couldn't go out today. Grey clouds had billowed past the window all morning, blown along by a chilly and furious, northern wind.

"I should be back in ten minutes – if not, call in the cavalry."

"Just be careful, Jen. Don't want you being hurled down the stairs or anything else like that," said Dayna. "I've got enough to do, without scraping you up off the floor."

"Ha-ha, very funny." Jenny edged towards the door. "Be back soon..."

The wind whistled around the railings at the top of the stairs. Letting go of the hand rail, Jenny stepped across the walkway. She rapped her knuckles on the front door, stood back and waited. And waited.

Looking across the car park, from this high level, Jenny could see the new housing estate in the distance. She wondered how many of the residents there knew that her shop existed, just a short side path away from them. It would be a shorter distance by foot, to travel to Jenny's shop than to go anywhere else in the surrounding area. In fact, Jenny's shop was nearer to the housing estate via any means of travel.

She tapped her knuckles on the half-glass door again.

"Who is it?" came a muffled voice from the other side of the door. A dark coloured curtain prevented Jenny from seeing the silhouette, in full, on the other side.

"Hello – this is Jenny, from downstairs."

"Who?"

"Jenny – I own the shop downstairs."

"What do you want?" The man's petulant voice was surly and unnerving.

"I'd like to talk to you if that's possible." Jenny bit her lip. *Was this the right thing to do?*

"What about?"

"Would it be possible to speak with you, face to face?"

"Why?"

"Rather than shouting through your door..." Jenny scanned the area, hoping that no one could hear her.

The front door clicked and opened slightly. "Spit it out then." The man spoke through the small gap although he still couldn't be seen.

"Look, I think we would both benefit from a quick chat about things. What do you think?" Jenny had now lowered her voice and felt far less vulnerable to any sort of repercussions that could have arisen by her shouting from the rooftops – well almost as high as the rooftop.

"Go on then..."

"I mean... well... could we arrange a meeting? Or could you come into the shop to talk to me?" Jenny thought for a moment. "Or could I come in to talk with you, here, now?"

"Naa..."

"Sorry?"

"Said, naa," repeated the man.

"Do you mean, no, you don't wish to talk about our issues?"

"Naa"

Jenny sighed, "Sorry, I'm confused. Can we talk or not?"

"Bout what?" The door opened a little further and Jenny could just make out a beady, dark eye, framed with wrinkles, glaring at her.

"About the notes that you have been posting." Jenny held her breath.

"What about 'em."

"Well this is what I mean – we need to have a chat – please. I don't want to be upsetting any of the locals and certainly not the residents here, which includes you," Jenny pleaded.

"Council can deal with it."

"But this is why I'm here. We could sort this out, between us. It doesn't need to go any further."

"Scared you'll get closed down…" the man sneered.

"No, I am not scared."

"Worried?"

A sharp, pointy nose protruded from the gap.

Jenny held her hands out to the sides and shook her head. "No. I'm here to help, not harm."

"Don't want your help." A little more of the man's face appeared. "Didn't ask for it – don't try and force it."

"I'm not trying to force it." Jenny huffed loudly. "I just want to resolve these problems with you."

"Speak to the council."

"I don't need to speak to the council."

"Will when I give 'em the notes." The man's creepy face came in to full view. "Taken copies, you know."

"Look, you don't have a leg to stand on…"

"You what?" The man's dark, empty eyes glared, frighteningly.

"You haven't got a leg to stand on – that's why I want to resolve it now."

"How dare you come round here and insult me. Who do you think you are?"

The man's raised voice sent a shiver through Jenny and she felt the prickle of her hair standing on end. She stepped back as he craned his neck round the door. "I have not insulted you in the slightest," she said, fretfully, as her face began to burn.

"You said I aint got a leg to stand on."

"Well you haven't... and if I was to be brutally honest, you have already been slandering my name in your notes and... and as for the banging noise... coming from your flat every day..."

The man flung the door wide open, furiously.

Jenny froze in fear.

Adrenalin pricked at her heart and raged through her veins.

She couldn't move.

Their eyes met.

A terrifyingly forceful pulse stuck in Jenny's throat and she gulped hard.

The man's murderously, savage eyes bore straight through Jenny's transfixed gaze.

Fearfully, in an attempt to look away, Jenny lowered her eyes and peered downwards...

Slowly, she brought both hands up to her mouth, which had just fallen open...

Sickness rose from the pit of her stomach...

The man held onto the door with long, spindly fingers. Dressed in a scruffy, un-ironed t-shirt and a pair of dirty, grey shorts, he continued to glare at Jenny's horrified, pale face.

Jenny took an involuntary step backwards, still clasping her hands to her mouth. Her eyes remained fixed and watery. Shaking her head, she couldn't peel her eyes away from the man's leg...

... The one that wasn't there...

"Oh my God," Jenny mumbled through her fingers. "Oh God... I'm... I'm so sorry..."

"Yeah... I 'aven't got a leg to stand on, you say. Well, I've got one good one, 'aven't I?"

Shaking her head from side to side, Jenny looked up at the man as the realisation of it all, struck her. "I'm truly sorry... really I am." Her watery eyes turned to single teardrops. "Please, can we talk?"

"Might as well now. Seen it all, 'aven't ya." The man hopped back towards the wall, inviting her to squeeze past him, into a long, dark corridor.

Shocked and afraid, Jenny walked through the door, abstractedly. Her senses fractured into a million pieces. The front door slammed shut, leaving her in complete darkness. Her heart pounded furiously. *Had this been a wise idea?* As Jenny's eyes adjusted, she noticed a glimmer of light filtering through, from underneath a door in front of her. "Through... here?" she whispered nervously, as she grappled around for a door handle. Her breathing had quickened and a dry mouth made it harder to speak, harder to gulp, harder to think...

"Go on..." said the man, right behind her.

She could feel his rancid breath on her hair and opened the door hurriedly. Bright light glared from the room, causing her to squint. Stepping into the room, she turned to see the man leaning against the wall in the corridor, fitting a prosthetic limb to the top of his left thigh.

"Sit down," said the man abruptly. "Go on, then."

Jenny turned round and saw a table and three chairs situated by the wide window, which she assumed was right above the shop front. Nervously she walked over to the table and pulled a chair out and sat down. To her right was a doorway to a very small kitchen and on her left a door to another room. Along the corridor there were two other doors, opposite each other. The room she was in smelt fresh and clean, almost flowery, although there were no flowers to be seen. The old, tattered furniture had probably seen the best of its days but it looked clean, all the same. Jenny rubbed her forehead and sighed as the man entered the room, with a limp.

"Go on then," the man said.

"Sorry?"

"What you got to say?" The man sat at the opposite end of the table and stretched his prosthetic limb out in front of him.

"I'm sorry... I didn't know..." Jenny struggled to find the right words. "I didn't know about your leg when I said... well... when I said what I said."

"About me not 'aving a leg to stand on."

"Yes, that."

The man shrugged his shoulders. "Probably 'aven't, 'ave I?"

"Look," Jenny said. "I really don't want to cause any problems for you. Could we possibly come to some sort of a truce?" Jenny sat with her hands clasped tightly together in her lap. A tightness grasped at her throat and her heartbeat thumped in her chest, furiously.

"Don't stress – it's sorted."

"Sorry?"

"Sorted. Forget it. Don't want knuckle-sandwiches do we..."

Jenny frowned and stared at the man. "I'm not really sure what you want from me."

"Me?" The man rubbed his plastic leg. "I don't want nothing. You came to my door... remember?"

"Yes I did. You've sent me two notes. I came to talk to you about them and see if we could come to some sort of agreement over the canopy and about the noise."

"Ah, forget it. Just bored – gave me something to do. Little moan here and there... does everyone good." The man stared hard at Jenny. "Get over yourself. You're not that important."

"Pardon?" Jenny didn't understand how this man was so hostile one minute and then so disinterested the next.

"Ignore the notes."

"Why the change of heart?"

The man shrugged his shoulders again and pushed out his bottom lip. "Got rhyming names..."

"Your name is...?"

Shaking his head, the man said, "Denny. And that's all you need to know."

"I'm pleased to meet you, Denny," said Jenny, extending a hand out, across the table.

Suddenly, Denny stood up and glared down at her. "Time to go. Goodbye."

Rising to her feet, shakily, Jenny looked at Denny pitifully. "Look, if there is anything I can do to help you out... at any time... please let me know."

"Don't need it, won't need it... will never need it. Goodbye."

Walking across the room, Jenny opened the door leading to the corridor. She now understood the thumping noise and could trace the pathway of noises by the layout of the flat. "Well, like I've just said – let me know if you need anything."

"Naa. Go."

Jenny hurried along the gloomy corridor, as fast as she could. Reaching the front door, she opened it quickly, allowing the daylight to flood in. Turning her head, she could see Denny stood at the other end. "I'll close the door for you."

Denny said nothing but his beady eyes continued to glare.

"Thank you for seeing me. Goodbye," said Jenny, as she stepped outside and closed the door behind her.

Inhaling a deep breath of cold air, she held it for a moment before letting out a long sigh. "Phew!" she breathed, before descending the staircase with shaky legs, and a puzzled mind.

Returning to the safety of her shop, Jenny realised how terrified she had been only moments ago.

"I was just going to send a search party out, Jen. Did it go ok? You look very pale."

Jenny nodded. "Err... I think it went ok..." Jenny felt the blood rushing back to her face and limbs. "...Actually, I'm not really sure at all." Moving across to the counter, she leant a trembling arm on the top of the till. "It was a very strange experience, Day. Really scary too."

"Go and enjoy the rest of your lunch break. You look like you need it. Put your feet up and I'll make a coffee. Then you can tell us about it," said Dayna, grinning. "I do like a bit of gossip."

Winking an eye at Tasha, Dayna left the counter and trotted off to the staffroom, two mugs chinking together in her hand.

"If there's no one in the shop, you come down too," said Jenny, forcing a smile.

Tasha nodded her head and smiled back. "I'll be down in a minute."

"Right, I'm off," said Dayna, reaching for her coat, hanging on a hook. "Hope you don't get any more weird notes before I return tomorrow... but if you do... let me go up there... please."

"I'm sure I won't... but if I do... no, you cannot go up there," replied Jenny sternly, but jokingly. "This is my problem if it continues, not yours."

"Only trying to help," Dayna smirked. "See you tomorrow then – Woohoo!"

Jenny looked at her friend, puzzled. "Why are you woo-hoo-ing?"

"Thursday," said Dayna with a surprised expression on her face, as if Jenny should know what she was talking about. "Tomorrow is closer to Thursday."

"What about Thursday..."

Dayna tutted and rolled her eyes upwards. "Thursday... Will..."

"Thursday will be what?"

"Will!" Dayna snorted. "You've forgotten haven't you? Mind you, it won't affect you anyway as I don't work Thursday afternoons."

"You've lost me, Day."

"Will – dentist – Xaylan's tooth – remember?"

"Oh, yes." Jenny smiled. "I did forget. Sorry. Woo...hoo."

Dayna tutted again. "See ya laters," she said, winking her mascaraed lashes, before walking out of the staffroom.

Hey, how are things going with you? Any more calamities since I've been away, lol. Aaron x

Jenny hugged her phone to her chest, while composing a reply in her head.

Not really any calamities, unless you can call the terrifying experience I had at lunchtime today, a public relations disaster? Jen x

Waiting for a reply, Jenny sifted through the paperwork on her desk. She came across the two handwritten notes from Denny, screwed them up and threw them in the bin. As far as she was concerned, the matter had been dealt with. As for the thumping sounds, well, they would be something she would have to live with and vice versa, Denny would have to live with the canopy being opened from time to time.

Sorted.

Jenny picked the garage repair bill up and looked at it. Reaching for the phone, she dialed the garage's number.

"Hello, my name is Jenny Fartor. I would like to pay a bill please. Do you take debit cards over the phone?"

Sorted.

Going in to a meeting now but I can call you later if you want to talk. Aaron x

Cool. Close at 8pm – should be home by about 8.45 at latest. Jen x

Something to look forward to. A chat with Aaron, this evening. Jenny was excitably-happy, at last.

Sorted.

Chapter 26

The hours ticked by way to slowly in the afternoon. The dreary weather seemed to have kept people away from the shop and the takings had slumped to a record low. Jenny kept both herself and Tasha busy with menial tasks of re-stocking, cleaning and dusting shelves, tidying the store room and sweeping the floors.

Peering up at the clock on the wall, Jenny noted the time was approaching five o'clock. "Thought the *Bits & Bobs* rep was coming out today," she mumbled. "Don't expect anyone will turn up now," she huffed, loudly.

"Ooh, I love their savoury snacks," said Tasha, cheerily. "I'll be buying loads of that stuff from you... my mum loves their stuff too."

"Hmm..." Jenny replied. "Well, it doesn't look like they'll be here today... unless of course they went to Marj's house instead. Now that wouldn't surprise me at all."

Tasha let out a snigger. "No, wouldn't surprise me either. Have you seen her lately?"

"No, I expect she's too scared to come in – especially now that her daughter has been in here."

"The horse-woman."

"Hmm... Hee-haw." replied Jenny, with a wry smile.

"Ooh!" blurted Tasha. "I get it. Hee-haw!" As soon as she'd said it, Tasha let out a burst of consecutive hee-haws, each one louder than the one before. She couldn't stop it. The more she tried the worse it became.

Jenny laughed too and soon came to the conclusion that Tasha's hee-haws were the highlight of their very dull afternoon.

"I'll see you tomorrow, Jen," said Tasha. "Is it ok if I call you, Jen?"

"Yes of course you can." Jenny laughed. "Call me whatever you like - I answer to most things."

Tasha smiled and walked out of the door.

As Jenny approached the door to lock it, a figure appeared from the darkness on the other side. The tiny silhouette of Marj stood against the door, peering in through the glass.

"Oh my God, Marj – you made me jump," said Jenny, pulling the door open wide. "You're lucky, I was just about to close."

Marj grinned sheepishly and stepped through the doorway. "I need some bird seed, dear."

Shaking her head, Jenny replied, "I still haven't got anything like that, Marj. Sorry."

"Oh, never mind – just some toilet rolls then. I really must have a clear out..."

"Sorry?"

"A clear out. The cage. They're messy little birdies."

"Oh, I see," laughed Jenny. "For a moment there I thought you meant that *you* needed a clear out..." Jenny laughed out loud. "You know, what with asking for toilet rolls. For a clear out" Bursting into a raucous guffaw, Jenny crossed her legs and held on to the open door. "Sorry Marj – I'm going hysterical these days." Then she laughed some more.

Shooting a swift, confused glance in Jenny's direction, Marj moved away and proceeded down the first aisle. "I'll just get some toilet rolls, thank you. I'll only be a minute and then you can close up."

"Ok," squeaked Jenny as tears rolled down her face. "Tell me, Marj, how do you use toilet roll?" She closed the door and stood at the top end of the aisle with her hands on her hips.

Marj turned and glared. "I beg your pardon?"

Jenny let out another roar of laughter and held her stomach as she leant over. "Oh dear," she spluttered. "You do make me laugh." Jenny looked up to see Marj scowling at her, whilst clutching a four-roll pack of turquoise toilet-rolls. This made Jenny laugh even louder. "Oh God, I'm sorry Marj – I've got a fit of the giggles tonight."

Marj frowned, fiercely. "I need toilet rolls to clear out the bird's cage." Marj thought for a moment and then added, "And you use our dear Lord's name in vain, far too often."

"Ok, I apologise," said Jenny, desperately trying not to laugh again. "While you're here though, could we have a very quick chat?"

"About what?"

"Your daughter came in to see me the other day…"

"Did she?"

"Yes, she's quite concerned about you." Jenny sensed that Marj already knew that her daughter had been into the shop.

"Huh…" huffed Marj. "You have to watch her you know. Trouble-maker, she is."

"I'm sure that she's just worried about you… and she cares about you."

"Huh." Marj tottered up the aisle and walked over to the counter. "She's trouble. Watch out my dear. Trouble with a capital T."

"Well anyway, I wanted to talk to you about the shop, not your daughter."

"I'm not giving you any more money for your shop, my love."

Jenny scowled, "What do you mean 'more money' for my shop?" She moved behind the counter and scanned the toilet rolls. "To be brutally honest with you, Marj, I'm surprised that you are actually paying for these toilet rolls today, let alone anything else."

Marj gave a questioning look and then pulled her fat purse out from her coat pocket. "Well they're not free anymore, are they? So that's why I'm paying for them."

Jenny clenched her teeth and puffed out her cheeks. Exhaling through gritted teeth, she rolled her eyes. "Marj, I think there has been an awful mix up somewhere along the line. My toilet rolls were never free."

"I see," said Marj, routing through the coins in her purse.

"No, I don't think you do see... And what did you mean about 'more money'?"

"You want more money?" Marj pulled a five pound note from a zipped compartment. "This is all I've got – will that do?" she asked, handing the note to Jenny.

"Yes, that will pay for the toilet rolls." Jenny quickly counted out some change and gave it back. "And here's your change."

"Oh, why thank you my dear. I get some change – that's very good of you."

"I always give change where change is due."

"Hmm," muttered Marj.

"Now, what about this money that you're on about?"

"I'll get it from the bank tomorrow, dear."

"Argh!" screeched Jenny, making Marj look up with a horrified expression on her powdered face. "I do not want your money, Marj. I really don't know where you have got this idea from." Clapping her hands to her cheeks, Jenny peered despairingly at the little old lady. A sudden fear rose in her stomach. What would she do if Marj did go and get money from the bank? What wacky notion would Marj come up with next? "This has got to stop Marj – please."

"You don't want the money now?" asked Marj, quite innocently. "Then why did you ask me about it?"

"I didn't. I never have. I never will. This has all been one humongous mess-up. I... do not... want... your money!"

"It was all your idea, dear. I really don't know why you are getting yourself so worked up about it. Being so het up is no good for you."

"Ok, Marj, let's just leave it at that shall we? I can't handle this anymore." Jenny sighed. "You're right, I really shouldn't be getting so worked up about it."

"You must be working too hard, dear. Take some time off – have a rest."

Jenny nodded her head in agreement but said nothing. Deflated and numb, she realised that she had been out-done by a little, old lady. She didn't have the will or way to fight against her anymore. "Will that be all, Marj?"

Marj nodded and grinned. "Yes thank you, dear. I'll be off now and don't forget to get some rest. Maybe a check-up at the doctors is in order. You seem to be deluded my dear – deluded I say…"

"I'm what?" Jenny's face burned with frustration but it was too late, Marj had scuttled out of the door and disappeared, leaving Jenny scowling alone.

The muffled ring of her phone made Jenny tut. *Damn, it's probably Aaron calling.* Her phone continued to ring inside her bag on the back seat of the car. She was late getting home and it was all due to Marj once again. After the silly old woman had left the shop, Jenny had flapped about in a furious frenzy, trying to concentrate on cashing up, ordering the milk delivery for tomorrow and locking up. She'd gone to pieces – maybe she did need to see a doctor. Maybe she was deluded. She wasn't sure that she knew anything about anything any longer.

After the third attempt to call Aaron's phone, Jenny sighed and gave up. She was too tired to care anymore and resigned herself to the fact that she needed a bath and bed as soon as possible. Another day at *J's Convenience Store* would be here before she could blink.

Sorry I missed your call, Aaron. Marj came in the shop late (just as I was about to lock up, actually), which made me late home, but that's another story. Hopefully catch up with you soon. Jen x

Opening her eyes in the darkness, Jenny glanced at the alarm clock. *Great, it's 4.15am*, she thought and turned over. And then she began to think about everything. Think, think and think. She could not get back to sleep. By 4.35am, she was angry. She had to be up, at the very latest, in 55 minutes. Think, think and think some more. What was she thinking about? Nothing really. She was just thinking about thinking which stopped her from sleeping. She sat up in her bed, in the darkness and sulked for a while. Then she laid back down... and began to think even more.

Shuffling through to the living room, Jenny picked her phone up from the coffee table and looked at it. A message from Aaron must have come through after she'd gone to bed last night (well, just a few, sorry hours ago, in fact).

Hi Jen, sorry couldn't get back to you, battery died and I ended up down in the bar having a few drinks until late. Aaron x

No problem, hope this message doesn't wake you up. I'm up at a ridiculous time of the morning, can't sleep. Speak soon, Jen x

Chapter 27

The familiar thumping noise was somehow comforting this morning. Jenny looked up to the ceiling and pictured the man upstairs, hopping from one room to another. She imagined that it must be incredibly hard work to hop around everywhere. Smiling to herself, she carried on sorting Jordan's newspapers, ready for his delivery, while the thumping continued above her head. It really didn't bother her anymore.

Jenny had used the extra hour awake to convince herself not to let things bother her so much in the future. After all, they never used to. She seemed to have lost the plot just recently, hardly surprising though, when she'd had to contend with the likes of the nursery manager and owner, the man upstairs, Marj and a strained income to boot. And then to top it all, Aaron had swanned into her life causing no end of confusion to her new, self-created, celibate existence.

Tasha arrived punctually, as always and wafted past the counter with a big grin on her face. "Morning," she chirped, before disappearing down the aisle.

The usual clique of oldies, chatted in a circle in front of the counter, while several dogs sulked or snarled outside, tied up to the rings under the windows.

Andrea from the nursery breezed past the window with a snooty air about her, carrying several carrier bags of shopping which she'd obviously bought from the *KO Store*.

Jenny chuckled to herself, if the stuck-up cow wanted to spend more time, money and effort getting her groceries down the road, then so be it. Jenny's laid-back attitude was going to get her through the morning, through anything that might crop up in this crazy neighbourhood and through the rest of the day. She hoped.

Lunchtime arrived before Jenny had realised how quickly the time had gone. Lost in her own little world out the back, in her office, she had drifted through the morning on auto-pilot.

Having placed an order with the *Bob's Bits & Bobs* rep earlier (the rep had apologised for not turning up yesterday because his grandmother had become ill suddenly. Hmm – not convincing), Jenny proceeded to do a bulk order of Christmas lines from her other suppliers. It was very late to be getting Christmas stock in but she had to at least make an effort to stock those festive essentials.

"Yoo-hoo, only me," said Dayna, poking her head around the door. "It's lunchtime, you know."

Jenny looked up through glassy eyes. "Yeah, I know. Been busy ordering Christmas stuff."

"Already?"

"No not already, Day. I should have ordered it back in September and got it straight out onto the shelves then."

"Hmm, suppose so. They all do that don't they? Bit stupid if you ask me. Some places put their Christmas stuff out while the kids are still having their school summer holidays."

Jenny laughed. "Yes, I know – well that will be us next year... if I last that long."

Dayna stepped into the office. "Course you will, Jen. Why do you say that?"

Shrugging her shoulders, Jenny huffed. "Ah, don't worry. I'm just tired that's all."

"Have a kip for a couple of hours," said Dayna, quietly. "We'll hold the fort and if anyone wants you, we'll say you're out."

Jenny smiled up at her friend. "Thanks, Day. I'm tempted, I have to admit. I was awake at stupid-o'clock this morning and couldn't get back to sleep."

"It's probably catching up with you."

"I think it definitely is."

"Make sure you have a nap... oh, and have you done those leaflets yet?"

"No... why do you ask?"

"When will they be ready?" Dayna shifted on her feet, looking decidedly cagey.

"I've done the leaflet. I haven't been out to get any ink for the printer yet though. Why?"

"No reason... I... I just wondered if you'd done them yet. You know, we need to get those customers rolling in don't we?"

"Yes – absolutely. Not sure how we'll get them all delivered though..."

"Ah, well don't worry yourself with that, Jen." Dayna grinned cunningly. "I have a plan."

"Oh no, not another one of your plans..."

"This is a good one – trust me... and I've got another idea too."

Jenny pulled herself up in her seat. "Go on then," she said, wearily. "I'm all ears."

"Ok, hear me out," said Dayna, closing the office door behind her. "Kids break up for Christmas about a week before Christmas day, right?"

Jenny nodded her head, nonchalantly. "Yes, go on."

"So for a week they are bored stupid – yes?"

"Yes, suppose so."

"They are, trust me, I should know." Dayna rolled her eyes. "Xaylan is an absolute pain in the arse just before Christmas."

"Ok," agreed Jenny. "Where's this going?"

"Jeffers-Bubble-Bon-Bon!"

"Jeffers-bloody what?"

"The balloon man – remember? We saw him down at the seafront last year." Dayna hesitated for a moment. "You must remember Jeffers?"

"I do vaguely remember a balloon man, yes," said Jenny, thoughtfully. "What's his name?"

"Jeffers-Bubble-Bon-Bon."

"What sort of a ridiculous name is that?"

Dayna lowered her head. "Yeah, I know. Stupid name... but he was good wasn't he?"

"Suppose so. But how can a balloon man with a stupid name help us here?"

"Well, I texted him last night, Jen. We...err... well, I still had his number." Dayna cringed and added, "We... no, I mean, I... err... ended up seeing him... last year. And err... I... well... I met up with him. And I... gave him a blow job, down on the common. So he owes me big time." Dayna flushed red and held her hands up in the air. "Yes, I know – I never told you about it. I was so ashamed afterwards. Yes, it's sickening."

Jenny stared at her friend in shocked horror. "No... you never told me... Oh God, Dayna. How could you? I can't believe you've never told me."

"Well there wasn't really anything to tell. It was all over in a few minutes. He blew his balloons and I blew him."

"Seriously? Oh no. Do you mean at the same time?"

Dayna nodded her head ashamedly. "Yep. He was a bit perverted. I didn't go back for seconds."

"I'm relieved to hear it," said Jenny, astounded by her friend's revelation. "So why have you contacted him again?"

"Saw an advert in the paper. He's doing Christmas themed balloon shows."

"Not sure we could have a balloon show in here."

"No, he would stand outside. Hopefully encourage kids to use the shop more. He's willing to do a doorstep display for next to nothing."

"And what do you mean by next to nothing exactly?" Jenny cringed. "I hope he doesn't think he's getting a double-whammy balloon blowing session?"

"No, of course not." Dayna tutted and rolled her eyes. "He'll do a big arched balloon display for our door, dress up as Santa and make Christmas themed balloons for the kids."

"And how much will all of that cost?"

"Seventy-five quid. Cash in hand. He said he could book us in on the 23rd December, for the afternoon."

"Go on then," replied Jenny. "I do hope that I'm not going to regret this."

"You won't – I promise you, Jen. He also has a little balloon-craft book which can be given away free if customers spend a certain amount in the shop. You'll have to work the percentage rates and costings out with him."

Jenny nodded her head, half-heartedly. "Ok, I suppose it won't hurt to give it a go."

Fumbling through her bag, Dayna pulled out a roll of A4 posters. "I printed these off from his website – we could start advertising the fact that he will be coming here in December, now."

Jenny took a poster and scanned the details. It seemed reasonable enough. "Why the hell does he call himself that?" asked Jenny, pointing to the swirly, turquoise writing at the top of the page. "Where does the 'bubble' and the 'bon-bon' bit come into it?"

"He blows bubbles," said Dayna, defensively. "Don't you remember?"

Jenny burst into laughter. "I don't want to hear gory details about his sex life, Day."

Dayna glared. "Very funny. Not those kind of bubbles, you dirty mare. Giant bubbles – you know, with giant wands."

"Oh, I see," said Jenny, suppressing a giggle. "And the bon-bon?"

Dayna tutted again. "Sweets – obviously."

"What does he do with those?"

"Throws them into the crowd. Jenny, don't you remember anything from when we saw him last year?"

"Yes, of course I do, now that you mention it."

"It was you who got smacked in the knee when a pile of kids threw themselves at your feet, trying to grab the sweets from the floor."

"Yes, I do remember now. What I don't recall is you disappearing off to give him a blow-job on the common. How did that happen?"

"Oh, let's just forget it..." said Dayna, screwing her face up. "Never doing that again."

"I should think not." Jenny screwed her nose up in disgust. "I do need to know though. Did you sneak off when I or Xaylan weren't looking?"

"No," Dayna scowled. "No I did not just sneak off. I'm not going to do that in broad daylight, am I?"

"Well I don't know, Day. Did you?"

"No! I went back that night. On my own," said Dayna, agitation rising in her voice. "Can we just forget it now?"

Jenny nodded her head and grinned. "All forgotten. So what's this other plan you have? Given anyone else a blow-job that I don't know about, have you?"

Dayna shook her head. "No, I haven't. You'll have to wait and see... just get those leaflets printed." Dayna smirked and then left the office.

Jenny couldn't decide between sleep or printer ink and as she sat in her comfy chair, pondering over the decision she had to make, her mind was made up for her. Within minutes, she fell into a deep and peaceful sleep.

Waking with a start, Jenny looked up at the clock on the wall. Five minutes to two. She'd been asleep for a good hour and a half. On the other side of the office door, she could hear the sound of the new till, bleeping away merrily. Dragging herself to her feet, she went through to the staffroom and flicked the kettle on, just as Tasha came in to collect her coat and bag.

"You alright?"

"Yes," Jenny replied, rubbing her hands over her face. "Just woke up actually. Can't believe I've slept so long."

"You must be tired, working here so long every day."

Jenny nodded her head and reached for two mugs. "Yeah, I must be. Can't believe I've slept so long."

"Is it ok if I go now?"

"Yes, of course. Tell Dayna, I'll be out in a minute."

"Ok. I'll see you tomorrow."

Carrying two coffees, cautiously along the aisle, Jenny paused midway and noticed that Dayna was stood behind the till mouthing something to her. With a contorted face, Dayna was desperately trying to say something but her words were totally indecipherable. Then she pointed to the other aisle and mouthed something again. Shaking her head, Jenny frowned and mouthed back, 'what?'

"I said 'Marj'. She's in here," said Dayna, as Jenny reached the counter and placed the two mugs on a shelf.

"Oh, is she? Didn't look like you said that."

"M, A, R, J. That's what I was saying."

Jenny laughed. "Do you think she can't spell now?"

Dayna gave a friendly slap to Jenny's arm. "Don't you want to speak to her?"

"She came in last night, just as I was locking up. It's hopeless. There's just no talking to her. She twists everything."

"Leave her to me, Jen. I'll deal with her."

"She's all yours. I can't get through to her." Jenny picked her coffee up from the shelf and stood by the window, slurping the sweet drink. "I'll stand here and watch."

"I'll go and see if she wants any help... probably wants more toilet rolls. Should I let her buy any?"

"Up to you. Her daughter did say that she's got piles of them stacked up next to her toilet but what can we do? Marj says she uses them for her birds – and she is actually paying for them again."

Dayna left the counter and walked over to the first aisle. "Afternoon, Marj," she said, before disappearing down the aisle.

The front door opened and a familiar looking woman walked in and went over to the magazine shelves to browse. Jenny had seen her face before but couldn't quite place her. Glancing up at the mirror, she could see Dayna and Marj, half way down the aisle, having a chat about something.

The woman by the magazines, peered up to the ceiling once or twice and by the third time she had done it, Jenny realised where she'd seen her before. She was the woman who came in one evening and commented about the banging noises coming from the ceiling. In fact, up until that time, she had been the *only* other person to have heard it.

Approaching the counter, with a gardening magazine and the evening news, the woman placed them on the counter top and drew her purse from her conservatively brown handbag. "Afternoon," she mumbled.

"Good afternoon," said Jenny cheerily. "Anything else?" she asked, having scanned the items.

"No, just those – thanks."

"That'll be three pounds, seventy five please." Taking the five pound note from the woman, Jenny grinned and wondered whether she should mention the ceiling noises again.

"Do you still get the noises all day?" asked the woman, raising her eyes upward.

"Well, it's not all day," Jenny replied. "Mainly first thing in the morning and last thing at night."

The woman nodded. "Bet it drives you up the wall."

"I have been to speak to him…"

The woman looked up from her purse, which she had been putting her change into, with a startled expression. "You've been up there?"

"Yes. I went yesterday. Had a few things to sort out."

"You're brave…"

"Why do you say that?" Jenny gave a puzzled stare. "Ok, I admit he's a bit scary but why do you think I was brave?"

"He's crazy." The woman's face was deadly serious. "I know him," she added, worriedly.

"Oh ok," Jenny replied, unsure of what to say, by the look of terror on the woman's face. "How do you know him?"

"My best friend… she… err… used to be his wife…"

Out of the corner of her eye, Jenny could see Dayna and Marj at the bottom of the second aisle, looking in the direction of the freezers. Then Marj quickly scuttled over to the freezer and almost threw herself in, obviously trying to reach for another cheesecake. Dayna shot up behind her and pulled her back, waving a finger in Marj's face and no doubt telling her off for overstretching. Dayna then reached over herself and pulled out a dessert.

"Oh, I see," said Jenny. "So… I'm assuming they're divorced now, as you said, 'used to be'."

"No…" The woman hesitated. "No… she's err…" Lowering her head the woman continued in a low, sombre voice. "She's dead now."

"Oh… I am so sorry to hear that." Jenny was uncomfortable and struggled to find the right thing to say. "So… err… the man upstairs – he is your friend's widow? I assume?"

"Killer," the woman snapped back.

"Pardon?" Jenny gulped hard, not liking the way this conversation was going.

"Killer," the woman repeated. "He's her killer."

"Oh my God... really? How do you know that?" Jenny shuffled from one foot to the other, feeling awkward and wishing that Marj would hurry up with her shopping so that Dayna could come to the counter.

"He got done for it."

"Oh gosh. I'm so sorry to hear this. How terrible."

"He's been up there..." said the woman, pointing to the ceiling, "...for the last three years – since he came out of prison."

Jenny cupped her hand over her mouth and stared wide-eyed as the realisation took hold.

"Went in a mental hospital for about eleven years and then he was in prison for the last seven."

"I... I can't believe it. So he got put away for 18 years?"

The woman nodded. "Yes... so be careful. Don't mess with him," she warned.

Shaking her head, Jenny mouthed a big, fat 'Noooo'. "No, I won't be messing with him, don't you worry. Err... well, umm... how did he... I mean, do you know?"

"How he killed her?" The woman finished the sentence for Jenny.

"Yes, do you know?"

The woman nodded slowly and then gazed down at her feet, sorrowfully. "Yes, I know... I was there..."

Dayna and Marj had finished routing through the freezer and were edging ever nearer to the counter. Willing Marj to hurry up, Jenny also sent a psychic message to Dayna, not that either of them had any psychic powers, but she willed her to get over to the counter, as quickly as possible. Jenny hated awkward situations like this and it was going from bad to worse by the second.

The woman continued. "I remember it like it was yesterday."

"That must be terrible." Jenny shook her head sorrowfully.

"Yes it is," the woman agreed. "It's like a living nightmare." Shooting a glance behind her and then around the shop the woman's twitchy eyes returned to meet Jenny's.

"I'm sure it must be a nightmare for you…"

The woman nodded and sighed heavily. "Me and Jessie were at the train station – going to London – work, you know. He'd dropped us off in the morning, like he always used to…" The woman's voice lowered, "…before he lost his license." She turned and looked behind her again, then out of the window and along the road. Turning back the woman peered down the length of the shop and appeared to shudder. "Does he come in here?"

"No, he has never been in here since we opened."

"Good," the woman replied and looked more at ease.

"So, you were saying – he lost his license, his driving license?" asked Jenny, curiously.

The woman nodded her head and continued. "Yes, dangerous driving. He got done for driving along the wrong side of the motorway. Could have caused a big accident. He had insisted on driving us to the station that day though, in Jessie's car. Said he wouldn't get caught and it was a one-off. He promised he wouldn't do it again. Said he wanted a go, one last time before his ban was made an order in the court."

"That's not good." Jenny began to chew her fingernails and then stopped abruptly and wrapped her arms around herself and tucked her hands underneath her armpits. A self-cuddle was the only comfort she could get as she continued to listen, intently.

"Station was only five minutes away so we thought it would be ok, just a quick trip, you know what I mean."

"Yes, of course… easily done, I know what you mean." Jenny shot a swift glance down the aisle. Marj was rummaging through the crisps, knocking packets onto the floor and creating a mess. Dayna picked the crisps up and tidied up behind Marj, in what Jenny thought was a very angry way.

"He had been acting strange though. You know, totally weird, since he'd gone up the motorway, three weeks before."

"Why did he do that?" asked Jenny, getting more and more intrigued but more and more worried that this man lived right above her head. And the really scary thing was that she had been alone inside his flat, only a short time ago.

"Said he made a mistake. Six miles and two junction slip roads is no mistake."

"God, no. He could have left the motorway surely."

The woman shrugged her shoulders. "Jess couldn't see it though..."

"See it?"

"Yea, see that he was getting weird."

"Oh, I see."

"Things she told me... I knew it wasn't right." The woman frowned and shook her head from side to side.

"I'm so sorry, it must be very hard for you," said Jenny, sympathetically. "You really don't have to tell me, if it's too difficult."

"No, it's fine. I don't ever talk about him anymore. It's just that my mum... well, she lives over the road. Bit awkward. We didn't know he lived here when my mum first moved in."

"Oh, ok. That is such a shame for you. And for your mum."

"Well, I suppose they had to put him somewhere... give him another chance. He can rot in hell as far as I'm concerned. We found out about a year ago, that he lived here."

The woman's face broke into a smile and Jenny smiled back briefly. "Sorry if I'm pestering you."

"No, not at all. I'm glad that you've told me. I met him yesterday, he is very strange. I found out why he makes thumping noises every day..."

The woman screwed her face up, in anguish. "Yes – nasty…"

"I did think there was something very strange about him, when I met him. He's very creepy, if you ask me."

"Yes, that's exactly how I used to feel about him… once he'd changed. Jess just couldn't see it. I tried to tell her. I tried. If only she'd listened…"

Jenny stared pitifully. "Please… don't be hard on yourself."

"I hope you don't mind me off-loading on you like this."

"No, not at all. I'm a good listener and I'm extremely grateful that you are telling me this to be honest."

The woman nodded and smiled weakly. "I thought you'd want to know – need to know."

Bravely, Jenny asked the pressing question. "So what happened after he'd dropped you both at the train station? Please don't feel that you have to answer the question. I'm just being really nosey now."

"No, that's fine. We were waiting for our train – it all happened so quickly." The woman's face turned serious again. "I thought he'd left the station after dropping us off. Me and Jess… Jess and I were stood on the platform talking." The woman paused and looked up to the ceiling. "He'd been waiting – on the platform – behind us."

"Waiting?"

"For the train." The woman's face twisted and contorted as she was obviously re-living the event in her mind. "Next thing I knew, he'd thrown himself at Jess, from behind." Rubbing her brow the woman flicked her eyes around again, scanning the shop and the road outside, before continuing. "They both… Denny and Jess… they went hurtling over the edge of the platform, together."

Jenny pulled her hands from her warm underarms and held them across her mouth. Reading between the lines, she knew what was coming next.

"The train. It hit them." The woman paused again. "Jessie was gone. Instantly – apparently."

Sickness rose in Jenny's stomach. "And he survived."

The woman nodded a furrowed brow.

"Is that why... his leg?" Jenny mumbled, through fingers still clutched around her mouth.

The woman nodded again and stared, silently, a pained expression etched on her face.

"You ok, Jen."

The sound of Dayna's voice brought Jenny down from her heightened state of alarm. Turning towards her friend she slowly pulled her hands away from her mouth and stared dumbfounded at her.

"Jen? You alright?"

Jenny nodded her head. "Yes... sorry. Err, right – Marj – Just that today?" Jenny picked the strawberry cheesecake up from the counter and scanned it as the woman moved away from the counter.

"I'd better be off," said the woman, tucking the paper and magazine under her arm. "Thanks for the chat."

"Any time," said Jenny. "And... thank you. For... for letting me know. Thank you."

The woman nodded her head. "I hope I'll see you again." She left the shop, hurriedly.

Jenny watched her walk across the road and then disappear out of sight.

"Jen... Jenny, are you sure you're ok?"

"How much, my dear?" asked Marj.

"Err... yes, err... sorry Marj, err..."

"Let me do it," said Dayna, shuffling Jenny away from the till. "You look like you've seen a ghost, Jen. Go and warm these coffees up, they've gone cold." Dayna passed the two mugs to Jenny and shooed her away.

"So who was that woman?"

She knows the man upstairs," said Jenny, carefully placing the steaming mugs of coffee back under the shelf. "She's just told me all about him."

"Must have been pretty bad by the look on your face."

Jenny nodded. "It was. It is. We seriously need to avoid him, Day."

"Why?"

"He's worse than we could ever have imagined..." Jenny paused for a moment and then added. "He's a murderer!"

Dayna stopped, mid sip of her drink. "Bloody hell. Are you sure?"

Nodding her head, Jenny continued. "Yep – sure. He's done time for it..."

"Blimey," Dayna replied and then took a sip from her coffee. "Guess I won't be going up there to have a word with him myself then."

"Why?" Jenny snapped. "Why were you going to go up there?"

"After he deliberately tried to spit on me the other day, remember?" Dayna cupped her hands around her mug and leant against the counter. "I was going to have it out with him."

"Well don't. Please Day, let it go – he's crazy."

"I can well believe that now. So come on," said Dayna, inching closer to her friend, "tell me more."

Chapter 28

Jordan's fresh, smiley face was a joy to see every morning. His cheeky smile was warming and always seemed to melt away any troubles or woes that Jenny might have at the time. He'd heard the thumping noises several times now and always looked up and commented about it. However, there was no way that Jenny would let him know what she now knew about the mad man who lived above.

Leaving the shop with a cheery smile and a wave goodbye as always, Jordan jumped on his bike and rode down the road, his fluorescent delivery bag bouncing about on his back.

Jenny sighed and looked up to the ceiling. That crazy man, Denny, had been on her mind permanently, since the woman had revealed all, yesterday. So much so that Jenny had googled the train incident, which happened over twenty years ago, and discovered that it had made headline news at the time – which wasn't surprising at all. The story behind Denny and Jessie's treacherous marriage, the suspicious death of their first-born child while in Jessie's care and her own string of sordid affairs was a harrowing report to read. But Jenny couldn't help herself. She could not stop thinking about him or what happened and she couldn't help feeling sorry for Denny. She didn't know why she felt sorry for him but she did.

Wouldn't Dolly just love to know the horrific story of the psycho living upstairs, thought Jenny, as she watched the queen of gossip tie her poor little pooch to a ring outside, brush something off her coat hem and then totter into the shop.

"Good morning Dolly."

"Good morning, dear. Lovely day again. Think we're still having that late, Indian summer – if there is such a thing and in November too – unheard of." Dolly chuckled and went to fetch her usual paper.

"Yes, it is nice. Better make the most of it. Could be pouring down or even snowing by this time next week."

"Snow?" said Dolly, stopping in her tracks. "Are we expecting snow?"

"No, Dolly, I was just saying that it would be possible at this time of year."

"Well anything's possible, dear. Why would you mention snow? Have you heard something?"

Jenny shook her head and tutted. "No I haven't – I was just saying."

"Why would you just be saying that? I do hope you're not trying to frighten an old lady."

"No, I'm not, Dolly. For goodness sake... I was just making conversation with you."

"Why? What do you know? What's going on?"

Jenny bit her bottom lip in frustration. "Nothing, Dolly! Can we just forget it?"

"Now you're telling me half the story. Either you tell me everything, dear, or don't bother at all." Dolly frowned. "I don't have time for silly games you know."

"Of course you don't," Jenny replied. *But I bet you'd have all the time in the world if I told you about the man upstairs*, thought Jenny. Trying to change the subject, she continued, "Have you got choir practice today?"

"Yes. We have a lot to do now, in preparation for the Christmas period."

Jenny nodded. "I'm sure you do."

"You should have some Christmas lines, dear. You won't do very well if you haven't got Christmas lines."

"I do have some bits out already," said Jenny, defensively. "I've got a lot more being delivered next week." *Not that you would bother to look or buy anything*, Jenny thought to herself.

"Hmm, a little late, if you ask me."

I'm not asking you. "Yes, it is but that's because I opened late," said Jenny, trying to keep her cool, like every other time that Dolly decided to give her unwanted opinions. *And what's it got to do with you anyway?*

The clickity-clack of Dayna's heels told Jenny that it was fast approaching eight o'clock. Dressed in an electric blue, shift dress and matching shoes, Dayna looked elegant as she waltzed into the shop. Her dark hair fell in swirls down her back and her expertly applied make-up was appealing. With a smirk and a wink to Jenny, she sauntered past the elderly social group and tottered down the aisle.

Ten minutes later, Dayna came padding up the aisle with two hot drinks. "Morning," she chirped, through a wide grin.

Jenny gave her a puzzled look. "Morning," she replied. "You do look funny in that dress... and flip-flops."

Dayna peered down at her feet. "Well I'm not wearing those shoes in here all morning. They'd kill me."

"So why are you wearing them at all?"

"Jenny," said Dayna, stiffly. "What day is it today?"

"Thursday..."

"Exactly." Dayna huffed and moved over to the till to serve a man who had been eyeing her up.

Waiting for the man to leave, Jenny watched as Dayna flirtatiously served him, chatted to him briefly, and then said her goodbyes. "So what does that mean – exactly?"

"Oh, Jen. You'd be dangerous if you had a brain and could remember anything."

Jenny raked through her mind but couldn't think of anything that might be happening on this day. Mind you, every day seemed to be full of surprises around here. "You've got me," she said, scratching her head, in thought.

"Duh – Dentist?"

Jenny tutted and rolled her eyes. "Should have known that by the way you're dressed."

Dayna grinned widely. "He fancies me – I know it. Gonna ask him out..."

"Really?" said Jenny, desperately hoping that her dearest friend was making the right decision. "What if he says no? Your son is his client remember – I'd imagine they don't date their clients or their client's mums."

"He will, Jen. Don't you worry. By the time I've finished with him he'll be begging for more."

Jenny cringed as a vision of Dayna, leaning over the dentist while he stretched out on the chair, entered her mind. "Don't rush it, Day."

"I'm not. Watch this space. He wants me – I know it."

"Just don't be a cheap thrill for him, Dayna. Do not go down the route of that bloody Jeffers-bubble-what-not, will you?"

"I'm hardly going to throw him on the treatment chair, yank his pants down and give him a blow-job, am I?"

"Well it's funny that you should say that. That's exactly what I was thinking."

"Jenny Fartor – you should think more highly of me. I'd at least lock the door first!"

Jenny laughed out loud. "Seriously, Day, don't you think you should hold off from asking him out directly?"

"So how do I do it indirectly?"

"Oh, I don't know... maybe don't ask him at all." Jenny thought for a moment and added, "Why don't you try and find out if he goes out drinking anywhere or if he has any hobbies. You know, just be a bit more casual with him. I really don't think you should go right ahead and ask him out... and how could you do that with Xaylan sat there anyway?"

Dayna shrugged her shoulders and pushed her bottom lip out. "Don't know," she replied. "I was thinking of slipping him a little note – it was going to be my plan B. There's a nurse in there with us too so I couldn't have asked him directly anyway – well not unless she disappears for a minute, which she does do now and again."

"Ok, but don't make yourself sound desperate (which I know you probably are). So what are you going to write in a note?"

"I've actually done it already." Dayna grinned. "Do you want to read it? Let's see if you approve..." Dayna promptly left the counter and flipped off down the aisle in her flowery, bright yellow flip-flops.

A few minutes later, she returned. With a beaming face, she passed the envelope to Jenny. "There you are – read it," she said.

Jenny took the envelope and opened it. As soon as she unfolded the sheet of paper a waft of perfume filled the air. "Ooh," breathed Jenny, "smells nice."

Dayna grinned, confidently. "I sprayed it."

Dear Will,

I really appreciate what you are doing for my son, Xaylan. And what you are doing for me too!

Jenny frowned and looked up. "What's he doing for you?"

"Carry on reading it," said Dayna, impatiently.

Unlike my son, I have always been so scared of visiting the dentist, however, you have completely changed my opinion on this matter. You have made me realise that dentists are real human-beings. They really are people with compassion and empathy. I thank you for this.

Looking up from the scented sheet, Jenny frowned. "Isn't it a bit over the top?"

"No," Dayna replied, defensively. "It's true."

Jenny continued to read.

I don't know how you feel but I really think that we have clicked since we first met. It would be a great shame to not see you again, once Xaylan's treatment has ended. I was wondering whether you would like to go out with me for a meal (as a way of thanking you for your efforts) one evening. I've included my mobile number here for your own personal use but you are welcome to call my house number (as stated on Xaylan's file) as well.

Yours sincerely,

Dayna Seeshy

p.s. There's a great American diner in town (should you fancy a taste of home) which I can thoroughly recommend (if you haven't tried it already).

Dayna x

"Oh my God, Day. What do you honestly think he is going to say about this?" Jenny stared disbelieving. "Are you really going to give this to him?"

With a hard glare, Dayna pouted out her lips. "Yes – why? What's wrong with it?"

Shaking her head, Jenny replied, "There's... there's nothing wrong with it. Just sounds weird, that's all."

"Weird? In what way?"

"Well... err... you sound a bit overly grateful..."

Dayna snatched the fragranced sheet from her friend. "I am grateful. You're just jealous because you don't have time for relationships now."

"You're probably right," called Jenny, as Dayna flip-flopped away with her treasured letter gripped between her hands.

Within five minutes, Dayna had reappeared and although the relationship between them had been a little strained a few minutes ago, there was no evidence of it now. Jenny and Dayna had known each for so long that their friendship was strong enough to cope with criticism, ridicule, confrontation or anything else that the pair could conjure up. Usually, Dayna was the conjurer of situations which arose and required a helping hand in one way or another. Jenny was the peace-keeper, mediator and decision maker. But whatever they were – it worked and always had done - thankfully.

"Right," chirped Jenny as she passed by Tasha, who was busy filling shelves, "I'm off to get some printer ink."

"Good," Dayna replied from the counter. "Hurry up and get those leaflets done." Glancing down at Tasha, Dayna winked. "We need Jen to get them printed A.S.A.P – don't we Tasha?"

Tasha nodded and smiled.

"Why?" asked Jenny, puzzled. "What are you up to?"

"You'll see," Dayna grinned cheerily. "See you later."

By the time Jenny's lunch break had finished, she'd managed to print off almost 100 leaflets. They looked great. She had been quite pleased with her efforts until a man, who was standing at the counter when she went flying up there to show Dayna and Tasha the first ever *J's Convenience Store* advertisement leaflet, opened his mouth.

"Problem with those things is, no one ever reads 'em," said the middle-aged man, dressed smartly in a grey pinstripe suit.

Jenny was hopeful that the man was completely wrong.

"Only two percent of leaflets posted into people's homes, ever get looked at – let alone read," the man continued. "It's a fact - I saw it in a magazine somewhere."

"Really?" said Jenny, feeling a little down-trodden. "Well I'll have to get a lot delivered then."

"You will if you want to make a difference. Good luck," said the man, before leaving the shop with a bottle of bleach and a pack of cleaning cloths stuffed into his briefcase.

"Haven't seen him in here before. I'm sure he doesn't know what he's talking about," remarked Jenny, before she scooted back to the office to have the rest of her lunch and continue printing the first of many hundreds of potentially pointless leaflets.

Dayna was buzzing. Her shift had finished and she was dithering around in the staffroom, checking her face, her hair, her dress, her shoes, her everything.
"Dayna, you look fine, now go and get Xaylan will you?"
"I've got a few more minutes yet. Are you sure I look ok?" Dayna turned round and peered back at her bottom, in the mirror. "Yeah – looks good," she answered herself.
"Yes you do look good – now stop fretting. You'll be a nervous wreck by the time you get there."
"But you still think that I shouldn't give him the letter."
Jenny shrugged. "It's up to you. You know him and if you feel comfortable doing it – then do it."
Dayna grinned and fluttered her eyelashes. "I'll let you know what happens."
"Ok, but be prepared for him not to text you. I don't think I could bear you moping around here for weeks and weeks."
"I'm prepared for the worst, don't you worry. But I'm also prepared for the best…" Dayna raised one eyebrow in an attempt to look sexy but only managed to look odd as she squinted her eyes and screwed up her face. "And then it's your turn tomorrow…"
"I don't want to go out with your dentist…" Jenny giggled.
"No, silly. Aaron. He's back tomorrow, isn't he?"
"Oh yes, he is," said Jenny, wide-eyed. "I'd forgotten about that."
"How can you forget, Jen?"
"I don't know. I haven't had time to think about it. Hardly going to see him am I?"

"Why?" Dayna continued to admire her figure in the mirror, turning from one side to the other and kicking a high-heeled foot out behind her.

"I'm working until ten tomorrow night."

"Ah, damn – forgot about that. Saturday then..."

"Dayna, just to remind you, I work until ten on Saturdays too."

"Rubbish! You really need to get someone else in, Jen... and soon. It'll kill you."

Jenny nodded her head in agreement. "Slowly, I'd imagine."

Not heard anything yet. He smiled when I gave it to him though – woohoo! Day xx

Fingers crossed then. How did Xaylan get on? Jen xx

Goes back in two weeks... afternoon, don't worry! Night sweetie xx

Goodnight, Day, and thanks for just being you. Love tired Jen xx

Chapter 29

Aaron – thought Jenny, the very moment she woke up. *He'll be back from Germany today.* A flutter of excitement filled her tummy as she laid in her warm bed and tried to picture his face. He was tall, lean and good-looking. His deep brown eyes captivated her every time she looked into them. He was a great kisser. Sensual and soft. He smelt good and his arms around her felt good too.

Glancing over at the clock, Jenny froze as the time dawned on her. Six minutes past six. How had she slept through the alarm, or in fact, switched it over to snooze on at least two occasions? In under 45 minutes time she had to be ready, in the shop, having done the papers, sorted out Jordan's pile ready for him to deliver, listened to the thumpity-thumps travelling backwards and forwards along the ceiling and opened the shop ready for the irritating Dolly's of the world. *Oh no*, Jenny breathed as she shot out of the bed and headed straight for the bathroom.

Jordan was helpful. In fact, Jordan was a lifesaver. No, Jordan's school was the saving grace. Inset days are really handy when the owner of the shop that you do deliveries for, hasn't got a clue what she's doing.

Jenny sighed. "Thank you Jordan – I don't know what I would have done without your help."

"Ah – no worries," he replied, politely. "Got an Inset, so it's no prob."

"I must have turned the alarm off in my sleep, this morning. Not like me to oversleep. You're my savior."

Jenny had turned up at 6.50am, ten minutes before the shop was due to open. If it hadn't been for Jordan, she would not have managed to get the papers brought in from the shed, sort them into their piles for displaying, got the A-frame loaded up with the 'Today's News' sheets and then sorted out Jordan's papers.

Jordan gave a little embarrassed laugh. "No worries. I'll get off now and deliver these." He picked up his bag and slung it over his shoulder. "See you tomorrow." With a cheeky smile and a wave, as always, Jordan was gone, quicker than *Usain Bolt*.

"Would you be happy for just one of us to work at lunchtimes?" Dayna asked, the moment she walked in.

"What do you mean?"

"Well... Are you ok if just me or Tasha work, while you're on lunch?"

Jenny looked oddly at her friend. "Why?"

"Just wondering if you'd be ok with it?"

"I'd be ok with you working on your own... but, like we've said before, Tasha is very young. Why would you work on your own? I don't get it..."

"So, if I worked on my own at lunchtimes, you'd be ok with that?"

"Yes but..." Normally Jenny could make out what Dayna was thinking but this time she didn't have a clue. "...why would Tasha not work at lunchtimes?"

"I'll reveal all later."

"Ok," said Jenny, unsure of what she might be letting herself in for.

"At lunchtime. When Tasha turns up – we'll explain."

Jenny nodded her head slowly as she mulled over the possibilities. She had no idea what they were up to.

Tasha strolled in at ten to twelve, wearing a big smile, tracksuit bottoms and trainers, which were not her usual attire for work.

"You been jogging?" asked Jenny, jokingly.

"Naah..." Tasha replied and blushed. "Where's Dayna?"

"Just nipped down to the staffroom."

"Oh, ok," she said, shyly and shot off down the aisle.

As the clock reached twelve, Jenny's tummy rumbled, signaling lunchtime. She hadn't heard from Aaron yet and wondered whether he would call, text or just turn up at the shop, unannounced. Checking the mirror above, she could see that there were no people in the shop so she wandered down the aisle to the staffroom. As she approached the room, the door slammed shut.

"Wait there a minute, Jen," came Dayna's voice from behind the door.

Muffled giggles and whispering could be heard coming from the staffroom and Jenny puzzled over what they might be doing in there. She desperately hoped that this wasn't another one of Dayna's daft ideas... she always had plenty of them to share.

"What are you two doing in there?" Jenny laughed, nervously. "I'm getting worried now..."

"Just a minute, Jen. Go up to the counter, we'll be up there in a sec," called Dayna, before giggling.

"Ok, but don't be long – this is my lunch break you know."

"We know," called both girls, in unison, before they started to laugh again.

"Oh... Jen?"

"Yes?"

"You've got to go with this... ok?"

"Err... ok... I think." Jenny hesitated. "Err... what am I agreeing to, exactly?"

"Hang on a minute," called Dayna, over the sound of strange rustling noises. "And you have to agree with what we say..."

"Yes... ok. I'm going up to the counter now – hurry up."

"Be there in two ticks," Dayna replied in a strange sort of muffled way.

Jenny walked behind the counter and stared out of the window. The road was void of traffic and pedestrians were scarce. She wondered how long, if ever, it would take for the shop to really take off. Would the leaflets that she had printed make a difference or would the man in the posh suit be right and it was all a waste of time?

"Do not look in the mirror!" Dayna shouted up the shop.

Instinctively, Jenny looked up at the mirror to see where Dayna was and could just make out her head, poking out from the staffroom door. "Ok, I won't," Jenny called back.

Turning back towards the window, she peered out absent-mindedly, as she listened to the scuffling of feet walking down the first aisle towards her.

Moments later, Jenny was aware of them standing behind her.

"You can turn round now," said Dayna, excitedly.

Swivelling around on her heels, Jenny halted and stared... and she stared, harder... then she blinked, disbelievingly. "What the..."

Dayna and Tasha stood side by side, grinning stupidly. "The best is yet to come," chirped Dayna.

"What? What are...?"

Simultaneously, Dayna and Tasha turned on their heels and stood, motionless, with their backs to Jenny.

"What do you think?"

Jenny was dumbfounded. "I... err... well..." Inhaling a deep breath, she continued. "Err... well... what does that mean exactly? I've heard it so many times but never really thought about what it means."

"What?"

"The 'be square' bit?"

"Uncool – obviously."

Jenny nodded her head, thoughtfully. "Ok, I think I get it."

"High five!" said Dayna, reaching a hand up to Tasha's and clapping them together.

"What's it all for? How much did that cost?" Jenny placed a finger across her lips and contemplated the vision before her.

Dressed in fluorescent pink waterproof trousers, matching jackets and high-vis, colour coordinated waistcoats, the two girls looked brighter than the Blackpool illuminations on a clear night. The bold, black lettering on the back of their waistcoats stood out, dramatically.

J's Convenience Store

Be there or

be square!

"Got them cheap from *Amazon*. Lettering was the expensive bit. We paid half each. We have a plan, Jen, so hear us out."

"I can see you have a plan," Jenny laughed. "What do you both look like?"

"Want to get noticed, don't we?"

"You'll definitely manage that," said Jenny, trying to keep a serious look on her face.

"I'll take mine off now, so I can serve if anyone comes in," said Tasha, shyly. "Cool aren't they, Jenny?" Tasha smiled and walked off with a rustle and a bustle as she went.

Shaking her head from side to side, Jenny snorted. "Oh dear, Dayna. You do make me laugh. So what's the plan? Oh... and I do hope that I haven't got one of those outfits... please tell me that I haven't got to wear anything like that in your plan."

"No, silly. It's just me and Tasha. We're going to deliver the leaflets."

"When?"

"Well, we had a little chat in the staffroom... and before you ask, I did not pressure Tasha into this. She's quite happy to do the extra."

"Extra?" Jenny stared, worriedly.

"We're both going to do an extra hour, each day."

"Really... but I can't..."

"For free..."

"Oh, ok." Jenny's troubled expression softened. "It's a bit much to ask of you both though, Day."

"That's the point, Jen – you're not asking – we're telling."

"Ok," Jenny replied, resignedly. "So when are you going to do this?"

"As we swap shifts around each day, we'll be swapping the delivery times round too. So, basically, one of us will deliver from eleven till twelve and the other from two till three."

Jenny nodded and smiled. "Ok, but are you sure that you're both happy to do an extra hour each day?"

"Yes – stop worrying. We've been talking about this for a week now. Tasha is bringing her bike here, so she can whizz around on that. I'm guessing it'll be fine to lock it up by the newspaper cupboard, round the back?"

"Yes, sure."

"That's that sorted then, we'll start on Monday. You know, Jen, we can both see that you're looking tired a lot, lately. The only way you're going to get any time off is if you can afford to get more staff in. The only way that you can afford more staff is if you get more customers. The only way you'll get more customers is if they know your shop is here in the first place."

"You're right, Day. Absolutely right. Thank you. I don't know how I can ever repay you. You've gone out of your way to do this and I am so grateful," Jenny said, humbly.

"We don't expect you to repay us, Jen. We want it to work as much as you do. We love working here and we'll do our bit to help you out." Dayna paused and grinned. "Now clear off and go and have your lunch break."

"Yes, Ma'am!" said Jenny as she stood to attention and saluted her dearest, but sometimes completely crazy, friend. "I'm going."

"Oh," said Dayna, "and check your phone – I heard it go off when I was down in the staffroom."

"Ok, thanks." Jenny scuttled off and passed Tasha on the way, who had already changed back into her normal, bog-standard, tame-coloured clothes.

"Well... you never know... it could be Aaron," Dayna called out.

Plonking her bottom down, Jenny leant back in her chair, clutching her mobile to her chest. *Is it him*, she wondered? She almost didn't want to look, in case it wasn't. Jenny could hear Dayna, in the staffroom, changing her clothes and making cups of tea. Holding the phone in front of her, Jenny swiped the unlock key on the screen and peered at the message notification. *Calvin. Bloody Calvin was still sending pathetic little, needy messages.*

How's the shop going? Heard you've had some problems with customers. Call me if you need any help. Calvin. X

Thanks, Calvin but I'm dealing with it. You know me – never give up, whatever is thrown at me.

That's my girl!

I'm not your girl, remember? Thanks for offer of help though. Jen.

Still tetchy I see. From cool, calm and collected Calvin.

Jenny listened to the chugging, clunking sound of the printer as she nibbled her way through a tuna sandwich. She'd reeled off 600 leaflets to date. She was guessing she'd need at least another 600 just to serve the area in closest proximity, without even venturing down Millen Road at all. Also, there had to be another 400 houses on the housing estate at the back. Did the girls realise just how many homes they would need to deliver to? Placing the rest of her sandwich back in the cellophane wrapper, she leant back in the chair and closed her eyes as the printer continued to do its thing.

A rap on the door woke Jenny from her doze. "Come in," she squeaked, sleepily.

"Jacob," said Dayna, handing the phone over.

Jenny looked at the phone sitting on her desk. "Blimey, I didn't hear the phone ring."

"Having 40 winks, were you," Dayna said in jest, before winking an eye and leaving.

"Hi Jacob, are you ok?"

"Yeah fine. Dad wanted me to ring – to find out how things are going. He's tied up with a big job at the moment."

"Oh, yes, everything's fine."

"What about the bill for that woman's car?"

Jenny paused and thought for a moment, she'd forgotten all about that. "Oh... err... I couldn't be bothered with it, Jay, so I just called them and paid it off."

"You idiot – why did you do that?" Jacob sounded annoyed.

"I've had too much other stuff going on to worry about that as well."

"Ok, well you know that you've been ripped off there – good and proper."

"Yes, I'm sure I have but I just wanted it out of the way." Jenny sighed. "The man upstairs has been enough for me to deal with – without anything else to worry about."

"He still giving you trouble?"

"Not any more... or should I say, not at the moment. But, Jay, you wouldn't believe it if I told you what I found out about him."

"Try me."

Jenny spent the next ten minutes telling her brother the gory details of Denny and Jessie Smith's torrid marriage, full of woe, deception and violence. "Look it up on *Google*, it tells you all about it."

"Bloody hell. I do hope that you won't be going up to his flat again."

"Absolutely not." Jenny heaved another sigh. "The council can deal with any problems that he thinks he might have with me in the future."

"Yes, do not get involved with him. And don't spread gossip around with your customers, it could cause no end of problems for you."

"Jay, I'm not stupid – of course I won't. I haven't even told Day and Tasha everything."

"They should know, don't you think?"

"Yes, they do know most of what the woman told me, but I just said to them to *Google* the rest... and no, they won't go spreading gossip. Tasha even said that she won't be telling her mum anything. Apparently, her mum would go broadcasting it around the world."

"Ok, well I'll tell Dad about it – obviously, he won't say anything to anyone."

"And give him a hug and a kiss from me." Jenny felt a pang of guilt wash over her. She hadn't called her dad or popped in to see him, on her way home from work, like she'd promised.

"Yeah, don't worry, he knows you're busy. Aren't we all?"

Jenny laughed. "Yep, ok, Jay, I'll see you soon. Love to everyone."

"See you soon Sis."

A few minutes later there was another knock on the door. "Yes?" said Jenny, suddenly wondering if it might be someone to see her. Someone like Aaron...

Dayna poked her head around the door. "I've got a text message," she squeaked, excitedly. Bouncing down the step, into the office, she closed the door behind her. "From Will."

"Will?" Jenny frowned. "The dentist?"

"Yes!" Dayna clutched her phone to her chest. "Can't believe he's replied to my letter."

"What did he say?"

"Well... err..." Dayna stuttered. "Well... he... err. Shall I read it to you?"

Jenny nodded her head and smiled, awkwardly. By the wobble in Dayna's voice, it didn't sound good.

Dayna breathed in deeply and looked down at her phone. "Hey, Dayna. Great letter! I thank you for your kindness and the offer of an evening out with you..." Dayna looked up and grinned.

"Ah, that's sweet," said Jenny, having empathy for her friend because, somehow, she felt that there was a 'but' coming.

Dayna continued, after another deep breath. "Somehow we seem to have gelled, over such a short time and very few visits..." Dayna paused and looked up with the biggest, cheesy grin, Jenny had ever seen.

"Go on," said Jenny, impatiently. Maybe there wasn't a 'but' in there.

"You're a beautiful lady..." Dayna clapped the phone to her chest again and looked up to the ceiling. "Aah..." she breathed.

"Oh bless him. Go on – go on." Jenny's heart was beating fast, in anticipation.

"It would be good to keep in contact and maybe one day we could go for that 'American Diner'... maybe even in America! Ha ha." Dayna looked up again. This time there was a sadness in her eyes.

"Is that it?"

"No, one more bit," Dayna replied, glumly. "I'm leaving the UK in the new year. I'm going back to the US to start a new practice over there. Hey, but keep in touch, won't you?"

"Ah, Day. I'm so sorry. I know you really liked him too."

Dayna nodded her head and peered down at her phone again. "Yeah... He's put his name at the end... but no kisses."

"You can hardly expect him to put kisses on a text message, Day – he hardly knows you. I think you've made a good impression on him. He clearly likes you. Bloody shame he's going back to the US though."

"Well, maybe I'll keep in contact with him and we'll fall madly in love and he'll... he'll ask me to go and live over there..."

Jenny nodded. "It's possible. I don't want you moving to the US forever though."

"Well, I've decided. I'm not giving up that easily."

"I would never have expected you would." Jenny laughed. "Just don't get hurt."

"The message isn't a 'put off'. I think he really does like me, he just doesn't see past his return to America."

"Yes, it does sound like he likes you. He didn't need to say all of that, did he?"

Dayna shook her head, determinedly. "No. So, I'm going to reply and say... well, I'll say, shall we go out sometime, for a couple of drinks and a bite to eat, before he leaves?"

"You've got nothing to lose," said Jenny, biting her lip, worriedly.

"He's still got a couple of months before he goes, so I reckon I'll push him a bit harder. He does sound interested – right?"

Jenny nodded. "Right – but just be ready in case he says no."

Dayna shrugged and puffed her cheeks out. "So, have you heard from Aaron, yet?"

"No," Jenny replied. "Not yet."

"Ah, perhaps he's been held up."

"Maybe..."

"You're not worried are you?"

"About what?" Jenny frowned.

"He will get in contact with you," said Dayna, positively.

"Oh, I'm sure he will. I'm cool – no worries."

Chapter 30

Hi Jen, I know I said that I'd come in to see you today but I managed to get held up in Germany – missed my plane! Great news though – struck up a deal – Europe-wide! I'll visit you tomorrow. Fancy lunch and an evening out? Aaron x

Pleased to hear your good news, Aaron. I can't do lunch tomorrow (unless you want to sit in my dingy little office, amongst the cans of coke and veggies) as weekends are less staffed. Don't finish until 10pm either. What a life! X

Damn! Forgot about that. I'm happy to sit between the carrots and potatoes, with a Costa coffee and a pre-packed sandwich, if you fancy that?

Deal! Only get an hour for lunch (at 12pm) but we could make out we're doing business to extend your stay (I'll have to let Dayna go to lunch by 2pm at the latest though). Look forward to seeing you. Jen x

Jenny heaved a sigh of relief, switched off the bedside lamp and snuggled under her duvet.

In comparison to yesterday morning, Jenny was wide awake before the alarm had had its chance to rudely interrupt her sleep. Springing out of bed, she headed for the shower with a skip in her step. She was going to see Aaron again today. She had plenty of time to wash her hair, put some make-up on and find something nice to wear to work. Jenny was half glad that Aaron hadn't been able to make it as previously planned. She'd been so late for work yesterday, that she hadn't brushed her hair and couldn't remember if she'd even cleaned her teeth in the morning.

"Morning," chirped Jenny, as Jordan walked through the door, ten minutes earlier than usual. "Beat you to it this morning."

Jordan chuckled. "I got here a bit early. Didn't know if you'd want me to help again."

"Ah, bless you." Jenny beamed. "No, I was up with the lark this morning."

"Lark? What's that?"

Bursting into a raucous laugh, Jenny held on to her stomach as it began to ache. "Oh... dear. You make me laugh. A lark..." Jenny caught her breath. "A lark is a bird. They sing a lot – I think. I suppose they must get up early too. It's just a saying – that's all."

Jordan nodded in acknowledgement. "Oh, right. I'll have to remember that. My brother lays in bed until one or two o'clock at the weekends. I'll tell him, I'm up with the lark." Jordan chuckled and then grabbed his heavy pile of weekend papers and pushed them into his bag. "See you tomorrow then... up with the lark."

"Bye, Jordan... and thanks again... for yesterday."

"No probs, bye."

The hours ticked by slowly as Jenny waited for ten o'clock to come round. Dayna's shift started then and she was with Jenny all day, until eight this evening. She hated to think it, time and time again, but it was so much more fun working with, Day. They were of the same age and they knew each other so well that they could almost finish off each other's sentences. And apart from any of that – Jenny couldn't wait to tell Dayna, that Aaron was coming in for lunch.

"I've replied," whispered Dayna as she shuffled past a couple of elderly women, standing a few feet away from the counter, gassing. "Just waiting to hear back."

"Oh wow, what did you say?" Jenny replied, with a hushed breath.

"Said he should come out with me and make the most of his last few months in England."

"Let me know the moment he replies." Jenny beamed and desperately hoped and prayed that he would reply to Dayna's text and he would say yes – her best friend deserved to have something good in her life, even if it was only for a few months.

"Aaron texted me last night..." said Jenny, feeling a surge of excitement rush to her head. "He's coming here for lunch."

"Oh, good. Gosh, we'll be going out in a foursome soon."

"Hmm..." said Jenny, thoughtfully. "I hardly think so... what with the long hours that I do."

"Ah, don't worry about that. Me and Tasha are hotfooting it around the area starting from Monday. They'll soon be rolling in here, spending all their money."

Jenny smiled, warmly, and then whispered. "Hope so – now go and make us a cuppa... oh, and there are some crumpets going out of date in the staffroom."

The two elderly ladies were oblivious to the conversation that had been going on at the counter behind them. Jenny watched as they gossiped and cackled like two witches around a cauldron, concocting a new spell. The large space, at the front of the shop, seemed to attract the elderly residents of Farehelm to congregate in small clusters, for a daily 'catch up' on all sorts of topics. In the time that the shop had been opened, Jenny had overheard many stories, ranging from the Grandson who had dropped out of university half way through his course, and then revealed his homosexuality to his whole family and left home to live with his partner, to the incident of 'poor old Fred up the road' who had gone out for a walk one day and never returned. Poor old Fred had been admitted to hospital, having been found wandering around the local copse in a confused state, three days after he'd left home. He then died two days later, apparently of natural causes.

It had crossed Jenny's mind as to whether she should start offering teas and coffees to the aging clique who populated the area in front of her counter but then she would be turning her shop into a café. The elderly folk did not spend anything like enough money in her shop to warrant a hot drink. Mostly, they purchased a morning paper and that was about it. In hindsight, perhaps Jenny should have opened a community centre/café for the residents of Farehelm. At least that way, she might have had a life. But no, this was what she'd wanted. This was what she'd strived for, for so many years... and this was what she was going to succeed at. And *then* she would get a life.

The fluttery butterflies had returned and now filled her stomach as Jenny watched Aaron's car pull into the side road, alongside the shop. He was so dependable and punctual. "He's here," she squeaked, excitedly. "I'm going for my lunch break."

"Don't feel that you need to be back out here on time, Jen. I should be fine for a couple of hours."

Jenny nodded her head. "Thanks, Day. Call me if you do need me though."

"Only in an emergency then. I mean... I don't want to interrupt anything do I?"

"Like what?" Jenny laughed, excitedly. "We're just having a sandwich together."

"Yeah, heard that one before," said Dayna, with a huge smirk on her face.

"Day, it's not like that." Jenny's face flushed. "Yet..."

Moments later the front door opened and in walked Aaron. Dressed in blue jeans, navy canvas shoes and a turquoise, checked shirt, he looked more gorgeous than Jenny had remembered. "*Costa coffee*, anyone?" Carrying three coffees on a tray, Aaron looked across at the girls.

"Ooh, goody," said Dayna, clapping her hands together. "Yes please."

Jenny smiled, sweetly. "Thanks Aaron. How are you?"

Aaron moved towards the counter, pulled a cup out from its holder and passed it to Dayna. "Here, there's no sugar in it – wasn't sure if you had it."

"Nah, sweet enough, me."

"I'm good thanks," said Aaron, meeting Jenny's eyes. "Glad to be back on home ground."

"Congratulations on getting the European contract."

Aaron huffed. "Thanks – it's been a long time coming. It wasn't easy either."

"I bet it wasn't," said Jenny, shyly.

"I thought we should buy a sandwich from the best place in town..." said Aaron, grinning.

"Oh, where's that?"

"Here."

Jenny laughed. "Come on then, we'll go and have a look what I've got left. They're on me."

"No they're not. I want to buy them."

"Are you sure?"

"Absolutely," said Aaron. "This is my treat. Call it a celebration, if you like."

"Well let's get the bubbly out then," chirped Dayna. "If we're celebrating we could have one of those big bottles." Dayna pointed to the top shelf to her left, which contained several large bottles of champagne.

"And serve customers in a drunken state all afternoon?" Jenny smiled.

"Nah – shut the shop."

Tutting playfully at her friend, Jenny walked slowly down the second aisle, towards the sandwich fridge, with Aaron in tow.

The atmosphere in the confines of the office, was heady and hot, while Jenny and Aaron ate their sandwiches and drank coffee. Making small talk, the two of them stared, longingly, into each other's eyes. The urge to touch him, kiss him, jump on him, made Jenny struggle to swallow the bread in her mouth. She hadn't realised how much she'd missed seeing him this week.

"So, that's my week – what about yours?" said Aaron, after giving a brief run-down of his week.

"Well," replied Jenny, thoughtfully. "I've had quite an interesting week, actually..."

Jenny proceeded to tell Aaron about the man upstairs and also about the hopeless conversation she'd had one evening, with Marj.

"So, I've given up trying to talk any sense to her. She's either completely lost it or she's winding me up. I cannot get through to her, at all."

Aaron had listened, intently, as Jenny told him about her week. Eating his sandwich slowly, his face had changed from one of amusement, to horror and through to disbelief as Jenny told him everything.

"I mentioned your shop to my mum..." said Aaron, looking down at the last piece of sandwich in his hand and discarding it back into the cellophane wrapper. "I told her about the crazy customers you seem to have around here. You know, all the things that have happened to you, since you've been here."

Jenny nodded. "What did she say?"

"Well, same as anyone would if you told them – she couldn't believe it. She hopes that you'll do really well here though."

"Ah, that's nice," Jenny replied, feeling warm and contented. "If I do anywhere close, as well as your mum, I'll be a very happy woman."

Aaron smiled. "Give it time." Moving his chair towards Jenny's he reached over. "I thought about you a lot, while I was away... I missed you."

Jenny nodded, just before she was engulfed by his arms. Tightly hugged, she wanted to melt away as she put her arms around his waist. Their lips met. Jenny's mouth and head filled with fizzy flickers of excitement. She wanted him. She knew he wanted her. It couldn't happen.

Pulling away with flushed cheeks, Aaron adjusted his seating and inhaled deeply. "Phew," he whispered. "Can't do this – you're driving me crackers. I'll end up turning into one of your crazy customers."

Jenny bit her bottom lip as the tingling sensation racing through her torso, began to subside. "I know."

Stretching up in the chair, Aaron stroked a hand across his mouth. "Shall I get us another coffee?"

Jenny shook her head. "I'm ok, thanks. Shall I make you one?"

"Joint effort," said Aaron, grasping Jenny's hand and pulling her up from her chair. "Come on."

It was no better in the staffroom. As the kettle heated up, Jenny found herself in an embrace again. Lips locked into a full-on kissing session. The kettle wasn't the only thing that was beginning to boil.

Aaron pulled away again as the kettle came to a climax and switched itself off. "I can't be around you for more than five minutes (and I have to be honest here), without wanting to molest you."

Jenny giggled. "Ah, so you admit now, that you want me."

"Yes..." Aaron breathed, before moving in for a third kiss, "I do... I want you."

Finally, the coffee was made. Two coffees, in fact. Jenny had changed her mind after all the thirsty work of kissing the life out of Aaron. It had to stop though. It wasn't right – not in the shop. The heightened state that they'd got themselves in to, was far too close to actually forgetting where they were and going for it completely – and possibly even, nakedly.

"Can I see you tonight?"

"I won't be away from the shop until about 10.30pm."

Aaron sighed. "And then you're back here at six in the morning, right?"

Jenny nodded. "Well, six fifteen at the latest. I get up at five."

"Does Dayna help you to lock up?"

"Oh gosh, no – she goes at eight."

Aaron looked puzzled. "So who's here with you until ten?"

"No one," Jenny replied.

"No one? You're here on your own at night?"

Nodding her head, Jenny smiled, sheepishly. "Yes, I know – I'm not even supposed to be here on my own. My alcohol license states that there has to be two members of staff on the premises at all times." Jenny hesitated. "I just can't afford anyone else, Aaron."

"But you can't be on your own – what if a dodgy character came in or even the man upstairs? What if you desperately needed to go to the toilet or something?"

Jenny nodded her head. "I know – I don't have any choice at the moment. The good thing is that the people from the council aren't likely to come and check late in the evening. So I should just get away with it... until I can get someone else in to work."

Aaron stared, thoughtfully. "Maybe I should come and help you."

"No, you can't do that!"

"I can – if you want me to."

Jenny shook her head. "No, Aaron – you've done enough for me already."

"But I want to help."

Touched by his kindness, Jenny moved closer and put her arms around him. "You're so sweet but I really can't expect you to do this."

"Well don't expect it. I'll surprise you each time." Aaron bent his head down and kissed her again. "You've just recruited your first volunteer."

By 1.40pm they had to tear themselves away from each other. How on earth was she going to work for two hours this evening with Aaron? The good thing, she supposed, was that they wouldn't be hidden away, out the back of the shop. They would hardly be able to kiss and cuddle on the shop floor, unless they dipped behind the counter for a quickie, or jumped in the freezer. But that wouldn't happen because they were both far too professional to risk doing anything so foolish. So that was that. Aaron was going home now and coming back at eight o'clock.

Dayna went for her lunch at a quarter to two. With a glint in her eye, she smirked at Jenny before she left. "Had a nice lunch have you?"

Jenny nodded.

"You've got that flushed look, Jen." Dayna giggled. "Just behave yourselves tonight."

Nodding her head again, Jenny gazed at her friend, like a love-struck teenager. "I will."

Chapter 31

It was so much fun working with Aaron. Thankfully, the needy desire to molest him had not arisen and the pair had worked very well together. He was great with the customers and on several occasions he'd referred to Jenny as 'his boss'. Proactive and conscientious, Aaron's help had been invaluable and refreshing. He'd come up with some great ideas to move some of the stock around, too. The last two hours of the day had whizzed by and Aaron's company had made the late evening at *J's Convenience Store* far less eerie and lonesome.

"Time to lock up," chirped Jenny. "Don't know where the time's gone. You've been great company, Aaron, and so helpful – I can't thank you enough."

"You can thank me later," said Aaron, with a smirk.

By 10.15pm, the money had been counted and bagged, the EPOS report had been printed off and the paper returns had been bundled outside to the cupboard. Jenny sighed as she looked at the report. "The footfall isn't increasing... neither is the average spend."

"You've only been open for a few weeks – give it time."

Jenny looked up and smiled weakly. "My 'time' is running out. I was expecting to double this by the end of the first three months."

"You may well do – Christmas is fast approaching."

"Hmm..." Jenny gazed into the middle distance, thoughtfully. "Christmas was supposed to be a bonus to sales figures – not the answer."

"When did you say that Dayna and Tasha are starting their leaflet distribution?"

"Monday."

"That might help. Makes me laugh though. The thought of those two going out in fluorescent pink gear and hi-vis jackets. And what's that motto again?" Aaron smiled, "Be there, be cool?"

"Be there or be square." Jenny giggled. "They do look funny. I'm surprised that Tasha agreed to wear it, she's quite shy."

"Thought you said she's well into dressing up in weird costumes."

"Oh, yes. Seems to be that way but she's still shy about it all."

By 10.20pm, Jenny and Aaron were walking out of the shop. Jenny locked the door and popped the keys into her jacket. "It's only twenty past and I'm out of here already. Thank you, Aaron – I could do with having you here every night."

"Can't do every night," Aaron replied, as they walked down the side road, towards the rear of the shop, "but I could help you on your late shifts – it's not a problem. And I want to do all I can to help you out. After all, you'll be owing me for the EPOS system in a year's time, so I'd better look after my assets." Aaron laughed. "And that wasn't a hint or anything, it seems that I'm compelled to see you succeed." Aaron pulled Jenny close to him. "And I'm compelled to kiss you now that we're not in the shop."

It was a short, soft kiss but lasted long enough for Jenny to wonder what she should do next. Once again, it was a case of, should she invite him back to her flat for the proverbial coffee – she wanted to? Or should she just say thank you and goodnight and be on her way, as she had to be up early again tomorrow?

"Do you want to come back to my flat? Err... you know... for coffee?"

Aaron looked down at her, longingly. "I would love to," he kissed her lips gently, "but I'm not going to."

"Oh," replied Jenny, disappointedly. "Ok."

"I came here tonight to help you – not hinder you." Aaron pulled away and smiled, warmly. "You've got to get up and come back here in a few hours' time – I dare not come to yours for coffee."

Jenny's euphoric state, during the evening, sunk. "Ok."

"But you finish at six tomorrow, yes?"

Jenny nodded. Once again she'd forgotten that it was Sunday tomorrow and she did indeed, finish early. "Yes – I always forget. The weeks fly by here."

"Then how about I take you out for a meal tomorrow night – and then we'll go back to yours for coffee, after?"

"Yes, ok, thanks, Aaron. I'd love to. But let me pay for it... as a 'thank-you' for what you've done this evening."

"Wouldn't dream of it. I'll pick you up at say... 7.15pm? Does that give you enough time?"

Jenny grinned and nodded her head, enthusiastically. "I'll make sure it does."

"I'll see you tomorrow," said Aaron, pulling Jenny into a dark corner of the car park and planting his lips firmly onto hers for what seemed like an age.

A few minutes later, Jenny watched Aaron climb into his car and slowly creep away. She too, crept away in her old jeep, leaving the peaceful, sleepy residents of Farehelm, far behind her.

OMG! He's text me! He's text me! Love, Day xxxxxxxxxxxxxxxxxxx

And?????

And... he's not sure he has any available time until next Saturday. xx

Well that's great isn't it?

During the day... Boohoo! xx

Why not in the evening?

He's travelling early hours of Sunday morning – Scotland – for a two day conference. Big dentist get together, apparently. xx

So you want time off?

How can I? xx

We could ask Tasha if she wouldn't mind swapping days. It's in both of your contracts to be flexible to changing your days at the weekends.

Oh, ok, woohoo! Can you ask her tomorrow? xx

Yes of course I can. Night night xx

One more thing, Jen. Is Aaron there? Woohoo! Have a good night's SLEEP!!!

No he's not. He went home after we finished at the shop. So I will have a good night's sleep, thank you x

You did it at the shop????!!!

No, Day! We did not do it at the shop.

Where then? Love Day xx

Nowhere!

Why?

Not time yet – now sod off and let me get to sleep. I'm up in six hours. All my love, Jenny x

You're dragging this one out or lying to me! Night hun, loves ya! Xxxx and don't forget to ask Tasha xx

I won't. And I'm not lying x

"Oh, while I remember, Tasha – would you be able to swap shifts with Dayna next weekend? It's short notice, I know, but Dayna needs the afternoon off."

"Next weekend?" Tasha looked horrified. "I... err... well, you mean, work Saturday instead of Sunday?"

"Yes. Is it a problem?"

"Err... well, I was going to go shopping with my mum... but... well, I should be able to cancel it... and you know, go with her the next time. Yes, so it's working until 8pm is it?"

"Yes – you wouldn't start until ten though. Can you do it?"

Tasha nodded, unconvincingly. "Ok."

"Were you just going shopping?"

"Well..." Tasha faltered. "Err, yes – just a bit of shopping."

"Ok, are you sure it's not going to cause a problem – you seem a little unsure about it, that's all."

"No, no. It'll be fine. I'll finish at eight o'clock, yes?"

"Yes." Jenny looked puzzled, at her young colleague. "Do you go shopping late then?"

"No, no... we were going out, that's all." Tasha shifted uncomfortably, from one foot to another. "Out for the evening... as well as shopping."

"Look, Tasha, if you have something important that you need to do, then we can sort it out – somehow. I mean, maybe Dayna could come back in the evening."

"No... no, it's ok. I'm sorry, Jenny. It's fine – I'll do it."

"Well, if you're sure..." Jenny couldn't work out why Tasha appeared to be so jittery about next Saturday.

"I'm sure – I promise. I'll get a lift from here at eight o'clock, straight to the..." Tasha stopped short. "Yes, it will be fine. Shall I make a coffee?"

"Please," said Jenny, looking perplexed as she watched Tasha tootle off down the aisle with a mug in each hand. "And you will get paid overtime for the extra hour, next week."

Tasha turned and smiled. "Thank you."

There was a strange, awkward silence for the rest of the day. Tasha was pleasant enough and helpful as always, but the atmosphere was a little strained. Jenny couldn't help wondering if there was something that Tasha wasn't saying, but then again, why should she tell her boss what she gets up to in her free time.

Tasha will change shifts with you next week but I don't think she was too happy about it. Be grateful, I get the impression she's missing out on something next Saturday. Hasn't said what. Been a bit odd all day. DO NOT say anything though. Be thankful that you can have your day with your dentist. Love Jen x

Oh shit! I forgot all about that!

What?

She's supposed to be going to Brighton with her mum. Her mum has a new pole-dancing act – in a topless bar!! xx

Really???

Yes – she tells me things, Jen. Forgot to mention it. Don't forget, you're her boss, she wouldn't want to tell you about stuff like that. Xx

Oh, ok!!

I'll talk to her. Can we do like, half shifts? I'll come back for 6pm, then she can go. Can we do that? xx

Do what you like, I don't mind. As long as I have one or the other, it's fine.

What about Aaron? Xx

Nope – not asking him to work here. He offered to help last night but I'm not going to ask him to cover for others.

Ok, I'll speak to Tasha and get it sorted on Monday. Ok? xx

Yes, ok, see you tomorrow, Day. Oh, and I'm going out for a meal with Aaron after work, tonight. Yay! X

Well, for God's sake, will you just shag him and get it over and done with? Lol xx

We'll see. He is a gentleman you know. X

Either antiquated or scared, I reckon! Lol x

Nope – just a gentleman. Treating me like a lady. Hopefully, your dentist will be the same – you might learn something! Love Jen x

With an excited energy, Jenny whizzed through the paper returns, after Tasha had left. There were just 45 minutes to go and then she could shut the shop. Having already begun to count up the small change and put it into plastic bags, Jenny was well ahead of time. She planned to get home as early as possible, jump in the shower quickly and be ready to go at 7.15pm, when Aaron would arrive to pick her up.

Through the window, Jenny could just see a taxi pull up, on the entrance to the side road. Moments later, a man struggled to get out of the back of the car. Through the darkness, Jenny could just make out the figure of Denny, the murderous man with one leg. He slammed the taxi door hard and limped away from the car, appearing to mutter something under his breath. Jenny moved back slightly, hoping to hide behind the middle panel of the window frame. Slowly, he hobbled over to the front of the shop. Jenny held her breath in fear. Was he coming into the shop?

Glancing up at the mirror, she could see that no one was in the shop. She was alone. Alone on a dark, Sunday evening, when everyone else was at home, tucked up in their cosy houses, bathed and hair washed, watching the TV, with full stomachs, having eaten a big roast dinner.

And here she was – about to stare death in the face.

Instinctively, she reached down for the phone under the counter, and then moved slowly back to her spot, behind the window's central frame.

Denny approached the door and peered through.

Jenny could just see her potential assailant, side on, through the window. *Oh God help me*, she thought as her thumb automatically dialed a number, the first number that she could think of. Placing the receiver to her ear, she waited for the phone to stop ringing, she waited desperately to hear someone's voice on the other end.

Denny moved sideways, away from the door, closer to the window pane where Jenny was hiding and cowering. He glared through the window.

"Hello?" A familiar man's voice said, from the phone.

"Dad? Oh... hi Dad. Err... right... how are you?"

"Jen, I've been meaning to call you – you've beat me to it."

Jenny laughed, nervously. "Ha – I've been meaning to... err... to call you too."

The man went back to the door and placed a bony hand on the handle.

"Everything going ok?"

"Yes..." Jenny tried to control her quivering voice. "Err... it's all going great."

As Jenny watched the handle creak slowly down, a lump grew in her throat. Gulping hard, she tried to remain calm. "So... err..."

The door opened.

"Jen? Is everything ok?"

"Oh... err... yes, Dad." Jenny raised her voice. "Yes, it's going REALLY WELL."

Denny stepped into the shop and narrowed his eyes at the bright lights.

"Yes... I've got them ALL working hard. Yes – they're ALL out the BACK OF THE SHOP, Dad. WORKING THEIR SOCKS OFF."

Denny glared across the shop to where Jenny stood, clutching the phone as if it was the only thing that would save her from a terrible ending of deathly doom.

"Jenny," said Dad, sounding puzzled. "What are you talking about?"

Seconds later, Denny slid away down the first aisle and out of sight.

"YES!" shouted Jenny, "AARON is in the STAFFROOM – IN THE SHOP. HE'S MAKING US A CUP OF TEA!"

"Jenny? What are you doing?" Dad called down the phone. "Talk to me – don't shout."

"I EXPECT AARON WILL BRING ME A CUP OF TEA IN A MINUTE..."

Peering up at the mirror, Jenny could see Denny standing just behind the first row of shelves. His head was swivelling from left to right, as if he was checking the aisle for people. Jenny gulped. It was as if the man from upstairs was on the lookout for any potential witnesses to his next murder...

"Oh, so you'll be HERE in a MINUTE too," Jenny shouted down the phone. "So we'll have EVERYONE HERE..."

"Jenny, have you gone completely mad?" What's going on?"

"EVERYONE WILL BE HERE IN THE SHOP – THAT'S GOOD."

Jenny froze as Denny began to snake down the aisle, going from one side to the other. Then he stopped half way down and stood motionless, in the middle of the aisle. His head suddenly began to flick from one side to the other. Then he stood perfectly still again.

In the mirror, Jenny could see Denny's shoulders and back rise and fall as he appeared to breathe heavily. Panting. Like a prowling dog.

"Err... YES – LIKE I SAID... THE GIRLS ARE WORKING..."

"For God's sake, Jenny," hollered Dad, angrily. "What..."

"THEY'RE JUST OUT THE BACK... I CAN CALL THEM OUT... OUT HERE... ANYTIME... I'VE GOT A BUZZER – RIGHT HERE!"

"Jenny – is there someone in the shop? Have you got trouble in there?"

"YES, DAD – you hit the nail on the head. THERE ARE LOTS OF US HERE." Jenny held the phone away from her mouth before screaming towards the end of the shop. "AARON! IS THAT TEA READY YET?" In a flash, Jenny returned the phone to her ear.

"Jenny!" Dad shouted down the phone. "Are you in trouble?"

"YES, DAD – WHY DON'T YOU COME ON OVER – RIGHT NOW?" The phone line went deathly quiet. Her dad had hung up on her. Jenny's heart raced. A tightness gripped at her throat. Sweaty and sick, Jenny gulped. "OH OK... YES, BRING MY BIG BROTHER HERE TOO," she continued. "OH, I SEE – SO MY BROTHER IS ON HIS WAY ALREADY? YES, SO HE'LL BE HERE IN SECONDS..."

Peering up at the mirror, Jenny's heart almost stopped as she watched the man slither down to the end of the shop and vanish from view. The one place in the shop where the mirror could not reflect, was at the very bottom of the first aisle, opposite the staffroom. And that's where Denny was. Lying in wait.

Waiting to butcher her.

The seconds ticked by prominently. Jenny's life was ticking away, quickly. Terrifyingly. Clutching the phone in her sweaty palms, she resisted the urge to cry. She would go down fighting.

"IT'S LOVELY CHATTING TO YOU – I DON'T KNOW WHERE AARON HAS GOT TO... WITH THAT TEA... HE'LL BE OUT ANY SECOND..." Jenny gulped hard as her throat tightened again. "YES... HE'LL BE COMING RIGHT OUT OF THE STAFFROOM – AT THE FAR END OF THE SHOP... ANY SECOND NOW!"

Denny came into view at the bottom of the second aisle as he turned the corner. He began to snake along the second aisle, towards Jenny.

Gripping the silent phone in her hand, Jenny pressed it harder to her ear.

Closer and closer.

The man's beady, black eyes, flicked from left to right.

Jenny's eyes were riveted onto his.

Denny moved closer. Crazy. Chancy. Cunning.

Jenny's life was about to end.

She would be cut into a million pieces.

Her dad, Aaron, Dayna, Tasha – they would all find her dismembered body, lying in a pool of thick, black blood. She would still be holding the phone... but her head would have rolled away, down the aisle, never to hear another word spoken.

Closer still.

Just moments away.

Jenny's life had almost come to its end.

Would she die quickly? Would it be painful? Would she have the strength to fight back?

Mad people are supposedly super-strong, aren't they?

Jenny stared, pleadingly, as Denny reached the counter and moved stealthily round it, on the prowl.

She could smell him. She could almost feel the sickly heat emanating from him. She squeezed the phone in her hand. *Goodbye*, she whispered, inside her firmly attached head. *Goodbye world*…

"Nice shop," grunted Denny, before moving across the floor to the front. Wrenching the door open, he limped out. Then he was gone.

Dropping the phone on the counter, Jenny clapped her hands to her mouth, drew in a deep breath and exhaled slowly. Letting out a nervous chuckle, she looked up to the ceiling and began an involuntary, convulsive sob.

She had overreacted – how silly of her.

In her moment of terror she hadn't even thought to use the panic alarm.

And thank God she hadn't.

How silly would she have looked?

The sudden, bursting sound of a siren brought Jenny back to her senses. Flashing blue lights lit up the shelving from outside.

The police.

Jumping from their car, two officers charged into the shop and halted by the door. "We've had a report of an attack, Miss."

Jenny shook her head, dumbfounded. "Not here," she replied.

"Are you Jenny Fartor?"

"Yes…" Jenny nodded her head. "I am." Discreetly, she placed a hand over the phone still lying on the counter top and pushed it aside.

"Have you had any problems, Miss?"

"No… no, not at all," Jenny squirmed, realizing just what had happened.

"We've had a phone call, Miss. Did you send out a distress call to your father?"

"No..." Jenny hesitated. "No, well, yes possibly. Well... err... no, not really. I think there has been a misunderstanding, officer."

"Is everything as it should be, Miss?"

"Yes... yes, absolutely, officer. I am so sorry about this. I think there has been a bit of a mix up." Jenny cringed. "I will speak to my father," Jenny tried to laugh it off. "He's a silly old sausage – honestly."

"Are you here alone, Miss?"

Jenny hesitated. "Oh... err... no... not at all. I... err... my colleague, well, she... err, she's just nipped out to the staffroom. The toilet – you know," she said, anxiously. "It's that time of the month." Jenny rubbed and patted her tummy and pulled an anguished look on her face.

The two officers nodded, embarrassedly. "Ok, if you get any trouble here, then please do call this direct line." The taller of the two men approached the counter and scribbled a number onto his pad, then he tore the bottom of the sheet and passed it over. "If you're all ok and sure that we can't be of any assistance, we'll be on our way."

"Thank you," Jenny replied. "Thank you and... err... I'm sorry that you've been called out unnecessarily."

"We will speak with your father, Miss. He should not be wasting police time. Good evening."

Jenny held her breath as she watched the policemen leave.

A few minutes later, as they drove away, a familiar looking van pulled up outside the shop and out stepped Jenny's dad.

"Jen – what the hell's been going on?"

"Oh God, Dad. I'm so sorry. I was... I was terrified. I'm so sorry. It was really silly of me." Jenny sighed. "I've gone and got you into trouble now, haven't I?"

"No – why?"

"The police, they were just here..."

"I know, I passed them."

"They said they're going to contact you, about wasting police time."

The front door opened and two people walked in. Then another three. It was plainly obvious that the residents of Millen Road were only here to see what was going on. At ten minutes to six on a Sunday evening, she'd never had so many people milling around the shop. Every single one of the potential customers eyed Jenny and her dad suspiciously, as they strolled around aimlessly.

"I thought you were in trouble, Jen. That's why I called the police – what else was I supposed to do?"

"I don't know. I really am sorry, Dad. I've been so stupid."

"So?" said Dad, softly. "What was going on?"

"It was the man upstairs." Jenny huffed and looked down at her shoes. "I thought... well, I thought he was going to do something..."

"Like what?"

"Like kill me..." Jenny smiled, weakly. "I know it sounds ridiculous. My imagination was working overtime."

"I've heard some stories about him..."

"Jacob told you?"

Dad nodded. "Yes – you were right to be wary, love."

"No... it was just me overreacting, Dad. He had only come in to have a look around – he's never been in here before." Jenny sighed. "As he left he said the shop was nice. God – what an idiot I've been."

"I'm not sure that I like you being here on your own, Jen. You are risking trouble – whether it's from him upstairs... or anyone else that may decide to come in and cause a problem."

Dad's serious tone meant that he would not be dropping the subject until something was done about it. But what could Jenny do? She could not afford someone else, she didn't want to ask Aaron to offer his voluntary services any more than he had already and Dayna and Tasha were putting in extra work by delivering the leaflets, which was more than she'd expected.

"I know, Dad. It's so difficult. Finances are not going as forecast yet. I can't employ anyone else either. Aaron helped me out last night."

"Aaron?"

"You know – the fella who put the EPOS system in. Aaron Frey."

"Good of him to help," Dad replied, curiously. "How did you manage that?"

"We've become friends – good friends."

"I see..." Dad curled the edge of his mouth up into a half smile. "Good friends – eh?"

"No, not like that. Well, we do get on very well. I'm supposed to be going out for a meal with him tonight." Peering up at the clock, Jenny noted the time. "The shop should be shut by now but how can I with all these people in here?" she whispered.

"Grab it while you can, love." Dad looked down the aisles on both sides. "About 12 people in here," he said, quietly. "I'll stay until they've all gone."

Anxious that she was not going to make it home in time for Aaron's arrival, Jenny huffed. "I could always tell them that the shop is closing now and could they bring any purchases to the till."

"And risk losing their custom?"

Jenny peered down the aisle and across to the mirror. As far as she could see, there was only one person that she'd seen before. "Ok, I know what you mean... and I think some of them could be new customers," said Jenny, resignedly. "Suppose I'll stay open until they've gone."

"What do you want me to do then?"

"Make a cup of tea?" Jenny grinned. "A sweet one – I need the sugar after the scare I just had. And I'm sure you're going to need one too, Dad. I'm so sorry – I hope the police will understand. Blame me for everything. "

Dad laughed. "Don't worry about me. You are a numpty sometimes though, Jenny. You're so like your mother was," he said, before leaving the counter area and trotting off down the aisle to the staffroom, dodging past people on his way.

Chapter 32

I'm running really late. Can we make it 8pm? Sorry, from Jen x

Kissing her dad on the cheek and saying sorry for the umpteenth time, Jenny jumped in her car and sped off. If Aaron was coming to pick her up at eight, she had about 45 minutes to get home, have a shower and find something decent to wear. No hope. Her dad had slowed her escape from the shop. Although his intentions were to be helpful and protective, all he managed to do was get in Jenny's way as she tried to whizz around the shop, checking things and turning things off. The money had to be counted three times due to the fact that both Jenny and her dad came up with two different figures. The third count tallied up with Jenny's first, so she went with that one – twenty two pence over the EPOS report. Bonus.

Sure, see you at 8pm. Hope you haven't had any more problems??? Aaron xx

The buzzer rang just as Jenny slipped on a pale pink silk blouse. Fully dressed, she went to the intercom. "Aaron, is that you?"

"Yes." Came Aaron's voice.

"Come up if you'd like, I'm almost done."

Racing back to the bathroom, Jenny pulled the sodden towel from her hair and reached for a brush. This evening she decided she was lucky to still have her head on her shoulders, after her imagined encounter with Denny. So the fact that her hair was still wet could only be thought of as a good thing – surely? A rap on the front door brought Jenny back from her muse.

"Hi – Aaron," she puffed, tugging her skirt down with the palms of her hands. "Only just ready." Aaron's puzzled expression made her want to laugh. "Yes, sorry, wet hair. Haven't had much time – all Dad's fault – he slowed me up." Snatching her coat and bag from a hook, Jenny walked out of the door and down the stairs with Aaron.

"Your dad's been in to see you?"

"Yes, he... err... well, it's a long story." Jenny smiled, shyly. "I'll tell you when we're in the car. I've been so silly tonight and poor old Dad is in trouble now. And it's not really his fault – it's all completely, one hundred percent, my fault."

Aaron gazed, amusedly, as they walked over to his car and climbed in.

By the time they reached the restaurant, Aaron's facial expressions had gone from fear, to horror, to one of disbelief (this was becoming the norm), to absolute hilarity. "Oh... Jenny. It always happens to you. I don't mean to laugh... but, well, it is funny. Surely you must see that now?"

Jenny wasn't laughing. "No, I don't. I've made myself look a right plonker. Dad could be in trouble with the police now. And... and Denny probably thinks I'm completely bonkers the way I was shouting down the phone." Jenny cringed. "And what are Dayna and Tasha going to think when they hear about it?"

"Sorry, Jen but I expect that they'll find it very funny too." Aaron burst into laughter again and held on to his sides, as if in pain. And he probably was. Splitting his sides.

Jenny chuckled to see Aaron laughing so much. Maybe it was funny. Maybe Jenny needed to lighten up. Maybe she'd experienced too many weird things going on at her shop. Maybe she desperately needed this 'Aaron time' to help her chill out.

No matter how much she protested, Aaron would not let her pay for the exquisite meal they'd just eaten. "No, you've had enough to contend with today. This is the least I can do." Aaron smiled through his dark eyes. "Now to get you home safely."

"Thank you," Jenny replied. "This was just what I needed. Time away from everything – away from the shop and its strange customers and even stranger neighbours."

"Come on then, let's get you home to bed," smirked Aaron, glancing down at his watch. "I'm sure it must be way past your bed time."

"Almost," said Jenny, noticing the time. "I've got 15 minutes before I turn into a pumpkin."

"You turn into a pumpkin at 10.30?"

"A shrivelled up one at that." Jenny chuckled.

Before getting in the car, Aaron paused and turned round. "It's been a lovely evening, Jen. Thank you." Leaning towards her, he kissed her gently on the lips.

"No. Thank you," she spluttered. "Back to mine for coffee?"

"A quickie..."

"Pardon me?" Jenny sniggered.

"A quick coffee – you mad woman. You're getting as bad as your customer and neighbour friends."

"Foe," replied Jenny, with certainty.

The coffee wasn't quick – it wasn't slow either. It was left, untouched, on the side tables in the living room. Somehow, Jenny and Aaron had made it through to the bedroom, where they stood in a passionate embrace.

"I should go..." Aaron breathed, deeply.

"You should..." Jenny fingered the buttons of his shirt.

"I will... now." Aaron's hot mouth pressed against hers.

"Go on then... now..." One by one the buttons of Aaron's shirt loosened.

"I'm going..."

Undressing.

Lying across the bed, half naked.

Their love making was fast and frenzied. Hot and hungry. Sustained and satiable.

Wrapped in Aaron's arms, Jenny closed her eyes as the heady aroma of sex engulfed her. Safe, warm and sleepy, she drifted away to a heavenly place where there were no tills ringing, no customers complaining and no strange locals looming.

The bleep of the alarm clock dragged Jenny away from her slumber. Reaching across, she turned it off. A warm body lay next to her in the darkness. Aaron. He was in her bed. Turning over, she slipped an arm around him and snuggled into his back. His soft skin brushed against her face. Closing her eyes, Jenny breathed in the musky scent of him and drifted off to sleep again.

"Oh God!" Jenny peered through the gloom at her clock. "Oh no." Leaping from the bed, she grabbed her dressing gown and put it on. "Aaron," she whispered. "Aaron," she said louder, shaking his shoulder.
Aaron groaned and moved his legs under the duvet.
"Aaron – wake up."
Lifting his head from the pillow, Aaron looked up, dazedly. "Yeah?"
"It's half past six – I'll never make it to work in time."
Grabbing fresh clothing from the wardrobe, Jenny rushed to the bathroom to get ready. "Get up – I need to go. You've got two minutes," she called back.
By the time Jenny had washed, dressed and cleaned her teeth, Aaron had also dressed and straightened the bed.
"Thanks," said Jenny, as she flapped about trying to find her shoes. "You didn't need to make the bed but I do appreciate it."

"Not a problem. Do you want me to come to the shop with you? I could help for an hour or so."

"No – I'll be fine. They'll just have to wait won't they?"

Aaron nodded his head, guiltily. "Ok, if you're sure."

"Sure – come on, let's go." Pecking Aaron on the cheek, Jenny ushered him through the front door and down the stairs. "Sorry to rush off. Bye," she added, before pecking his cheek again and heading towards her own car.

Pulling up alongside the shop, Jenny could see Dolly and Jordan waiting by the door. As she walked towards them, Wilbur, who was tied up on his usual ring, wagged his little stumpy tail, fervently.

"Sorry, sorry," said Jenny, holding her hands up in the air. "So sorry, Jordan."

"Poor boy has got to be off in a minute. He has school you know."

"Yes – I'm well aware of that, Dolly." Jenny pulled the keys from her pocket and unlocked the door.

Jordan stood silently with a sheepish grin on his face. "I can help sort the papers out. I...I'm not sure I'll have time to deliver them though."

Dolly huffed as she followed behind them into the dark shop.

"Just wait there, I've got to deactivate the alarm," called Jenny, as she rushed behind the counter and switched it off. Next, she turned the lights on, both inside and out. Even though the gloomy day was beginning to dawn, the looming grey skies would necessitate the outside light being left on for a few hours this morning. "I'm really sorry, Jordan. I've done it again, haven't I?"

"And what about your customers, lovey? We're going to have to wait until you've sorted yourself out, before we can get a paper." Dolly exaggerated a false sigh. "Oh dear, you should go to bed a bit earlier, my dear."

"Yes, yes – I know." Jenny looked at Jordan and raised her eyebrows. "Look, Jordan. Why don't you get off and I'll get one of the girls to do your round."

Jordan peered down, sulkily.

"I will still pay you – this is all my fault."

"I should think so – it's hardly his fault that he can't do his job."

"Yes, I know Dolly, that's what I've just said." Jenny could feel anger beginning to rise in her stomach. "Go on, Jordan. I promise you, this won't happen again."

Jordan nodded. "Ok... and... thanks, Jenny. I'll see you tomorrow." Jordan smiled at Dolly and said goodbye, before disappearing out of the door.

"Dolly, could you do me a real big favour?"

"No, dear, I can't deliver your papers for you!"

"No, I don't want you to. I wouldn't dream of asking you to do that." Jenny frowned. "Could you just watch the shop for a minute... just while I go out the back and bring the papers in?"

Dolly puffed her cheeks out. "Yes I could. How long are you going to be. I... I can't leave poor Wilbur tied out there for too long." Dolly pointed to the window. "Looks like we'll be getting some rain."

"I'll only be a minute," said Jenny, edging away down the aisle to the end of the shop. *And you really don't mind leaving poor Wilbur out there for bloody hours when you're having a good old gossip in here – do you?* Jenny thought to herself and wished she had the nerve to say it out loud. Unfortunately, if she did do that, Dolly would poison the entire, elderly population of Farehelm against her and half of her customers would probably disappear.

After three trips and three disgruntled glares from Dolly, Jenny had hauled the bundles of papers through the shop. "Thanks," she panted, "do you want your usual?"

Dolly shrugged her shoulders. "Not sure I can wait any longer, dear. Maybe I should have gone to the *KO Store*. They're always open on time... and they open at six every morning too."

Well, thanks for nothing – why don't you just sod off down there then? "I can have these untied in a jiffy, Dolly. How would you like it for free today, just for the inconvenience I've caused you?" Jenny went behind the counter and grabbed the scissors.

"That's very kind of you, my dear. Thank you."

"Don't mention it," said Jenny in a disgruntled tone. "Here," she said as she passed the top paper to Dolly.

"Can I have one a bit further down please? This one is creased..."

Would you like me to frigging well iron it for you? Jenny pulled a paper from the middle of the pile and passed it over. "Is that one all right?"

"Yes, lovely, dear. Thank you." Tucking the folded paper under her arm, Dolly walked towards the door, pulled up her coat sleeve and looked at her watch. "Oh my goodness, look at the time. I must get off now."

"Bye, Dolly, and thanks for watching the shop."

"Never mind, dear. I shouldn't think it will do much good for your business if you keep being late though. Early nights, dear – that's what you need."

Jenny forced a smile and nodded her head. Then she watched as Dolly went outside, bent over the dog hook, untied Wilbur and trotted off with an air of opulence about her.

Cantankerous old cow.

The dairy delivery, the bakery delivery, the wholesaler's delivery. Deliveries, deliveries and more deliveries. Therefore, there were invoices, paperwork and payments to make. Tasha had turned up promptly, as usual, yet Jenny hadn't said more than two words to her. Those two words had been, 'Morning Tasha'.

At 8.35am the phone rang. Jenny left the stock room and reached for the phone on her desk. "Good morning, *J's Convenience Store*, how can I help you?"

"My papers – I haven't had my papers this morning." The man's voice sounded aggressive.

Jenny froze. *Oh no.* She'd completely forgotten that the papers hadn't been delivered. "Ah... err... yes, I can only apologise about that, Sir. We... err... we've had a slight problem this morning... but... err... I can assure you that they will be with you very shortly."

"I do hope so. I expect to have them here when I get up in the morning. This has inconvenienced me somewhat. I won't be able to read them until this afternoon now. They will be old news by the time I get to read them."

"I am so sorry, Sir. I can assure you that it won't happen again."

"What time will they be here?"

"You'll have them within the next half an hour."

"Thank you. Goodbye."

"Bye..." Jenny replied but it was too late, the man had already hung up the phone.

"Tasha – the papers haven't been delivered. Either you go..." Jenny peered out of the window at the splodges of rain hitting the glass, "...or I'll go in the car. But you'll be here on your own for a while."

Tasha's eyes widened. Shooting a cursory glance through the window, she looked back to Jenny. "I don't mind staying here if you want to go. Or... I'll go if you want me to."

"It would be quicker if I go. Are you sure you'll be ok?"

Tasha nodded, timidly. "Yes, I think I'll be fine."

"Can't believe I've forgotten to do them. If anyone else rings, tell them they're on the way."

"Didn't Jordan turn up this morning?"

"Yes – it was me that didn't turn up. Well, not on time anyway. He had to get off to school."

"Oh, you were late then?"

Jenny nodded. "Yes... yet again."

Quickly, Jenny put together a pile of papers from the Monday delivery list. "Right, I'm going. I'll be back as soon as possible."

Mr Johnson must have been waiting behind his front door. As Jenny approached the letterbox of the dark green wooden door, the man whipped it open. "Ooh..." squeaked Jenny, as she almost fell through the doorway, while clutching several, damp newspapers. "Sorry."

"About time," said Mr Johnson. Towering above her, the man glared down. "I was just on my way up to the shop."

"Sincere apologies. We... there was a slight problem this morning. I'm the owner of J's – I've had to come out and deliver them myself." Blinking away the raindrops dripping from her fringe, Jenny glanced up at the man, sorrowfully. "I do apologise."

"Do you have a phone? I tried looking for your number. Couldn't find it anywhere. I can tell you – I was not best pleased about trekking out in this weather."

"Yes, of course. You should find it on your paper bill."

"Tried that – didn't work. It's the wrong number."

Jenny puzzled over this latest piece of news. "Are you sure?"

"Are you calling me an idiot?"

"No, not at all?" Jenny replied, shakily. "I will check it when I get back to the shop. Once again, I can only apologise."

"I'm sure you'll find that your number is wrong. On the bill, at least." The man's voice had softened.

Jenny smiled, weakly. "Thank you, I will look at it." Turning to leave, she brushed her wet, bedraggled hair away from her face.

"Good bye," she muttered, politely. But the man had already closed his door.

Soggy, tired and troubled, Jenny delivered the last two papers and then travelled the short journey, back to the shop.

"Aaron's here," mouthed Tasha, as Jenny walked through the door, feeling the warm air tingle on her face. "He's making you a cup of tea." Tasha leant over the counter and continued in a whisper. "I wasn't sure if I should let him go in the staffroom. He said you wouldn't mind."

Jenny smiled, warmly. "No, it's ok. He can."

Reaching the staffroom door, Jenny pushed it open. Aaron was standing by the kettle, dressed in a dark grey suit, pale purple shirt and a dark, maroon tie. He looked so handsome. So tidy. So dry.

Two large croissants sat on two plates and Aaron was carefully stirring three frothy cappuccinos.

"Oh dear – look at you," he said, with a smirk on his face. "Is this all my fault?"

Jenny shook her head and a drop of water dripped on to her nose. "No, it's not," she said, wiping the wetness from her face. "I should learn to get up when my alarm goes off."

"And I should learn to help you get up when your alarm goes off." Aaron grinned, cheekily. "I'm leaving at ten – thought you might have some breakfast with me before I go."

"Thank you. That's sweet of you."

"I won't be back until late tomorrow evening... maybe I could see you Wednesday night?"

"Yes, of course. More meetings?"

Aaron nodded. "Manchester. It's a pain but I need to go and show my face at these places."

"That's what comes from being such an entrepreneur." Jenny grabbed a hand towel from the wash basin and rubbed her hair dry.

"Yeah – it's not all that it's cracked up to be."

Peering in the mirror, Jenny growled. "Look at the state of me – I look like the *Blair Witch*."

"No you don't. You look beautiful, as always... Ok, maybe you do look a bit *Blair*-ish."

A warming hug and a tender kiss, made Jenny's morning so far, so much better. And even if she did look like a witch on a wet and windy morning, it was obvious that Aaron liked her – warts and all.

Chapter 33

It had rained for the last three days, practically non-stop. Or at least it felt like it had. The footfall and spend decreased considerably and Jenny guessed that the bad weather had something to do with it.

Staring at the pile of invoices to be paid, Jenny veered off into a day dream. If December didn't pick up, she wasn't sure how she was going to pay her next month's rent on her flat – let alone buy any Christmas presents for anyone. Or eat food. Or pay her electric bill.

Dayna and Tasha had been steadfast in their mission to deliver the leaflets. Their illuminous pink suits had protected them from the elements and they hadn't once moaned about the weather. For some strange reason, they seemed to be enjoying their little trips out around the area.

"I reckon we must have delivered about 350 leaflets between us, by now," said Dayna, boastfully. "They'll soon be rolling in, Jen. You just wait and see."

"I hope you're right."

"Even if people don't read the leaflets, we've had enough cars tooting at us and passers-by commenting on our clothing." Dayna grinned. "I say to everyone – be there or be square."

"Did you sort out what you're doing on Saturday?"

"Oh, with Tasha you mean?"

Jenny nodded.

"I'm coming in at six, then she can go."

"Ok, good."

"Are you all right, Jen – you seem a bit down."

"Yes... yes I'm ok."

"No you're not. Are you seeing Aaron tonight?"

"Yes, he's bringing a take away round to mine at nine."

"So what is it then?" Dayna wasn't stupid. She could always sense when something bothered Jenny.

"Same old stuff. I'm really hoping that these leaflet drops will work."

"They will, Jen. They've got to. There are hundreds and thousands of people living round here – you've probably only seen a fifth of them. Give it time... you'll see."

"Hmm... I just don't know how much time I can give it."

Dayna stared at Jenny's downtrodden expression. "That's not like my Jenny. Come on, get a grip. You're usually so determined."

Smiling weakly, Jenny left the counter and headed to her office. The bills were calling her. The payroll was summoning her. The paperwork was demanding her attention and a lack of sleep was taxing her. She had to keep going.

The evening arrived quickly. Jenny had been so absorbed in sorting out all of her tasks that the time had flown by. Dayna had popped her head around the door from time to time, offering cups of tea and high spirited hope. The shop had been fairly quiet all afternoon and Dayna had managed to clean all of the shelving down one aisle.

"Right I'm off now," said Dayna, cheerily. "I've bagged up some of the coins from the till." Dayna passed over handfuls of money bags. "Do you need me to do anything else before I go? I'm guessing you'll be wanting to get away early."

"No, that's fine. Thanks, Day. You go – I'll be finished here very soon."

"Ok, see you laters."

Locking the door after her friend had left, Jenny grabbed the till's tray and went down to the office and waited for the EPOS report to be printed off.

The sheet of paper popped out from the printer and Jenny picked it up to read.

Total amount today: £737.56

Considering that she was expecting to be taking somewhere in the region of £1,500 to £2,000 per day by now, and even more at the weekends – this amount was barely half.

Jenny's face reddened as a fear welled up inside her. The takings were going down, not up. She'd hit the £1,000 mark only twice in the time she'd been here and had put the low figures down to a slow start. It appeared that her 'slow start' was not even starting anymore.

Driving home, Jenny frowned and cursed again and again, as she pondered over the poor figures. Her head began to thump and she'd lost her appetite of earlier.

Her flat was warm and cosy and Jenny had managed to get home in record time but grabbing her phone from her bag, she sent a text message.

Aaron, so sorry, can we cancel tonight? I've got a banging head and need to go to bed. Can't seem to get enough sleep at the moment. Jen x

Moments later a message came back.

Not a problem, Jen. I totally understand what it's like when you're running your own business. Perhaps we could do Saturday night? I can come in and help out again, if you still want me to. Sorry, can't help on Friday though – got another big job on this week. Aaron xx

Sounds great! Thanks for being understanding. See you Saturday x

Trudging through to the bedroom, Jenny changed into her Pyjamas. Although she couldn't be bothered to see Aaron, she did miss him. She wished it could be easy – if only he could just turn up, say a quick hello and then go to bed – to sleep! Their relationship would work for her that way – for now.

It had rained, non-stop, all week. Noah would have been very busy building an ark, Dayna had said, after one of her trips out to deliver soggy leaflets. Tasha didn't seem quite as enthusiastic about the leaflet drops as she had at the beginning of the week, but Dayna had tactlessly reminded her that it could be the difference between them having a job or not having a job and to get over it – it was just a bit of rain for heaven's sake.

Saturday morning was no different from any other damp morning this week. Poor Jordan had turned up early, every day, with the same cheery smile. Not once had he moaned about the weather, even though he was practically soaked through to the skin before he'd even begun his deliveries.

In contrast, however, Dolly had moaned constantly. She'd moaned about the weather, groaned about the price of Wilbur's new raincoat and she'd grumbled about the Christmas hype, everywhere she went.

"Your shop is the only place that isn't decorated so early on. I expect you will be putting some up though. Have you got decorations?"

"No, Dolly, I haven't. Suppose I'd better get down to the town and get some." *Before you ram your unwanted opinions down my throat.*

"Well, yes, if you want to keep up with the other shops, you will. Just don't go over the top, dear."

Tasha arrived at ten o'clock and just for a moment, Jenny wondered why she was here on a Saturday.

"Yes, ok – just clicked. You've swapped."

Tasha giggled. "We thought you might have forgotten."

"I can't believe that Dayna hasn't been going on about it all week."

"She's been worried, I think. She didn't want to bother you with any more than you had already to worry about."

"Worried? About what?" Jenny looked questioningly at Tasha.

"She said that you've got a lot on your plate." Tasha paused. "And... and she didn't want to upset you by going on about it, you know... because you haven't seen Aaron." Tasha's face had turned a deep pink colour. "That's what she said, anyway."

"Oh for goodness sake. I'm fine – and it was me who put Aaron off. I'm just too busy to see him most of the time or he's too busy." Jenny sighed, "When things are better... well, things will get better – you know what I mean."

Tasha nodded her head in short, quick movements. "Yes. Of course."

The fact that Aaron's text message, only half an hour ago, had bothered her and it wasn't fine, only seemed to enhance her last statement, 'things will get better'.

As soon as Tasha had made some tea and arrived at the counter, Jenny went down to the office to read Aaron's text message once again.

Really messing things up now, Jen. I can't make it tonight – need to switch over this new system, it didn't go as planned last night. They shut at 8pm. It's going to take me a couple of hours to do the changeover. **Begging now** – can we do tomorrow night, like last Sunday? Can't believe a whole week has gone by and I haven't seen you. Aaron xx

As long as I can get up on Monday morning, lol x

Don't drag me into your bedroom then! Lol xx

Don't remember dragging you – I'm sure it was you who used persuasive powers to entice me in. x

The day dragged on and on. It was unfair to say that it was because Tasha was working and not Dayna but that was the case.

And it didn't help that Jenny did not have the evening to look forward to with Aaron.

How are things going? Love Jen x

"I've just texted Day," said Jenny, excitedly. "Wonder how she's getting on with her dentist."

"He might be giving her a filling as we speak."

"Pardon?" Jenny stared at Tasha, briefly, before laughing aloud. "A filling?"

Tasha gasped and covered her face with her hands. "Oh... I didn't mean like that..."

"Are you sure?" said Jenny, in jest.

Nodding her head, Tasha murmured, "Yes, I was joking..."

"I know you were." Jenny smiled. "Oh... that might be her now," she said as her phone vibrated. Reaching underneath the counter, she picked it up and looked at the message.

Good – I'll be there at 6pm. Tell you then xxxxx

They both kept on looking up at the clock. Even Marj did, when she noticed Jenny and Tasha peering upwards, clock-watching.

"Are you waiting to close?" Marj asked, as she approached the counter with a pack of four white toilet rolls.

"No – why do you say that?"

"You keep looking at the clock, on the wall." Marj pointed up to the wall above the window.

"Just waiting for Dayna to arrive. These are white ones, Marj." Jenny held up the toilet rolls, in front of her. "Don't you want the turquoise ones?"

"Oh no, dear. Bill and Ben have left home." Marj grinned, snidely.

"Left home? Bill and Ben? Are they your birds?"

Marj nodded, a sorrowful look creeping over her face. "Gone. Flown away, dear."

"Really? Did they escape?"

"Yes, I forgot to close their cage door... then they left."

"Oh, I'm sorry to hear that. Did you have the cage outside?"

"No, indoors. They were flying around the house for a couple of days – I couldn't get them back in." Marj poked around in her purse and then pulled a £20 note out. "Do you have change?"

"Yes, of course. So how did they get out and fly away?" Jenny was curious now.

"When I went down to the bank... that silly daughter of mine... she let them escape, didn't she?" Marj growled.

"I'm sure she wouldn't have done it on purpose."

Marj grunted. "Anyway, I've got two new white ones now. That's why you haven't seen me in here for about six months."

"Sorry?" Jenny puzzled over Marj's last words. "Six months?"

"It took me a long time to get over Bill and Ben. I've just got Florence and Fiona today. The man at the pet shop brought them round to me. Kind man – very kind man."

"You were in here the other day, Marj."

"Oh no – you must have me mixed up with someone else. I've been indoors. Grieving over Bill and Ben. It must be at least six months since I was in here."

"Marj – I haven't even been open for six months." Jenny shook her head and rolled her eyes to the ceiling as Tasha came walking up the aisle with a grin on her face.

"Oh," Marj giggled, "the one before you then. The other shop."

"This shop was closed for a year, Marj and I'm sure you wouldn't have used the tanning salon that was here before that."

Tasha covered her mouth with both hands, suppressing a horsey belch of laughter.

"Yes I did, actually. I do like a tan."

"Ok..." breathed Jenny, resignedly. "So you have two new birds now."

Marj nodded her fluffy head. "Florence and Fiona."

"So why not the turquoise toilet rolls?"

"They're white birds, dear. I'm sure I just told you that."

Jenny didn't dare look across to Tasha for fear of her starting to hee-haw. "Ok... so white toilet rolls for white birds – yes?"

Marj nodded again. "Yes. Bill and Ben were turquoise blue budgies – remember?"

"Oh yes, of course they were. I suppose that Florence and Fiona have to have white toilet rolls then."

"Yes, of course they do. I've told you all of this before, dear. Have you forgotten?"

"Seems I must have, Marj. I'm sorry."

Tasha darted away from the counter and swiftly moved down the aisle, clutching at her mouth. Hee-haws were blurting out, sporadically, as she ran down to the end of the shop.

"Here's your change, Marj. I hope that you'll be very happy with Fiona and Flo." Jenny grinned, cheesily.

"It's Florence," said Marj, disgustedly, before leaving the shop in a huff.

Dayna passed by Marj at the door and walked into the shop with a huge grin. "Yoo-hoo only me," she hollered. "She still going on about paying you some money for the shop?"

"No. She hasn't mentioned it in a while – thank God."

Dayna grinned. "Hopefully that little episode is over with then."

Jenny nodded, agreeably. "So... How did it go?" she asked, impatiently.

"Let me put my coat and bag away first." With a cheeky flick of her eyebrows, Dayna tottered off to the staffroom.

Tasha left the shop hurriedly, smiling shyly, as she went. "See you on Monday, Jenny. Bye."

Moments later Dayna appeared, at the counter. "So, Marj ok, was she?"

"Huh – yes, same old Marj. Are you trying to stall the big question?"

"No," Dayna snapped, "I haven't seen her for a while –I was curious."

"She's on the white toilet rolls now, but don't bother asking her why she's changed the colour – you'll get a very confusing story about the disappearance of Bill and Ben and the arrival of Florence and Fiona."

"Don't worry, I won't ask… well, I won't ask her anyway."

"So… how did it go?" Jenny rubbed her hands together, in anticipation.

"Well… yeah, it was good."

"Good?"

"Yeah, I had a nice time…"

"Go on then, tell me all." Jenny frowned, "And don't be worried about me – Tasha mentioned that you've been worrying about me."

Dayna shrugged, "I didn't want to rub it in, Jen. You don't seem to have much fun these days and I didn't want you to get annoyed if I kept going on about it."

"Dayna – I love hearing about other people's fun. Ok, maybe I don't have a life, myself, at the moment but I do love to hear about yours – especially if exciting things are happening. I've been so wrapped up in my own problems, that I'd completely forgotten to ask you how you were feeling about going out today. I wasn't trying to avoid the issue."

"No, I know, Jen. I just didn't want to go on about it."

"Well, you should – so now's your chance – go on then."

"We went bowling first," said Dayna. "And then we went for lunch at that restaurant on top of the hill."

"Oh, yes. I know the one."

"Then we parked up in a layby on the hill, and watched the world go by for the rest of the afternoon."

"And?"

"And that was it."

"Nothing else?" Jenny quizzed her friend. "What did you talk about?"

"Oh, all sorts of stuff. His life story mostly."

"Anything else?"

"My life story." replied Dayna, sheepishly.

"And that was it? You went home after talking?"

"Well... yes... eventually."

Jenny sensed an elusive pause. "What do you mean, 'eventually'?"

"Well... after our chat..."

"So nothing else happened?"

"Not really – I'm seeing him again though, next week." Dayna's tone of voice changed from one of cautiousness to elation, in her last few words.

"Hmm," said Jenny, grinning suspiciously. "So you didn't get your hands on him or anything else?"

"Not really."

Jenny frowned. "Not really? Did you or didn't you?"

"Oh God, Jen. I shouldn't have done it..."

Jenny stopped frowning. "Oh no... done what? Please don't tell me this was another one of those 'Jeffers-bubble blow-jobs'."

"Jeffers-bubble-bon-bon blow-job," Dayna corrected.

"Bon-bon, yes. Sorry. Well, was it?"

"Not fully..."

"Oh my God. What do you mean, 'not fully'?" Jenny shook her head in disbelief. "A half one then? Or was he blowing balloons at the same time too?" Jenny giggled.

"No – there were no balloons. It was just sort of..." Dayna peered down at the floor. "Look, Jen, I didn't realise that weird people hang around up there, on the hill, when it gets dark."

Jenny stared, wide-eyed. "Oh no. I know what you're going to say next." Bursting into raucous laughter, Jenny doubled over and held on to her stomach. "Oh no... Dayna..." she spluttered. "Really?"

"What?" Dayna's cheery voice, of earlier, had turned into a contrite tone. "You know about it then – what goes on up there?"

Jenny snorted and tried to catch her breath, as a young couple walked in the shop. Browsing the magazines, the couple remained at the near end of the aisle. "Tell me later," whispered Jenny, tears of laughter stinging her eyes.

"Jen, I feel really bad now... having thought about it all." Dayna looked serious. Her bubbly bubbles had popped.

"Go on, tell me what actually happened." Jenny peeped around the shop and could see that they were alone. "Hurry up, before someone else comes in."

"I don't want anyone to know about it – ok?"

"I promise," said Jenny, holding a hand to her heart.

"We parked on the bit of wasteland up on the hill. It was just getting dark at about four o'clock, I think. There was no one else there." Dayna tutted, "I'd heard of that kind of thing before but I never thought it really went on."

"Oh, I believe it does. I'm surprised it was so early though."

"It was about five when we... err... got a bit carried away with things."

"So you did give him a..."

"Started to." Dayna rubbed at her forehead. "Next thing we know, a man is stood outside the car, peering in."

Jenny's mouth fell open for a moment. "Oh no, Day." Shaking her head in disbelief, she added, "He was watching?"

Dayna nodded. "He was doing something down his trousers."

"Oh my God..."

"The man made Will jump in fright. As poor Will shouted at him to go away... well... *It* nearly choked me, Jenny."

Jenny looked up to the ceiling and burst into more laughter. "I'm sorry, Day... that... is... so funny..."

"It wasn't funny. We were really scared. And I could have choked to death. I couldn't stop gagging. I've still got a sore throat now." Dayna bit her bottom lip. "Then the man ran off with a big dog following behind him."

"So you didn't finish where you left off, then?"

"No, we drove away quickly as I was still gagging in the car. Then he took me straight home, to Mum's."

"Oh no, Dayna. How do you manage to get yourself into these predicaments? Has he asked you to see him again next week?"

Dayna nodded. "Yes. Hope it's not just because he wants to finish what we started. I know I shouldn't have done it – not so soon. I can't help it, Jen. It just sort of happened."

"You do pick some funny places though. Why didn't you ask him back to your place?"

Dayna shrugged her shoulders. "I don't know. Suppose I thought it would be ok, you know, as we were just going to talk."

"What's done is done, Day. You can't change it. However, I'm beginning to think that you must be the blow-job queen of the South. Gagging or no gagging." Jenny chuckled. "Go get 'em girl."

Forcing a disconcerted grin, Dayna picked up a duster and walked away from the counter.

Chapter 34

In comparison, Jenny was far more reserved than her best friend. On the, now two, occasions that things had heated up between her and Aaron, they had been in her flat.

After a peaceful evening of TV watching, an Indian takeaway and some fruity wine, Aaron had been the one to instigate a full-on sex session, which started in the living room, went through to the hallway, into the kitchen and finally, the bedroom. Maybe Jenny wasn't quite as reserved as she liked to think she was.

Determined not to oversleep, Jenny set the alarm on her mobile phone, as well as her clock. "If you wake up before me, kick me out," she whispered, to an already sleeping Aaron.

Once again, a disgruntled Dolly, bored Wilbur and forgiving Jordan, waited at the front door. Jenny was late again. Her phone had run out of battery power during the night, and the clock had not done its job of being backup plan. She'd ignored it. Twice.

"This is getting to be a little too often," said Dolly, keeping a friendly hand placed upon Jordan's shoulder. "Poor Jordan here, can't be late for school. He's in those very important years."

"I'm well aware of that, Dolly." Jenny frowned. "And this is only the second time you've waited here."

Once again, Jenny could only apologise, profusely, and offer to pay Jordan's wages for the morning. Once again, she would have to remember to deliver the papers as soon as Tasha arrived, at eight. Once again, Jenny was going to have a bad day. She could feel it in her veins.

December arrived far sooner than Jenny would have liked. It meant that her rent would be due soon. It meant that more invoices would have to be paid, for the previous month's stock. It meant that it was even more imperative that her sales figures went up. It meant that she was skint.

Dayna had been floating around the shop all day. It was Saturday evening and she was going to see Will again.

"Just play it cool, Day. Try not to be so 'giving'... if you know what I mean."

Dayna nodded. "I'll try."

Aaron arrived at five minutes to eight, just as Dayna was getting ready to leave. His offer of help, was invaluable, once again. He managed to take Jenny's mind off things. He was lively, funny and thoughtful.

"You know," said Jenny, matter-of-factly, "I've been thinking..."

"Does it hurt?" Aaron joked.

Playfully, Jenny shoved him away. "No, listen. I'm going to put a 'Christmas Opening Hours' sign up on the door."

"Good."

"I'm going to shorten some of the hours on Christmas Eve and Boxing Day. I could even close early on New Year's Eve. What do you think?"

"Go for it. You need a break, Jen."

"Yes, I do. At first, I was so excited that I was going to be having Christmas day and New Year's Day off altogether. But then I got thinking... why open for normal hours the rest of the time?"

"Exactly. You should work out what you might save on electricity by closing early. You know, weigh it up against potential sales."

"Hmm... electricity verses sales... I think electricity wins, hands down," said Jenny, sarcastically. "I just don't know what's going on around here. Day and Tasha have delivered well over 900 leaflets now. At a two percent read-rate, I should have at least 18 new customers."

Aaron laughed. "How do you know that you haven't got 18 new customers? Are you doing face-recognition, EPOS summaries now?"

"Ha, ha – very funny."

"It's true... you will have to deliver a lot more leaflets, to see results. I think so, anyway."

"Dayna seems to think that our problems will be solved when this stupid Jeffers-bubble-what-not comes in."

"Bon-bon are the words you're looking for." Aaron grinned. "Look, try not to worry too much, Jen. I can talk to my mum – see if she can come up with any ideas, if you want me to."

Jenny nodded her head. "Yes, go on then. There might be something that I just haven't thought of yet."

"I'm sure there will be, now get those Christmas hours sorted out. Then you can spend a bit more time with your family over the holidays. You should get a sign up as quickly as possible."

"I will and maybe we could spend a bit more time together... more than just one evening a week?" Jenny laughed, bashfully.

"Ah... well I'm not going to be around over Christmas." Aaron looked down, guiltily. "I'm sorry – I thought I'd told you."

Jenny shook her head and smiled, weakly. "No."

"It's my crazy auntie, in Wales. She has pestered me for so long about staying with her over Christmas one year, and this year, my cousin and his wife will be there, so I agreed."

"Oh... ok."

"I wish I wasn't now, to be honest."

"Why?"

"Well, I would much rather see you a bit more."

"Would be nice... So, why do you call your auntie 'crazy'?" asked Jenny, attempting to sound cheerful.

"She's mad. In a nice way, of course. She's my dad's sister – but nothing like my dad, whatsoever. She's so funny."

"And your dad's not funny – right?"

"Dad's just Dad. Nothing more I can say really." Aaron grinned. "No – he's a good dad. Hard working."

"Like you then…"

Aaron shrugged. "Suppose so."

"Well I'm glad that you've told me you won't be here – I might as well work some more."

"No, Jen. Take a bit of time off. This place will be dead most of the time."

"What? More 'dead' than it is already?"

"I'd imagine so. Mum closes early at least four days and shuts completely for two. She says that she only sells newspapers and the odd jar of pickled onions at Christmas."

"Ok, I'll go and have a look at the dates and come up with something," said Jenny, before pecking him on the cheek and walking away to the office.

"Are you coming back to mine?" asked Jenny, as she locked up the shop.

"For a coffee?" Aaron laughed, cheekily. "And then you won't get up in the morning."

"Yes I will. I'm not going to oversleep just because of a coffee."

"Ok, yes. Coffee it is. Then I'll go home." Aaron looked at his watch. "It's nearly half ten now."

Grabbing her phone from the bedside table, Jenny peered at the brightly lit screen, cutting through the darkness of her bedroom. Squinting her eyes, she noticed a message notification. She hadn't heard her phone go off earlier but then again, would she have noticed while in the throes of a sexual frenzy on the sofa. Aaron slept silently beside her. Exhausted, they had both ended up moving off the sofa and climbing into her bed and that's where they'd stayed. Before setting the alarm on her phone, Jenny thumbed through to the text message.

OMG – hope it's not too late. I can't sleep. Will is wonderful. True gentleman. I'm staying at his tonight. Mum's ok with it. Xaylan's having a bit of a grump but he'll get over it. He thinks I'm staying at yours. So hush, hush. Love from, loved-up best bud, Day xxxxxxxx

Glad you had a good time. No worries, my lips are sealed. I can't sleep either but I should – it's now 2.20am and I need to be up in three hours!! Did you finish what you started last week? Hope there weren't any spectators this time, lol xx

No... no... not again. A rising fear and jagged fragments of thought flicked through Jenny's mind as she frantically dressed. "Ready?" she panted as she glanced at the clock for the umpteenth time. "I've got to go."

"This is my fault," said Aaron as they sped down the stairs.

"No – it's mine. I really should get up. This is getting ridiculous. See you tonight..."

At least there was no one waiting at the front of the shop, however, within minutes of Jenny arriving, Jordan was rapping on the front door. "Sorry Jordan. God, I don't know what's got into me lately. I'll pay you extra if you could sort the papers out for me first."

Jordan nodded his head and smiled warmly. "Yes, sure I can."

"Thank you – you're a lifesaver."

Luckily, Dolly didn't know about Jenny's late arrival – not that it was any of her business, anyway. As the old lady twittered on and on about trivial things, Jenny did her utmost to suppress the constant stream of yawns, invading her headspace.

"You look very tired again today. Is it getting too much for you?"

"No, not at all, Dolly. Sundays are great – I finish early."

"I'd get some cucumber on those eyes of yours, dear. You've got dark rings around them."

"Hmm... thanks, Dolly. I might just do that." *Maybe you could get some hooks over your ears, to tie up those crinkled, saggy bags, under your eyes too.*

"Goodbye, dear. There's a northern wind on the way, I must get Wilbur home before he gets too cold."

"Bye, Dolly." *Get your broomstick out and hopefully the wind will be strong enough to blow you all the way to Kansas.*

Ha ha, no spectators. I'm in Will's penthouse suite, down by the harbour. OMG! xx

Blimey! He must have some money then.

Yeah, I reckon so. Not bad under the sheets either. Bit kinky though! xx

Kinky? In what way? x

Wanted me to be his school teacher! xx

Oh dear. Really? x

Don't mind – it was fun! xx

Each to their own, I guess x

See you tomorrow... if I can walk! Ha ha! Xx

Oh dear xx

The cold wind was beginning to howl through the letterbox and just as Dolly had predicted earlier, the northerly weather front had turned the late autumn into winter, in just a few hours.

"It's freezing in here," said Jenny, rubbing her hands up and down her arms. "Are you cold?"

"A bit," Tasha replied. "Hands are cold."

"I've got a small heater out the back, do you want it behind the counter?"

"What about you?" Tasha placed her hands underneath her armpits. "You'll get really cold out in the office."

"Hmm... true. I should get another one. The heat from the back of the fridges and freezers, won't keep the shop warm enough all over the winter."

Tasha nodded, politely. "Yes – one more should do it."

"I'll get one tomorrow lunchtime."

Tasha smiled and shuddered as the front door opened and an elderly man blew in. Waddling down the aisle, he bent down awkwardly, and picked up a couple of papers. As he approached the counter, his reddened, weather-beaten cheeks, cracked into a smile. "Morning."

"Good morning," said Jenny as she moved across the counter, took the papers and scanned them through the till.

"Here you go," said the man, passing a ten pound note across.

Jenny took the money and began to collect the change from the till drawer.

The old man held his hand out as Jenny counted the money into it.

Drip.

A droplet fell onto the back of Jenny's hand. Looking up, horrified, she noticed that the man's nose was dripping. Another globule quivered on the rim of his left nostril.

Tasha gawped at Jenny's hand, in horror. Then she gaped at the man's nose. "Ugh..." she gasped, before clutching at her mouth.

Wiping the bead of fluid from her hand, discreetly, Jenny gave the man the rest of his money as quickly as she could – whilst watching his nose all the time. "Thank you," she said, just as the other drop fell from the man's nose and landed on the counter top.

The elderly man left the shop, completely unaware that he had left two women reeling in disgust, behind the counter.

Six o'clock couldn't come round soon enough. Jenny could not feel her toes anymore, her fingers had stiffened and her nose ran, at the most inappropriate moments. She understood how the man, of earlier, could have a runny nose in this cold weather but she didn't get why he didn't know about it. Surely he must have felt the drops hanging from his nose – it tickles? Maybe he didn't – maybe it was an age thing. Jenny sniffed and wiped her nose again. She didn't want to end up with an oozy, drippy nose, when she met up with Aaron in an hours' time. They'd made an agreement – spurred on by Aaron's insistence. She would meet up with him at their favourite restaurant, have a meal with him and then go home for an early night – on her own, straight after.

And she did. It was hard. But she did it.

Chapter 35

Surprisingly, there had been a bit of hype, leading up to the 'Big, Bubble' day. Apart from the festive feel of the shop, clad in glittery ceiling decorations and tinsel banners, and the approaching holidays, there seemed to be genuine interest in the arrival of Jeffers-Bubble-Bon-Bon. The name still grated on Jenny's nerves every time he was mentioned, but the fact that the parents from the nursery had started to come back into the shop again and ask about his visit, made up for the skin-crawling thoughts that Jenny had of him.

Bubbly-Bon-Bon, as he called himself, in a high pitched, squeaky voice, had visited the shop, under cover, a few days ago. Dressed in a fawn coloured, full-length raincoat and a tweed fedora with a dark green ribbon around the base of its crown, Jeffers looked like your typical pervert. A flasher type of pervert. In fact, Jenny was more than relieved when he kept his coat on during their meeting about the costings and promotional deals.

As soon as Jeffers had left, Jenny approached the counter, where Dayna was serving a string of customers and she waited for the last one to leave. "Oh my God, Dayna. How could you?"

"What?" Dayna replied. "What do you mean?"

"Him," Jenny gestured towards the front door. "That Jeffers bloke."

Dayna huffed. "Long time ago."

"It was only last year."

"Yes – I know. A long time ago. I've gone up in the world since then."

"I suppose you have. You do attract the weird ones though."

"Are you calling, Will, weird?"

"No... no... but... well, isn't he a bit unusual as well? What with all that school teacher stuff?"

"It's just a harmless game," said Dayna, defensively. "Just because it's all prim and proper with your little entrepreneur, Aaron."

"It's not prim and proper – I can assure you." Jenny sighed, "I don't want to get into an argument, Day. I'm pleased that you have gone up in the world. It's about time."

"Hmm... so just forget about Jeffers-Bubble-Bon-Bon. We'll never have to see him again after this."

A rap on the door brought Jenny back from her daydreaming. Peeping her head around the door, Dayna smirked. "Miss bloody Doo-glass is here – wants to speak to you."

"Oh, really? Wonder what she wants. And it's Douglas."

Dayna shrugged her shoulders, "Yea, I know – stuck up cow – do you want me to tell her to clear off?"

"No." Jenny leapt to her feet. "I'll see what she wants first."

Andrea Douglas waited by the counter, a smug look plastered across her face.

"Hello again," said Jenny, cynically. "What brings you back in here today?"

Andrea smirked, "Boss says we can come in here for our stuff again."

"Oh, does she now?"

"Yes, it was nothing to do with me, you know. She stopped us from coming in."

Jenny shook her head, disapprovingly. "Silly really."

"She said you've paid for her car, she's not suing you and we can use your shop again." Andrea smiled, uncomfortably.

"Got ripped off, more like," said Dayna, aggressively. "Sue? She wouldn't have stood a hope in hell – silly bitch."

Jenny scowled at her loud-mouth friend, before turning back to Andrea. "Well that's very good of her to let you come in here again. So... I take it that I'm no longer considered to be a psycho? Or a crazy bitch? I take it that she thought long and hard about suing me for her bruised bottom and obviously made the right choice not to, in the end." Jenny folded her arms in front of her, defiantly.

"She's the boss – what are we supposed to do when she says we can't get our stuff from here? And as for her bruised bum – well, we all think it's funny but we daren't mention it in front of her – she goes mad." Andrea's face flushed. "And I don't know about any psycho stuff, either."

Jenny shrugged, huffily. "Really? Well, ok, never mind about that..." Pausing, thoughtfully, Jenny unfolded her arms and then added, "Ok, give me a list and we'll reinstate your account."

Andrea pulled a piece of paper from her pocket and passed it over the counter. "Can we start from tomorrow... and I'll pay you up front for the week?"

"Ok." Jenny glared across at Dayna who seemed to be biting her tongue in a torturous way. "We'll start tomorrow. Same time as before?"

Andrea nodded and gave a half smile. "Thanks," she said quietly, before turning round and exiting the shop quickly, with her head bowed.

"Should have said no," barked Dayna. "Bloody cheek if you ask me."

"I'm not asking you. Think about it, Day. I lost a fair whack of money when they stopped buying from here. We need them as much as they need us."

"Ok," said Dayna, resignedly, "I don't have to like her though."

"No you don't – but just keep your mouth firmly closed. I don't want to upset anyone else around here."

"Lips sealed," mumbled Dayna and gave a sarcastic, tight lipped grin.

On the afternoon of Jeffers' balloon delights, the shop was full of parents, toddlers and screeching, traumatised babies in pushchairs. Jeffers-Bubble-Bon-Bon did not go down well with everyone. Dressed in a sickly-green Santa outfit and a well-worn yellowing beard, Jeffers' balloon models weren't so popular with the smallest of children. Even the odd bellow of giant bubbles couldn't convince the tearful tots.

The balloon-arch display around the front door seemed to entice, not only passers-by but also the parents who hadn't wanted to come to the shop. Children dragged their apathetic parents inside the shop, after seeing Jeffers do his thing with the balloons. Somehow, he'd managed to convince the parents and children alike, that they too, could learn how to make things from balloons.

"Never seen the shop so full," Tasha exclaimed. "He's pretty cool isn't he?"

"Err... I wouldn't describe him as cool, Tasha. "Think 'weird' would be a more appropriate word."

"Ah, I like him. Quite tasty for an older man, too."

"No." Jenny stared, wide-eyed. "No – seriously? Tasha, he's a freaky, lecherous piece of filth."

"Don't you like him?"

"No I do not." Jenny peered out of the window at the small gathering of mums clustered around him.

"Why did you have him here then?"

"It was Dayna's idea, wasn't it?" Jenny sighed, "I suppose he has helped to pull the parents from the nursery back into the shop."

"So that's good then?"

"Yes, I suppose it is." Jenny continued to watch through the window, as Jeffers twisted his khaki green balloons into Christmas tree shapes and the white ones into angels. Then some of the parents came into the shop, asked for his 'balloon craft' book and got a free lollipop... or two.

It went on for several hours. Jeffers was lively, loud and ultra-friendly to Jenny's customers, creating a healthy beeping of the till and a growing stack of notes in the tray.

"It's going well," said Dayna, cheerfully. "I bet you've taken more today."

Jenny nodded. "Yes, it looks like it."

"So it was worth having him here for the afternoon?"

"Yes – ok, Day. You win. I don't want him back again though – gives me the creeps."

"If it works, don't knock it." Dayna grinned, conceitedly. "Going to make Jeffers a coffee, anyone else want one?"

Jenny had to admit that her friend was right. At the end of the day, the till was almost bursting at the seams. Ok, it was overflowing with coins, more than notes, but she had a good feeling about it.

After three counts, Jenny pressed the summary button on her computer and waited to see if the figures were true. And they were. The takings had increased considerably. Not quite doubled but well enough. The only problem was, she couldn't have Jeffers in the shop every afternoon and there was no doubt that eventually, he would have worn out his novelty appearance. Jenny sighed and looked up as the evening's 'thumps' jumped across the ceiling. At least she had the nursery's orders back – that would help. Wouldn't it?

Locking the front door, Jenny felt a swirl of excitement swish through her body. Tomorrow she'd be closing earlier than normal. Tomorrow she'd start her Christmas holiday's opening hours. Tomorrow she would feel like she was getting her life back, albeit temporarily. Tomorrow, there would be no Aaron. He'd gone. Wales would have him for Christmas and sadly, she wouldn't.

If you're going to be out in the sticks – I'll wish you a happy Xmas now. Hope you have a good time at your auntie's. See you when you get back. Happy Xmas! Jen x

Chapter 36

You too, Jenny. Just crossed the Severn Bridge, pouring down now. Stopped for a Costa – happy days! Have a good rest over Xmas. Oh, and Mum said she'll pop in to see you over the holidays. Said she might have a few ideas for you. No pressure, told her we're good friends, so don't start panicking that you're meeting the mother-in-law or something ridiculous like that, lol. See you soon. Aaron xx

A lie in. Except that Jenny was wide awake by twenty to six. *Who gets up at six o'clock on Christmas day*, she thought, before turning over and closing her eyes again. *Only families with young children.* That counted her out then. Drawing a deep breath, she let out a long sigh before drifting off again.

Dad had cooked a super-size turkey with all the trimmings. A feast of Christmas home cooking, which he loved to do. And sprouts. Hundreds of them.

"This is the first proper meal I've had in months," said Jenny, feasting her eyes over the spread. "I'm full-up just looking at it."

"Get it eaten then. It'll be no good hanging around here when you've all gone." Dad sat down and smiled. "Happy Christmas to you all."

Picking up their glasses of wine, Jenny, Jacob and his bossy wife, Becky, returned the goodwill.

Jenny didn't like Becky very much either but she didn't hate her like Dayna did. Jenny and Becky were two completely different personalities and sometimes they clashed. But for the sake of Dad, they always made polite conversation and smiled at each other a lot when he was around. It all felt very false but it made Dad happy and that was all that Jenny cared about. As for Jacob, he didn't care much either way. Quiet and placid, Jacob tended to keep himself to himself and deliberately not notice his wife's bossiness or indeed, react to it. So Becky usually harped on about trivial things, moaned, childishly, about everything or bossed people around, to her heart's content. No one seemed to care too much.

"Thanks Dad. I've had a really lovely day. And the food was amazing. I'd forgotten how good your roasties were."

"Well I've told you many a time, Jen. You are welcome to come for dinner on a Sunday… and bring your man friend along too, if you like. What's his name? Aaron?"

"Oh, yes… Aaron. Ok, thanks Dad. I may just take you up on that."

Dad nodded his head and winked. "Just tell me when you're coming."

"I will." Jenny smiled, warmly, and threw her arms around him. "Right, I'd better go – got to be up for the papers tomorrow morning."

Jacob muttered, "See you soon, Sis… don't work too hard."

"Yes," added Becky. "Take it easy… if you can. Bye."

Jumping into her car, Jenny drove away with a sense of sadness. It was Christmas day and families were gathered together having fun, eating too much and watching festive TV. Jenny was going home to her empty, undecorated flat, to get an early night before work in the morning. It was a lonely existence, owning a failing shop and having to work non-stop. She really hadn't put this into the equation when she'd submitted her business plan to the bank.

Happy Christmas. Have you been working today? Hope not. Give me a shout if you get fed up and/or lonely. We could go out for a drink?

Thanks, Calvin – Happy Christmas to you too. No, haven't worked today, went to Dad's for dinner. Back to work tomorrow… Jenny paused, thoughtfully. Should she tell him that she's seeing Aaron? Or leave it for another day, just in case it spoilt Calvin's Christmas entirely? One way or another, she had to get the simple message, that she had no further interest in him, across to Calvin... *Thanks for the offer but it wouldn't be a good idea to go for a drink, Calvin, we're finished – remember? Enjoy your holidays and take care. J*

Woohoo! Happy Crimbo, Jen. Sorry so late – been hectic here. Xaylan has been so spoilt by everyone. He loves the game you bought him (well, I bought it and you paid for it, lol). Guess where I've been invited tomorrow? Love and hugs Day xxx
America? To meet Will's family? Lol x
No, don't be silly. Going to spend the day at his penthouse suite! OMG! Sex-filled Boxing Day!
Better get your school books ready then, lol. Have a fab day x
Ha ha, might ask Tasha if I can borrow her nurse outfit – have a change of theme. Hope you've had a good day off and enjoy your shorter day tomorrow. Love ya! Day xxxx

Jenny stared up at the ceiling, thoughtfully, from her warm and cosy bed. *Hmm...* at least she was only working until four o'clock tomorrow. Maybe life wasn't so bad after all. At least she could catch up with her washing and ironing in the evening, cook her frozen chicken, meal-for-one and watch some Boxing Day TV, whilst munching on a mince pie or two. Heavenly. Almost.

Jenny really didn't know why she'd bothered opening the shop, at all. Apart from Dolly and the other regular newspaper buyers, no more than twenty other people had come in. No more than £80 had been taken in the till. It had probably cost more to run the shop for the day. Jenny grumbled under her breath. Although the nursery were using her services again, they were closed for the next two weeks. "I don't know what I'm going to do if it's dead like this for the next two weeks."

Tasha stared, worriedly, at Jenny, not knowing what to say.

"Well, there hasn't been much point in us being here today, has there?"

Tasha shook her head, apprehensively. "It'll be better tomorrow, won't it? We've still got lots more leaflets to deliver."

"Yes, sure it will. I'm sorry, Tasha, I don't mean to sound grumpy. Just tell me to shut up."

"No – I couldn't do that. You're my boss."

"Yes you can – you don't have to put up with a grumpy boss, you know."

Tasha laughed, nervously. "I don't mind... really I don't."

Tasha had been right. Custom had picked up by the following day. Everyone seemed to have run out of bread and milk. Even the newspaper buyers had stretched their pockets to buying a loaf or a small carton of milk. Jenny was taken aback that they'd actually bought something else, apart from their paper. So they did have money. And there she was, thinking that her stock wasn't good enough for the elderly clique or that they just didn't carry any other money in their pockets. But Jenny had now decided to change her tune. Instead of saying that things were going well, when asked by polite and friendly customers, she was now going to tell them that if they didn't start using her, they'd lose her. "Use it or lose it," she said, over and over again.

"Blimey, you're going for it today," said Dayna, placing two mugs of hot chocolate under the counter. "Can't believe that you said that to those two old men."

"Well it's true, Day. If they don't start using us and buy a bit more than a paper, then we won't be here in a year's time."

Dayna puffed out her cheeks. "Yes, I know, but maybe you could say it in a nicer way. You sounded quite abrupt then."

"Did I?"

Dayna nodded, "Yes, you did."

"Well I'm fed up with being polite to them... especially when they come in here, buy a cheap old paper and then stand around chatting to all their friends for bloody hours."

"Go to your office," said Dayna, picking Jenny's drink back up and passing it to her. "Go and have a chill out. I'll do the till."

Resignedly, Jenny left the counter and stomped down the aisle to her office. Maybe she was a little grumpy still.

On way home today. My granddad died suddenly, last night. Be in touch soon. Aaron xx

Oh no, I am so sorry to hear that, Aaron. My thoughts are with you and your family. Love Jen x

Thanks. Don't expect my mum will come to see you now. Sorry, Jen. I'll see you soon, I hope xx

Hope so, too. Take care and let me know if there is anything that I can do. Jen x

"Well... God knows when I'll be seeing him again," moaned Jenny, miserably. "Just had a message. On his way home – his granddad has died, suddenly."

"Oh dear, I'm sorry to hear that. You are really not happy at the moment, are you? And this just adds to everything else."

Close to tears, Jenny stood at the end of the counter, stared past Dayna and out through the window. "Oh, ignore me. I'm fed up, that's all. Everyone is enjoying their Christmas hols... except me."

"And Aaron now, by the sound of it." Dayna moved closer to her friend. "Do you want a hug?"

Tears seeped into Jenny's eyes. "No – you'll make me cry."

"Cry then. You probably need a good cry, Jen."

Shaking her head, Jenny left the counter and walked off down the aisle. Lips quivering, she was not going to give in. Things had to change. Somehow.

The week was flying by. Things were pretty much back to normal. The shop was barely ticking over. Barely making enough to cover all of the overheads. Just normal.

Jenny hadn't seen Aaron at all. He'd text her once, to let her know that his brother was coming over from somewhere in Germany, for the funeral and that he hadn't seen his brother for a long time. Well she hadn't seen Aaron for what felt like a long time too. A selfish thought, she knew.

However much she tried, Jenny couldn't shake off the negative feelings she had about practically everything – including Aaron.

"I don't see the point in trying to have a relationship," she said, stubbornly. "I don't have time to mess around and on the one day a week that I might see Aaron... I'm worn out. So what's the point?"

"Jen, you've got a right negative head on just lately. What's up with you?" Dayna stared, anxiously. "You're a fighter – not a loser. Come on, get a grip."

"I'm ok... I just can't do both."

"Both?"

"Shop... and boyfriend. One's got to go."

Dayna shook her head in despair. "Sounds like you're quitting, Jen. You like Aaron a lot. Don't give up on him."

"I can't give up on the shop, Day – not yet."

"No, of course not. Stick it out Jenny Fartor. You could end up having it all. This does not sound like the girl I once knew."

Sorry haven't been in touch much. Lots going on at home. Funeral on the 7th Jan. Great start to the New Year – not! On the upside, can I take you out New Year's Eve? A meal? See the New Year in together, somewhere? How about going up the hill? Great views of the harbour and the fireworks up there. Missing you, Jen. Aaron xx

Sounds good, would love to. I finish at six o'clock... and best bit, I get a lie-in on New Year's Day! Hooray! Meet you somewhere or are you coming to mine? Jen x

I'll pick you up. 7.30pm ok? Xx

Fine. Looking forward to seeing you again, feels like ages. Missed you too. J x

Jenny's sombre mood of late had lifted. Aaron's text message had melted away the hopelessness. She was going out to celebrate the New Year and she *was* going to celebrate, in style.

Pulling her ruby red shift dress over her head, Jenny stood back and peered in the mirror. *Sexy,* she thought and smiled at herself. This was going to be a wonderful evening, more so, because she didn't have to worry about getting up in the morning.

"Wow – you look amazing," said Aaron as Jenny clambered into the car, in her tight-fitting dress and dangerously high heels.

"Thanks," she replied, coyly. "You look pretty good yourself."

Dressed in black trousers, a lemon shirt and a thin black tie, Aaron leant over the gearstick and kissed her softly. "I've missed you."

Jenny's face flushed as a raging heat raced around her body. "Me too." Smiling nervously, she gripped her glittery, red clutch bag with both hands.

"Come on then, let's go. The Sea View restaurant has a live band in the bar tonight. Thought we might have a look, after our meal." Aaron glanced across and smiled before pulling away. "If it's no good, we could go to the hill. What do you think?"

"Sounds good to me."

Although Aaron hadn't been able to drink all evening, he held no resentment and actively encouraged Jenny to have several. Straight to her head, it went. Straight to her head, the fatigue came. Struggling to keep her eyes open past eleven o'clock, Jenny suggested they go to the hill. At least she would get some fresh air there and the wind whipping across her face, would hopefully keep her awake. The fact that they would have to stand to see the fireworks, would help too. She couldn't fall asleep standing upright, could she?

It was totally romantic. Dizzy with drink, Jenny stood watching the fireworks, wrapped in Aaron's arms. They'd kissed, briefly, during the midnight celebrations and then joined in the well-wishing with the many other couples and families, spectating on the hill.

"That was so nice," said Jenny, dreamily, as the finale came to an end. "I'd heard that people came up here on New Year's Eve but I didn't know it was this good. Thank you, Aaron."

Aaron gazed down at her. "Used to come up here when we were kids... with Mum and Dad... and... well... grandparents too."

"Ah... I'm sorry. It must have been hard for you to come up here."

"I'm ok." Aaron gazed out across the harbour, "Going to miss him..."

Jenny squeezed her arms around his waist. "I bet you will. You'll always have your memories of him, tucked away safely in your heart – no one can take those away."

Aaron pulled her in closer. "A nice thing to say –thanks."

"Shall we go? Coffee? Lie-in?" Jenny's head was spinning round and round. The cold air had increased her alcohol-addled mind.

Aaron looked back and smiled. "Yes, lie-in. Let's do it."

Weightless. Floating through the air. Dreamily wafting towards her big, cosy bed. Lowered onto the firm mattress, Jenny felt the gentle tug of her shoes being removed. Then the quilt covered her clothed body. Lips dampened her cheek, momentarily. Darkness. Dizzy. Sleep.

"Do you want that coffee now?" said a voice, next to her.

Turning her aching head, Jenny squinted at Aaron. "Please..."

"You've had your lie-in. It's almost eleven."

Turning back, Jenny peeped open one eye at the clock. "Oh God. I fell asleep. Oh dear, sorry, Aaron – I can't believe I've slept so long."

"I can. You needed it." Jumping off the bed, dressed only in his trousers, Aaron headed towards the door.

"I don't remember coming home." Peering under the cover, Jenny could see her scrunched up dress gathered around her waist.

"I thought it best to leave it on you," said Aaron. "You were practically unconscious by the time we arrived here. I carried you up the stairs and into bed."

"Oh no – I am sorry about that."

"Don't be sorry. I'll get that coffee."

Two coffees, an hour of talking and a lot of smooching later, Aaron removed his trousers and climbed back into bed.

It would be almost four o'clock before he got out of bed again.

Chapter 37

"I spent practically the whole day in bed," said Jenny, grinning widely. "He left at nine... he was going to stay the night but he was worried that I or we, wouldn't get up this morning."

"It's nice to see you with a smile on your face again." Dayna gave Jenny a quick hug and headed off to the staffroom to put her coat and bag away.

Following behind her, Jenny arrived at the door just as Dayna switched the kettle on. "Did you have a good New Year?"

"Hmm... Ok, I suppose." Hurriedly, Dayna found two cups in the cupboard and went about preparing coffee. "Didn't do anything... sat round Mum's... with Xaylan, New Year's Eve. Then he fell asleep so me and Mum watched the TV."

"Family time – that's nice."

"Yeah... suppose."

Jenny leant on the doorframe and folded her arms. "Are you ok? Seems like we've switched roles."

"Yeah... fine." Dayna grabbed the milk from the fridge and slammed the door shut with her hip. "Been thinking about Will. Saw him for a couple of hours last night"

"That's nice."

"I'm not sure about him, Jen."

"Oh, why do you say that?"

"All he wants to do is play games." Dayna plonked herself down on a stool and stared at the kettle, absent-mindedly.

"Thought you liked it..."

"Once in a while is ok but not every time I see him. Said he's going to transfer Xaylan over to the other dentist, Andrew Clift, as well. Now he's even tastier than Will." Dayna smirked.

Jenny rolled her eyes and tutted. "You're a nightmare, Day. So, why isn't he going to finish the treatment?"

"Says it would be awkward now that we're seeing each other. He thinks it will be better if he goes across to his colleague."

"Fair enough." Jenny picked up the boiled kettle and poured water into the cups. "I think that's a sensible idea and very professional too."

"Hmm... I'm not bothered by it. I just can't make my mind up about him though."

"Are you having fun?"

Dayna nodded, half-heartedly. "Suppose so – don't want to play games all the time though."

"He won't be around for long, Day. Make the most of it while you can."

"Yeah... I know." Dayna shrugged her shoulders and looked up. "Suppose I could always work my magic on the other dentist. He is like a Greek God."

"You're insatiable," Jenny giggled.

By the first Sunday of the New Year, the girls were back on track. Dayna and Tasha had been true to their word and delivered leaflets every day for weeks, apart from over the Christmas period. The printer printed flyers continuously and Jenny had now bulk-ordered black and coloured ink. The street map, on the wall in the office, was beginning to look artistic, with its coloured-in streets and roads, in various fluorescent marker pen hues.

Yet still, there was no apparent increase in the footfall or sales, apart from the prospects of the nursery's daily orders, which would start again next week. Even Dayna and Tasha were telling customers to 'use it or lose it' and to pass the message around.

Dolly's only comment to Jenny was, 'Well, dear... if only you got up early enough and opened on time, you would be able to serve your customers with their early morning papers – that would help, wouldn't it'?

Smiling sarcastically, Jenny had muttered a few expletives under her breath, as Dolly walked out of the door.

Jenny sighed. Although it was the shortest day of her week and Sundays had become her favourite, spending time with Aaron all evening, it was not going to happen today. He hadn't helped out in the shop last night, either. His grandad's funeral was tomorrow and his brother had arrived from Germany, hence, it seemed, that there was a lot of family time going on in his life. And understandably too. Yet Jenny couldn't help feeling neglected, feeling selfishly irked, feeling totally fed-up again. With everything.

Hi Jen. Hope everything is going ok. Miss you. Can we do lunch during the week? Obviously, not tomorrow. Aaron xx

Yes, sounds good. I look forward to seeing you. I'll be thinking of you all tomorrow. Send your mum my condolences. Miss you too J x

Will do. I'll bring lunch then – let's say Thursday? Xx

Thursday's good for me. Take care, love Jen x

You too, love Aaron xx

"Should I clear these shelves off, ready for the new stuff, tomorrow?" asked Tasha, tentatively.

Jenny realised that her mood was having a negative effect on her colleagues but she tried her best to be upbeat about things. Dayna could handle it but Tasha was timid, worried and an anxious employee.

"Good idea, Tasha. You're certainly more on the ball than me. I should get those things returned. I'm sure that no one will be wanting packs of Christmas cards or wrapping paper now." Jenny smiled, guiltily, she'd hardly said two words to Tasha all day. Wrapped up in her own muddle, Jenny's insular existence was no good for anybody. Especially not her.

Glancing at the clock, Tasha replied, "I should just get it done before I finish. I can box it up, if you like."

"Yes, please do. And Tasha..."

"Yes?"

"Please don't feel worried about things. I'll get around all of the problems – somehow. I usually do."

In an attempt to keep her mind focused and her gremlins away, Jenny caught up with a few things on her 'to do' list. She recalled Mr Johnson's complaint, when she'd delivered his newspaper to him. Upon inspection, Jenny found that the phone number on the header of her newspaper bills, did indeed, have a digit missing from the end. Puzzled by this careless mistake, Jenny wondered how the other concerned customers, who had waited for their deliveries that day, had managed to phone the shop.

Done, she told herself.

The printer continued to print, relentlessly.

Done... or at least, doing.

Invoices filed, bills paid, orders made, stock wastage recorded, overdue pay-slips created and printed...

Done, done, done, done, done...

And when it was all done... Jenny felt just as empty and miserable as she had before.

Chapter 38

January jolted by in irregular bursts of activity. Good days. Bad days. Leaflet drops were the only consistent system that gave Jenny any hope for the future. It had to work. It had to make a difference. Even Jenny's so called relationship had jumped into January in a very itsy-bitsy way. There was never enough time to enjoy each other's company in a relaxed way. The whole affair was governed by how quickly they could eat a meal, move on to the amorous stuff and then fall asleep before the alarm clock woke them, far too early, the next morning.

"Jen – there's a woman waiting to see you," whispered Dayna, as Jenny walked back into the shop, having nipped down to the bank, in her lunch break. "She's down there." Dayna pointed a finger towards the second aisle. "Alex – her name's Alex." Dayna lowered her voice further. "Is she *the* Alex? Aaron's mum?"

A fearful expression swept across Jenny's face as she nodded. "Yes. Oh God. Didn't know she was coming in... Aaron never said." Inhaling a deep breath, Jenny thrust her shoulders back and held her head high as she tentatively walked towards the aisle.

A middle-aged woman with reddish brown hair, wearing black trousers and a pale pink raincoat, was scanning the products, along the shelves, at the end of the shop. She looked up and smiled as Jenny approached.

"Hello, Alex." Jenny stretched out a hand. "Lovely to see you again."

Grasping Jenny's hand in her two, Alex shook it enthusiastically. "Jenny. Good to see you too. I've heard all about you – from Aaron – you know what he's like, chatter, chatter."

Jenny laughed, nervously. "I'm so surprised to see you here. He didn't mention that you were coming. Maybe it's only you who he chatters to."

"He's a sod," she whispered. "I told him I would pop in to see you today. He said you might need some advice."

Jenny nodded her head, fervently. "Yes, that would be really helpful and no, he didn't tell me. He's probably too wrapped up in his own businesses, isn't he?"

"Hmm..." Alex rolled her eyes and tutted. "I keep telling him... there's more to life than working every hour of the day, every day of the week."

"I know how it feels though, I have to admit..." Jenny paused and met Alex's eye briefly, "I didn't think it would be this hard."

Alex nodded and shook her head, respectively, while holding a hand up, under her chin. "I know, honey. It's really tough when you first start out."

"Would you like a tea or coffee while you're here?"

"I'd love a cup of tea... and no sugar – thank you."

"Oh..." said Jenny, "And...err... can I just say how sorry I was to... err... hear of your loss. I hope that Aaron passed that message on to you, a few weeks ago."

"He did. Thank you." Alex peered down at the floor momentarily and then looked back up, with a beaming smile. "Ok, let's have that cup of tea and then I can do a walk around the shop with you, if that sounds all right?"

"Thank you for giving me your time. I really do appreciate it." Jenny beckoned to Alex to follow her to the staffroom. A quick glance behind her and Jenny smirked at Dayna, who was watching from the counter. "I'll bring you a coffee... in a minute," she called back to her friend.

"Seems like a nice girl."

"Yes, she is. She's my best friend actually – we go back a long way, Dayna and I."

"That's good. So it's just the two of you?" Alex appeared to be showing a genuine interest.

"No, I have a younger girl, Tasha. She works alternate shifts with Dayna." Jenny prepared the cups and offered a stool to Alex.

"Thanks," said Alex, lifting herself up, onto the high stool. "And I suppose *you* work all of the time – every hour God sends?"

Jenny nodded, "Yes. I knew that I would have to, when I first thought about having a shop. Was it the same for you?"

"Oh yes..." Alex said, thoughtfully. "Years ago... well, I never thought that I would have a life ever again." Gazing into the middle distance, Alex paused. "Unless folk experienced it for themselves, they would never really know how extremely hard it can be. Bringing up the kids and juggling a work/life balance. It feels impossible. At the start."

Jenny acknowledged every single word, agreeably. "Don't know how you did it, Alex. I'm really struggling now and I don't have any kids."

"I had a husband – that helped. Well, most of the time anyway." Alex laughed. "Don't get yourself one of them too soon though, they can be a help – but they can also be a big hindrance."

Jenny giggled, nervously. She was unsure of how much Alex knew about her relationship (of sorts... or was it just classed as a part-time fling?) with Aaron. "I'm in no rush – I wouldn't get time to have a real relationship anyway."

"So, tell me about your shop. Have you had a steady increase in numbers of customers and takings?"

Jenny shook her head and frowned. "No. It fluctuates from week to week. Just when things look like they're beginning to pick up – it all comes crashing back down again."

"Ok, well don't feel disheartened. That can happen. I did notice a couple of things. More to do with the layout of the shop, that might help, if they were changed."

"I'm open to any suggestions that you might have, Alex. I aspire to be like you."

"Oh, you're making me blush now," said Alex, wafting a hand across her face. "Another thing I have thought of too..." Alex peered out of the staffroom and up the first aisle, before turning back. "Have you used the local paper's indie-store promotion yet?"

"No, I haven't. Do you mean their promotional frog thing, 'Neville the News Newt'?"

"Yes – that's it. Sounds silly but it's definitely worth a try. I can give you a contact number, if you'd like. Mention my name and I'm sure that they will get your promotion fast-tracked."

"Really?" Jenny passed a cup of tea to Alex. "That sounds great, thank you."

"Not only will Neville the newt spend an afternoon in the shop, promoting the local paper and giving away free chocolate bars, but the promotions team will also put an advisement in the paper, for a week, beforehand."

"I had noticed in the small print that they do these promotions for independent stores, as well as the big-wigs, but to be honest with you, I hadn't thought about giving it a go before. For some reason, I had it in my head that I would have to be selling more papers before I could use it."

"They do have a threshold, yes," said Alex, before taking a slurp of hot tea. "But as long as you're not too far away from the figures, you shouldn't have a problem. Like I said, mention my name. I don't see it being an issue if you don't meet the requirements." Alex chuckled, "Catch 22 isn't it? If they don't help with the promotions, how can you sell more of their papers?"

Jenny smiled, thankfully. "Your advice is priceless, Alex. It's not for a want of trying. The girls here have been dropping leaflets for the last couple of months..."

Alex shrugged. "I don't mean to sound harsh but about 98 percent of those will get binned."

"Hmm... someone else told me something like that too."

Taking another slurp from her tea, Alex plonked the cup on the counter and stood up. "Shall we take your friends coffee up? I assume you have drinks behind the counter?"

"Oh yes – It's probably a health and safety issue, having hot drinks behind the counter but maybe, once we're busy enough, we'll have mini-breaks in the staffroom." Jenny laughed. "For now – we just sit drinking tea and waiting to fight over who's going to serve the next customer who walks in the door."

Alex laughed and beamed an Aaron-like smile. "First things first. Come on – let's get this shop sorted out for you."

"What an amazing woman," said Jenny, as both her and Dayna watched Alex climb into her *TOYOTA RAV4* and pull away.

"Hmm... nice car too." Dayna sighed. "So – let's have a look at the list then."

Jenny passed a sheet of paper over. "If this doesn't help, then nothing will."

"Blimey," said Dayna, eyeing the list in astonishment. "We've got a lot to do."

"I know – but I'm sure that it will be worth it."

"Wants to be. Where do we start?"

"I'm going to start with a phone call. Get this promotion set up." Jenny grinned. "We'll be in the paper, Day. How cool is that?"

"That is pretty cool. I'll make a start on the moving of stock then, shall I?"

"Thanks, Day. I'm sure that between us all, we'll have everything moved around within a week."

"Does she..." Dayna pointed a thumb out of the window. "Does Alex think that this will make a big difference?"

Jenny nodded. "Uh-huh. It'll make people walk around the shop more. If you think about it, the likes of Dolly never go past the newspaper shelves."

"So they don't have a clue about what else we might sell in here."

"Exactly."

Just as Alex had predicted, the local paper arranged to do a promotion in the shop, with their mascot, Neville the News Newt, within two weeks. Three large posters arrived with the papers on the following Monday.

Support your local independent store with
Neville the News Newt and the Daily News.
Come and see Neville and the news team
on
Wednesday 30th January
Here!
Free sweets with every paper

"Ooh, it's exciting, isn't it" said Tasha, arriving on time, as always. "Are we moving all of the papers today?"

Jenny nodded. "Yes – it's all systems go. We've cleared enough shelves down the end – so let's do it."

"It will look really different in here."

"Hmm... wonder who will be the first to moan about it."

Simultaneously, Jenny and Tasha blurted out, "Dolly." Then they both laughed – except Tasha neighed, more than she laughed.

They were all correct. Even Dayna and Jordan had joined in the stakes.

"I'm really not sure why you have done such a thing. It's terrible."

"Sorry, Dolly?"

"Why on earth have you put your papers...?" Dolly pointed a shaky, gnarled finger down the first aisle, "...all the way down there? Good heavens, you can't expect the elderly folk to walk all the way down there, dear."

"They manage to walk here in the first place, Dolly."

"Yes but..." Dolly moved towards the counter. "It's too far. Why should they have to go all the way to the bottom of the shop to get their papers?"

"Do you have a problem with it, Dolly?" Jenny asked, calmly.

Dolly hesitated. "Well... hmm... yes I do, dear."

"Then I apologise to you, sincerely."

Dolly looked puzzled. "Why would you do that?"

"It's just that I know there isn't a hope in hell of you ever buying anything else in this shop – apart from your paper – so I want to apologise to you for the inconvenience it may cause to you, personally. But, I need to look at the bigger picture here, Dolly. This is a sales strategy, you see."

"What do you mean?"

"There is a small chance that other paper customers, may well look around the shop a little more and possibly discover that some of my prices are as cheap as the supermarkets in town. They may see things that they haven't noticed before. They might even buy more than just a paper." Jenny paused and peered at Dolly's angry, twisted face. "Dare I say it... they could even stretch to supporting their local, independent store before it collapses. They would be the first to moan if it disappeared, due to a lack of support."

"And so would I," Dolly huffed. "But if the staff can't get here on time, practically every day, and they weren't so darn rude to me – on several occasions, I would probably support them a little more. And moving the papers away is surely going to upset some folk. Don't you see?"

"Like I said, I apologise, Dolly." Jenny shot a sarcastic smile at Dolly's face of fury. "Did you want to get a paper today?"

"I... I'm not sure... oh, yes, of course I will – I haven't come all the way up here, with dear old Wilbur, for nothing."

Jenny nodded, nonchalantly, "That's good."

Turning around, Dolly hobbled off down the aisle, with a forced limp.

"Oh, Dolly," called Jenny. "Have a look around on your way back – you might find something else you'd like to buy, as well."

"Huh," she puffed, from the first aisle.

Jenny listened and watched through the mirror, as the cantankerous, old woman tottered down the aisle, muttering and mumbling under her breath. All of a sudden, her false limp disappeared, as she was out of sight. Or so she thought...

The parents from the nursery were just as excited as their children. It seemed that Neville the Newt was going to be a big hit. Jenny watched as the mums and, sometimes, dads, approached the shop window, with their toddlers in tow and pointed to the giant poster, while babbling on about Neville's visit to *J's Convenience Store*.

"Look," Jenny exclaimed, poking the paper lying on the counter. "There, in the kids section. Look – we're there."

Surprised by Jenny's child-like outburst, the moment she arrived at work, Dayna walked across the front of the shop and scanned the Neville the Newt's News section, enthusiastically.

Next week, Neville will be appearing at:
Beasley's News, Hayford – Monday 28th January
The News Store, Rowlands – Tuesday 29th January
J's Convenience Store, Farehelm – Wednesday 30th January
Dittons, Ribchester – Thursday 31st January
Harwood News, Hillington – Friday 1st February
Don't miss out on Neville's goody-bags
and free, Newt News, stickers

"Cool," said Dayna, casually. "I'll buy one. Take it home and show Xaylan – he'll think you're famous."

"I am," said Jenny, beaming smugly. "Do you want my autograph?"

"Only if it's on a big cheque. Coffee and crumpets?"

"Absolutely – let's celebrate."

Celebrate what?"

"The future success of *J's Convenience Store*, of course." Jenny placed her hands on her hips and sighed deeply. "Ahh... I can feel it in my bones. Good things are coming our way."

"God, I do hope you're right."

"Come on, Day, get some positive vibes going. I have to force myself sometimes."

"Yeah... I will. Last time I'm going to see Will tonight though." Dayna said, remorsefully. "He leaves next week."

Jenny peered at her friend in dismay. "Oh, Dayna... I'm so sorry. I've been so selfish and wrapped up in my own crap... I'd... I'd forgotten all about that."

"No worries. It's ok, really. I don't think it would have lasted much longer anyway. He's just not my type. Think I'd prefer the English, stuck-up gentleman sort, to be honest." Dayna gave a half smile and walked off to the staffroom. "I'm cool with it..." she called back, raising her hand in the air and pinching her thumb and index finger into an 'Ok' sign. "...before you ask."

Heaving. That was the only way to describe the shop, during Neville's visit. The crowds of nursery parents and children, attracted passers-by and even the odd vehicle pulled over to see what was going on inside the shop.

However, Neville the Newt was not quite what Jenny or Dayna had expected. Neville was a young, overweight and profusely perspiring woman, dressed in a warty, brown jumpsuit and a frog-like head piece. She smelt terrible. Her tail piece must have been at least four feet long and was trampled on by the young children, on several occasions. Georgia (aka Neville) was the most miserable looking, grumpy woman that Jenny and Dayna had ever seen. It was plainly obvious that she and her colleague, David Hughes, the sales rep from the Daily News, did not want to be there. With forced smiles and false pleasantries all round, David dished out the goody-bags and stickers while Georgia, thankfully, kept her frog head on and stood in the breeze from the opened door.

"Bloody miserable pair, aren't they?" whispered Dayna, half way through the afternoon. "Suppose it's not a very exciting job, spending your time dressed as an overgrown tadpole."

Jenny agreed, "Hmm... and David has to hang out with a fat newt all day long."

Dayna suppressed a giggle. "Yeah, and give out sweets and stickers to screechy little brats too."

"Well, I don't care whether they like it or not. Look what it's doing to our sales today."

Dayna nodded, heartily. "Wouldn't want them in here every day though."

"I would... if the till was full like this every day." Jenny looked down at the wad of twenty pound notes, wrapped up in a plastic money wallet, in her hand. She bent down and discreetly hid it away, under the counter. "Better get that lot put into the safe soon."

"Do it now and make us a coffee while you're down there."

"I will but I can't bring it up here, Day. You'll have to drink it down in the staffroom. There are too many people in here to be walking up the aisle with hot drinks."

"Take it in turns to go for a slurp, shall we?"

Grabbing the money wallet back from underneath the counter, Jenny winked at her friend and headed off through the audience of shoppers and bystanders, all waiting to get a piece of Neville, the nauseous newt.

Chapter 39

How did it go today? A xx

Hi Aaron – on top of the world! It was really good. Almost tripled sales! Couldn't believe it. X

Brilliant. Knew it would help. Let's hope it continues. See you Saturday for my late shift, lol xx

It hadn't helped. As soon as smelly Neville had left the scene – so did everyone else. Back to normal. Back to the mundane mornings with Dolly and her band of merry men, forming a community centre for the moaners of the world. Back to the pitiful sales figures. Back to the rarest of moments when the shop looked busy. Back to the sleepless nights of worry and woe. Back to the turquoise toilet rolls. Yes, that's right – turquoise.

"How can you lose four birds in as many weeks, Marj?" puzzled Jenny.

"I didn't lose them, my love. They've changed colour."

"Really? You're telling me that your white birds have changed to turquoise?"

Marj grinned over her brown teeth and nodded. "Yes, dear. It happens you know."

"I'm sure it does in your world."

Tottering out of the shop with her toilet rolls tucked under her arm, Marj stopped right outside the door and peered back, through the window. Grinning widely, she suddenly threw her head back and cackled. Pointing a little, crooked finger at Jenny, Marj mouthed, what Jenny could only make out as, 'Tricked you, tricked you, hee hee'. Then she disappeared.

The frost set in hard for February. Icy temperatures kept a lot of the familiar faces away, for days on end. The shop was a cold place.

Freezing, in fact. Jenny had now purchased three heaters in total. One behind the counter, one in the staffroom and one in her office. Her concerns were growing. The additional costs of keeping the shop at a workable temperature and the lack of custom was beginning to show in such devastating ways. Having paid her bills, the wages and the stock invoices for January, Jenny had been short of money for her own rent. Aaron had offered to lend her enough to cover the shortfall and some extra for her living expenses but Jenny declined. There was no way she would get into debt with a part-time boyfriend and he'd done enough to help her already. Dad was the only one who Jenny could turn to.

"I don't know what else to do." Sitting at the end of her dad's breakfast bar, hands propping up her chin, Jenny sulked.

Once again, Aaron was off, somewhere in Europe, building business and meeting with clients. Sundays were supposed to be their time for seeing each other, even if it was only for a few hours in the evening, but today Aaron had left in the afternoon, to catch his flight at four o'clock.

"You've done everything you can do, Jen. I don't know what else to suggest. I would have thought it should have picked up by now."

"I know," said Jenny, resignedly. "I can't think where I've gone wrong."

"You haven't gone wrong – it's the area that's wrong. They'll all regret it if you pack up and leave."

"Huh – not to mention poor Dayna and Tasha. What do I do about them? I can't fail, Dad. I just can't."

Dad dished up his famous roast potatoes, on to two warm plates. "You haven't failed, Jenny. The area has failed you. The residents of Farehelm have not appreciated the gift of their very own, independent shop."

"I can't see me lasting until the summer, Dad. It's that bad." Jenny's eyes watered and she quickly blinked away the wetness.

"If it becomes that bad, Jen, pull out of it. Between you, me and Jacob, we'll get through it somehow."

"Yeah... thanks, Dad. There's got to be a light at the end of this long tunnel though – there's got to be." Helping to load the plates with colourful vegetables and thick slices of succulent chicken, Jenny tried to forget about the shop and enjoy this rare moment, this exceptional twinkle of time, sharing a meal with her dearest dad.

"They've forecast snow," said Dolly, the second she was through the door. "Tomorrow."

Wrapped in an over-sized, purple padded jacket, a pale blue bobble hat covered in green dog print, a bright red, thick knitted scarf and yellow wellington boots, Dolly looked like she had recently returned from an outrageous-costume-designs competition in Antarctica.

Jenny peeped out of the window to see Wilbur suffocating in a designer dog-wear, luminous green puffer coat. "Yes, I've heard. Mind you, these weather people get it wrong sometimes, don't they?"

"Not on the *BBC* weather report, dear. We'll have snow tomorrow. I must get some salt and grit today."

"From here?" Jenny asked, sarcastically.

"No, dear, I'm going into town later."

"Thought as much."

Dolly trotted off down the aisle, to fetch her paper, oblivious to the hundreds of products she had to walk past. It was guaranteed that she would never buy anything else from her local independent store. And neither would the other early morning dog walkers. A paper and a gossip were their only requirements each day.

The ideas had been evident when Alex paid a visit to the shop but the lack of shoppers and a stubborn streak, which ran through most of them, meant that Jenny's efforts had been fruitless.

Alongside Dayna and Tasha's laborious leaflet drops, there had been no results whatsoever.

"Might get a dusting if we're lucky," said Jenny, deliberately.

"If we're lucky?" Dolly harrumphed. "No. They've forecast several inches." Dolly slapped her paper on the counter. "You'll be scuppered if you get no custom, won't you, dear? And we're hardly lucky, are we?"

"I've heard it all before, Dolly. They say it's going to snow and we're usually the only town that misses it."

"Sounds like you want it to snow."

"Don't mind a bit of the fluffy white stuff, now and again. It looks nice."

Dolly huffed. "Ok for you, I suppose. Just wait until you get older, dear. You won't be so eager then. It can have devastating effects on the elderly, you know." Dolly peered into her purse and pushed some coins around. "Fuel bills increase in this cold weather… and that's hard on pensioners. Not to mention the risks of going outside. Older folk have brittle bones which break easily. A fall could be fatal – you really have no idea do you?"

"Dolly…" said Jenny, exasperatedly, "… it might not even happen here. Stop fretting."

"I'm not fretting, my dear. How dare you say that I'm fretting. It's about time you saw sense – living in your dream world of lie-ins and false promotions." Dolly's face flushed a deep scarlet and she quickly resumed her faffing with the coins in her purse.

"Think we both got out the wrong side of the bed this morning."

Throwing a couple of pound coins onto the counter, Dolly puffed her saggy cheeks out. "I have no problems getting out of bed in the mornings, dear. And I get out of the right side. Now let's just stop this silly nonsense. Mark my words – there will be snow tomorrow." Extending a hand to collect her change, Dolly grinned smugly, before walking out of the shop.

A polar wind blew through Jenny's hair as she locked the shop's door. It was eerily light under the orange and peach coloured night sky. *Snow clouds,* thought Jenny as she pulled her coat around her tightly, buried her face into the furry collar and walked round the corner to her jeep.

Snow. Not a blanket covering. Not even a dusting or a peppering. Approximately one flake per square metre, to be more precise. However, more pale grey clouds billowed across the sky in undulating waves, threatening to burst their contents on the earth below.

"It's coming," said Dolly, smugly. "Told you it would snow."

"I'd hardly call three flakes, snow," replied Jenny, folding her arms across her midriff, defiantly. "I expect we'll get another three and that will be it."

Dolly peered out of the window at the sky. "No, they said it's all coming today. Just wait and see, Jenny."

"Ok, you win. I'm sure you'll be right, Dolly." Jenny looked out of the window too and watched a clumpy flake of snow fall to the ground and then start to melt. Little Wilbur shivered under his padded jacket and shook his head as another flake landed on top of his nose.

"I'd better get Wilbur home – he doesn't like the snow. Too cold for his little feet."

"I'd image it is – poor thing. You should get him some snow boots."

"Oh no. I won't be taking him out in the snow, dear. He's far too small and delicate. Goodbye."

It was quieter than usual. And that really is quiet. Apart from Dolly and her gang and the nursery's miserable staff collecting their order earlier, there had hardly been anyone else in the shop, at all. Millen Road was bereft of pedestrians and vehicles. Even the nursery's morning rush hadn't rushed. The snow had continued to fall, sporadically, during the morning but every tiny snowflake that landed safely, suddenly disappeared into a miniscule pinprick of a puddle.

"It looks like it's getting heavier," said Dayna, turning round from the window and taking her hot chocolate drink from Jenny.

"Yes, it does a bit. Great – that's all we need. This place doesn't need snow to look like a ghost town."

"Ah, it'd be nice if it laid. I love the snow. Me and Xaylan could build a snowman."

Jenny shot a cursory glance through the window and leant back against the counter, gripping her hot mug in both hands. "Yeah… it's nice to look at… until someone goes and spoils it by walking through it."

"It is laying, you know…" Dayna looked harder, through the window. "Yes, it is now," she said, excitedly. "Look!"

By midday, Jenny and Dayna estimated that there was about one centimetre on the ground. "Blimey, it's really coming down heavy now," said Jenny. "Perhaps we should put salt out on the pathway."

Dayna nodded, in agreement. "Yep, we'll do it while you're having lunch."

Jenny looked out at the snow covered houses across the road. Somehow, snow always managed to make any place look picturesque and serene. A sense of calm washed over her as she gazed, absent-mindedly, at the curtain of frosty white specks cascading down in swirls and twists as the northerly wind blew stronger and stronger.

"Might give the leaflets a miss today, if that's ok?"

"Oh God, of course it's ok, Day. I didn't expect you to do it in the first place, let alone carry it on for months, whatever the weather."

Tasha walked through the door and dusted the snow from her coat, her rosy cheeks and bright red nose suggested it was extremely cold outside. "It's freezing out there," she said, pulling her gloves off. "It's the wind. Makes it like a blizzard."

Lunch break over and an hours nap thrown in, Jenny stood up from her chair and stretched. The warmth rising from the heater next to her desk, had zapped every ounce of energy from her earlier, but now she was raring to go. Stepping into the shop, she was surprised to see the bright glare from the windows at the far end. Everything in sight was white. There was certainly a blizzard going on now.

Dayna had got the 'Wet Floor' signs out and placed two at the front of the shop. The new, wide mat at the front door was soaking wet and little drifts of snow had built up, all along the window frames, outside.

"Wow," said Jenny, mesmerised by the dramatic transformation in just two hours. "You going to be ok getting home in that?" She looked at Dayna and then turned back to the whitewashed view out on Millen Road. "Even the road is covered – how are you going to drive down there?"

"I'll be ok. It's you two I'm worried about." Dayna rubbed her hands up and down her arms. "If it carries on like this you'll both get stranded up here."

"Four wheel drive, don't forget – I'll be fine. And I can run you home, Tasha, if you'll be prepared to wait."

Tasha smiled, "Thank you but my mum's got a jeepy-thing – it's got special wheels for snow – so she says, anyway." Tasha stared out of the window, alongside Jenny and Dayna. "She'll pick me up."

"I'm going now, wouldn't be surprised if Xaylan's school closes early. It might have shut already and he's at home with Mum. I'll phone first, come to think of it."

"Go on then – otherwise I will be taking you home. Look at it now."

The evening came and the blizzard continued, relentlessly. Opening the front door, Jenny guessed that the snow was at least six centimetres deep now. Her car was good in conditions like these but momentarily, Jenny doubted the safety aspect of driving home in it. Locking the door, she pulled her hood over her head and tentatively trudged round to her car and jumped in.

The ride home had been treacherous and Jenny sighed a breath of relief as she went inside her warm, cosy flat. Along the route home, she'd spotted several abandoned vehicles, particularly at the bottom and top of Millen Road. The road's steep inclines had prevented a lot of cars and vans from going up or down.

Have you got home ok? Tried ringing the shop. A xx

Yes, home now. It's really bad out there. What's it like in Birmingham? X

Nothing here, makes a change. Normally the other way round. Seen it on the news – can't believe how bad it is down there. Xx

Let's hope it's gone by the morning. Xx

Hope so. Expect it's been dead in the shop, has it? Xx

Reasonable, considering. X

Ok, got to shoot – out with clients. See you on Saturday, miss you madly xx

Miss you too, have fun x

Jenny flicked the TV on and turned to the news channel. Snow. Everywhere. More snow to come. Stranded vehicles on the motorway. Mayhem across the south. How the UK can't cope with a sudden onset of extreme weather. Not enough grit for the minor roads. Accidents, stories of courage, stories of woe, tales of dramatic rescues. And on and on. Jenny flicked the television off and padded through to her bedroom, making a mental note to apologise to Dolly if she turned up tomorrow morning.

A last peep through the curtains before she went to bed, Jenny watched the giant snowflakes continue to fall. Each clump of icy perfection that reached the ground, would add to the ensuing havoc in the morning's rush hour if it carried on like this.

Chapter 40

It certainly was highly risky. Jenny managed to cautiously steer her way through the minor roads and out on to the deserted main road. There were no indications of a morning rush hour forming later and the snow continued to fall, softly and silently. It wasn't as heavy as the previous day's onslaught but still damaging enough as it fell on top of yesterday's compacted, frozen landscape. A grit lorry, struggling to cope with the conditions on the roads, passed by Jenny as she skillfully maneuvered her vehicle through the crispy, white town. More abandoned cars and vans. Eerie and still the town lie under the thick snow, waiting to be rescued, waiting to cope and already waiting for the melt.

"Jordan," said Jenny, surprised to see him, yet worried only moments ago, that he wouldn't come. "I didn't think you were coming."

Jordan brushed the snow from his coat and grinned. "I walked here – sorry I'm a bit late."

"No, don't be sorry. I'm surprised you're here at all. Can't believe you've walked." Jenny smiled at his rosy cheeks and red nose. "Are you sure you want to do it? I mean, I could probably go in the Jeep."

"No, it's cool. School's closed – I can walk. I like the snow."

"Well, if you're sure, they're here." Jenny passed the bundle to Jordan and watched as he put them in his bag. "If it gets too much, bring them back and I'll go later. They'll all have to be patient and wait, I mean – what do they expect in these adverse weather conditions?"

Jordan sniggered. "If you get lots of phone calls, tell them I'm on my way. It might take me a bit longer though."

"I will and I might even tell them that they should pay some danger money for your efforts." Jenny looked out of the window at the relentless weather. "Seriously though – you be careful, won't you."

Nodding his head, Jordan smiled and walked out of the shop, cautiously.

While Jenny listened to the elderly dog walkers (excluding, Dolly) harping on and telling tales of hardship, having squabbles about who had the deepest snow drifts around their properties and discussions about the weather reports of more snow to come, the phone rang. "Excuse me," she said, politely and picked up the phone.

"Hello, it's Andrea – from the nursery. We'll have to cancel our order today. The nursery's shut."

"Ah, thanks for calling, Andrea. Somehow, I didn't think you would be opening today."

"I'm surprised that you are," Andrea huffed down the phone. "You'll be wasting your time – no one will go out in this today."

"Well, I need to be open, so we'll see. Let me know when you'll be back, it's not a problem to do an order on the hop."

"Ok, thanks... oh, and good luck with the shop today."

Jenny laughed, "Thanks – I might need it."

Jenny watched through the window as Tasha climbed out of her mum's *Nissan Qashqai*, closed the door behind her and stood waving as the car reversed slowly, from the parking bay. The snowfall had subsided over the last hour but the depth on the roads, was treacherous, not to mention the pavements.

"Hello," called Tasha from the front door. Stamping her feet on the ground, she flicked the snow from her fur-lined boots, before coming inside. "Mum's going to pick me up later – it's terrible, isn't it?"

Jenny nodded, agreeably. "At least it's stopped now."

"Weatherman said we've got more this afternoon."

Rolling her bottom lip, Jenny folded her arms and wondered whether Andrea had been right earlier. "Haven't had many people in here. It's like a ghost town. It'll get worse if there's more snow to come."

"Hmm," replied Tasha. "Shall I make us a warm drink?"

"Yes please and then I'll get some paperwork done, while we're quiet."

Jen, I won't be able to get in unless you can come and get me. My car won't make it up those hills and there are no buses running. Unless I start walking now, lol xx

I'll come and get you at 11.30. Tasha should be ok – we're dead here x

Paperwork hell. Jenny was boggle-eyed and brain-dead. But she had to make use of this time. She had to sort out her finances and see the real picture of where she was in the 'will I make it/will I fail?' stakes. Surprisingly, out on the shop floor there had been some noise. The sounds of people talking. Tasha laughing, in a controlled manner for a change. And most importantly, the till beeping.

Snatched from her reverie, Jenny bolted upright as the office door opened.

"Jenny, I'm sorry to disturb you but... the milk... it's almost gone. You've got four cartons left."

"Really?" said Jenny, surprised.

"And the bread..." Tasha swivelled her head back and peered at the shelf behind her. "Yes, there are one, two... five loaves left."

Jenny rose to her feet and looked past Tasha. "Where's it all gone?"

"Sold it. I couldn't get down here sooner – I've been so busy." Tasha looked worried. "Sorry."

"Don't be sorry, I'm amazed. You should have pressed the buzzer though, if you've been that busy."

"Sorry... I was too busy to think about it."

The front door opened and three people walked in, stamping their feet on the rug and staring around the shop, with astonished expressions on their faces.

"Loads of people have been in... said they didn't know you were here..." said Tasha, before she shot off up the aisle, to the counter.

After four cartons of milk, five loaves and a till drawer bursting at the seams, Jenny thanked the last customer for coming to her shop for the first time.

Gone.

The salt had gone, along with all of the bread and milk. Even the dishwasher salt had disappeared.

"Blimey," breathed Jenny, "what's going on? I'm running out of everything. I'm going to have to go to the wholesalers – get some bread and milk, at least."

The door opened again and in walked two more people. "Didn't know this shop was here," said the larger of the two young women. "How long you been here?"

"Oh, quite a few months now," said Jenny, trying to contain her excitement.

"You got any milk?" The smaller woman asked. "*KO Store's* got nothing. They can't get any deliveries."

"Oh really?" Jenny sighed. "I'm afraid that I have just sold the last of my milk... but..." Jenny eyed Tasha, desperately. "... but we'll have some more... within an hour."

Tasha nodded her head. "Yes... we will."

"Are you sure you'll be ok if I go to the wholesalers?" whispered Jenny, concerned about leaving Tasha alone but realizing that this could be her opportunity to turn the shop around.

"Yes – you need to," Tasha replied, earnestly.

"That's good – so can we wait here? We'll have a look around the shop while we wait," said the larger woman, peering down the first aisle.

"Yes... of course," replied Jenny, meeting Tasha's eye again. "You sure?"

"Yes – go."

"Jenny?"

"Yes, hi Tasha – everything ok?"

"Yes... err... I've phoned to say that you might want to pick up loads of bread and milk... I've... err... got a queue of people waiting. And salt too. Everyone is asking for it."

"Blimey. Ok, I'll go back round and get double of everything. Should be back in twenty minutes."

"Oh good... err... Jenny... one more thing..."

"Yes?"

"Are we doing deliveries to vulnerable pensioners who are housebound?"

"What?"

"I've had five or six phone calls from people, asking if we deliver and saying that they didn't know we were even here. They are all phoning back in half an hour or so."

"Oh my God – yes! Tell them I will deliver."

"You might want to triple your order then... I've got a shop full here and the pensioners want loads of stuff."

"Right – I'm on it, Tasha. Be back as soon as poss."

"Oh... don't forget that you've got to pick Dayna up too."

"God – yes, I'd better do that on the way. I would have forgotten her. Thanks Tasha – you're a star. See you soon."

Dayna just squeezed into the car but had to keep her knees tucked up to her chin. The car was full with bread, milk, salt, dishwasher salt and a few other odd bits that Jenny had been meaning to order from her suppliers. Maneuvering through the deserted town, Jenny cautiously headed for the steep inclines of Millen Road.

"There's no way that I would have made it up here," said Dayna, staring wide-eyed through the windscreen. "It's madness – you're braver than me, Jen, to even attempt it."

"Haven't got much choice. Got to keep the shop open and I'm glad I did now."

As they pulled up to the shop, both Jenny and Dayna stared in amazement.

"Bloody hell," said Dayna. "How many people…"

"God – it's full."

Stepping out of the car, Jenny was met by at least eight people, who had just poured out from the shop.

"Have you got bread?" asked a man in a dark suit and matching overcoat.

"Can I have some milk please?" A young woman called out, from the back of the growing crowd.

"We'll bring everything in. If you could all wait a couple of minutes more please," shouted Jenny, over their heads. Peering across to Dayna, Jenny gave one of her flabbergasted looks before opening the boot.

A stream of crates, boxes and shrink-wrapped packs entered the shop. One person after another (mainly men), helped to unload the car and carry things into the shop. Jenny couldn't thank people enough for their help. The people couldn't thank Jenny enough for being here, for selling bread and milk when no one else could and for being 'such a friendly shop' and the best bit of all was when the countless people said, 'We'll come again – now we know you're here'.

Many of the newcomers looked puzzled when Jenny and Tasha told them that they had sent leaflets out to every single house in the area. Dayna boasted about how the leaflet drops had been her idea and how she'd bought the luminous pink outfits... even though it hadn't been quite as successful as she had hoped.

The phone calls came and Jenny went. Delivering goods to the local, elderly residents all through her lunch break. After 15 deliveries Jenny came to realise that this was indeed a service that she should provide. There were so many elderly folk around and many of those were housebound or at least they couldn't make it past their front drive, without aid. They struggled to meet the minimum requirements for deliveries from the giant supermarkets in town, Jenny had learnt, and relied on family and friends to get their 'bits' in. The service that Jenny had provided, in the space of two hours, had given the pensioners a sense of independence, a sense of worth and a friendly face to open their doors to.

Jenny's tired, old Jeep slipped and slid its way back to the shop.

"This is crazy," she said, walking over to the counter with a wad of notes and a bag of loose change in her hands. "Bring on the snow." She passed the money over the counter. "Put it in the box for me – unless you need any of it for the till."

"You're kidding aren't you? Dayna looked smug. "I've emptied it again since you've been gone, Jen."

"Never..."

Dayna nodded her head. "Yep, and you'll have to get more bread and milk if this carries on." Dayna swivelled her eyes to one side, indicating to the second aisle.

Staring down the shop, Jenny could see more people. Single people, couples, groups. So many of them. And all looking around, picking things up from the shelves and having discussions amongst themselves.

"You haven't had a lunch break, Jenny," said Tasha, worriedly. "I've got to go in a minute – Mum's coming to pick me up."

"That's fine, Tasha – don't worry about me. I'll get something to eat quickly. I don't need a lunch break – I am buzzing."

Epilogue

It felt like the whole world had ground to a halt. After three consecutive days of snow, the working world outside had stopped, but life in *J's Convenience Store* was thriving.

Boom.

The takings had been phenomenal and far more than Jenny could ever have imagined at this point in the shop's life.

With no time for doing anything but serve customers, stock up from the wholesalers, drive around the area delivering shopping bags to the elderly and going home to sleep, Jenny hadn't replied to Aaron's two text messages and one missed call. She had to find the time to contact him. They barely saw each other, let alone talk or text.

Stuck in Birmingham for longer than expected, during the snow-days, Aaron's journey home would be fraught with danger. Although some of the major roads were now cleared, there were still problems with grit shortages and freezing temperatures.

Hope everything's ok, haven't heard from you. I'll be sliding home tomorrow. If I skid past your window, get the lasso out and reel me in, lol. Aaron xx

Hi, Aaron, sorry I haven't replied – been manic here, you wouldn't believe it! Err... if I'm going to reel you in, then surely I'll need a fishing rod rather than a lasso? Lol x

Clever girl – just checking you're awake. See you Sunday night??

Absolutely! X

It went as quickly as it had arrived. Mushy pavements and sludgy roads made walking or driving anywhere a very messy affair. Why did the snow always have to turn a nasty brown colour as it melted away?

As the snow disappeared, Jenny half expected her new customers to disappear. She waited for the triple-takings to dwindle and the delivery phone calls to stop. But they didn't. As life returned to normal, in Farehelm, Jenny's business did not. The footfall had increased by 241%, according to the EPOS summaries and spend, per customer, had risen dramatically too.

Jenny spent her lunch breaks shooting off to the bank or the wholesalers, in an attempt to keep up with the ever growing demands.

As soon as the delivery lorries were able to get back up Millen Road, she increased her orders considerably. It was manic, all round.

"It's getting too hectic in here," said Dayna, one crispy-cold morning. "We need to use the other till for more than just newspaper delivery payments."

Jenny placed the last bottle of *Blossom Hill* on the shelf and turned towards the counter. "If we had the other till working properly, we'd need someone else to use it."

"So do it. Get someone else in. You don't stop, Jen. You can't keep doing all of these deliveries every day, and then run around the shop, stacking shelves all day as well. You've got black bags under your eyes and you look like you've lost weight."

Jenny peered down at herself. "Oh good, could do with losing a bit and I have been thinking about Tasha's friend... err... Jane someone."

"Thornton, I think," said Dayna, thoughtfully. "Go for it, Jen. You definitely need a break and... well, I've been thinking..."

"Ooh, sounds dangerous."

Dayna smirked. "Well, I thought that maybe I could open or close the shop sometimes, if we had someone else to work – you know, just so that you can come in later in the mornings or go earlier at night. I could cash up, if you show me how. I've even spoken to Mum and she's ok with having Xaylan for a bit longer each day. He's doing football after school now as well, so he seems to have settled down a bit. All it would take would be a spare key."

It smacked her right between the eyes. Yes. Why hadn't she thought of that? Of course Dayna could open and close the shop, if she had someone else working with her. "Yes, you could. Ok, I'm going to call Jane Thornton – see if she's still interested. God – I might even get a life..." said Jenny, excitedly. "We can do this, Day, can't we?"

"Yes. We can, Jen. Dream-team."

Jane Thornton was sweet. An ideal candidate for a part-time position. Having just completed two years at college, Jane was looking for work to see her through a gap year. She was far too timid and homely to go off travelling for months before she went to university, but she wanted to earn some money of her own. Her parents had also decided that she shouldn't rely on their generous handouts, now that she had reached adulthood. She would still get them but she was not to rely on them.

How Jane and Tasha had become school friends and then continued that relationship after the age of 16 was a mystery to Jenny and Dayna. They were entirely different people, from very diverse backgrounds and they seemed to have absolutely nothing in common.

In comparison, Jane was a petite, dainty little thing with wide blue eyes and blonde wavy hair, tumbling down her back. When Tasha and Jane were together, the friendship was not apparent at all. In fact, it seemed to be very one-sided and Tasha was the one who worked doubly hard to please her friend.

"I'd like you to start on Monday, if you're happy to do that?" said Jenny, passing a form across the table. "Could you complete this before then?"

Jane nodded her pretty head, nervously, and her hair seemed to shake. "Yes – thank you. Certainly."

"It's a three month contract – subject to renewal at the end."

"That's wonderful. Thank you."

"I'm afraid you'll be on opposite shifts to Tasha – I need you to work mainly with Dayna."

Jane sat hunched in a chair, opposite Jenny, clutching her tiny hands together and smiling or nodding at the appropriate moments. Dressed in a smart, pale blue trouser suit and a contrasting navy, floral, silk scarf, Jane's attire made Jenny feel frumpy. Wearing black jeans, a long, woolen jumper and black trainers, Jenny's 'deliveries' clothing did not reflect her position in the interview.

"I may have to shuffle things around, from time to time, but you'll get plenty of notice. Does that all sound ok?"

"Yes, thank you very much, Miss Fartor."

"And please, call me Jenny... or Jen, even."

"Yes, thank you very much, Jenny."

Jenny smiled warmly and then showed Jane the door. "Thank you for coming at such short notice. I'll email the work rota to you this evening."

"Thank you... very much. Bye, bye."

Jenny watched as Jane glided up the aisle in her conservative, navy, one-inch heels and stopped at the counter to speak to Tasha.

A sense of excitement filled Jenny as she thought about the pending time off available to her. Time to spend with Aaron, time to build on their previously restrained relationship and time to catch up with her life.

OMG! I've now got Saturday evenings off! Happy days. Fancy an evening at the cinema? X

Absolutely, Jen. This Saturday? Told Mum about your snow-success, she's real happy for you. Told her we're VERY good friends as well – so she knows now. A xx

I'm cool with that. What did she think about it? X

She's happy – thinks we make a nice couple, lol. Xx

Ah, sweet. And your dad? X

Don't know if Mum's told him but he just grunts and groans in his reclining chair when he's at home – doesn't say much. He's been tinkering in his shed a lot lately as well, since Grandad died – doesn't get on with my Grandma, who comes round a lot more now. Why am I telling you all of this over a text message? Lol xx

Lol – 'cos you're probably sat in a meeting or behind someone's counter fixing tills, bored stupid and hiding your phone while texting me. X

Yep – you're right on one count. Waiting for an EPOS to fire up. See you Saturday. For a whole evening!!! About time xx

I'm getting the keys cut this week. Dayna is opening the shop on Sunday. Lie-in for us – yay! Xx

Us? Ok, you've persuaded me. Guess I'll be staying for another coffee then. Loving you Miss Fartor xx

Loving you too xx

The last month's takings were extraordinary. Jenny pored over the summaries, the income and expenditure spreadsheets and the final figures. Since the snow, the business had steadily increased and Jenny now had to decide whether she would reap the rewards or put them to good use. Maybe in the employment of another part-time staff member? That way, the girls could have their well-earned holidays without Jenny having to worry about who was covering who.

"Think we could get someone else in, Day."

Great news! That would really help – and maybe this till working properly would help even more?" Dayna smirked. "Didn't Aaron say...?"

"Yes, he did and it's all sorted. He'll be doing it a week on Sunday – he's got too much on at the moment."

"Woohoo! A two-till shop – we're really going up in the world."

Jenny nodded. "Yes, I know. Exciting isn't it? But I'm going to have the other till set up properly for the paper delivery accounts and also, the grocery deliveries..."

"What? So we can't use it for normal stuff? What about when we have those big queues?"

"If you'd let me finish, Day. And it will be for 'normal stuff' too. Aaron's going to change it into a three-way till – somehow." Jenny paused and looked at Dayna, thoughtfully. "I'm going to make you the official manager of the shop too. What do you think?"

Dayna was speechless and could only gawp.

"Well? What do you think? It comes with a pay rise."

"You're going to make me cry," said Dayna, as her eyes began to water. "I think it's an amazing idea... are you sure you can afford it?"

"Yes, and I need you to take more of the responsibility, you know, learn more of the management side of things. You in?"

"You bet I'm in."

Hey, Jenny. Heard about your recent success, from your dad. Congrats. Let's celebrate. How would you like an all-expenses paid meal at our old-time favourite, The New Delhi?

Thanks for the offer, Calvin but I must decline. It's kind of you to congratulate me and yes, thank heavens for snow! Calvin, I am seeing someone now and think that the best way forward is for us to forget about any reconciliation or evenings out together. I'm sorry but I have moved on and I'm very happy. Kind wishes, Jenny.

It was only a friendly invite, Jen. Your boyfriend can come too?

Thanks, Calvin but I think it best that we leave it. I'm sorry to disappoint you but I'm very happy now.

Yet again, your loss. Good luck with whoever he is.

Thanks Calvin and I wish you a happy future too. Take care, J.

"Heard from Will at all?"

"No – said he'd email me once he was settled but to be honest with you, Jen, I'm really not bothered."

"What about the Greek God dentist you were on about?" Jenny raised her eyebrows, suggestively.

"No. He's spoken for, I do believe. Well that's what Joanne was telling me, anyway. Hooked up with someone over Christmas – fell head over heels in love, apparently."

"Who's Joanne?"

"The receptionist. We're going out on the town in a couple of weeks – she's a single parent too."

"Ah, that's nice. I'm pleased for you, Day. About time you went out for a girlie night."

"Absolutely! And we are so going to *hit* the town – big style."

"Oh, Dayna," said Jenny, beckoning to her friend to move closer. "Make sure you keep your mouth shut then."

"About what?" Dayna frowned.

"Not about anything. Keep it closed should any stray willies head your way."

"Oh," blurted Dayna, "Oh, you're funny." Dayna laughed aloud. "My lips are sealed."

"Pleased to hear it."

"Unless of course... they break through."

The girls laughed together, although the shop was pretty full. It didn't matter though. The clientele these days, seemed to enjoy the light, airy, fun-filled feel to the shop and would spend more time than perhaps they should, joining in the banter and frivolous chats.

But maybe, just on this occasion, Jenny and Dayna's chat about sealed lips had to remain private, for their ears only.

Even Andrea Doo-Glass Douglas had lightened up and now actively supported the shop and her new acquaintances.

It seemed to annoy Dolly – Jenny was sure of it, although she hadn't broached the subject. Yet.

"Morning Dolly," said Jenny, chirpily. "I hear you stayed with a cousin of yours while the snow was here."

"Second," replied Dolly, grumpily. "She's my second cousin."

"Oh, sorry – your second cousin then. How long have you been back? We haven't seen you in weeks."

"I came back weeks ago. Soon after the snow had gone."

"Ok. So, why haven't you been in before now then?"

"It's too busy in here."

"How would you know that if you haven't been up here?" Jenny quizzed the grizzly old woman.

Dolly cleared her throat and leant across the counter. "Look, dear," she whispered. "My legs are not so good and I can't stand around in long queues, waiting to be served with my paper."

"It's hardly that busy first thing in the morning."

"Hmm... well I heard that you've turned things around and you are very busy. I've been getting my paper from *KO*." Dolly pulled herself upright and placed a hand around the small of her back. "This waiting around is no good for us elderly folk."

"Dolly – I've had enough of your moaning and groaning, to be honest with you," said Jenny, cringing at her own words. "So why are you here today then? Winging and whining about anything you can think of?"

Dolly said nothing and stared up at Jenny with a pathetic look on her face.

"Well? Spit it out, Dolly. Why are you here now? You should watch out – there might be a mad rush in a minute and then you'll be crushed by the surge." Jenny knew her words were spiteful but she couldn't stop herself from saying exactly what she'd been thinking for a long time.

Still, Dolly was silent.

"Are you all right?"

Dolly nodded her head.

"Say something then…"

"I missed you." Dolly lowered her gaze. "Although we argue quite a lot… you're like a real friend to me."

"Marj. Hello, how are you?"

Marj peered around the shop, looking surprised by the number of shoppers, and then grinned at Jenny. "Good morning."

Gesturing to Marj to come towards the counter, Jenny leant over the top and spoke in a low voice. "What did you say, the last time you came here – as you were leaving? Before the snow came."

"Me?"

"Yes – through the window – as you left."

"I've no idea what you're talking about, dear." Marj looked genuinely puzzled.

"Something like, 'Tricked you, tricked you'."

Marj shook her head from side to side. "I haven't a clue what you mean, dear. Please don't say things like that to me."

"Like what?"

"I've only come in to buy toilet rolls – do you have those?"

"Yes, of course we do." Jenny frowned. "So what colour birds do you have now? Haven't seen you for a while – I guess you stayed home during the cold weather."

"Birds?"

"Yes – your birds."

"I don't know what you're talking about, dear. I don't have any birds. Please show me where you keep your toilet rolls and I'll be on my way."

"Tasha," called Jenny, "could you show this lady to the toilet rolls, please."

Tasha peeped around the corner of the first aisle. "Yes, sure," she said, with a smirk.

A few minutes passed and Marj appeared at the counter with a pack of four pink toilet rolls.

Serving her silently and swiftly, Jenny made a conscious effort to leave out any further questions. She did not particularly want to know whether there were pink birds living at Marj's house now. Or even if the turquoise ones had miraculously turned pink. Or even if she had multi-coloured ones which had flown away, creating giant rainbows in the sky. It really didn't matter anymore – at least she was paying for her toilet rolls.

No, I mean, I'm really loving you, Miss Fartor. Xx

Ah, that's sweet. Oh, go on then. You know, I think I could go with a four-bed mansion and acres of landscaped gardens. Maybe a summer house and a shimmering, Olympic-sized pool at the bottom of the garden too. Yes, I think I could stretch to that. Ha ha, no, seriously, I'm joking. Really loving you too, Mr Frey xx

I knew you'd make it Jen. I've made it too. I've also fallen in love with you and you can have it all. We'll have matching pool towels as well – I'm serious. You will have it all xx

Busy Busy

It's seven o'clock and the shop is opening

In they come for their fags and mags

And later on the children are hoping

To have some sweeties in their bags

Shelves stacked full in strict array

With labels brightly showing

Customers queue so they can pay

Their baskets over-flowing

Potatoes, milk, bread and butter

Cards, pens and paperclips

You can have a little flutter

With your lottery lucky dips

By Joan Stevens (2014)

Thank you for reading this book
Please spare a moment to leave a short review on Amazon
Hugely appreciated
Tara ☺

Printed in Great Britain
by Amazon

12119156R00254